Can a vampire break a curse?

When Janie Robinson says "I do," she might as well call the morgue. Two days after her wedding, David died in a car accident. The day after she accepted his proposal, Justin fell to his death at work. The day after she agreed to move in, Aaron died in a freakish drone accident. Now Sam wants to date her because she's some kind of Perfect Mate. If she's perfectly anything, she's perfectly cursed and she's not about to risk Sam's life.

Sam Kincaid is a vampire. He has been searching for Janie since the day he let her go. Her so-called curse doesn't bother him until he becomes the killer's next target. He's never feared for his life before, but if he lets her go again, it wouldn't be worth living.

I0741587

Other books by Stacy McKitrick

Bitten by Love Series:
My Sunny Vampire
Bite Me, I'm Yours
Blind Temptation
A Vampire Wedding
Biting the Curse

Ghostly Encounter Series:
Ghostly Liaison
Ghostly Interlude

Short Stories in the Following Anthologies:
Home for the Holidays
Love's a Beach

Short Stories:
Forever Thirty-two
Savannah's Destiny

Biting the Curse

(Bitten by Love #5)

Stacy McKitrick

Dayton, Ohio

Mythicalpress.com

Copyright © 2019 by Stacy McKitrick

Cover designed by Maria Zannini of Book Cover Diva
http://bookcoverdiva.blogspot.com/
Edited by Michele Stegman and Stephanie McKitrick
Formatted by Enterprise Book Services
http://www.EnterpriseBookServices.com/

All Rights Are Reserved. No part of this book may be used or reproduced in any manner whatsoever without written permission, except in the case of brief quotations embodied in critical articles and reviews. The unauthorized reproduction or distribution of this copyrighted work is illegal. No part of this book may be scanned, uploaded or distributed via the Internet or any other means, electronic or print, without the author's permission.

This story is a work of fiction. Names, characters, places, and incidents are either products of the author's imagination or are used fictitiously. Any resemblance to actual events, locales, business establishments, media title, or persons living or dead, is entirely coincidental.

Published in the United States of America
First Electronic Edition: July 18, 2019

Print ISBN: 978-1-7331762-0-0

Dedicated to Janis Mastrino
Thanks for being a friend.

Chapter 1

Strangers in the night.

Of all the stupid and idiotic things Janie had done, walking back to her car—in the middle of the night no less—toting a container full of gas and no flashlight to guide her, was perhaps the most stupid and idiotic.

But could she really expect her brain to work when her heart was aching? How else could she explain not checking the tripmeter after passing that last gas station? Because heaven forbid the stupid gas gauge worked correctly. Not that she would have noticed that, either.

She stayed on the edge of the road where the blacktop met the gravel and prayed for no slithery things to come her way. So far, so good. Besides the occasional breeze through the dry brush and some missteps as she kicked the gravel, no other sounds existed. Not even a cricket. Driving in the middle of Nowhere, Arizona was bad enough, but to be stranded after midnight was plain creepy. The smart thing would have been to buy or borrow a flashlight back at the gas station, but she was far from being smart.

Janie wiped her eyes as tears started to fall. This was not how the weekend was supposed to end. If only she had told David she was coming over. But her friend, Megan, insisted she surprise him for his birthday.

If she had called, she wouldn't have caught him with that other girl. And she wouldn't have been driving back to campus in the middle of the night. Then again, she wouldn't have caught him.

And she probably would have married a two-timing jerk.

She shook her head and took a cleansing breath. At least the temperature had cooled since sunset and the sporadic wind made for a comfortable walk. As comfortable as it could be lugging an eight-pound gas can. The mile walk to the gas station hadn't been so bad, but why'd she think it would be a breeze going back?

Yep. Stupid and idiotic. She should get that tattooed on a prominent part of her body, so everyone would know.

Twenty minutes and two aching arms later she reached her SUV. Or would it be David's? He'd given it to her as an engagement present. If they were no longer engaged, would she have to return it? If he insisted, she would. Then she'd make sure to buy a car that had a working gas gauge. After emptying the gas can into her dry tank, she tossed the container into the back and quickly climbed inside the car. Safe and sound—or as safe and sound one could be stranded in the middle of who knew where.

Because heaven forbid she would have remembered to bring a charging cord for her phone. And heaven forbid she'd remembered to check after buying the gas. She nearly banged her head on the steering wheel, but with her current luck, she'd end up with a broken steering wheel. Or a concussion. Or both.

She started the engine—oh, what a wonderful sound—and pulled a u-ey toward the gas station. As she rolled up to the pump, bells ding-dinged her arrival. Gosh, she couldn't remember the last time she'd heard those. Probably from an old movie. She grabbed the container out of the back and placed it by the door as instructed. She opened the door to the store and another bell announced her arrival.

The grandfatherly gentleman sitting behind the cash register put his book down and smiled at her. "I see you made it back all right."

"Yep." And happy to see a friendly face. "I'm just thankful you're even open. I can't imagine you get much business at night. That road is just plain deserted."

"And what might have happened to you if I weren't open? Nights aren't so bad and I haven't got anything else better to do. I'm just sorry I couldn't drive you back to your car." He slid the five dollar bill on the counter toward her. "Here's your deposit for bringing the can back."

Janie slid the bill back. "No, you keep it. You don't know how much I appreciate that you were open at all." She rummaged through her purse and pulled out a credit card. Slapping it on the counter, she said, "I'm filling up."

The old man nodded and Janie left the store. As she leaned against the SUV waiting for the tank to fill, a man strolled his way to the station, his cowboy boots kicking up dirt.

Guess she wasn't the only one who'd run out of gas.

He walked into the light and she nearly gasped. Her heart might be breaking, but her eyes were fine with the view. He wore a white T-shirt that hugged him like a second skin and showed off a well-built chest. Those jeans fit just right, too. What a hottie, and she hadn't gotten a look at his face. Yet. His shaggy dark hair—nearly black—whipped around in the breeze, obscuring his features. He certainly didn't worship the sun god. His skin was much too pale.

Paying her no mind, he entered the store.

Hmmm… She wasn't particularly vain, but she couldn't remember the last time she hadn't caused a guy to turn his head her way. Maybe the hot cowboy was gay. Seemed most of the hot guys were.

Not that she was looking for one. Not yet, anyway.

The pump kicked off and she replaced the nozzle before securing the cap. She sniffed her hands and grimaced. Ah, what did she expect? To end up odor-free?

When she entered the store, Hot Cowboy was in the back staring at the beer case. Okay, so maybe he hadn't run out of gas. But where the heck did he live to walk here for a beer? She grabbed a Diet Dr. Pepper and a bag of Combos, being careful not to touch the stuff too much with her stinky hand, and placed them on the counter.

"Do you have a charge cord for an iPhone?"

The owner placed her items in a bag. "Naw. Technology changes too fast for me to keep anything like that on hand."

Okay, now she didn't feel one-hundred percent stupid for not checking earlier. Only ninety-five percent. "Where's the ladies room?"

"Outside, 'round the back." He placed the credit card receipt on the counter, which she signed. "It was a pleasure doing business with you, Miss Robinson. Stop back soon."

She leaned over the counter and grinned. "No offense, but I hope I'm never out this way again. Thanks again for your hospitality." She lifted the bag off the counter. "Do I need a key to get in?"

"Naw, it's open. Saw no need to lock it. Most people leave me alone out here. Just make sure to turn the light out when you're finished."

"Will do." She placed her bag on the passenger seat, locked up, and headed toward the back of the store. When she turned the corner and lost her only light source, she stopped. Her eyes were practically useless.

Damn it, if she didn't have to clean her hands so badly, she'd just turn around and forget it. She palmed the rough bricks of the building and kicked the pebbles in her path—just in case some snake or scorpion she couldn't see decided to check her out—and felt her way to the restroom.

The rough brick turned to smooth metal and her hand hit a door knob, but reading the door sign was impossible. She reached inside and flipped the switch. The light stung her eyes and she squinted. Ah, good. It was the ladies room. Even better? No creatures.

After washing her hands a good five minutes—gasoline smell was a bitch to remove—she made sure she'd have no other reason to stop before she reached Tucson. Once finished, she turned out the light and stepped outside.

Oh great. Blind again. Should have bought that flashlight. Following the same routine that got her here, she back tracked her steps. Four steps later she ran into a hard body. She about jumped out of her skin.

"Hello, Janie," he said as he placed his hands on either side of her. "Damn, girl. What kind of perfume is that? It smells absolutely scrumptious."

A lump formed in her chest. Had David sent someone out after her? No, no, he couldn't have. "I think you've mistaken me for someone else. Let me pass."

"Now, Janie. Don't be like that. I'm your good friend, Sam." He kept her caged against the wall and inhaled in a lazy kind of drunk way. "Be a good girl and give me a kiss hello."

He was close enough for her to make out the white T-shirt and shaggy hair. Holy shit, he was Hot Cowboy. Okay, so not gay. And man, did he smell good. No way she knew him, though, so how the hell did he know her? And what was with his eyes? They practically shimmered, but from what light source?

What did it matter? She'd known guys like him. Thought because they were bigger or more important that she should do what they want. Words didn't work on them. No, only action.

So instead of arguing with the guy, she grabbed his arm to get by. Erotic charges surged through her body and accelerated her already racing heart. Even her nipples became hard. What the hell was happening to her and why'd it feel so damn good? She leaned her head back and dropped her arm.

"Whoa," he said. "What was that?" He grabbed her upper arms, his hands feeling better than they had a right to feel. "Sweet Jesus."

Sweet Jesus, indeed. His touch was wreaking havoc with her body. She should stop him, but in a way she wanted him to continue.

"What are you doing to me?" Her voice came out all breathy-like and, before she could say anything else, he planted his lips against hers and claimed her with a hunger she'd never experienced before.

Her body quivered as he held her head and probed her mouth with his tongue. Without any directive from her brain, her arms wrapped around his neck. Erotic-like senses shot through her body and she tightened in need.

More. She wanted more. She lifted her leg and pulled him in close, bringing his erection to rub her just the right way.

He broke the kiss and left a burning trail of kisses to her neck, where he stopped to nuzzle. Her lips missed his presence, but her neck was more than happy for the attention until his sucking created a momentary prick of pain.

What the hell? Was he biting her? No, no. Couldn't be. It would hurt more. Wouldn't it?

He moaned in pleasure. She almost joined him.

Her brain finally woke up and took charge. He *was* biting her. And it *should* hurt, not feel good, but damn if it didn't feel better than good. She lowered her leg, put her hands up to his shoulders, and pushed. Well, that got as much reaction as pushing a boulder. "Stop! You're hurting me."

Which was a big, fat lie and he probably guessed that right away. Because just as he stopped biting her, she orgasmed. Wave after wave of pleasure rode through her, turning her legs into rubber. He wrapped his arms around her waist and held her up.

As her heart rate slowed, her head cleared. She was engaged, for Pete's sake. Didn't matter if David had cheated, she wasn't going to do the same. No matter how drawn she was to this…stranger. She grabbed her neck, squirmed free and slapped him across the face. "What did you do to me?"

He grabbed her hand and stared at her with those shiny eyes, as if she should do something.

She should be furious, but somehow the anger wouldn't come after the best sex-not-sex she'd ever had. What did that say about her? About David? No, no. This wasn't about him. She yanked her hand free. "I know you speak English. What did you do to me?"

"I haven't done anything to you. You ran into me. Remember?"

"You call kissing and biting nothing? What kind of freak are you?"

His eyes widened. "I…uh…"

"What kind of answer is that?"

"I'm so sorry. I thought you were someone else."

"Sure you did, you pervert." Heck, maybe it did say "stupid and idiotic" on her forehead. Or just "easy prey." In an effort to get away, she stumbled over her own clumsy feet. He caught her before the ground could do damage to her face. And damn it, his embrace wreaked all kinds of havoc on her body.

"Let me make it up to you. Help you to your car maybe?" He scooped her up into his strong arms as if she weighed no more than a pillow.

"Hey! Put me down. I can walk on my own." Although, her body said, "Nah, let him continue," as it enjoyed his touch way too much.

What the hell was wrong with her? It was like her brain and body were bickering with each other. She didn't know which one to believe. She'd always gone by her instincts before. Now her instincts were shot. Had he sucked them all out of her?

Ignoring her demand, he carried her around the building. When he came into the light, his shimmering eyes were actually a beautiful brown. They didn't necessarily sparkle—it was more subtle than that. Still, they didn't seem…human.

Which was silly, really. Aliens didn't exist. Did they?

But if they did and he was one... Holy crap! Had he probed her mind? How else would he have known her name?

He reached the driver's side of her vehicle. As he released her, he licked her neck. "Now, wasn't that easier than trying to walk?"

She should be furious. She should at least be scared out of her mind. Instead, his lick sent more erotic charges and desire through her. A desire to get to know Hot Cowboy—or rather, Sam—better. And that was just crazy. The man had practically assaulted her. And then there was the strange thing with his eyes. His beautiful, beautiful eyes. No, no. He was an alien and she had to get away before he did any more probing.

She slapped him again, unlocked the door, and hopped in her car.

But as she sped away, an uneasy feeling came over her as if she'd made the worst mistake of her life.

Chapter 2

500 years later. Okay, only four and a half. It just felt like 500.

Sam Kincaid stood behind the bar in Wings and rubbed the spot where Janie Robinson had slapped him all those years ago. Had it only been four and a half? Might as well be five hundred. And right on cue, his boner returned, along with his fangs.

After their encounter, he'd been worried she'd tell someone—that she'd been assaulted at least, something he wasn't proud of—but as time went by with no mention of vampires being seen in the Arizona area, the worry faded. Didn't mean he'd forgotten her or her wonderful scent, and he'd tried. Boy, had he tried. Instead he fantasized about a woman he'd be foolish to pursue. Because a mortal who couldn't be controlled was a dangerous person and he had no desire to harm Janie Robinson.

Then seven months ago he'd read the announcement on the Committee website about the appearance of Perfect Mates—a rare mortal who couldn't be turned and couldn't be controlled, but when bonded with a vampire, could make a vampire almost feel mortal again—and a thought took hold. What if she was one? As luck would have it, Sam was invited to John and Sarah Pennington's wedding—the first known bonded couple—the following month. And one enlightening conversation with John confirmed what Sam had wondered after the announcement: Janie Robinson was most likely a Perfect Mate.

Everything John had said about his initial encounter with his wife, Sarah, explained why Sam had a strong urge to follow Janie after that slap she'd landed. Explained how she could even get away with slapping him. Or the fact that everything he'd thrown at her mental-wise bounced off her like a tennis ball on a racket.

Then there was the warmth he'd felt after touching her. And the taste of her blood. He'd been sure he'd died and gone to heaven.

All this time he'd been thinking he'd run into a freak and was damn lucky not to be outted. Instead, he'd discovered a rare breed and had let her go.

Technically, he should have killed her. Vampires weren't allowed to leave those who could out them. But killing Janie would have been too severe. Wasn't her fault he failed to test her mind first.

And now he was super glad he hadn't killed her. Because she was a Perfect Mate and she could be his.

If he could only find her. John promised to help, but only if Sam contacted Victoria, another vampire who had found her own Perfect Mate. It'd been hard for Sam to admit such a thing to her because she was a Committee Member and would be expected to report the find. He didn't want another male vampire finding Janie before he had a chance to woo her the right way. Because he was pretty sure there had to be more to the whole bonding thing than him being a vampire and her a Perfect Mate.

Victoria had ended up being great about the whole thing, though. Not only had she offered her help, she'd promised to keep his secret until Janie could be found. But seven months later, he still had no idea where she'd gone.

It was like she was a ghost.

Except a ghost wouldn't have given him the best sexual experience of his life. And they hadn't even had sex. If John and Sarah were any indication of how great a Perfect Mate couple could be, Sam could only imagine sex with Janie would be the be-all and end-all of his existence.

"He's gone again, Johnny. I don't know why you keep him," Perry said from the other side of the empty counter, twirling on the stool.

Sam retracted his fangs and turned toward the one man he had to keep his discovery from at all costs. It was no secret that Perry Davenport was searching for his own Perfect Mate. Sam wanted to make sure it wouldn't be Janie. "I'm just thinking. Something you should do from time to time."

"Thinking? About what? How Johnny can stay in business?" Perry laughed. More like cackled—high pitched and loud. No one joined him.

Wright Wings Sports Bar and Grill, Wings for short, was rather quiet, but then it was only Thursday and the temperature had dropped significantly during this January day in Dayton, Ohio. Or at least that was the complaint of the few customers who had appeared. Vampires couldn't feel temperatures. Except when they touched a non-mated Perfect Mate. Even the sun didn't feel hot to a vampire. It was the damage the sun did that was painful.

John crossed his arms and leaned against the back counter. "Why are you still here, Perry? I thought you were going back to Atlanta with Barnet."

Atlanta was home to the Committee Headquarters, and Barnet Groves was the Head of the Committee. He still didn't know about Janie, thanks to Victoria. And while John suggested several times that Sam should confide in Barnet, that Barnet wouldn't be an issue, Sam didn't want the extra competition. Because what non-bonded vampire wouldn't be interested?

Perry continued spinning on the stool. "I've been in Atlanta long enough. It's time for a change."

"Susannah still mad at you?" John asked.

"Maybe. Probably." Perry stopped and hung his head. "Yeah."

"What'd you do to poor Susannah?" Sam had heard the newbie vampire was adapting fairly well to her new world, as unexpected as it all was since she'd had no idea vampires even existed until her turning. Probably helped that her brother, Ben, was the Perfect Mate bonded and married to Victoria.

"How many times do I have to say it? I didn't *do* anything to her."

"No," John said. "You just told her she wasn't a Perfect Mate."

"Well, she isn't. She's a vampire. And a friend. Or at least I thought she was a friend. How was I supposed to know she thought I wanted more?"

"Because you don't have female friends?" Sam interjected. "I'm surprised you didn't read her mind." Sure, it was frowned upon by the vampire community, and almost impossible to do with an older vampire, but it didn't stop anyone from actually doing it if they wanted.

"I try not to do that with friends. They get kind of prickly." Perry gave John a knowing glance before returning to his twirling. "Now I just have to figure out where I want to go for a while and let her cool off."

"You can always cover for me while I'm gone."

"And bartend for bossy Johnny here? I don't think so. Where are you going?"

"Up to Detroit. Victoria asked me to check in on Richard...Daugherty." Sam regretted the words as soon as they popped out of his mouth. And not because Richard was a Perfect Mate who'd nearly been killed by one of them.

"Why would Vic ask you to do anything? Last I saw you weren't the Committee's lackey."

What could he say to that? No one but John knew of Sam's association with Victoria.

"She only asked him because I said I wouldn't leave Sarah and Sean," John said, saving Sam's ass big time. "Do you really think she'd ask you to do anything and expect you to do it?"

"Well... I guess you have a point there," Perry said. He turned toward Sam. "So, when do we leave?"

"We?"

"Yes, we. You have to take me. I'll go stir crazy if I stay here. All Johnny and Sarah want to do is look at the baby. Talk about boring!"

Sam couldn't fault John for being fascinated with his son, Sean. Vampires became sterile upon turning, but apparently being bonded to a Perfect Mate reversed that procedure. The news had freaked out Victoria a bit—something about not wanting to go through her monthly cycles—but so far she hadn't noticed any changes since bonding with Ben.

And frankly, the thought of being a father fascinated Sam. To be a parent with Janie, even better. But he had to find her first and hope she felt the same toward him as he did toward her. Provided she could forgive him for assaulting her. It would probably take some groveling. Lots of groveling.

John threw a hand towel at Perry. "Everything I do is boring to you. I'm sure you'll change your tune the day you find your own Perfect Mate and want children."

Perry stopped twirling and caught the rag. "Are you kidding me? My Perfect Mate will not want to have kids. That's what will make her perfect. That, and the fact her blood will do amazing things for me."

"And of course it's all about you," Sam said, trying his best to keep the sarcasm light. "So, if you want to go to Detroit, go. Why do I need to go?" No sooner had he asked the question, he realized the answer.

"You really think Vic will believe anything I tell her? Come on. Be a sport. We'll have fun, just like in the old days. Check in on Richard Daugherty then go bar hopping for some tasty snacks." Perry smacked his lips.

If Sam really wanted Perry out of competition, helping him find his own Perfect Mate would be the way to do that. But the thought of bar hopping only turned Sam's stomach. There was only one woman for him and she smelled of peaches and cream.

Ahh, Janie Robinson. Where are you?

* * * *

Janie held her breath as she knocked on her cousin's door. She should have visited long before now, like when she'd first heard of his bizarre behavior, but that required coming home, and home was not a place she wanted to be. If not for his even stranger phone call the other day, she wouldn't be standing here now.

The door swung open and a man she barely recognized smiled at her. His eyes were the same brilliant blue, though. "You came."

"I said I would." She entered his apartment and froze. Every available wall space was plastered in newspaper and magazine articles. "What the hell is this?"

"I'll explain later." He pulled her in for a hug. "Oh, Janie. It's so good to see you again. How's life treating you in Nashville?"

"Nashville was last year. I'm in Cleveland now and for another six months."

"I don't see how you can stand moving around all the time. When are you going to settle down?"

Settle down? She was beginning to think that would never happen. Not when the men she'd been involved with dropped like vampires in the sun. She'd been a fool to think Aaron would be any different. "And give up living on the corporation's dime?"

"Ahh, Janie. It's been four years. You need to move on."

Problem was, she had moved on. Twice. Had someone put a curse on her? Because it sure felt like it. But that wasn't the conversation she came for. "What did you want to see me about?

Mom mentioned something about drugs. Is that why Julie left you?"

"Your mom knows? Of course she knows. My mother doesn't know how to keep her mouth shut. But I'll tell you what I told her and she didn't have the sense to share, I'm not on drugs. I've never done drugs. That's just what they want you to believe." He plopped down on his couch and the papers on the wall fluttered.

So many papers. So many articles. "They? Who're they?"

"I want to tell you. And I will. I just don't want you to think I'm crazy."

"Did you tell Julie? Is that why you broke up?"

"Julie didn't understand. Mom didn't understand. But I'm hoping you will. Eventually. I just need to ease you in, you know? So you can see I'm not crazy." His stomach rumbled.

"When was the last time you ate?"

"I, uh, I don't know." He ran his hand through his dark hair. "Yesterday?"

"What? You haven't eaten all day?"

"It's not what you think. I'm not on drugs. I just get involved and forget to eat."

And that forgetting was probably the reason his clothes hung on him loosely. Either he bought his clothes big or he'd lost twenty pounds. "Why don't I take you out to dinner and you can tell me everything as slowly as you want? How about Delmonico's?"

His eyes lit up. "Delmonico's?"

Relief rushed through her as he recognized their favorite hangout. Maybe he did have a good explanation. And no one would bother them there. "Yeah. You got clean clothes in that bedroom of yours?"

"Yeah. I'm not a slob, despite what I look like."

"You look pretty bad."

He chuckled and scratched the beginnings of a beard. "Yeah, I guess I do. Give me a minute."

While he left to go change, she walked over to one of the covered walls. Pictures of mutilated bodies and articles about animal attacks stared back at her. Whatever her cousin was obsessed with didn't look good. Didn't look good at all.

* * * *

Sam parked along the curb, across the street from Daugherty's apartment building. The drive hadn't been so bad. Perry could be amusing when Sam stopped fretting about Janie.

"I wish we could just wear sunglasses," Perry said as he inserted a contact into his right eye.

"That wouldn't look suspicious at night, now would it?" Sam kind of wished the same, though. Contacts were a pain and hard to stay in. They kept wanting to pop out, when they weren't scratching like crazy. But if by some chance Richard Daugherty saw them with their sparkly eyes—and that was how a Perfect Mate recognized a vampire—their plan to check on him discreetly would be blown.

Perry closed the contact lens case and placed it in the cup holder. "How long are we supposed to hang around here to make sure he's okay?"

"Victoria said to make sure the apartment is empty before we go inside and investigate. If everything looks fine, we can leave. If we see anything suspicious, then I call it in."

"Great. And we can only observe during the night which means we could be waiting for days." Perry groaned and leaned his head against the seat back.

"You could have stayed in Dayton. No one forced you to come."

"Believe it or not, this is still more interesting. Don't mind me. I'm just a little grumpy."

"You? Grumpy?" Sam laughed.

"It still kind of burns that Vic didn't ask me to do this. We've been getting along a lot better since she married Teach."

Teach being Victoria's husband, Ben. The day Perry called anyone by their given name was a rare day, indeed.

"Maybe she's changed her tune since you insulted her sister-in-law."

"I didn't do it on purpose. Plus, I apologized. Anyway, I doubt Suzie even told Vic. Believe it or not, those two aren't all that chummy."

After Sam blinked several times to ensure the first contact remained seated, he took the second lens from his case. He needed to change the subject. Perry would blow a gasket the day he discovered his friends had kept a Perfect Mate from him. Sam didn't want to be anywhere around when that happened. "I'm sure

Victoria only asked John because of his proximity to Detroit. It's not like she was going to ask Dalton, now was it?"

"Dalton is an idiot. I mean, you'd have to be if you can't tell when someone isn't under your control."

Sam missed his eye and the contact landed on his black T-shirt. Stick him in the idiot column, then. At least he hadn't nearly drained Janie dry like Dalton had done to Daugherty. Now, where was that blasted lens?

"Vic knew I was in Dayton, though. And she knew Johnny was busy being a daddy."

"I don't know what to tell you." Definitely not the truth. The lens reflected the headlights of a passing car. On the second try, Sam stuck the second contact in successfully. "I'm surprised Barnet didn't just round up all the single female vampires and hold a lottery for the guy."

"Well, actually, the Committee might have been throwing that suggestion around."

"No shit?" All the more reason not to tell Barnet about Janie. Sam didn't want her up on the auction block. "Then why the subterfuge?"

"Because they want to make sure the man hasn't gone totally bonkers. Which is another reason Johnny would have been bad for this. Daugherty's seen him before. He hasn't seen me."

"Maybe they thought he'd be discreet."

"Discreet? If you wanted discreet, you shouldn't have come in this bright yellow tank."

"John's Xterra is hardly a tank. And why pay for a rental when he offered his car?" Sam opened his door. "Come on. Let's go see if Daugherty's here. No use waiting around if he's already gone."

"Sounds good to me. The sooner we get this over with, the sooner we can hit the bars. I'm getting a little parched."

Snow started falling as they climbed out of the vehicle and crossed the street. Maybe John's SUV was a bit on the bright side, but it wasn't the only bright vehicle on the street. A neon green Jeep was parked a few spots away.

"For someone who wanted to blend in, you're not exactly dressed the part." Perry, wearing a wool coat, pinched the collar of Sam's jean jacket and tugged.

"It's fine." Sam yanked free from Perry's grip. "I'm just walking from the car."

15

Perry opened the entryway door and stopped. Sniffed. "Hot damn. This is my lucky day. I got dibs."

"What are you talking about? Dibs on what?" But Sam got his answer as soon as he stepped into the foyer. The scent hit him. Hard. Peaches and cream. He was instantly transported back to that summer night in Arizona. It was like she was here. But he knew she wasn't. Unfortunately his dick wasn't getting the message. His boner returned.

"There's a Perfect Mate in the building," Perry said.

No shit, Sherlock. But Sam couldn't let on. If he admitted it, it was like telling Perry he'd already met an unbonded Perfect Mate, because once a vampire got a whiff of one it wasn't too hard to spot another. They all smelled the same to that one vampire.

"Well, duh," Sam said, playing it dumb and willing his erection to wilt. "But I thought you couldn't smell the males. Unless there's something you're not telling me."

"Very funny. It's not Daugherty I smell." He sniffed the air and followed an imaginary trail leading them straight to Daugherty's apartment.

"You sure about that?" Sam nearly burst out laughing at Perry's confused expression.

"Of course I'm—" Perry shook his head. "Go ahead, yuck it up. But just remember, I called dibs. She's mine."

Sam shook his head. He didn't believe for a minute that that was all it took to claim a Perfect Mate. But if Perry actually found his own Perfect Mate, then he wouldn't be a threat where Janie was concerned. Didn't seem all that fair that he'd find one before Sam found his. Not that he'd been actively looking for four and a half years, but damn…it'd been four and half years since he'd seen Janie. Whereas, Perry had been technically looking for only a year, after he'd first met Sarah. Sam wasn't quite convinced that the reason Sarah wasn't interested in Perry was because she'd met John first. There had to be more to it than a first meet. There'd been a connection between John and Sarah, one that had occurred because they'd gotten to know one another better. So Sam was making damn sure no one else got to Janie before he could re-establish their connection.

Because they'd had a connection. He was sure of it. If only she had a unique name, or lived in a major city, maybe he would have found her by now. She certainly wasn't living in Detroit. He'd asked Victoria after she requested he check in on Daugherty.

Perry put his ear up to the door. "We're in luck. No one's here." He pulled out a set of lock picks and made quick work of the door. Man definitely had skills.

Sam followed Perry into the darkened apartment. No need to turn on the light and alert anyone to their arrival. Their vampire eyes adjusted fine with what little streetlight came in through the windows. Even with the stupid contacts in.

The scent of peaches and cream was definitely stronger inside. No amount of will power was getting his penis soft. Hopefully Perry wouldn't notice. "So what exactly are you smelling? I smell peaches and cream."

"Shit." Perry walked over to the far wall.

"You smell shit?" Sam bit back a laugh. "And you still *want* a Perfect Mate?" Okay, that helped dim his arousal a bit. It was a rare day when Perry left the door open like that. Still, what scent did Perry smell? What scent reminded him of home?

"What? No, asshat. This." Perry pointed to the walls. Walls that were covered in newspaper and magazine articles.

Sam never got around to checking out what Daugherty did for a living. "He's a detective?"

"He wasn't when they brought him to Headquarters last year, but I suppose he is now. Seems he's looking for us. Or rather, vampires."

Vampires? Oh yeah. Shit, indeed.

Chapter 3

Sparks flew.

"Enough of the small talk," Janie said as she placed her napkin on the table. "Either you tell me what you wanted to see me about or I'm going back to Cleveland."

Because frankly, if she'd wanted the low down on family business, she could have called her mother.

Her cousin put down his fork. He'd only eaten about half his meal. "You're right, you're right. I'm sorry. This is just very hard for me. I value your friendship and I don't want to ruin that."

"I promise that whatever you have to say it won't ruin our friendship."

He took a deep breath and leaned in close. "Okay. Last summer, when I was on my supposed drug binge, I was bitten by a...vampire and nearly died from blood loss."

He'd said the word so quietly, she wasn't sure she caught it right so she mouthed, "Vampire?" When he nodded, Janie's heart raced and she almost brought her hand up to her neck. She could have sworn she'd been bitten once—by an alien, no less—but the lack of bite marks had calmed her down some. "Why do you say that?"

"What else drinks blood? I was just walking home from a late-night baseball game and this guy jumps me. Bites my neck. I started yelling, but he clamped a hand over my mouth until I lost consciousness. I woke up in some kind of hospital room, chained to the bed, surrounded by more of them."

"How do you know? Did they sparkle or something?" Her biter—Sam, the hot cowboy—had eyes that glimmered in the dark. Except Sam had been apologetic. And again, she never did find any evidence that he'd actually bitten her. But what were the odds?

"No. Nothing sparkled. That's exactly what Julie asked. Stupid *Twilight* book. I'm being serious here."

"So what makes you think you weren't in a hospital?"

"Because when the female touched me this electrical charge ran up my arm and, excuse me, but it started giving me an erection."

Those odds were getting better. Hadn't Sam affected her the same way? Vampire made more sense than an alien, except...vampires didn't exist, either. Did they? "You're saying it was erotic? When she touched you?"

"I'll say. She pulled away before anything happened, though. Well, unless she took advantage of me later. When I started screaming to let me go, they gave me something to knock me out. They could have done anything to me then. When I finally came to, I was in another hospital and was told I'd been roaming the streets, hallucinating. I don't remember any of that. They gave me something, I just don't know what."

"But why?"

"Because they wanted people to think I'm crazy when I tell them vampires exist. Why else? So I figure I need proof first."

"Proof?" She leaned back as it hit her. "You mean those articles you have posted on your walls."

"Yeah. They can't all be animal attacks. Some of them have to be vampires. They just have to."

"Rick, don't you think that's a little far-fetched?" Although if she told him about her own encounter, he'd probably want her to corroborate his.

"I know what I remember. And I wasn't doing any drugs. I swear."

She believed he wasn't doing drugs, but could he be having a psychotic episode? "So where did he bite you? Your neck looks fine."

"That's just it. There isn't any evidence that I've been bitten. They must have a way to heal me or something. How else would they be able to get away with biting everyone?"

Heal? Like from saliva? Sam had licked her after that bite. Could that be why? But if vampires or aliens actually existed, and they were biting everyone, why weren't there more reports? Unless… Sam had sure looked at her funny after he'd bitten her, like he'd expected her to forget. And she hadn't. Just like Rick. Oh shit. "You're not going to find any evidence."

Rick placed his hand over hers. "I know it sounds far-fetched, but I swear, it's the truth."

That wasn't her point, but she'd get back to that later. "Do you remember what the guy looked like? Any of them?"

"The one who bit me was black, about my height. The female who touched me was a kid, high school age. The other guy in the room was a little older than us, had light brown hair and blue eyes. He almost seemed like a doctor."

None of them sounded like her hot cowboy. "A high school girl and a doctor?"

"I know. It was strange. And if it weren't for that touch and the fact I'd been bitten and they covered it up, I would have thought they were human."

Sam had looked human, too. What did that mean? Janie took a sip of her drink. "What do you hope to accomplish once you get your proof?"

"You believe me?"

"I don't believe you're lying. I just…"

He lowered his head. "Think I'm crazy. Like Julie."

"You're not crazy. But if you really want people to think differently, you can't be spewing this vampire story. Again, what do you hope to accomplish? Pandemonium?"

He lifted his head and there was a fire in his eyes. "You don't think people have a right to know they're food? That their lives are at stake?"

"But are we food, really? These people let you go. Why would they do that if you were just food?"

"I…I…I don't know what to think anymore." He covered his face with his hands. "I wish I could forget it all."

She wished she could forget it, too, but Sam had invaded her dreams more than once. And they weren't all that unpleasant. "Have you thought about seeing a therapist?"

He tossed his napkin on the table. "Now you're sounding like Julie. If I told a doctor without any proof, they'd put me away."

"And if you don't talk to someone who can help you deal with this, you *will* go crazy."

"I can talk to you, can't I?"

"I'm not a therapist."

"No. You're better. You're a friend."

He couldn't be serious. A friend would have been here when he'd been hospitalized. Sure, they'd been close as kids, but now? Distance had put a crimp in all that. But he was family and maybe that's all he needed. "Okay. Do you really want to forget it all?"

"Yeah, I think I do. That's if you think people aren't in danger."

"If they killed you, I'd think people were in danger. But they let you go. That tells me they aren't a threat."

He nodded. "See? That's why I need you around. You make me see sense. So what should I do?"

"First off, you need to stop searching for something that doesn't want to be found. And you need to throw out all those articles."

A chuckle erupted out of him. "You must really think I'm nuts."

"I don't think you're nuts. I think you had a horrible experience and you were coping the best way you knew how. Hopefully, now you know better."

And hopefully she wasn't misleading him. But if Sam were one of these vampire/aliens, he had let her go, too. That had to mean something.

* * * *

Sam badly wanted to adjust his jeans, but not in front of Perry. There'd be no explaining his actions if he did. The scent alone was pleasing and alluring to a vampire, but the carnal desires didn't hit until first contact. Or so it seemed. It was still being studied and there was much the Committee didn't know. But to Perry, Sam shouldn't *know* the peaches-and-cream scent that invaded his brain was from a Perfect Mate and he shouldn't have any reaction below the belt.

Was this what he had to look forward to until he bonded with Janie? God, if she were only here. He'd come clean with Perry. But she wasn't here. Victoria would have told him. So he kept his mouth shut.

"Hand over your phone," Perry said.

Thankful for the interruption, Sam reached into his back pocket. "What's wrong with yours?"

"Dead."

21

"I don't know why you bother to even carry one."

Perry snatched the phone out of his hand. "So I'm not caught in a lie when they ask if I have one. Duh." He pushed the on button. "Password?"

Sam took the phone back. "Like I'm gonna tell you." He placed his thumb on the screen and opened it up. "Here. What do you need it for?"

"To call this in, what else?"

"Shouldn't I do that?" Sam's answer was Perry's back as he left the room. Whatever. At least he could adjust himself now. He had to do something to keep his mind off Janie, because the scent wasn't diminishing any. He perused the walls while Perry made his call. Each article was about brutal animal attacks.

Daugherty must still remember being attacked even though he'd passed out from the loss of blood. All because Dalton didn't know what to do when he couldn't control Daugherty, so he'd nearly bled the guy dry. But Daugherty had been healed by the Committee and kept unconscious. He hadn't been left like this. But if this was what happened when a Perfect Mate was bitten by a vampire and was set free…

Crap. Had he done the same thing to Janie? Could she be wandering about going crazy wondering? Or had she been institutionalized? Was that why he couldn't find her? Oh man, what had he done?

Perry stepped back into the living room and handed over the phone. "Come on, let's go. We're done here. Barnet's going to plan this to death, but will eventually capture him when it'll look less suspicious."

"And how is it suspicious now?"

"Because he's not alone. He's with another Perfect Mate. Remember?"

"You told Barnet?"

"I had no choice. He's probably freaking out as we speak. But she's mine and don't you forget it."

"Won't she have a say in that?"

"Not if she meets me first. So we'll wait outside in the car, and when she shows up I'll follow her and make sure to run into her when Daugherty and you aren't in the picture."

Sam nearly laughed. Had he sounded that crazy when he first talked to John about Janie? Probably. It was a heady feeling, one that had overwhelmed him in the beginning. Now he was just merely obsessed. But hey, if he could help Perry bond with this Perfect Mate, he wouldn't be a threat for Janie. And wouldn't that be a relief?

Perry locked up the apartment and they headed for the exit. Sam barely got his foot out the door when Perry dragged him over to the side of the building and into a pile of older snow. "What are you doing?"

"I just saw Daugherty in a car." Perry peeked around the corner. "And a woman is driving. Hot damn. They're going into the parking lot. All right, this is my chance. You wait in the car while I go accidentally run into my Perfect Mate."

"What if she's already taken? By him?"

"Daugherty isn't married."

"But *she* could be." Sam nearly laughed at the irony. Hadn't John been telling him the same thing about Janie?

"I'll worry about that later." Perry zipped away to the parking lot.

Sam brushed the dirt from his jacket and shook his feet free from the snow he'd been pushed into. When he finally found Janie, he would not act that paranoid. Except he sort of was already. Why else not tell Barnet about her?

His phone pinged. A text from Victoria saying to call when he was alone. Who knew how long Perry would take? Sam made the call, already knowing what the conversation would be about.

She didn't even bother to greet him. "There's another Perfect Mate?"

He knew Barnet wouldn't keep that news a secret. "Seems so. What are the odds, right?"

"Did you see her?"

"Not yet. Any word on Janie?"

"Sam…" She drew his name out, but didn't continue. Probably because every time he'd asked her about Janie, she'd given the same answer.

"I'm sorry," he said. "I know you said not to ask, that you'd tell me when you got news. That there's only one of you and a million Jane Robinsons."

"I didn't say there were a million."

"Might as well be. It's just that smelling that Perfect Mate made me…antsy."

"Was it that strong?"

"Strong enough." At least the fresh air had cleared his head and loosened his pants. "Is it possible she's in a mental institution? After seeing Daugherty's apartment, I'm wondering if maybe she went a little crazy after what I did to her."

"What you did to her was nothing compared to what we did to Richard Daugherty, but I'll start checking those next."

"Would it help you if I finally told Barnet?"

"I really don't know, but I won't ask you to do something I couldn't even do. Let me know when you get a look at this other Perfect Mate so I can start making notes."

"Right..." Sam laughed. "You think Perry's going to let me do that? He went after her in the parking lot. Making his move as we speak."

"What? Shouldn't you make sure he's not making his move on Janie?"

"What are you talking about? You just said you didn't know where she was. And you told me earlier she wasn't in Detroit."

"She's not *living* in Detroit. Doesn't mean she's not visiting. Do you want to take that chance?"

Oh, hell, no. Damn. What had he done?

* * * *

Janie parked her car just as her phone rang. Megan Reynolds. Her one and only friend. Well, of the female variety. Megan was the big sister, or fun aunt, that Janie never had. They'd met shortly after Janie had left Detroit for good and had remained friends. It was all texts, e-mails, or phone calls, but that made her the best kind of friend. She didn't impose on Janie's life like some family members wanted to.

"You go on inside while I take this call, okay?"

"Sure. See you in a bit." Rick climbed out and shut the door.

Janie answered her phone. "Hey, Megan. What's up?"

"I was worried. How'd your meeting go with your cousin? Or are you still with him?"

How much could she tell her best friend? Certainly nothing about the crazy bits. Rick deserved much better than that. "I'm still with him, but he just left for his apartment while I'm out here in my car talking to you. I think I'll stick around for a couple of days. His break-up hit him hard and he needs a friend right now. And to tell you the truth, I feel a little guilty that I haven't been around for him."

"Hey, what have I told you about that? You've got to stop feeling guilty about everything you can't control."

"Easier said than done." Before she'd let Megan get on her about that, Janie continued, "Listen, it's cold out here and it's snowing. I'll call you before I turn in." She climbed out of her car only to find some guy at her tire. "Hey! What are you doing?"

The man held his hands up. "Nothing. It looked flat so I was checking it out."

"Is something wrong? Are you okay?" Megan asked.

Janie sighed. "I'm fine. Seems I have a flat tire."

"Just your luck, huh, kid? Give me all the details later. Love ya, girl."

"Same atcha." Janie disconnected the call and stared at the flat. When the hell had she done that?

"Do you need any help? I'm pretty handy with a tire iron."

The man was slender and tall, wearing khakis and a wool winter coat. If it weren't for that blond ponytail he sported, she'd consider him handsome. In a way. But she wasn't fond of guys whose hair was longer than her own. Not that hers was long anymore. And blond really wasn't her preference. Dark. That's usually what did it for her. But from afar. No more up close and personal. It just wasn't safe.

"Thank you, but no. I'll call the rental agency. Let them worry about it." Too bad Rick's apartment building didn't come with a garage. That might have been useful. She grabbed her purse and locked the car doors. As she headed for the building, the man blocked her path.

"But you might ruin the rim letting it sit here. Hate to see you get charged for that. I don't mind helping. Honest."

"Maybe so, but it's dark and cold and snowing, and I really don't care."

"It's not that cold to me." The man blinked as if he had something in his eye. A moment later something flashed through the air and he covered his right eye.

"Did you just lose your contact?" She bent over, but the security light was useless. Turning the light on her phone, she scanned the blacktop, but even it was turning white with snow.

"There it is." He picked up something, wiped it against his sleeve and put it in his eye. "Thanks. Now I must repay you. If you don't want me helping with the car, would you care to get a drink?"

Was this guy for real? "Don't you need to wash that off first?"

He blinked several times as if testing the contact. "It's fine. Honest. Now, about that drink?"

"I'm sure you're a nice guy, Mr.…."

"Davenport. But you can call me Perry."

"Perry." And damn, the guy just grinned big when she said his name. "I don't make it a habit to go out with guys I met in a parking lot. Hope you understand."

"You're not even going to give me a chance? Tell you what, you pick the place and I'll meet you there. I'm sure once you get to know me you'll want to go out. But no pressure. Honest."

"And I'm going to get there with what car?" She pointed to the flat tire.

"Oh, right. How about tomorrow night?"

Persistence must be his middle name. He was cute, and trying so hard, and maybe, before Aaron, she might have met him for coffee. But Aaron had been the last straw. The police might not think she was guilty of his death, but that didn't mean she wasn't to blame. Cursed, that's what she was. And she wouldn't endanger anyone else's life. But before she could turn Perry down—again—a man called out his name.

Gooseflesh broke out on her arms and her nipples tightened. That voice. She knew that voice. Or more importantly, her body responded to that voice.

"I'll be there in a minute. Stay put." Perry smiled at Janie. "So, where should we meet?"

"Who is that?"

"A co-worker. No one important. Please, just name a bar and I'll meet you there."

Why was he being so persistent? And what was that business with the contact lens, unless… Was that why Rick didn't notice any sparkly eyes? They wore contacts? She was probably stupid to even do what she planned, but then she'd been known to be stupid. A lot. She grabbed Perry's hand. Just as she suspected, an erotic charge coursed through her body and she gasped. "You're one of them."

26

Perry didn't answer. His mouth hung open and he closed his eyes. Might have even moaned a little. She released his hand.

Although pleasant, Perry's zap wasn't near as strong as she'd gotten from someone else. Someone else she was sure was here. "Sam?"

"Janie?" The man from her past, her dreams, her yearnings, stepped around the building and under the security light just as an explosion sent her flying on her ass.

Chapter 4

The truth bites.

Sam rolled to his hands and knees and shook the gravel from his hair. What the hell just happened? And had he really seen... "Janie!"

When he'd taken a peek around the corner, he hadn't been able to get a good look, but the woman had short hair, not long. So he'd just assumed it wasn't Janie and let Perry have his way. It wasn't until she'd called his name, and he'd heard that angelic voice of hers, that he realized his mistake—she'd just cut her hair. But was she okay? Had the explosion hurt her any? He rushed to where she'd been standing, and came upon Perry holding his hand out to her. A violent urge came over Sam and he tamped it down.

"Are you hurt?" Perry asked her. "You need help?"

"What just happened?" She stood without Perry's help and looked up at the hole in the apartment building. "Oh my God. Rick!"

Perry wrapped his arms around her waist as she tried to make a run for the building. "You can't go in there."

Sam stood still, his heart aching. All this time he'd waited to find her and she was with someone else. And another Perfect Mate at that. What were the odds? Guess Daugherty's life was just as much of a black hole or else the Committee would have known he was involved with someone.

"What the hell did you two do?" she wailed. "He was going to take them down."

"Do?" Sam turned toward the building. "You think we did that?"

Sirens sounded in the distance and people were pouring out of the building, converging in the darkened parking lot. The blast had taken out every security light in the area.

"Why else are you here?" She squirmed in Perry's arms. "Let me go! I have to find him."

"Wait," Sam said. "I'll go."

"Sammy, if there's a fire…" Perry didn't need to say any more. Fire wasn't a good thing for vampires.

Sam nodded. But he had to go, if only it would prove to Janie that he had nothing to do with the explosion. "I'll be right back."

The blast had happened on the top floor, the same floor where Daugherty lived, but from another apartment. By the time Sam reached the staircase, all mobile residents had departed the building.

No sign of Daugherty, though. Shit, that couldn't be good.

As Sam stepped up to the top floor, he was met with a war zone. Drywall and insulation littered the area. Doors to all the apartments but one were either left or blown open. The apartment containing the blast was missing its door, and most of the wall.

Gas fumes filled the air, but no fire. Not yet, anyway.

Sam edged his way to Daugherty's apartment. The wall containing his display of attacks had toppled into the living room and the ceiling was partially gone. Snow floated down. "Rick? Are you here?"

He stilled and listened. The sirens messed with his hearing. He narrowed his focus. A faint heartbeat came from what was left of the bedroom. As Sam climbed over the destroyed wall, the rest of the ceiling came crashing down. Falling to his hands and knees, he yelled out as a beam landed across his back. Pain radiated from the impact. Might have broken a bone or something, but it would heal. Eventually. He waited a beat, just in case something else decided to fall. When all was steady, he unearthed himself and crawled over to the bedroom. His back throbbed from every movement. Yep, definitely broke something, but he'd live. Rick was buried under a pile of debris. Lucky dog was saved by his bed. It had kept the debris from crushing him.

The floor creaked as Sam uncovered Rick. No way did he want to fall through the floor if he could help it. One broken bone was one too many. He flattened down onto his stomach and grabbed Daugherty's arm.

"Come on, buddy. Please don't be stuck."

Rick moaned, then coughed. "What happened?"

"Explosion next door. Can you move? Are you stuck?"

A moment passed before Rick spoke up. "Not stuck. Help me out."

Sam pulled the man free and helped him stand. "Be careful. I'm afraid the floor might give."

Gingerly, they made it out the door to the staircase just as firemen appeared below.

"You two okay? Any more up there?"

The scent of blood was strong. Too strong. A small cramp flittered across Sam's abdomen and his fangs extended. He retracted them before anyone could notice. "I don't know if anyone is left up here. I'm fine, but he's hurt. Bleeding."

* * * *

Snow mingled with dust—or was that insulation?—and Janie shivered. Rick had to be okay. He just had to be. She'd had too many deaths in her life.

She tugged on Perry's arms. "You can let me go, now." There was no need for her to go running up to Rick's apartment. The fire department arrived and she was more than willing to let them do their job.

"Yeah, sure." He released her and stood back. "So, you know Sammy?"

Why'd his voice sound mad and sad at the same time? "I don't *know* him."

"But you met earlier. Knew his name."

"I guess you could say that. He fed from me." *And kissed me and invaded my dreams too many damn times to count.*

"I'm sorry? He what now?" Perry blinked shimmering green eyes. He must have lost the lenses in the explosion.

"Oh, don't give me that innocent look. I know what you are." Well, sort of. But he didn't know that. "You didn't have to blow up the building, you know. Rick was going to stop looking for you."

"We didn't blow up the building. And what are you talking about? Did something land on your head?"

Well, this conversation was going nowhere. "Why were you hitting on me?"

Perry flashed his pearly whites. "You're a beautiful woman. Why wouldn't I hit on you?"

"Right. Whatever. Know what? I think I'll sit in my car and wait." At least it would be warmer there. But where was it? The blast had taken out the security lights and sent her several feet away. She pulled out the key fob and pressed the lock button.

Lights flashed under a pile of brick. "Oh shit."

"Guess you don't have to worry about that flat tire now, huh?" Perry said.

She couldn't help but laugh. This whole night was bizarre. But her humor died a swift death when something in the building crashed and debris fell to the ground. Some people around her even screamed.

"You think they're okay?" Because it sure didn't look okay. How could Rick have survived that blast? Heck, she'd been blown several feet.

"Well, the building isn't on fire. Smoke inhalation is the worst for—is the worst."

She turned toward Perry. "For who? Humans?"

"That's not what I was going to say, but yeah. For people. And animals."

She shook her head. He was so full of it. What was he hoping to accomplish? That she'd forget? She hadn't forgotten what Sam did to her.

Firemen exited the building, helping her cousin to the ambulance. She ran to them. "Rick!"

He looked up. "Janie!"

She hugged him tight. "I thought you were dead."

"Ma'am, we need to take him to the hospital." A fireman stood with a stretcher beside him.

"You're hurt?" Blood soaked the side of Rick's shirt. "Oh my God. Are you okay?"

"A little woozy."

She stood by while the paramedics stabilized Rick before strapping him onto the gurney and settling him in the ambulance. She wanted to go with him, but they wouldn't let her ride in the ambulance.

"I'll take you."

She'd nearly forgotten that Sam was even there. But she couldn't mistake him now. He still had the sparkly brown eyes and hot body. Still wore the faded jeans, although he was wearing a jean jacket over a black T-shirt. His hair was a little shorter but otherwise hadn't changed. Had he even aged? "Thank you for getting him, but I'll just get a cab."

"Don't be silly. I have a car here. You'll be out of the cold and at the hospital much faster."

"Why should I trust you? I don't know you."

"But you already know I won't hurt you. Don't you? And you can ask your questions, because I'm sure you have a ton of them."

She did. "Fine. But no funny business."

"No funny business. I promise. Come on, it's over there."

"Sir." A fireman grabbed Sam by the shoulder. "You're injured. Your arm."

Sam turned. He yanked a chunk of wood that had stuck out the back of his arm. "It was just caught on my sleeve. I'm fine. Thank you."

Like hell it was caught. That thing had been imbedded and now he was bleeding. Couldn't the fireman see that? But he was leaving. "Wait. He's—"

Sam grabbed her arm. "Don't bother him. It's just a scratch. I'm fine."

Of course he was fine. He probably healed fast because he was a vampire. Or an alien. She just wasn't sure which.

* * * *

Her scent was driving Sam nuts. It took everything in him to keep his fangs from extending.

Man, he really needed to feed.

"You okay?" Perry asked as he met up with them.

"Nothing a...meal won't fix."

Janie snorted. "A meal? Is that what you call blood?"

They were heading for the SUV, but had walked through a group of people when she'd uttered the "B" word. He turned toward her and spoke softly. "I know you're angry and confused, but can you save the snark until we're in that bright yellow car over there?"

"Tell me again why I should go with you?"

"Well..." Perry said. "You don't have much choice. Your car is a pancake and I doubt you'll get a taxi from here."

Using the key fob, Sam unlocked the vehicle. Janie climbed into the back. "This is all your fault," she yelled, then promptly slammed the door.

"This is going well, isn't it?" Perry asked with a smirk. "I can't believe you didn't tell me you met a Perfect Mate."

"Not now, Perry."

"Oh no. Yes, now. Why didn't you tell me?"

"I didn't know she was a Perfect Mate until the announcement, okay?"

"That was seven months ago. How long ago did you meet her?"

"Get in the car." What could he say to Perry that wouldn't hurt his feelings more? Sam slowly settled behind the steering wheel. His back was screaming at him to get some rest, his stomach was in knots wanting some blood, and his fangs wouldn't stay locked up in his gums.

Perry entered the vehicle. "Does Johnny know?" When Sam kept quiet and drove the car away from the curb, Perry slapped the dashboard. "Damn it. You told him at the wedding, didn't you? And Vic. Of course she knows. She didn't call Johnny about this trip, she called you. What about Barnet? Are you all shutting me out?"

Janie poked her head between the seats. "Do I need to be here for this?"

Perry turned her. "When did he feed from you?"

"Perry!" Sam shook his head. It took everything in him to keep the car on the road. "What are you talking about?"

"She already admitted that you had. Plus, you couldn't wipe her memory. Right?"

Sam gripped the wheel. This wasn't happening. Perry was going to ruin everything. Sam would never be able to talk to Janie now. Convince her they weren't dangerous.

"You can wipe memories?" Janie asked.

"How else do you think we can stay hidden? But don't worry. We can't wipe yours or else you wouldn't have remembered anything. So when did he feed from you?"

She stared at Sam in the rearview mirror. "Four and a half years ago. On July 12th."

"You remember the date?" It was etched in Sam's memory because he never wanted to forget how she made him feel. Was that why she remembered?

"Only because it was my then fiancé's birthday and I was on my way back home after finding him with another woman."

So much for being memorable. Sam's heart ached.

"What did you do to Rick? Why'd you blow up his apartment building?"

"Ummm… Sweetheart," Perry said. "I told you. We didn't do that. We came here to make sure he was okay. Except he's not. Is he?"

Sweetheart? Perry had no right calling her that. Sam nearly cracked the steering wheel and let up on his grip. She was his, damn it. Well, not his technically, but would be. Should be. If he ever got a chance to make it all right.

"No, he's not." Janie broke eye contact and looked out the side window. "What did your people do to him? Try to beam him up to your spaceship?"

"Spaceship?" Perry laughed. "Wait a minute. You said you knew what we are."

"She doesn't know," Sam said. "She's only guessing. Just like Rick is. Am I right?"

"Well, you're not human. I can tell by your eyes. And you know I can tell by your eyes. Why else wear contacts?"

Perry turned in his seat. "So we can see?"

"Yeah, right."

Her scent was intensifying in the enclosed vehicle and Sam nearly lowered his window. But it'd only make her cold and he was more concerned about her comfort than the raging boner going on in his jeans. He turned up the heat. "What happened to your boyfriend was an accident, okay? We tried to fix it."

"Boyfriend?" She scrunched her face then smoothed out in understanding. "Rick is not my boyfriend. He's my cousin."

The tension that had coiled up inside Sam's gut released a little. She may not be Rick's girlfriend, but she could still be someone else's. Or worse, their wife.

"Cousin?" Perry looked at Sam. "Barnet's going to have a field day."

"Who is this Barnet fella? And why should he care that I'm Rick's cousin?"

Sam couldn't lie to her. Hell, he wanted her for his mate; she'd know all this stuff eventually. "He's trying to find a connection between all the people we can't…"

"Control?" she asked.

"Not the word I was going for, but yeah, control is one of the things we can do."

"Is that what happened to Rick? The alien couldn't control him so he tried to kill him?"

"Aliens?" Perry said. "I'll have you know I was born in this country."

Janie's face paled. She grabbed her neck with one hand and her stomach with the other. "Rick was right. You're vampires."

Sam gritted his teeth. Man, this was not how he expected their second meet to go. Or even their third or fourth. He figured he'd get her to like him first before laying the vampire thing on her. Now she knew and he couldn't change her memories. Couldn't make things better through coercion. He could only do it with his words or actions. He only hoped they would be good enough.

* * * *

Sam stared at Janie through the rearview mirror, his eyes mesmerizing. "Yes, we're vampires. But we don't kill people for food, okay?"

Janie kind of figured that or she and Rick would have been dead. So why was she relieved when Sam confirmed her theories? It didn't make sense. He was a freakin' vampire! But there it was. Relief.

"Not to mention," Perry said, "we like to feed from people whose memory of the incident can be erased."

Oh God. They couldn't erase her memories. She should have taken that cab. They weren't going to let her go now. "What are you going to do with me? With Rick?"

"Do?" Sam asked. "We don't want to do anything."

"But we know your secret."

He pulled into the hospital parking lot. Before he killed the engine, she yanked on the door handle without success. After flipping the lock, the door still wouldn't open. Trapped. She was trapped in the car with two vampires.

Sam turned around and winced. Had he gotten hurt getting Rick? And damn, his eyes were more beautiful without the mirror between them. "You've known my secret for quite awhile now. Did you tell anyone?"

She shook her head.

"How come?"

She gave him a "duh" look. "Like anyone would have believed me." Plus, he really hadn't hurt her that night. What was there to tell?

"Did Rick tell anyone?"

"Just me," she lied. Why give these two vampires more people to go after? "And only after I confronted him. You really messed up his mind."

Sam opened his mouth to say something when his fangs descended. Holy shit. They were real.

"Dude," Perry said.

Sam turned around, his face out of sight. He said something quietly to Perry, but she couldn't make out a word of it.

"Are you going to let me go see Rick?" Why else bring her to the hospital? These two were confusing her more and more.

Perry leaned his elbow on his seat back. "Sure, we'll let you go. In a moment. But you need to understand, we have no intention of hurting you or your cousin. In fact, I want to…date you."

Date her? What the hell?

Sam growled.

"Hey, you had your chance. I can't help it if you blew it."

"I didn't know what she was back then. I didn't even know they existed."

"What I *am*? What *am* I?" she asked.

Perry grinned at her. "A Perfect Mate."

She snorted. She couldn't help it. If only they knew. "I'm not a perfect anything."

"You are to us." He rested his head on his arm. "We can't read your mind. We can't control you. And your blood—"

"What?" She grabbed her neck again.

He sat up. "Is not important. You're safe with us. Honest."

"You know, I'm getting a little sick of your honest."

"So am I," Sam said. The locks clicked free. "Go on. We'll see you inside."

Janie opened the door and slipped out before they could change their mind. She checked in at the desk to find that they'd sent Rick to surgery. They told her where the waiting room was located.

At least this wasn't the same hospital she used to candy-stripe at all those years ago. She could only imagine who she might run into there.

Only one other person sat in the room, a woman in her forties reading a book. Janie went to the other side, sat in the corner, and pulled out her phone. It was after ten-thirty. Would they still be up? Did it matter?

Rick's mom, her aunt Susan, picked up. "Hello, Janie. Is something wrong?"

She would ask that, because why else would Janie be calling so late? "There's been an explosion at Rick's apartment building."

Aunt Susan gasped. "Oh my. Is he okay?"

"I think so. He got hurt, but he's in surgery now. Most likely to stitch him up. No use for you coming out here now." Hell, the vampires would probably send her aunt back home. "I'll stay and keep you posted."

"Thank you, Janie. Were you able to talk with him?"

"We had a nice long talk earlier. I think that's all he really needed." Janie hated lying to her aunt, but what choice did she have?

"Call as soon as you hear something. I doubt I get any sleep until I know."

"I will. Love you." Janie disconnected the call. One down, one to go. If she didn't call Megan and Megan watched the news…

"Turning in already?" That was Megan. No, "hello." No, "how ya doing." Just straight to the conversation.

"Not yet. Just wanted you to know that I'm okay." Janie then went on to explain what little she could. It would have been so much nicer to be able to dump everything that had happened, but until Janie could grasp exactly where she stood with those two vampires, her lips were sealed.

Besides, if she did blab, they'd probably kill her. Perfect Mate or not.

Chapter 5

Perfect madness.

When Janie slammed the car door, Sam could only stare at Perry. The pain in his back and stomach were no longer an issue. Anger had taken up residence. "I want to date you? Really?"

"Weren't you the one who said I should let her decide?" Perry crossed his arms. "Well... I'm letting her."

"I found her first."

"And weren't you the one who said that shouldn't matter?"

"Will you stop telling me what I said?"

"I'm not stepping away and you can't make me. Hell, with the way you look right now, I could probably take you out in one punch."

Sam couldn't refute that. Hell, Janie could probably take him out. "This is why I didn't tell you about her. Or Barnet. Or any unbonded vampire."

"No. This is happening because you *failed* to tell me. When are you going to learn to trust people?"

"Right, like you would have told me if you'd found her."

"Guess you'll never know now, will you?" Perry opened the door and climbed out. "I thought you were a friend. I'm beginning to wonder if I have any." He slammed the door and headed for the hospital.

A strong cramp gripped Sam's stomach. He should go feed, but he couldn't let Perry be alone with Janie. Couldn't let them...bond, in the non-vampire way. Not that she seemed all that interested.

Still, she could change her mind. Perry could change it for her. So instead of doing the smart thing, Sam followed Perry to the waiting room.

On the left side of the room, an older woman was reading a book and looked up as they entered. Janie sat in the corner on the right side of the room. They certainly wouldn't have any privacy talking here. Just as well. He wasn't sure what kind of stupid stuff would spew from his mouth. Somehow he would have to get Janie alone, but with the way Perry was acting, that feat would be damn near impossible.

Perry went to sit beside her, but the glare she gave him caused him to leave a seat between them. Sam would have laughed, except she basically gave him the same look. Couldn't really blame her there. They hadn't exactly acted like adults. He moved to sit on the other side of her when his legs gave way and he crumpled to the floor.

Oh great. His broken back was having the last laugh. He sent a mental command to the woman to ignore him and then planted his hands on the seat behind him and lifted. But all that accomplished was another slide to the floor and more pain to his back.

Janie leaned over. "Are you okay?"

"Not really." It would most likely take a feeding before he could move his legs again. He'd ask Perry for help, but didn't think the man would bother. He could use the lady from across the room. Would that freak out Janie?

She turned toward Perry. "Are you going to help him?"

"Nope."

Bingo. Sam called that one.

Perry rested his arm along the empty seat between them. "How's your cousin?"

"He's in surgery."

"Surgery?" Sam said. "I'm sorry. I didn't think he was that bad off."

"If you're not responsible for blowing up the building, then it's not your fault. Are you sure there isn't anything I can do to help you? You look…uncomfortable."

He kind of liked that she was concerned for him. Maybe he stood a chance with her after all?

"Ah, he's fine." Perry smiled. "Aren't you, Sammy?"

The words, "screw you," were on the tip of Sam's tongue, when a cramp seized his stomach. Blood would solve his body problems, but for some reason he didn't think her idea of help included that specific donation. Besides, the last time, the only time, was so erotic, he wasn't sure it wouldn't be again. Which was definitely the wrong thing to remember. Not everything below his waist was paralyzed. His boner returned.

Smooth, Sam. Smooth.

* * * *

Janie widened her eyes as Sam's crotch grew. What the hell was turning him on? And how big was he?

The only other occupant in the waiting room—who surprisingly hadn't even flinched when Sam had fallen—stood up and moved to the seat beside Sam's head. She then extended her arm.

"Dude," Perry said. "Shouldn't you go somewhere more private?"

"Private? For what? What's going on?" Janie asked.

Sam glowered at Perry, but didn't take the woman's arm. "Priceless. Got any more gems you want to disperse?" He took a deep breath. "I'm sorry, Janie. I need to feed so I can walk again, so if that bothers you, you might want to leave."

Perry cackled. "Oh my God. You are so pathetic."

"You can't walk?" Then she remembered the roof falling in. "You *were* injured." And it'd left him paralyzed. Guilt slammed into her. "Don't you need a doctor?"

Perry leaned in close. "He doesn't need a doctor. He needs blood."

Was that why Sam was getting a hard-on? He was thinking about drinking that woman's blood?

Perry shook his head at Sam "Why didn't you feed before coming in here? Oh wait, don't tell me. You didn't trust me."

"You didn't exactly give me the warm fuzzies."

"Will you two cut it out?" They were worse than Rick and his brother back when they were little. "Are you going to hurt her?" But that wasn't the question she really wanted answered. Just didn't seem right to ask if he was going to give the woman an orgasm.

"No. She won't even know what's going on. So excuse me while I heal." He no sooner had exposed the woman's wrist when two teenage boys entered the room.

"Mom?"

Janie froze. How would Sam be able to explain what he was doing to their mother? But before she could utter a word, they both grabbed their crotch and ran out of the room.

"Don't say I didn't do anything for you," Perry said. "I'd hurry if I were you. They might not really have to go."

"What did you just do?" But then the answer didn't matter when Sam bit down on the woman's wrist.

Something like jealousy struck her. Why would he feed from a stranger? Wasn't her blood good enough? And how long would it take before the woman writhed in an orgasm? Janie almost didn't look.

But upon closer examination, the answer to that last question was a big fat never. Those boys' mother just sat still with a vacant look in her eyes. As if in a trance. Nothing sexual flittered across her face. Janie relaxed.

Perry spoke softly. "I made sure those boys didn't see their mother and told them they had to go to the bathroom. Now."

"You told them?" Janie whispered, since he'd seem so covert about the whole thing. She hadn't heard him say anything to those boys, though.

"Telepathically."

"That's how you control them? That's how Sam is controlling her?"

"Yeah."

Damn. That was some kind of power. No wonder they've stayed hidden. "But you can't do that to me. Or Rick." Was that why it had felt erotic? Because Sam couldn't control it otherwise? But he'd been turned on. Except… Maybe not. He no longer sported an erection. Hmmm…

"You're catching on."

"How much do you take?"

"Less than what you'd donate to a blood bank. We're not killers. If we were, there wouldn't be any mortals left and we'd starve."

"Good point." And nice to know Sam hadn't taken that much from her four and a half years ago. Which made sense. She hadn't gotten dizzy or light headed. The wobbly legs had more to do with the wonderful orgasm than from blood loss.

Sam licked the woman's arm. Still in a trance, she stood, grabbed her purse, and exited the room.

"Where is she going?" Janie asked.

"To the vending machine." Sam leaned back against the chair and wiggled his feet. "Ah, thank God."

"Why the vending machine?"

He turned those beautiful, brown eyes her way. "I told her she was thirsty for some orange juice. Hopefully it has some. I had given you the same command back then, but you weren't actually listening to me."

"Awww. Ain't that sweet of you," Perry said sarcastically.

It *was* sweet of Sam and Janie smiled. "You care."

"Don't let him fool you," Perry said. "We all care."

"Oh, like you send your donor off for food after," Sam said.

"You only did that to impress Janie. Admit it."

"I did no such thing."

Janie nearly screamed. "What is wrong with you two? You're acting like five-year-olds."

Sam lowered his head. "You're right. I'm sorry."

"I'm sorry, too," Perry said. "Guess we're not making a very good impression, are we? It's just that it's not every day we're in the presence of a Perfect Mate and we're probably acting a little…crazy."

More like a lot, but why insult the vampires? "Would you stop calling me that?"

"But that's what you are."

Sam slowly rose, using the seat for leverage as he had the last time. This time he managed to stay on his feet and the seat. "This is not the way I thought we'd meet again."

"You were looking for me?" How much different would her life had been if he'd found her sooner? Would Justin and Aaron still be alive?

"Yeah. Since I realized what you were seven months ago. You're not an easy person to track. Did you change your name?"

He only started looking seven months ago? Justin had been dead by then, but Aaron would have stood a chance. That was if she seriously considered hooking up with Sam, assuming that's what his plans were. "How did you even know my…oh, my credit card. But it says Jane and you called me Janie."

"Because that's what it said on the book inside your car. Property of Janie Robinson."

All this time she'd thought he'd been an alien and had probed her mind, when it really just came down to being observant. She nearly laughed. "What were you planning on doing once you found me?"

"I'd like to hear the answer to that, too," Perry said.

Sam ran a hand through his hair. "I don't know. Never thought that far. I just needed to find you."

"Because I'm a Perfect Mate."

"Yeah," both guys said in unison.

"Would all your kind act crazy around me or is it just limited to you two?"

"Not all," Perry said. "But most."

"And Rick? Does he drive you crazy, too?"

Sam shook his head. "We're heterosexual, as I assume your cousin is. Except for being unable to read his mind or control him, he smells the same as any other mortal."

"Which is just wrong," Perry said. "Not that I made up the rules."

"I smell different?"

They both nodded, but neither elaborated.

"So why was Rick attacked? He said it was a man."

"It was a man," Perry said. "A stupid man who didn't bother to make sure he could control your cousin before feeding from him."

Sam grimaced. "Yeah, right. Go ahead. Call me stupid."

"You attacked Rick?" Which didn't make sense. Sam wasn't black.

"No." He shook his head. "You. What I did to you was stupid."

"Oh." The night of July 12th. The night of her dreams. Funny, they never seemed stupid. Confusing, sure, but stupid? Nah. He'd reacted to her pretty much the way she'd reacted to him. She hadn't been able to control that so why would she expect he could?

"After you stormed off, I realized that I hadn't been treating my female donors with much respect and for that, I'm sorry. It was never my intention to hurt you. Guess you could say I grew a conscience that day."

Janie smiled. She had done that to him? Maybe he wasn't such a bad guy after all. "So if you didn't blow up Rick's apartment building, would this other vampire do it? The one who attacked him before?"

"No. He's under strict orders to stay away." Perry strummed his fingers on the seatback beside her. "It had to be an accident. None of us had any reason to attack your cousin."

She was willing to believe him until the cops came looking for her.

Chapter 6

Targeted, cursed, what's the difference?

Sabotage? Could this day get any weirder?

Sam had listened to the policemen explain to Janie that the explosion hadn't been an accident. That they were gathering information to find out who in the apartment building could have been targeted.

Certainly didn't help his and Perry's case any in trying to convince Janie that they were innocent. At least she waited until the officers left the waiting room before asking, "Wanna tell me again how you had nothing to do with it?"

Thank goodness the room was empty on this late Friday night. Hardly anyone passed by in the hallway, either. Sure made conversation easier. Especially when vampires were the subject matter.

Sam stretched his now moveable legs and winced at the pain in his back. He might be mobile, but it would take more time, and probably another feeding, before he was one hundred percent. "If someone in our organization was responsible, I know nothing about it."

She snorted. "Organization? Really? Good one. How do I know you haven't been responsible for all the other deaths in my life?"

"Deaths? What deaths?"

"Like you don't know. Do David, Justin, and Aaron ring a bell? All this time I thought I was cursed, and it was you keeping me from getting attached to anyone. And now you're going after my family."

"Whoa, wait a minute. I haven't killed anyone. I didn't even know where you were until today." And who were all those men? Family members or...husbands? Did he really want to know?

"Sure, a likely story." She glared at Perry. "You're probably in on it, too, huh?"

"If I had known you existed, I would have made myself known. Hell, I would have just mentally sent any suitors away. Trust me, a vampire who discovers a Perfect Mate doesn't let them get away. Except for stupid over there."

Sam couldn't dispute that fact. He was stupid for letting her go. "In my defense, I had no idea Perfect Mates even existed."

"But if you didn't..." She covered her face. "I *am* cursed."

Sam fisted his hand. Why oh why had he let Perry accompany him on this trip? If not for that one little mistake, Sam would be alone with Janie now. Comforting her. Trying to fix the huge mistake he'd made four and a half years ago. "Janie, what's been going on?"

She slowly lowered her hands. "You might want to re-think that Perfect Mate thing. Every guy I've ever been close to has...died. And now I guess I'm affecting my relatives."

Perry stood and backed away, as if she were contagious. "Died? How?"

"David." Her eyes glistened and she swallowed. "He was in a car accident the day after our wedding."

"Wedding?" So she had been married. Was that why Sam had never been able to find her? Because she'd changed her name?

She swiped at her eyes. "You think no one would want to marry me?"

"No. That's not it. I didn't even think you'd changed your name."

"I didn't. Never had the chance." She looked away. "He was gone before we even had a honeymoon. Afterward, there was no point to it, was there?"

"I'm so sorry, Janie." He hated seeing her in distress, even if it was for another man. "What about the others?"

"Two years ago, Justin proposed." She eyed him to say something, but he kept his mouth shut. "The next day he fell to his death at work. No one knows why he was there. Authorities figured he lost his footing. Then six months ago, Aaron asked me to move in with him. A day later he died in a freakish drone accident." She lowered her head. Tears dropped onto her jeans and she sniffled. "I tell you, I'm cursed."

"Damn," Perry said. "That sounds pretty cursed. A drone? Really?"

"I said it was freakish." She rummaged through her purse and pulled out a tissue.

"No one's cursed." Sam moved closer to Janie. "Are you sure they were accidents?" Because it sure sounded more than coincidental to Sam.

She wiped her eyes and blew her nose. "The police said they were. And if you guys weren't responsible, why would someone kill them?"

"To frame you?" Perry asked.

"What?" She stood and paced the room. "No. No. That's not possible. I mean, I was the first person the police looked at. And I had solid alibis in every case. Hell, I didn't even gain anything from their deaths. Well, except for David."

"Because you were married to him." Just thinking about her with someone else, even when those someones were all dead, grated on Sam. If he'd only known back then. She never would have been involved with those men. He'd have made sure of it.

"Yeah." She sat down. "I inherited his estate. And life insurance policy. It was quite substantial."

"How substantial?" Perry asked. "Enough to hire out a killer?"

And she was up again. "I didn't kill anyone."

"I'm not saying you did. Just that those other cases could be re-opened if this one looks like you're involved."

She covered her face. "Oh my God."

Sam smacked his so-called friend. "Perry, why would you say that?"

"Just stating the truth. She should be prepared."

Janie resumed pacing. "Why? Why would someone do that to me?"

"Crazy people don't need whys," Perry said.

"Oh God. My life just got way more complicated, didn't it?" She stopped and faced Sam. "Do you think... Do I need a lawyer?"

"Not if you become my Perfect Mate." Perry grinned as if that were the best idea ever.

Mouth open, she stared at Perry. Couldn't have been more gobsmacked.

"What the hell, Perry?" A smack was too lenient. Sam pictured his right fist going through Perry's face.

"Well you're not asking her. Why shouldn't I?"

Sam could list a lot of reasons why Perry shouldn't. Number one being: she wasn't his.

Janie grabbed her head. "Oh my God. You're nuts, that's what you are. Be your Perfect Mate." She elaborated those last two words with air quotes. "Oh sure, that would solve everything...not. News flash! I'm not going to be anyone's Perfect Mate. I don't even know you guys."

Sam stood and put his hands out. "No one's forcing you to." That wasn't the way it worked, he was sure of it, but Perry... Damn man.

"Fine," Perry said. "No bonding...yet. But you would be safer with us. At Headquarters."

Sam nearly exploded. It was his worst nightmare coming true. "Are you shitting me? You want her near Barnet and every other male vampire who isn't bonded?"

"Headquarters? You have a Headquarters?"

Perry jumped to his feet and zeroed in on Sam, ignoring Janie's question. "Man, you just don't trust anyone, do you?"

"It's not a matter of trust, and you know it." Sam was more worried about losing his sanity. If he lost that he wouldn't have a chance with Janie.

"Then what do you propose?" Perry put his hands on his hips. "And don't go saying she can stay with you and Johnny. She needs to hide."

"She'd be better off there than Headquarters." The man had lost it. Plain and simple.

Janie wedged between him and Perry. "Shut up and sit."

"Ooh, bossy. I like it," Perry said.

Janie just glared at him. Sam was ready to punch the guy, but took his seat instead. Perry followed suit.

She stood facing them. "Did anyone tell you, you two are impossible?" She put her palm out when Perry opened his mouth.

"Don't answer that. But here's the thing. I can't go anywhere right now. It'll just make me look guilty."

"Then don't get a lawyer until you need one," Perry said. "Innocent people don't have one on retainer."

"That's not true," she said. "Is it?"

Sam so much wanted to take her hand in his. Not only to feel her warmth, but to offer her some reassurance. "I wish you'd reconsider. You'd be safe with us until this all blows over."

"Safe? Like your Headquarters? Where is that? In New Orleans?"

"Please. That's so Anne Rice," Perry said. "We're in Atlanta. The Underground. Which is where we'll be taking your cousin once he's able to travel."

Janie's eyes widened. "What? Why?"

Sam hated having to dump more bad news on top of bad, but she had a right to know. "Because he's not stable right now. The Committee made a mistake letting him go the way they had. They aren't planning on hurting him, I swear."

"Plus," Perry interjected, "there are a few females who might be interested—"

"Are you kidding me?" Janie interrupted, her face turning red. "You want to hook him up with a vampire?" She practically hissed that last word. Either out of disgust or she didn't want anyone to overhear.

Perry leaned forward in his seat. "You make it sound like it's a bad thing. We can offer some pretty wonderful perks."

"What the hell, Perry?" Sam smacked him again. "We're not interviewing for an employee."

"I'm just trying to help."

"Yourself, you mean."

"Yeah, like you don't want her for yourself."

"Stop it!" She stamped her foot and glared at them.

Perry grimaced. Sam had never been so turned on. Such spirit. Such fire. He could only imagine what she must be like in—okay, he was so not going there. But damn. What she must think of him.

She paced the room. "You can't take him. If he goes missing, what'll that look like for me?"

"We can't have him blabbing about us, either," Perry said.

"I know. I know. But if he's able to talk to you like I am. Without the *bickering*, that is." And yeah, Sam might have winced at that remark "He'll probably reconsider. I mean, he was already reconsidering. He'll be relieved to know he's not going crazy. Can't you give him that chance?"

Sam wanted more than anything to give her and her cousin a chance. Unfortunately, that wasn't his call.

＊＊＊＊

Janie smoothed her sweaty palms against her thighs and sat back on the chair while Sam stepped out to make a phone call. Of all the conversations she'd had in the past, tonight's had to be the weirdest one on record. Vampires and Perfect Mates. Their Headquarters were in Atlanta, of all places. It was just so unreal. Her heart was still racing.

What was even more unreal was that she sat there hoping these two vampires would talk to her cousin, a so-called Perfect Mate, and help him understand.

If that were even possible. *She* didn't really understand.

But if they took Rick away to their Headquarters, and the police started looking into her past, she was sure to be charged with something. Probably murder. Damn it. She didn't want to go to jail.

She rubbed her still sweaty hands on her thighs again and asked Perry, "So, who's Sam calling?"

"My guess? Vic. Victoria. She's on the Committee."

"You have a Committee? At Headquarters?" Of course they did. Bizarre.

"We're very civilized. Honest."

She turned to tell him to cut the crap about being honest all the time and found him leaning into her space. Sniffing her. She jerked back.

Perry straightened. "I'm not going to bite you."

"Right." She couldn't suppress a giggle. "You just want to date me."

"Is that so bad?"

Maybe she *was* a Perfect Mate. For vampires. She'd been killing off all her mortal suitors. A vampire was probably more...sturdy. But if she were to pick a vampire to get to know better, it wouldn't be Perry. "I'm sure you're a nice...guy, but—"

"Don't say it." He leaned his head back. "It's because you met Sam first, isn't it? You like him better."

"I don't know either one of you enough to like you or not. But I'm sorry, it's nothing against you as a person, but I don't get the same…feeling from you as I do from him." She was certainly attracted to Sam. Drawn to him more. Was it because they'd met first? Or was it because of that earth-shattering kiss? A kiss she wouldn't mind recreating. Some day.

"See? I knew it. You'd rather rip his clothes off than mine."

"I'm sorry to burst your bubble, but I have no desire to rip anyone's clothes off." At least, not yet anyway. "Why does it matter that I met him first?"

He shrugged. "It just seems to."

"Who did Rick meet first?" Could it be he already had a perfect vampire for a mate?

"Vic. Victoria. Before she bonded with her own Perfect Mate, she wanted to see what kind of reaction she got from touching your cousin. Plus, it was the best way to determine that he is indeed a Perfect Mate and she didn't want to involve another female vampire since they were keeping it all hush-hush back then."

"So it's not who you meet first then, is it?" Otherwise, Rick would be craving Victoria and he didn't seem so interested. Not like she was with Sam.

"I don't know. We don't know that many."

"Rick mentioned seeing a teenager. Was that Victoria?"

Perry cackled. "Yeah, that was her, but don't let her hear you call her that. Sure, she was turned when she was seventeen, but she's nearly 400."

"Four…hundred?" Janie placed a hand over her heart. "Just how old do you get?"

"Don't know. The oldest vampire I know about is over three-thousand years old."

Holy crap. Just how old was Sam? He and Perry both looked to be about her age.

Sam returned, but he still walked stiffly. "Victoria and Ben will be here tomorrow night. They left a couple of hours ago and should make it to John's before sunrise."

"They were already on their way?" Janie asked. "Why?"

"Because I called in your cousin," Perry said.

"They're coming to get him? No." How could she rescue Rick?

"Relax," Sam said. "I told Victoria what you said. She agrees with you. If Rick is okay with the whole vampire business, they won't take him to Atlanta."

Janie was beginning to like this Victoria person, teenager or not.

Perry stood. "If you'll excuse me, I need to get a bite to eat."

Sam grabbed Perry's arm and seemed to be communicating. Telepathically, maybe? A moment later Perry yanked free and left the room.

"What was that all about? You now bickering telepathically?"

"That obvious, huh?" Sam shoved his hands in his pockets. "I was just surprised he left me alone with you."

"You two don't trust each other, do you?"

"Something like that. This whole Perfect Mate business is a lot to take in. Even for us. Doesn't help matters when there aren't that many of your kind and you've just now started to show up."

"Perfect Mates haven't existed before now?"

"Nope. Not that anyone has admitted to anyway. It's possible Perfect Mates have been found earlier and…killed because their memory couldn't be wiped. Sounds harsh, but it would have been the only way to keep our secret."

"So that vampire who attacked Rick. He wanted to kill him?"

Sam sat in the chair catty corner from her. "Yes and no. Rick was lucky. Dalton called for help because he wasn't sure what to do. It was only because Perfect Mates had recently been reported that Rick was brought to Headquarters. In the past, especially before cell phones, a vampire probably wouldn't have bothered. I mean, I had a cell phone and didn't bother."

"But you didn't kill me, either. Why is that?"

One side of his mouth curled up in a grin. "Why would I kill someone who filled my heart with warmth? Who lit my soul on fire? Who smelled like home? Hell, I didn't even want to let you go, but I was afraid that if I kept you and it didn't work out, I'd have had no choice but to kill you. At least back then. It's different now. Perfect Mates and vampires who discover one are protected now."

Her heart did a little stutter-step. She'd done all that to him? With just one kiss? "I smell like home?"

"What I remember home to be. And it's very alluring. I just want to…" He sighed.

"Bite me?"

His eyes widened. "No. I mean, yeah, but no. Not like that. I want to touch you. And maybe kiss you again. But I won't. Because what Perry said earlier is true. I want to date you, so we can get to know one another better. See if there's an actual connection between us."

She liked the way he thought. That's how she entered every one of her relationships. To find out if they were compatible before making any major life changes. It was the only way to go. "And if there isn't a connection, if I didn't like you, could you walk away?"

"You don't like me?"

She laughed at his expression. "I don't know you yet. But could you? Walk away?"

"It would be hard, but I'd do it. For you. But fair warning. Another vampire would most likely seek you out in that case, hoping they were the one. That's why I'm surprised Perry left."

"Well… I may have let on that he wasn't my type."

"Oh?" Sam smiled and her insides turned to goo.

Was there a connection between them? She'd had that thought four and a half years ago, after she'd driven away. And then there were the dreams. God, the dreams. To have that in real life would be exciting. But there was more to a relationship than lust. "Dating me may still be risky. You know. My curse."

He chuckled. "Number one, I don't believe in curses. Number two, I'm pretty indestructible. As long as I stay out of the sun."

"Because you're a…and you burn. Got it. I'm surprised Perry hasn't returned yet, because I don't think the cafeteria opens until six."

"He's not looking for that kind of food."

"He's not? Oh. Because you two are…and you don't eat. Got it. You don't happen to turn into…" She flapped her arms. "Do you?"

"Birds?"

"Very funny. You know what I mean."

Sam laughed. "Sorry. Couldn't resist. What you see is what you get."

Nice to know, because what she saw was very nice indeed. Oh hell, did this mean she was going to date a vampire?

She grinned. She could think of worse things to do.

* * * *

Tricia Crawford calmly turned off the TV, but everything inside her wanted to throw the remote through the screen. Aaron had only been dead six months and Janie already looked to be involved with someone else.

What a slut.

How many more times would Tricia have to get involved? How many more men would have to die for Janie to get the message?

Apparently one more. Cameras didn't lie. Tricia had seen the way that hunky fellow stared at Janie. Maybe it was time to just end it. At least she wouldn't have to travel far.

The front door squeaked opened then closed. Her daughter called out, "Mom?"

"In the TV room, dear." TV room. What a joke. It was just a stupid spare bedroom. No fancy media room. No special any kind of room at all. Not like she used to have. Not anymore, damn it. All because of Janie.

Rachel—her beautiful daughter and the only thing keeping Tricia sane—dropped her backpack on the floor and plopped down on the recliner. "You're up late."

"And you're home late."

"Sorry. Got distracted with Mary and the guys. Did you hear about the explosion? Tore the roof completely off some apartment complex."

"It was on the news. Terrible. They said no one died, though." Too bad for that. If it weren't for bad luck, she'd have no luck at all.

"I heard. Were they lucky or what? Those kinds of things usually start a fire. The firemen said it was fluky this one hadn't, but not unheard of. Glad we don't have gas."

"You talked to the firemen? What were you doing over there?" Tricia's heart skipped several beats. She did not need her daughter involved in Janie's mess, or anywhere near it.

"No, Mom. Snapchat. Everyone is talking about it."

Snapchat? What the hell was that? "Don't worry me like that."

"You okay? Have you taken your meds? You look a little depressed."

As if medication could ease the pain. The sorrow. "I'm just tired. Probably should go to bed. What are your plans tomorrow? Think you can spend some time with your dear old mom?"

"Well... I do need some new shoes. Can we go shopping? I promise not to spend a lot."

Rachel shouldn't have to promise such a thing. She should have whatever she wanted and Tricia should be able to give it her. But a person needed more than a social security check for that. Shoes, though, Tricia could handle. "I suppose we can do that."

"I'd also like to get more practice in. Want to shoot some arrows after?"

Archery was Rachel's favorite sport. If one called it that. But Tricia was more than happy to play along with her daughter. And it wouldn't cost any extra. Hell, the target practice alone was invigorating. All Tricia had to do was picture that slut's face as the target. "If you load up your car, I don't see why not."

"Thanks, Mom." Rachel stood and kissed Tricia on the cheek. "I'll see you in the morning." She then blew a kiss to the picture on the wall. "Night, Dad. Love you."

Tears threatened to fall. Rachel should have a father in her life, but Janie took that away, too. Nothing Tricia had done seemed to cause Janie the same kind of pain Tricia felt every day. That's because Janie was a slut. She cared for no one but herself.

So maybe it was time to stop going after the men. Janie clearly didn't care. Time to go after the little slut herself. And then maybe the pain would go away.

Chapter 7

As if two vampires weren't enough.

Hospitals might be the hubbub during the day, but after midnight? It was practically a ghost town. Even on a Friday night. Or would it be Saturday morning now? Sam emerged from the public restroom into the deserted hallway. One donor later—well, actually two if he counted the one from the waiting room—and the pain was gone. Sometimes being a vampire had its perks.

Oh great. Now he was thinking like Perry.

No sooner had he thought of his old friend, or possible enemy now, Perry appeared. He leaned up against the wall and crossed his arms over his chest. "I take it we'll be spending the day here."

Sam's donor—a male nurse or medical technician of sorts—exited the restroom, none the wiser. Sam waited until the man was out of earshot. "We're not supposed to leave Rick alone." Or Janie, for that matter, but why give Perry ideas? "By the way, he came out of surgery fine. Janie's with him."

"And you're not there clinging to her? Making sure I don't make a move on her? Will wonders never cease?"

"Listen, I'm sorry, okay? I wasn't thinking straight."

"No, you weren't thinking at all. You met her first. Fed from her. No one else has a shot with her. Don't you get it?"

"You don't know that. No one knows that." And no one would until more Perfect Mates were found.

"Well, I know she's not into me. Like my touch did nothing to her. Like I wasn't even on her radar."

Sam held back the smile that itched to form. Now was not the time to gloat. Although he wanted to. He wanted to badly. "I'm not sorry about that, but I'm not so sure she's into me, either."

"But I bet she's giving you a chance. Am I right?" Perry waved Sam off. "Yeah, I'm right. Because: She. Met. You. First."

Sam would so like to believe Perry's theory, but it just didn't make sense. The chemistry between vampires and Perfect Mates couldn't be any different than the chemistry between two mortals, could it? Either they were attracted to one another or they weren't. Why couldn't Perry see that?

"Then from your premise, Rick will go bonkers when he sees Victoria again. Then what? He's ruined for life? No other vampire has a shot? I highly doubt that. And that's because: It. Doesn't. Matter." Oh hell, why was Sam encouraging the man? Perry had already stepped away; did Sam really want the competition?

"But see, Vic didn't feed from Daugherty. You fed from Janie. Therefore, she's attracted to you and she's yours."

"According to John, you fed from Sarah before he did. Explain that."

"Well, not so much fed, but sampled."

Sam rolled his eyes. "That's not the point. You took her blood first and she didn't leave him for you. What do you have to say about that?"

"But…but…"

"Yeah, but. Your theory has holes in it."

"Shit. You're right. So you're saying I still have a shot with Janie?"

"No." Damn it. "Didn't you just say she wasn't interested?"

Perry cackled. "I'm just messing with you. You should have seen your face. Doesn't mean I'm still not mad at you. You should have told me. I thought we were friends."

"We are friends. And I didn't tell anyone except another bonded vampire. It had nothing to do with you personally, okay? Except maybe what you did with Sarah. That wasn't right, man."

Perry shoved his hands in his pockets and leaned against the wall of the hallway. "I know that now. Why do you think I'm trying so hard?"

"Maybe that's the problem. You're trying too hard. Not that I want you trying with Janie."

"Okay. Fine. You're forgiven for not telling me. You're still a distrustful bastard, though."

"Hey, I'll have you know my parents were married."

"Smartass." Perry pushed off from the wall. "Should we go guard Daugherty's door now? So he doesn't escape?"

Sam nodded and headed toward Rick's room. "It's this way. Just don't go in."

"What? You still don't trust me?"

Unfortunately, Sam didn't trust the guy. Probably wouldn't trust another vampire within a mile of Janie. But it sure helped that she wasn't interested in Perry. "That's not why. Rick can't know we're here and Janie isn't supposed to say anything until Victoria and Ben arrive."

As they approached Rick's room, another vampire came strolling toward them. Damn it. What was Dalton doing here?

* * * *

Janie entered the little bathroom in Rick's room. No place to really sit, so she leaned against the wall and placed her call. She wouldn't be in here long anyway. "Sorry to call so late, but you wanted an update."

"Sleep is overrated," Megan said. "How's your cousin doing?"

"Doctor said he was lucky. Nothing vital was injured, although he might have a concussion. He should be able to go home tomorrow."

"Home where? Wasn't his blown up?"

"His parents'. They don't live far." That's if the vampires let him. And they would once Janie made sure Rick understood his situation.

"Do you need me there? I could hop on a plane. Be there in the morning."

Oh shit. Janie straightened from the wall. "Don't be ridiculous. I'm fine. We're fine. I'm about ready to head back to my hotel room and get some sleep. I just wanted to make sure Rick was okay before I left."

"Then what's your room information? I want to send you something."

"That's not necessary."

"Of course it's necessary. And if you don't give it to me, I'll hop on the plane and deliver it in person."

"You're impossible." Janie gave her the details. "Please don't go to any trouble."

"It's not trouble when it's for a friend. I am your friend, aren't I?"

"Of course you're my friend. You're like the big sister I never had."

"More like a young aunt, but I'll take big sister. If you change your mind about me coming over..."

"You'll be the first to know." She hated lying to her friend, but if Megan came over, would Sam and Perry feel the need to wipe her memory? No one was touching Megan's memories.

Janie said her goodbyes and slipped the phone back into her purse. Her head ached. Her back ached. A bed sounded really good right now. She left Rick's room in search of her two new friends and found them in the hall with a strange man. A tall black guy with brown, sparkling eyes. And he settled his sights on her. Oh shit. Another one.

"What's going on?" she whispered. "Why is he here?" Was her scent that powerful she was bringing vampires in off the street?

"Dalton was just leaving," Perry said as he put an arm around the man's shoulders. "Weren't you?"

Not just another vampire, but Dalton. The vampire who attacked Rick. Double oh shit. "He's the one who—"

Sam held his hand up, halting her words. Yeah, they knew who Dalton was. What was she thinking?

"She knows?" Dalton said. "Why? That's not allowed."

"It's not for you to know," Perry said. "Victoria is on her way, okay?"

Dalton's eyes widened. "Victoria is coming here? I thought she never left Atlanta."

"She does now. And she's coming to fix it and make it all better. You understand?"

"Because he's a Perfect Mate." Dalton stared at her. Sniffed the air. "Is she one, too?"

"She is," Perry said. "You've never met a female one before, have you?"

Sam moved in front of her, blocking her view. Or protecting her. She peeked around his massive body.

Dalton shook his head. "She smells nice. Can I touch her?"

Sam practically vibrated as he stood there and his scent became stronger. She placed a hand on his shoulder. He stilled and turned his head her way.

So far Dalton didn't seem like such a threat. Janie smiled at the man. "Why do you want to touch me?"

"To see if it's true." Dalton turned to Perry. "She's not bonded is she?"

"She's not bonded," Perry said. "Sammy?"

Wait a minute. Why was he asking Sam? Wasn't it her—

"It's not my decision to make," Sam said.

Oh. She relaxed for a moment, then tensed right back up. Did she want another vampire touching her? Her instinct was to say not only no, but hell no. But these vampires knew so little about Perfect Mates. And they seemed to almost worship her. That in itself was a heady feeling.

Sam turned around. "I won't let him hurt you, but I understand his curiosity."

Curiosity. Yeah. Guess that's what she was to the vampire community. A curiosity. A curiosity they seemed to worship. "Do you trust him?"

Perry piped up. "I think we already determined that Sammy doesn't trust anyone."

Sam rolled his eyes, but didn't say a word.

"Okay, then." Hopefully she wouldn't live to regret it. She took a step toward Dalton, but Sam lifted his arm.

"Not here. In the parking lot."

Why that mattered, she had no clue, but it seemed that's where they were headed.

* * * *

This is wrong, wrong, wrong. That phrase kept pounding inside Sam's head, but what could he do? He had no rights to Janie. None at all.

Perry took Dalton via the stairwell and Sam joined Janie at the elevator. Her peaches-and-cream scent mixed in with something a little sweeter.

"What are you afraid of?" It hurt to think she might be afraid of him.

She straightened. "Who said I was afraid?"

"I can smell it on you. It's quite strong." And mixed with her natural scent made it damn hard to control his fangs. Maybe vampires in the past thirsted on the sweet taste of fear, but he never had. If only his fangs could get with the program. "I hope you know I won't hurt you."

"I'm not afraid of you. Or Perry. But Dalton?"

Yeah, Dalton was…different. Mostly okay, but sometimes unstable. Why he'd ever been turned was a question for his maker, but unfortunately his maker no longer existed.

"If you don't want him touching you, then say so. We'll make sure he abides by your decision."

The elevator doors opened and he followed her inside. Her scent intensified in the small enclosure. Maybe they should have taken the stairs, too, but she'd gone to the elevators and he wasn't thinking.

She pushed the button for the lobby. "Why does he want to touch me? I thought I just smelled different. Do I do something to you?"

Do you ever. "When a vampire and a Perfect Mate of the attracting sex touch, the vampire will feel warmth." And a male vampire would quite possibly sport a boner and, oh damn, Dalton was going to get a boner. If Sam told her that, would it change her mind?

"Different than touching a regular person?"

He smiled. Regular person. She was so cute. "We can't determine temperature. So yeah. It's different."

"But you can feel the sun when it burns you. Right? That doesn't make sense."

"We can feel the pain of damaged cells, but not the heat. When we touch a regular person, as you put it, our temperature will match theirs. It's nothing anyone notices, though."

"So, you're never hot or cold?"

"That's right. We dress appropriately for the weather because that's what people expect."

"Do you think I should let Dalton touch me?"

No. Never. Tell her about the boner! "It's not my call."

"But if it were?"

If it were, he'd have taken her away and holed up somewhere private. Where they'd make love all day long. Every day. But they hardly knew each other and he wasn't about to scare her off like that. God, she was killing him. "How about I just say that I don't want anyone to touch you."

"Except you?" She smiled.

He shrugged. "Well...yeah."

"Do you want to touch me now?" She held out her hand.

Holy shit. More than anything. But for some stupid reason he could only stare at what she offered. When the doors opened to Perry and Dalton, she lowered her hand.

Opportunity wasted. Damn, what a fool he was.

* * * *

Janie stepped out of the elevator, Sam close behind her. Why hadn't he taken her hand? Was she afraid it'd go farther than a hold? He seemed to be fighting back...something. His fangs, maybe? She wouldn't mind getting a glimpse of them again. They were kind of sexy.

Together they followed Perry and Dalton to the parking lot. Of the four of them, she was the only one making breath trails in the cold air. The only one shivering, too, she bet. Would regular people really notice that, though? She'd have to ask later. Now didn't seem like such a good time.

It was closing in on three a.m. and the place was practically deserted. Probably why Sam insisted on coming outside. If Dalton tried anything, they'd be able to restrain him without much notice.

God. Restrain. Was she making a huge mistake?

For a big man, Dalton smiled shyly and ducked his head. "Thank you for letting me do this."

Perry grabbed Dalton's shoulder. "Don't make her regret it, either. Now stand against the wall over there."

Dalton did as he was told. Sam stood in front of Dalton, but a little off to the side. "Stand behind me," he said.

"Is this really necessary?" she asked.

In a blink, Perry appeared before her. "Do you get why the precautions?"

"Man, you move fast." There certainly would be no running away from one of them.

"Exactly. Now stand behind Sammy and me. That way if he tries a grab, he'll have to get through both of us."

What the hell? She looked at Dalton. "You're not going to try a grab are you?"

"No, ma'am."

Perry whispered, "I'm sure it's not in his plan, but once he gets a sample, he may not have much control."

"Will you shut up?" Sam said. "You're starting to freak *me* out."

Oh, great. Now the vampires were freaked. What did that make her? Janie laughed. "I'm sorry. This is just so bizarre. You sure you don't want to put me in a cage first?"

"A cage would be useless." Sam turned around. "If you've changed your mind, just say the word." His eyes nearly pleaded with her to do just that. But she had a feeling his pleading was stemming from his own insecurities and had nothing to do with Dalton as a person. Just as a male vampire. So maybe Sam was only freaking out because of that and nothing more.

Because, frankly, Dalton didn't seem like such a threat right now. And he was following orders without any question. He was just curious and she was beginning to be curious, too. What exactly would she feel? The same thing she felt when she touched Sam or closer to what she felt after touching Perry?

"Yeah," Perry said. "No one is forcing you to do this."

No, if anything, Sam would prefer she not touch Dalton. But Sam had relaxed when he realized Perry was no longer a threat. Dalton certainly couldn't be that much different and could possibly ease Sam's mind some more. Especially if Dalton didn't have any kind of reaction. Why Sam's mind and well-being even mattered was a thought for another day.

"I'm good. Let's get this over with." She indicated to the guys to turn around and then stood behind them. Slowly, she lifted her arm between the gap they left, toward Dalton. Her steady hand was no indication of the beating going on behind her rib cage.

Dalton hesitated a moment, glanced at Perry, glanced at Sam, then took her extended hand. He gasped and gripped her wrist while a faint, pleasant wave coursed up her arm. Not erotic like when Sam or Perry had touched her. But nothing revolting, either. It was just…nice. Like being hugged. She took a deep breath and the feeling dissipated. Huh.

"I feel heat," Dalton said. "Her scent is stronger, too."

"Yeah? What do you smell?" Perry asked.

"Roses. Like in Mama's garden. She had a beautiful garden." Dalton stared at her, his bronze colored eyes practically glowing. "Are you for real?"

"As real as vampires are, I suppose." She offered a smile and tugged on her arm to let him know she was finished, but he held on. Just how long did the guy have to hold her?

Sam grabbed Dalton's wrist. "You can let her go now."

Oh thank God. While his touch had been pleasant for a brief time, being held against her will was most definitely not. Janie yanked to get free, but Dalton continued to hold her tight. Not enough to hurt her—yet—but she might as well be shackled, her freedom was just as encumbered.

He set his sights on Sam. "Have you claimed her?"

"She's not a possession, but she's agreed to date me. Now let her go."

Date. Yeah. Guess she did agree to that. And it was nice to know he didn't consider her a thing to be possessed. At least he made a good show of it. Was he meant for her? She'd love to touch him again, maybe even take that touch further, but she couldn't base their future on just that. She had her priorities. Whereas with Dalton, she'd just like to have her hand back.

"So I'd have to…" Dalton stopped in thought, but kept hold of Janie. She continued to pull gently, hoping the guy would get the message.

"Let her go," Sam growled.

"Yeah, man," Perry said. "You're not being cool."

Dalton's pupils grew larger, his eyes were nearly black. Damn it. Was he getting ready to grab her? Even Perry couldn't pry her free and he was tugging on Dalton's fingers.

"Challenge you."

Janie froze. So did Perry.

"Excuse me?" Sam said. "Challenge me for what?"

Dalton bared his fangs. Okay, those were not sexy. They were scary as hell. She gave her arm another good yank. Before she could even process her freedom, she flew backward and landed on her sore butt while Dalton attacked Sam.

Chapter 8

Alone at last.

Sam had been half expecting Dalton to grab Janie and run off. The man was crazy and Sam didn't think Perfect Mates came into play at all. But when Dalton had said "challenge," Sam had lost focus. And maybe his grip.

Dalton growled and wrapped his hands around Sam's neck. Vampires couldn't be strangled, but they sure could get their head ripped off. Yeah, that wasn't happening. Sam grabbed Dalton's arms, fell back, and flipped Dalton over. The impact caused Dalton to loosen his hold.

Now free, Sam jumped to his feet. "What the hell, Dalton? We're out in public."

If Dalton heard, he didn't care. His eyes were huge, wild. The whites stood out against his dark skin. He charged at Sam again.

Prepared this time, Sam zipped around and grabbed Dalton from behind, pinning his arms against his body. The man writhed like a fish on a hook.

"You okay?" Perry asked. "That was quite a spill you took."

Janie. Sam spun, keeping the squirming Dalton in his arms. She was sitting on the ground and Perry was offering a hand up.

"Two falls in one day. I think that's a record." She stood without assistance and brushed her backside. "I might have bruised something back there, but I'll live."

She sounded okay, but she didn't look it. Red rings circled her wrist. "Your wrist. Did he break it?" Because if Dalton had, Sam wouldn't care if the vampire never saw another day.

She rubbed her wrist. "It's not broken. I probably did more damage than he did. You know, trying to get free."

"He shouldn't have held you to begin with." Sam squeezed Dalton. "Why? She was being nice and you do this?"

Dalton squirmed. "I must fight you for her. I must have her."

John had insisted, Perry had insisted, even Victoria had insisted, that a vampire would only be curious about a Perfect Mate. That they wouldn't get violent. And maybe most of them wouldn't. Just his luck he tripped over one who was. "You do realize we don't live in the dark ages anymore, right? It's the twenty-fucking-first century. Why are you doing this?"

"Yeah," Perry said. "We don't fight for women anymore. They don't like it so much."

Janie snorted. "Are you telling me that women used to like it?"

"Oh sure. To have two men fight for her hand was an honor."

"I don't believe this," she muttered as she rolled her eyes.

Sam wasn't believing it, either. Dalton had been a slave. Nothing in the way he was treated could have amounted to this kind of violence. Except, maybe to his maker, who was now dead.

"But that is exactly what you're supposed to do for a Perfect Mate," Dalton said. "Fight to the death."

Sam could see fighting to save her life, but nowhere in the Perfect Mate story did it say you had to fight to win her hand. "Where did you hear such garbage?"

"I think I know." Perry patted Dalton's cheek. "Dalton, buddy. Anton told you a fib. Vampires don't fight over a Perfect Mate. The Perfect Mate picks the vampire."

Dalton stopped squirming. "They do? But Master Anton said we fight."

"Because Anton enjoyed a good fight. All of his stories included one, didn't they?"

Dalton nodded. "He did like to fight. He liked to watch me fight, too, even though I didn't like it so much. Is that why he fibbed? So he could watch me fight?"

"It's possible. It's also possible he just liked his version of the story better. We'll never know now, will we?"

"But he told me about the pull. He didn't make that up. I can feel her pull me. Don't you?"

Sam knew all about the pull. He'd nearly followed Janie after their first encounter. Even now it was nearly impossible to leave her side. Would paranoia set in next, or did it already have its claws in him?

"Actually, I don't," Perry said. "Huh."

Sam had already suspected as much. Perry hadn't been making an effort to be by her side. It was nice to hear him admit it, though. One down, one to go? "Are you going to fight me anymore? Or are we going to have to stake you and turn you over to the Committee?"

"Noooo. Don't turn me over. I've already messed up once. Barnet said I had to behave. I thought I was doing the right thing. Please don't tell them. Please."

Something didn't sound right to Sam, but he released Dalton anyway. His fear of the Committee was strange, but useful in this case. "Why did you come to the hospital tonight?"

"You weren't going to hurt my cousin again, were you?" Janie asked.

Dalton straightened his shirt. "Your cousin? Noooo. I saw you on the news. Found out where you went. Thought you might need some help. Am I in trouble for that?"

"No," Sam said. "But you have to stay away from Daugherty. He can't see you. Committee's orders."

"Because Victoria is coming."

"That's right. She wants to talk to him."

"Okay." Dalton wobbled on his feet and then took a step toward Janie.

Sam grabbed his arm. "Your home is the other way."

Dalton glanced at Perry and Sam as if they were playing tennis. "Will you two be coming over later? After sunrise?"

No way in hell would Sam ever set foot in Dalton's home, but he didn't need to be rude about it. "We can't. We have orders to stay here."

"Oh. Are you going to tell Victoria what I did?"

Frankly, Sam wasn't sure that Dalton behaved unnaturally in the presence of a Perfect Mate. Well, except maybe for that fight-to-the-death part. "I won't tell her you continued to fight when we told you to stop, but Barnet will want to know your reactions to

Janie. I won't keep that information from him. So expect a call from him."

Dalton nodded. "I miss him, you know. Master Anton. He always knew what to do."

"That's not true," Perry said, patting Dalton on the shoulder. "He didn't know how to stay alive. You did."

Dalton shrugged and walked away.

"Is he all right?" Janie asked.

"Right now I'd say no," Perry said. "Anton was a sick bastard. The Civil War was ending and he didn't want to lose Dalton as a slave, so he turned him. And poor Dalton still considers himself Anton's slave. It's sad, really."

Those blue eyes of hers became two beautiful circles and she shivered. "Slave? When did Anton die?"

"A couple of years ago," Perry said. "I doubt Dalton has adjusted."

Sam fought the urge to wrap his arm around her shoulders to offer warmth. Hell, he wasn't sure he *could* warm her up. "You look cold. Why don't we go back inside?"

She hugged the coat close to her body. "Actually, I was hoping you could give me a ride to my hotel. I'd like to get some sleep."

Damn. It'd been so long since he'd hung around mortals, he'd completely forgotten that she'd need rest. If only he could accommodate her. "I'm sorry. We can't let you do that. I wasn't lying to Dalton when I said we had orders to stay here."

"And that includes me?" When Sam just tilted his head in answer, she said, "Right. Silly me. What was I thinking? Couldn't one of you come with me and the other stay here?"

"No can do," Perry said. "We got the Committee involved, so we do this the Committee's way. Which means we're spending the day in the hospital. I'm sure you could borrow a bed somewhere."

"But can't one of you take me to my hotel long enough so I can take a shower and change my clothes? I'll be quick. The sun doesn't rise until eight, right?"

Sam smiled. A quick trip to her hotel room? Some alone time with Janie? He didn't even bother to get Perry's permission. "That, I can do."

* * * *

Janie gave Sam the address to her hotel and gingerly climbed into the front passenger seat of the Xterra. She'd hurt her butt after the explosion, and the recent fall had only aggravated the area.

Sam climbed into the car. "You *are* hurt."

"Nothing a good, long soak in the tub wouldn't cure." Well, maybe. She hoped she hadn't broken anything back there. What kind of ribbing would she get at work if she ended up needing to sit on one of those donuts for the next few weeks? Hell, would she ever be allowed to go back to work?

"I'm sorry, Janie. I wish you had time for one of those."

"It was just wishful thinking." She wasn't so sure she wanted to be naked like that with him waiting in the next room anyway. Of course, a shower probably wasn't much better. But she was still picking sand and rocks out of her hair from the explosion. Talk about grody. "I'm glad you and Perry didn't argue over who was taking me. Dalton wasn't too far off on that fighting bit. You two just go at it with words." So far.

He groaned. "I guess we have been behaving pretty badly. I expect it's over, though. The arguing."

"Why is that?"

"Because he admitted that he wasn't drawn to you."

"You mean that pull that Dalton talked about? Do you feel the pull?"

He hesitated a bit before nodding. "I do."

Holy crap. She was affecting him? But he seemed so…calm. "Are you fighting it?"

"Not so much fighting as controlling. Am I struggling more than usual? Sure, but I won't lose control, okay? That's not the way I roll."

Why did that sound like a challenge? And why was she considering it? Maybe she was being drawn to him, too. His earthy scent was sexy as sin, and so far he seemed like a nice guy. Of course, there was still her curse to consider. "What's going to happen to me after Victoria comes? Will I be allowed to go home? Back to work?"

"You seem to be adjusting well with the knowledge. And since you've agreed to get to know me better…probably. Where is home?"

"Right now it's Cleveland."

"You move around a lot, don't you?"

"Part of the job. I do contract work for a software company. I go where the work is and the company pays for my keep. Kind of a sweet deal, actually."

"But you never settled down."

"Curse. Remember?"

He shook his head. "Oh, don't give me that. You are *not* cursed."

"We'll see about that. If we end up becoming serious, just watch out, okay?" Holy crap. Whatever made her say "serious"?

He smiled. "You hoping?"

Was she? Yeah, maybe she was.

He parked the car and managed to exit and appear at her door before she'd even unbuckled her seatbelt.

"That's some skill you have there," she said.

"I'm a man of many talents."

"I just bet you are." Maybe her curse didn't stand a chance against him. Then again, he could accidentally get caught in the sun, all because of her, of course, and then no more Sam. What a depressing thought.

"Why the frown? Can't you walk?"

"I can walk just fine." She took his offered arm, being careful not to touch his skin, and climbed out of the vehicle. She got the feeling he would have carried her if she'd asked. Her body was screaming for her to do it. Instead, she kept mum and led him up to her room.

"Do you want me to stay out in the hall?" he asked.

She swiped the keycard in the slot and opened the door. "Is that necessary?"

"Only if you think it is."

Perception was a funny thing. Did she think she was safer with him out in the hall? "I have a feeling the door wouldn't stop you if you had a mind to do anything nefarious."

"Nefarious?" He laughed. "You definitely do need to know me better. If only to see I am nothing like that."

Deep down she knew he wasn't. He just wanted to date her. And people who dated tended to be on their best behavior. The only way she'd see the real him was to get him to lower his guard. And for him to do that would require more contact. Not necessarily physical—although she wasn't opposed to that—but intimate. Like now. "You can come in."

"Thank you. And I promise to behave."

Well, he didn't have to go *that* far. She shut the door. "I'm sure glad I had the sense to check in before visiting Rick. Or else my suitcase would be a flat mess, I'm sure. That's if I could even get to it."

"I would have been able to get it out for you." He flexed his arm. "Vampire muscle."

"Sweet. I'll have to remember that next time I'm trying to open the pickle jar. Do you need to use the sink before I go in there?"

"For what?"

"To check your arm?" Had he really not noticed the looks he'd gotten while walking through the foyer?

"My arm?"

"Yeah. Your arm." She pointed. "Where the wood was stuck."

"Oh." He removed his jean jacket and fingered the hole. "Think this could be fixed? I kind of like this jacket."

"Don't look at me. I'm a programmer, not a seamstress."

He laughed. "You sound like Dr. McCoy."

"Well, he was my favorite character on *Star Trek.*" David had forced her to watch the original series at first. The second and third times had been her idea.

"Mine, too." His smile transformed his face and her body reacted.

Down, nipples, down. She needed to get her mind off how sexy he looked. "Aren't you worried about the blood stain?"

"Nah. That washes out." He fingered the hole again. "I guess I could ask Sarah to fix it."

"Sarah?" Pain slashed her heart. Why was he going after her if there was another woman?

"John's wife. She's his Perfect Mate."

"Oh." Color her stupid. Oh wait, she already was. Why should she feel jealous anyway? They weren't a thing and they wouldn't be a thing until she got to know him better.

He slid the sleeve up, exposing his bicep. Man, what a bicep. She itched to touch him and then nearly laughed. Maybe she wasn't the only one sending out pulling vibes. She kept her distance and inspected his arm. Dried blood surrounded the area where he'd been hurt, but no hole. Or scar.

"Wow. That's some pretty fast healing."

"Neat, huh? I guess I could wash it up some. Do you mind?"

"No, be my guest."

He slipped the shirt over his head. His skin was practically white, not a tan line in sight, but the muscles. Oh yum, the muscles. She'd never seen such perfection. Even had a smattering of dark hair on his chest, just the way she liked it. Along with a nice trail of hair leading to someplace she should not be staring at.

He chuckled as he headed toward the sink.

Damn. Caught in the act.

* * * *

Sam grinned on his way to the bathroom. Janie had been checking him out and he couldn't be more pleased. If all it took was to bare parts of his body, well then, he'd bare them. The public parts, anyway. She'd have to ask him to bare more.

But not until she got to know him better. That seemed important to her, and he wasn't about to have her doubt her true feelings for him.

"I don't need to pack up, do I?" she yelled from the other room. Eventually she'd learn she could whisper to him across a room and he'd hear her.

He wet a washcloth and started scrubbing his arm. "I wouldn't worry about it."

"Right, because you'll pick up my stuff if you decide to whisk me to Atlanta, right?" She appeared in the doorway. "Do you need any help with that?"

While he enjoyed her ministrations with her gaze, her touch was a whole 'nother matter. "I'm good. I got it."

"Yeah, that's why you missed this part. Give that to me."

Before he could object, she grabbed the washcloth from his hand. "You're using cold water?"

"Isn't that what gets out blood?"

"In clothes, yeah, but skin? I don't know. Most people prefer it warm."

"Because they can feel it."

She blinked a few times. "I keep forgetting you can't tell the difference between hot and cold."

Except when they touched, and then he noticed warmth. Her warmth. She'd been very careful not to touch his skin since they left the car. Would she continue to be careful? Or would she experiment? God, could he handle one of her experiments and not totally lose control?

She had taken off her coat and the sweater she'd worn. In just a T-shirt, her arms were exposed. The muscles in her biceps stood out as she scrubbed the soap onto the washcloth. For a computer person, she wasn't a slouch. Probably worked out in a gym or something. He wouldn't mind watching her work out, either.

"Turn around," she said.

He swallowed hard. If she put a hand on him… The thought no sooner left his brain when she gripped his arm. She gasped and he held his breath. Heat spread from the touch, down his arm, across his chest, into his heart. God damn, he was in heaven.

His jeans became tighter in the crotch and his fangs lowered.

Oh great. One look at those and she'd run for sure. As he willed his fangs away, he grabbed onto the counter. The marble was cool to the touch. Holy shit. It was like she'd turned him back into a mortal.

A horny mortal.

If she wasn't his Perfect Mate, how the hell could he go on after this? Of course, she could end up doing something so disgusting that he wouldn't want her around, but he couldn't imagine anything she did would be disgusting.

So far she just seemed so…perfect.

She jerked her hand away and he mourned the loss of her touch. "I'm so sorry. I didn't mean… But, damn."

Yeah, damn. The counter was no longer cool and he risked breathing again. He figured he could handle her scent or touch alone. But combined? That wasn't an experiment he was willing to try. Yet. "A little overwhelming?"

"If that's a little, I'd hate to see your definition of big." She managed to scrub his arm without touching him again. Did she not want to touch him or was she trying to be nice? "There, I think I got it all."

"Thanks. I'll let you take your shower." He headed for the door with his back toward her so she couldn't see how she'd affected him.

If he wanted her on board with their relationship, it couldn't all be about the Perfect Mate attraction. Although, isn't that what made it perfect? God, it was giving him a headache.

"Sam?"

He stopped. "Yes?"

"Do you have a last name?"

He looked over his shoulder, his fangs safely tucked away. His boner was still an issue, though. "Kincaid. Why?"

"Thought it would be nice to know your full name. Since we'll be dating and all."

"And all?"

She shrugged. "Whatever comes with dating."

Sex. She meant sex. Damn, could his nuts explode? "Are you tempting me, Janie Robinson?"

"I thought I was already doing that with my scent." She flexed her fingers. "And touch. I am sorry about that."

"Don't ever be sorry for touching me, okay? I swear, I won't lose control." He'd rather walk into the sun than scare her.

"Even if I want you to?"

Holy shit. She did not just say that. His boner was never going to leave now. "You know, on second thought, maybe I will wait out in the hall."

He said he wouldn't lose control and it appeared the only way to keep that promise was to leave the room and her alluring scent.

Chapter 9

A blast from the past.

Back at the hospital parking lot, Janie sat in the Xterra and closed her eyes while Sam grabbed a fresh shirt from the back. Had she been trying to tempt fate? Or had she been so horny she couldn't keep stupid words from flowing out of her mouth?

She'd apologized numerous times. So much so that he'd told her to stop. He wasn't so much as mad as frustrated, and she really hadn't meant to frustrate him to the point of leaving her room. She had hoped for a kiss instead.

But really, would he be able to stop at kissing? Would she? And not just because it had been months since she'd last had sex. When she'd touched him earlier, it had taken every bit of willpower to stop. And that was just from a touch. A touch. A damn touch.

Could that be why he left her room? He wanted it to be more than just touching and sex? Or was he simply abiding her request: that they should figure out if they were compatible in other ways first? And here she went and practically propositioned him. God, she was so stupid.

Sam opened her door. "Are you coming out?"

If they were to work, they couldn't be afraid to touch one another. But every time they touched…was heaven. Yeah, heaven. There had to be some way past that. "Do we need to get acclimated first? Is that it?"

"Excuse me? Acclimated to what?"

"To each other. You know, sort of like how the guy will jack off before a date so he's not feeling so stressed."

His eyes widened. "You want me to jack off?"

"No. That's not what I meant." Although, God, he probably could. He sported quite a bulge in his pants and all it took were words from her mouth. Or was it her scent? Whatever, it appeared she affected him big-time.

Sam leaned on the door wearing a cocky grin. "Then please, tell me what you meant."

Right. Eye contact. And damn, if she couldn't drown in his gaze. But she had to focus. "Touching. Would holding hands, just holding hands, help relieve some of the tension?"

He stood back on his heels and scratched his temple. "I don't know. Maybe."

"An audience would certainly keep us in line. Right?"

He smiled. "An audience? You mean Perry?"

"Perry. Nurses. Technicians. It is a hospital and it will get busy." Then again, hospitals had a lot of rooms to hide in. A lot. Oh hell, what was she thinking?

"I suppose we could try getting acclimated." He held out his hand. "Shall we start?"

Janie held her breath and placed her hand in his. Sensual waves spread throughout her body, causing her nipples to harden and her sex to clench. Standing seemed impossible. "Give me a moment, would you?"

"Take all the time you need." He inhaled deeply and leaned his head back.

"Are you enjoying my rosy scent?"

He opened his eyes and stared at her. "You don't smell like roses to me. It's peaches and cream. It's always been peaches and cream."

"I don't smell the same to everyone?"

"No. It's the other way around. For me, all unbonded, female Perfect Mates smell like peaches and cream."

"So you would react the same to another Perfect Mate?" Somehow that didn't make her feel all that special.

"I don't know, but I doubt it. I've only met one. You."

"Then how do you know?"

"Perry and Victoria. Especially Victoria. She's met three and they all smelled the same to her. As for the other reactions, you could ask them how different each encounter was."

She wasn't sure she wanted to ask Perry. Wouldn't that be like slapping the poor guy across the face? There might not be an attraction, but that didn't mean she disliked him.

"Although, you probably already know the answer. You've touched three vampires now. Have they all felt the same?"

She shook her head. "With Perry, the erotic wave was brief and not as strong as yours." Even now she basked in the waves Sam's touch was creating. "And Dalton's affect fizzled almost right away."

"Really? That's interesting." He might have tried to sound serious, but his lips twitched just a bit as if he'd been pleased. Super pleased. He looked out over the parking lot and frowned. "I saw that neon green jeep over at your cousin's. I hope no one else was hurt in the blast."

She peered through the windshield at where he'd indicated. "I hadn't heard, but those green jeeps are all over the place. Must have been a popular color."

"But it's the same license plate."

"It is?" She squinted. Heck, she couldn't even see the plate. "That's some eyesight you got there."

"It comes in handy."

"For what? Catching prey?"

"For seeing beautiful women at the gas station." He winked.

Her. He was talking about her.

"Your heart rate has slowed down. Think you can walk now?"

Man, he was observant. Was he feeling her pulse or hearing her heart beat? She wouldn't be surprised if he could hear an ant fart. But could she walk? The erotic buzz was still there, but not nearly as strong as when they'd first touched. "I believe I can."

He helped her from the vehicle and locked it as they headed for the hospital. "I know this...attraction we have is overwhelming. I just want you to know that I'm trying my best not to let it be the only thing driving me. I really do want to get to know you, Janie."

His statement almost made her teary eyed. She prayed that her cursed days were over.

* * * *

Tricia sat up in the car as the love birds walked into the hospital. She should have gone to bed when Rachel had, but sleep was the last thing she wanted to do.

Hell, sleep never came all that easy anymore, anyhow.

She had hoped what she'd seen on the news was wrong. But nope. After finding which hospital Rick Daugherty was staying in, she'd driven over hoping for an opportunity to kill the slut. But as Tricia left the vehicle, Janie and that hunk exited the hospital, drove off together, and went to the slut's hotel. The hunk had parked in the arrival area, so Tricia had waited until the man left, but when he returned, the slut was still with him. They'd probably done the nasty inside. And if that hadn't steamed Tricia even more.

To top it all off, when they arrived back at the hospital, they held hands at his car for the longest time. Looking all lovesick at one another.

It took everything inside her not to yell "Slut!" Now more people would have to die and it was all on Janie. If she'd just grieved after the first one, there wouldn't have been others. And when Tricia finally finished her duty, the slut would know exactly who was at fault for all those deaths: Janie, herself.

* * * *

Acclimation suited Sam and he grew more envious of John. He had this peace all the time, probably even better since he was bonded. Sam wanted the same, to hold onto Janie forever. But for forever to occur—for her to become immortal—she would have to agree to bond. If he were a betting man, the odds seemed to be in his favor. Because she had suggested acclimation. And they were holding hands.

The doors swished open as they approached the hospital entrance. Still quiet before the dawn, the foyer was empty. They headed for the elevators.

"What are you going to do if they release Rick this morning?" she asked.

"Well, for one, they won't. And second… I guess there isn't a second."

She laughed. "So sure of yourself, are you?"

"It's a gift," he said as he wagged his eyebrows.

A woman in scrubs appeared down the hallway. Janie gasped and buried her head in his chest.

As much as he enjoyed holding her, her scent turned sweet. "What's the matter? Do you know her?"

"Is she coming this way? Please tell me she's not coming this way."

"She's coming this way." In fact, she was making a bee-line toward Janie. "Is she an enemy?"

"Damn it. No, nothing like that. Can you make her go away? You know, use that gift of yours?"

Before Sam could intercede, the woman had already spotted Janie. "Janie? Janie, is that you?"

"Oh great," Janie muttered and lifted her head.

Sam stared at the woman and sent a command. "*You are mistaken. As you approach her, you will see she is not Janie Robinson.*"

"Oh, I'm sorry. For a minute there I thought you were someone else. Forgive me." The woman continued on her way.

The elevator doors opened and Janie pulled him inside. She pushed the button to Rick's floor and the doors closed. "Wow. Gift is an understatement."

"Want to tell me what that was all about? Because if she sees you again she'll still recognize you."

"Just someone I used to know. If she sees me again, I'll deal with it. I just didn't want to deal with it now. Thank you."

"A blast from your past, huh? So you're from Detroit."

"Born and raised."

He supposed Victoria had been looking for where Janie was currently living, and not where she used to live. "How did you end up in Arizona?"

The doors opened on their floor. She made no move to exit. "Do you think anyone would notice if we stayed in here awhile?"

He let the doors close. "Probably not, but wouldn't you be more comfortable in a waiting room?"

"There are people in waiting rooms, and then we couldn't talk without using your gift, which I'm sure comes with a price. Right?"

"It takes more energy than usual, sure. But don't let that stop you from suggesting I use it." He kind of liked having her comfortable enough to ask. And frankly, he'd do anything for her.

"Well, maybe I'd prefer not to have Perry within earshot. I'm guessing you hear better than the average mortal. So let's see, how should I start? A long time ago in a hospital far, far away—"

He laughed. "You like *Star Wars*, too?"

"Loved it. Loved them all. But that's not what we're talking about, is it?"

"No. What happened a long time ago?"

"There was this girl who wanted to be a nurse."

"You. You wanted to be a nurse?"

She nodded. "I thought so at the time. David's mother was—is a nurse, and she suggested I volunteer to be a candy-striper. That woman you sent away, she was in charge of the candy-stripers. In charge of me. Her name is Liz Delaney. She's David's mother."

"I sent away your mother-in-law? Why wouldn't you want to see her?"

"I haven't seen her since the funeral. Didn't really want to get into where I've been or what I'm doing."

And apparently she'd been to lots of places and done a lot of things. Was she willing to tell him what drove her away from her home?

* * * *

Janie smiled. Sam's hand was warm. Just warm. Seemed acclimation was exactly what she needed to hold a coherent conversation. Or her bone-tiredness was helping to keep the libido away. Whatever the reason, she took it. She wanted Sam to know.

"So what happened?" he asked. "To change your mind about being a nurse?"

"Hospital politics, I guess. There was this doctor, Dr. Ian Crawford, who... Well, he wasn't very nice."

"Abusive?"

She nodded. "Started out with harmless flirting. Or so I thought. But when I kept ignoring him, he became more insistent. Cornered me in the supply closet one day. Told me if I didn't do what he wanted, he'd have me relieved of duties. I told him to go ahead, I was only a volunteer. So then he threatened to take down Liz. I asked him what he wanted me to do. He said he wanted me to go down on him. I was only eighteen. I'd never done that to anyone, not even David. Wasn't even sure what it was and said so. He grabbed my hair and told me not to be such a tease. Then someone opened the door and he released me. I'd never been so relieved in all my life. I immediately went to HR and reported him."

"Good for you. That couldn't have been easy."

"Easier than I thought. I was so mad. Then I got madder when nothing happened. He was still working. It was like he was only slapped on the hand or something. At least he didn't go after Liz, probably afraid it would have made him look guilty. Still, I couldn't stand by and see him be treated as if he'd done nothing wrong. So I reported him to the local news."

"Wow. And that got him fired?"

"Yes and no. It got me canned. Insubordination. Slander. Hell, he was ready to sue me when several other women, girls, actually, came forward and admitted the same thing. His sterling reputation was clearly ruined and the hospital had no choice but to let him go. I heard later that he'd been murdered. Some people blamed me for that, even though I had an air-tight alibi. Said if I'd kept my mouth shut, he'd still be alive. Yeah, well, if I'd kept my mouth shut other women would have been hurt. They didn't see it that way, though. I couldn't stay here. David had graduated a year before me and was going to college in Arizona. After I graduated, I left, enrolled in a college near him, and never came back. Until now."

"You said some people blamed you. Liz?"

"No. Not Liz. She'd always suspected the doctor was abusing her girls, but never had any proof. Because no one would ever tell her the truth. They were too scared."

"And you weren't scared?"

"Well, I didn't say that." Hell, she'd never been more fearful of anything in her life. Not even after learning vampires existed.

"So you were engaged to David when we met, huh? Wait a minute. Didn't you say your fiancé cheated on you?"

"I did. That's why I was alone that night. And not thinking. At all."

"But you ended up marrying him anyway?"

"It had been a stupid misunderstanding. I thought his roommate was a guy. So when I showed up at his apartment and found a girl... Well, he should have told me she was a lesbian. I would have understood. Heck, I did understand. She ended up being one of my bridesmaids." Her legs wobbled and she fought a yawn. She should get some sleep, but she also liked being with Sam. Holding his hand. Talking with him.

"I think it's time to leave this elevator so you can get some sleep," he said.

She smiled. "Sleep does sound good. How about you? Are you and Perry going to take turns crashing so as not to leave me and Rick unwatched?"

"We don't sleep."

"At all?"

"Nope. Awake all the time."

"Wow. No offense, but that would suck. I can't imagine never sleeping."

"And you would never have to worry about it, either. Bonded Perfect Mates still sleep." He hovered his finger over the open door button, since the elevator hadn't moved. "Shall I?"

She wanted to ask him more questions. Learn more about him and vampires in general. But if she didn't find a bed or chair soon, she'd probably fall asleep right here in the elevator. "Yeah, might as well." She squeezed his hand. "Acclimating has been good, don't you think? Or maybe I'm too tired to act on anything."

"No, you were right. Acclimating was good." He pushed the button and the doors opened.

"There's a recliner in Rick's room. I think I'll use that to sleep. That way when he wakes, I'll be there. Hopefully he won't wake for a few hours."

Still unwilling to release him just yet, she pulled Sam into Rick's room. Rick was still asleep.

Sam lifted their joined hands. "You ready?"

No, but she couldn't ask him to stay. Or could she? She got the feeling he'd do anything she asked. But if Rick woke and found him in here, yeah, that wasn't happening. After sitting on the recliner, she released his hand and instantly mourned the loss. Man, would it always be like that?

Sam found a blanket and covered her. "Sweet dreams."

Still no kiss. Not even on the forehead. But she was okay with that. For now.

Chapter 10

If only you could choose your relatives like you do your friends.

With a headache that would probably take a whole bottle of Excedrin to disappear, Janie finally escaped to the windowless waiting room where Sam and Perry had been sitting most of the day.

She'd forgotten what it was like dealing with family. Or maybe she just didn't want to remember. Her headache reminded her. Big time.

Rick hadn't been the problem this time. Just as Sam had said, the doctor had told Rick that he should stay at least another day, to make sure infection hadn't set in and to monitor his concussion. Whether or not the doctor was coerced into saying it was something Janie didn't bother asking, because it didn't really matter.

Her cousin was more than willing to stay in the hospital, not that he'd had a choice. Said he wasn't looking forward to going back to his parents. Even for a short while.

And Janie had learned why soon enough. Aunt Susan and Uncle Tom arrived between breakfast and lunch. Tom seemed content to just sit and chat or watch the sports highlights on TV, but Susan couldn't sit still. She was up getting water. She was up fixing the blankets. She was up checking Rick's IV and alerted the nurse when it was empty. She wanted to know what happened. Who else was hurt. If Rick had some enemies she didn't know about.

Blah, ba-blah, blah, blah.

After an hour of that torture, Janie had tried to make her first escape—politely, of course—but Susan wouldn't hear of it. "It's been too long since we've seen you, Janie. Tell us everything you've been up to."

And by everything, she'd meant everything.

Janie had never been so happy to see someone leave before. Even Rick needed a nap after all that.

Sam smiled when Janie entered the waiting room and just like that, her headache disappeared. Man, how could she have it so bad for him when she hadn't even known him a whole day? Her body didn't seem to care in the least, though.

Then again, it never had.

"Have you been scaring the other visitors away?" Not another soul—besides the two vampires—sat in the room. The television on the wall was showing a home improvement channel, the sound low.

"I haven't. Don't know about ugly, here." Perry grinned and patted the seat next to him. As if she'd take it.

Janie sat in the seat beside Sam and placed her hand, palm up, on her thigh. About time to start some acclimating. And if someone—okay, Perry—saw her get horny, so what? She needed something pleasant after the last torturous hours.

"That bad?" Sam hadn't taken her hand yet. What was he waiting for?

"Let's just say I wouldn't have picked them to be friends."

He laughed. It was a wonderful sound and her heart clenched a little. If he wouldn't take her hand soon, she might have to take action. Thankfully, he stopped her from looking like a fool.

He linked his fingers with hers and she sighed as the erotic wave rushed through her. Yes. This was what she'd been yearning for all day. Bliss. Sheer bliss.

"Is it official?" Perry said, indicating their clasped hands.

"We're just getting acclimated," she said. But it might take hours before that erotic buzz went away. Not that she wished it away. It could stay all the time, because really, who wouldn't want to feel this good 24/7?

"Ha! Is that what you call it now? You know, I'm beginning to think you aren't my Perfect Mate. Because my Perfect Mate would want to find a closet and act like bunnies."

"Just because I'm not acting on it, how do you know I don't want that?"

Sam shook his head. "Please, don't say that."

Uh ohh. His growing erection reprimanded her. Stupid mouth. Stupid words.

Perry cackled. "Oh please. Do get him more frustrated. It's the most fun I've had all day."

"So glad I can entertain you," Sam said. "And here I thought you had fun with that nurse."

"Nurse?" Alarmed, the buzz faded. Had her story meant nothing to Sam? She yanked her hand away and glared at Perry. "Did you coerce a nurse?"

"Sorry, Janie," Sam said. "I didn't mean it like that. He didn't coerce anyone."

"That's right," Perry said. "She came on to me."

"But if you wanted to, you could? You could make them do anything, right?" And here she was getting comfortable with them. Just because they couldn't coerce her didn't mean they couldn't, or wouldn't coerce someone else. Shit.

Instead of answering her, Sam stood as a tall, young man and small, teenage girl entered the room.

Perry waved. "Hey, Vic. Teach. Wait a minute. What time is it?"

"I was going to ask the same thing," Sam said. "Did I misread the time?"

Not a teenager, but a four-hundred-plus-year-old vampire who could pass for the head cheerleader at a high school. She had the blonde wavy hair for it, too. But how had she arrived in the middle of the afternoon when these two couldn't leave the hospital?

"No. We took the company van." Victoria approached Janie. "And to answer your question, yes, if these two wanted to, they could coerce. But it's frowned upon by the Committee."

Janie looked up at the vampire. "Frowned upon doesn't really ease my mind all that much."

"I don't suppose it would." Victoria held out her hand. "You must be Janie. I'm Victoria. This is my husband, Ben."

Ben, not Teach. Or at least he was Teach to Perry only. Janie wasn't sure she'd ever understand Perry or why he did what he did.

She stood and ended up looking down on the vampire. Not even Victoria's heels brought her to Janie's height. Janie took the extended hand. No zip. No nothing. "Thank you for giving Rick a chance."

Perry tapped Victoria on her shoulder. "Back the train up here, Vic. The company van is fine for short distances in a low-setting sun, not all day with it blaring high in the sky. The UV windows can only block so much. What'd you do, cover yourself with a tarp in the back? You took a big risk. And Teach, I can't believe you let her."

"She wasn't covered," Ben said. "She sat in the back, out of the direct light."

This news didn't seem to surprise Sam, yet he lowered his head as if in shame. Perry, on the other hand…

His eyes widened. "You can tolerate the sun now?"

"Victoria…" Ben placed a hand on her shoulder. "I thought you said everyone knew."

"No, I said we would eventually tell everyone. We just haven't done that yet. So yes, Perry. Since we've bonded, daylight doesn't sap my strength like before and I only burn in direct sunlight."

"Damn it!" Perry eyed Janie, fists at his side.

"What'd I do?" she asked.

"Nothing." He turned toward Sam. "Did you know?"

"Ummm… John might have mentioned it."

"Damn it!" Perry punched Sam's arm as he stormed out of the room.

"What was that about?" Janie asked. "Did he hurt you?"

Sam rubbed his arm. "I'm fine. He's a little pissed because I knew something, again, that he didn't."

"Perry will get over it," Victoria said. "Now, is Mr. Daugherty alone for us to talk? Or do we need to move him?"

"His room is private," Janie said. "But if he starts yelling for help…" And why wouldn't he once he got a look at Victoria.

"Then you need to prepare him for our visit. If he cannot remain calm and rational, then we'll have no choice but to drug him and take him to Atlanta. Do you understand?"

"You're not going to hurt him, though. Right?"

"No one is going to get hurt. But while we want what is best for him, we have to think of ourselves first. It's the only way to insure our anonymity. Unfortunately, he knows too much, and after today he'll know even more. If he can't come to terms with that, we would hope that more interaction would be beneficial."

They hoped because they didn't know shit. "And if it isn't, then what? You'll kill him?"

"Janie," Sam said. "She just said no one is going to hurt him."

"So he'd be a prisoner instead?"

"Trust me," Victoria said. "It will not come to that. Especially if he becomes someone's Perfect Mate. We would introduce him to several female vampires who are interested. Eventually he will come around."

"You make it sound like he's up for auction. He's not a slave."

"I know it sounds bad," Ben said. "But think about it. You've had ample opportunity to leave today, but you didn't. Why?"

"They would have just stopped me."

"But you didn't even try, did you? Because you met someone who lit your soul with one touch, right? It's hard to leave someone who can do that. And that's how your cousin will feel when he meets the right vampire."

Was Ben right? She hadn't even thought about leaving. But it was because of Rick. Or was it? How hard would it have been to get him out of here when his parents visited? Instead, all she'd thought about was escaping into Sam's presence. Not escaping from him. Shit. Janie practically fell onto the seat and bit back a moan. Her butt still hadn't recovered from the two falls yesterday. "But it could be his choice if he's okay with vampires in general. Right?"

"That is correct," Victoria said. "So let's not worry about something we can't control. Go on and talk to your cousin. Ben and I will be in the hallway waiting. And you." She pointed to Sam. "Go talk to Perry."

* * * *

Tricia entered the hospital foyer. That yellow SUV was still parked in the same spot as last night, which meant Janie and her boyfriend were still here. Good.

It would be the topping to the fun morning she'd had with Rachel and the start of a lovely weekend. Shoe shopping had cleared Tricia's head and ideas burst forth. She hadn't felt so alive before. And her torment would end forever once she got rid of that tramp. But not right away. First, there was another boyfriend to tend with.

Let Janie think her curse struck again before the truth was revealed.

But that meant Tricia couldn't be spotted. By the boyfriend, yes. The tramp, no. And as luck would have it, Boyfriend emerged from the elevators not wearing a coat. Great. But as he searched the area, she almost panicked. Was he looking for Janie? If she was down here then Tricia would have to hurry.

She moved the broach to her right sleeve and gripped the syringe in her right hand, thumb on the plunger. Hurrying toward the elevator as an old woman on a mission, she made sure Boyfriend was in the way. It helped that he hadn't paid her any mind. She bumped him on her right side and stuck him in his hip with the needle.

"Oh, I'm so sorry, ma'am," he said, rubbing his hip. "I didn't see you. Are you okay? I think your pin is loose. It stuck me."

She looked down at her sleeve. "My broach! Oh, thank you. It's a family heirloom. I hadn't even noticed that it had fallen." She placed it in her purse after examining it. "I really must get the clasp fixed on this thing. I didn't hurt you, did I?"

"I'll live. Are you okay?"

"Yes, I am. Thank you." And she'll feel even better once the drug took effect. Too bad they were in a hospital. But who in their right mind would think a big hunk like that would have a heart attack?

She headed toward the elevators and then turned around. Boyfriend wasn't looking her way and she dodged around the corner. Shouldn't be long now.

It would be even more perfect if the slut was in the area. Maybe he could die in her arms. Wouldn't that be fitting?

Instead, the person he'd been searching for was another hunky guy sitting in the corner. Too bad. Guess she couldn't have everything. Boyfriend kept rubbing his hip. *Good, get it into the blood stream faster.* "That's the way." The two men shared words and then stepped into the stairwell.

Well, damn it. She'd hoped to have witnessed his demise. Guess she couldn't expect to watch them all. She adjusted her purse and headed back to her car. One down, one to go.

Ahh, yes. It was going to be a lovely weekend.

* * * *

Sam rubbed his hip. That's what he got for not watching where he was going. Although his mind was pretty much back with Janie.

Was he the reason she hadn't tried to bolt? He'd never even considered she'd leave, so if she did have a mind to do it, would he have been able to stop her? Perry probably would, but then he wasn't consumed with Janie. At least that he showed.

But Sam had come down here to find the man, not nearly knock over an old woman. He rubbed his hip again. Stupid brooch. He searched the foyer and found Perry sitting in a corner, safely away from any windows.

Perry glanced up for a moment then went back to staring at the floor. "What do you want?"

The words landed on Sam's shoulders, weighing him down. In the past, Perry hadn't always been someone to count on. But since the arrival of Perfect Mates? He'd changed. A lot of it had to do with wanting to find his own Perfect Mate, but maybe he was also trying to just be a better person, period.

"I'm sorry. I know it's not enough, but I honestly forgot about that sun bit, okay? I wasn't intentionally keeping it from you."

"Maybe so, but Johnny did. I just don't get why you're all so secretive about what Perfect Mates can do for a vampire."

"Hard to share when we're not sure who we can trust."

"You mean me. You can't trust me."

"Not just you. You'll understand when you find your own Perfect Mate. And the paranoia that sets in. Even Victoria didn't tell Barnet everything. Although, I guess she has if she admitted the sun thing to you."

"Barnet is a bit obsessed, isn't he?" Perry chuckled. "Okay, maybe Vic has a point. It just hurts that no one trusts that I can keep a secret."

"You have to admit, you've been known to blab first, apologize later."

Perry leaned his head back and cackled. "Touché!" He stood. "What's wrong with your hip?"

Sam hadn't realized he was still rubbing it. The pressure was irritating. "I don't know. Can we go somewhere private?"

Perry indicated the door marked stairs. "How about there?"

Looked good to Sam. He stepped inside the stairwell and unbuttoned his jeans.

"Dude, I'm not that kind of vampire," Perry said.

"Will you shut up? There's a bump where a lady poked me with her pin." It shouldn't irritate that much. Hell, getting stuck with the wood hadn't even bothered him.

"Why would a lady poke you with a pin?"

"It wasn't on purpose. I ran into her by accident."

"And she stabbed you with a pin? I wish I had seen that."

"Will you stop?" He opened up his jeans and exposed his hip.

Perry crouched down and examined the site. "That's not a pin poke. You've been injected with something."

"What? How can you tell?"

"Because there's this big bubble on your butt. I bet you can pop it easy enough."

"Pop it? Like a pimple? Ewww."

"What a wuss." Perry backhanded Sam's hip. Liquid squirted out and the tightness alleviated. "Got a tissue?"

"No."

Perry wiped his hand on Sam's leg. "It's your mess."

"Whatever." Sam zipped up his jeans. The irritation gone. "Wonder what it was? And why would she inject me?"

"Because you're dating someone who's cursed?" Perry bent over, cackling. "Oh my God. She *is* cursed. You're so screwed."

Or someone was making Janie feel like she was cursed. "Damn it." He rushed out of the stairwell and headed for the elevator. "She's gone."

Perry caught up. "You didn't think she'd stick around, now did you?"

If she'd gone outside, there wasn't anything Sam could do. The sun was out. But if she'd gone upstairs…

"Janie."

* * * *

Leaving Victoria and Ben in the hallway, Janie entered Rick's room and prayed her cousin would see reason.

Rick turned off the TV. "Where have you been? I'm going stir crazy."

She cringed at his terminology. After their talk, he'd probably think everyone but he was crazy. "How are you feeling? About what we talked about earlier?"

"Earlier?" He scrunched his forehead briefly. "Oh, you mean at the restaurant."

Janie dragged a seat over to the side of the bed and sat. "Yeah. Are you still freaking out about that?"

"I've been freaking out for the last several months. You listening to me made a difference. I am calmer now."

How calm would he stay, though? She patted the back of his hand. "But it still bothers you, doesn't it?"

"Yeah it bothers me. I want to know why. Why they did it. Why they let me go. Why they want me to think I'm going crazy."

"What if I found someone to talk to you about that? Would that help?"

He leaned his head back. "Shit. You got a therapist? I thought you believed me."

"I do believe you. Okay? And she's not a therapist. At least I don't think she is. I just need you to not freak out when you see her. Keep an open mind and think of your questions. Can you do that?"

"And this person can answer them? Why?"

"You'll find out soon enough. But you have to stay calm. It's important you stay calm." Janie had thought she'd have to go get Victoria, but the vampire probably heard the whole conversation anyway and appeared in the doorway.

"Hello, Mr. Daugherty."

Rick's eyes widened. "Oh shit. Janie, she's one of them. The ones I told you about. What's she doing here?"

He tossed the covers aside and moved as if he was going to bolt, but Janie took his hand and held it firm. "What did I say about staying calm? No one's going to hurt you."

And she honest to God hoped Victoria hadn't lied about that.

Ben settled into the corner while Victoria stood at the head of Rick's bed. "I'm here to talk. To answer your questions. And to apologize."

He yanked his hand free, but as he swung his feet over the edge, he grabbed his side, where he'd been hurt. "Why, Janie? Why?"

Janie latched onto his arm and urged him back to the bed. "Will you calm down and listen? Please? It's important. You wanted answers. She has them."

It took several moments of him glancing back and forth between Janie and Victoria. "How can I trust her?"

"Because I trust her."

His eyes watered. "You do?"

Janie nodded. She needed him calm. So he'd listen. His future depended on it. "No one's here to hurt you. She just wants to talk."

Rick leaned back against his pillow. Swiped at his eyes. "Fine. Whatever. Go ahead."

"I understand you've figured out what we are," Victoria said.

"Vampires." Rick pointed at Ben. "He's not, though. Is he?"

"You are correct. My husband is a rare breed of human, as you are."

"Rare breed? I don't understand."

Janie leaned forward. "We can't be controlled and they can't wipe our memories. They call us Perfect Mates."

Rick snorted. "Now you're starting to sound crazy."

"Oh?" Janie said. "And why is that?"

His eyes widened. "Shit. I didn't mean... Why did you include yourself?"

"Because they can't control me or wipe my mind. I met one of them four years ago. My vampire just happened to let me go before he did any damage."

"What?" Rick sat forward on a wince. "Why didn't you tell me this last night?"

"And what would you have done with the news at that time?"

He had the decency to look ashamed. "Point taken. So what makes us special? Did we eat something we shouldn't have?"

Ben laughed. "Wouldn't that be something? Here, have a donut. Become a Perfect Mate. But truthfully, they aren't quite sure what makes us special. Just that it has something to do with our genes or DNA, and last I read, no food could change our genome. We probably share the same great-great-great-whatever grandparents. I know the three of us are related, anyway."

Victoria paced in the small room. "To say we mucked up where you're concerned is an understatement. I'm sorry for what you've been going through. We had no intention of making a bad situation worse, and it seems we've done just that.

"So to answer your questions," Victoria continued. "Why you? That was a mistake. Dalton didn't check to see if he could wipe your memory first before feeding. So he fed from you until you passed out and then he called us for help."

"Us?"

"The Committee. There are five of us who maintain order within the vampire community."

"Just five?" Janie asked.

"That's all we've ever needed."

"You never took me to any hospital, did you?" Rick asked.

"No. We gave you blood—intravenously—healed you, and kept you sedated until we knew what to do with you."

"So you woke me on purpose? Why? So you could touch me? And what the heck was with that anyway? What did you do to me?"

"Yes, we woke you on purpose. To confirm our suspicions. That you are a Perfect Mate. Since a female vampire was needed, I volunteered. You see, I had met my own Perfect Mate at that time, without the Committee's knowledge. We hadn't bonded yet and I wondered if I would get the same reaction from you as I got from him. You don't know how happy I was to find out I did not. But Barnet wanted to know if you felt a draw to me. Your anger pretty much confirmed I wasn't the one for you. As for the touching, I didn't do anything to you, Mr. Daugherty. It is the reaction you get when you touch an unbonded female vampire."

Well, not every unbonded vampire, but Janie would let Sam explain that later.

"And it's kind of my fault," Ben said. "I thought the connection Victoria and I felt was due to some chemical reaction when we touched. That I didn't have any free will where she was concerned. So of course she wondered the same thing."

These poor vampires seemed to be fumbling in the dark. Janie could say she had all the free will required against Dalton and Perry. Sam was another issue, though. She hadn't even tried to leave him. Was that free will or what?

"Did you take advantage of my arousal?" Rick asked.

"I most certainly did not. I am not a rapist."

"No, just a kidnapper and torturer."

Janie smacked Rick's arm with the back of her hand. "Rick, she's trying to apologize for that."

"Why are you defending them? What they did to me wrong."

"You are right, Mr. Daugherty. In our process of understanding Perfect Mates, we've made mistakes. Our largest mistake was in letting you go before giving you a chance to understand the situation. I'm trying to give you that chance now."

Rick glared at the vampire. "Meaning what? I don't understand and you chain me up? Or do you just kill people like us?"

"We don't kill," Victoria said.

"So then chained."

"Rick, please," Janie begged. "It doesn't have to be that way. Life as you know it has changed and there's no going back. You know what they are. They know you know and they can't wipe your memory. Don't make them do something drastic."

"How can you be so calm about this? They feed off people. That's not right."

"Why? Because you think we're at the top of the food chain? Well, we're not. And if they were killing to feed, it would be different. I know it sounds horrible, but they don't take that much and the person doesn't even know what happened. They're probably more humane with us than we are to animals."

"You sound like you...like them."

"I kind of do. They aren't bad people."

"They aren't people, period. They're...monsters."

Janie shook her head. Was there no getting through to her cousin?

Chapter 11

Insanity: it's what's for dinner.

After discreetly searching the entire floor—and conducting a little mind coercion—neither Perry nor Sam found any sign of an old woman hanging around. Sam didn't know whether to be relieved or worried. Relieved Janie wasn't in danger, but worried she might be later on.

While Perry settled himself in the waiting room, Sam headed for Rick's room. Janie's voice echoed softly in the hallway.

"You are so fucking stupid. One of those so-called monsters saved your life."

"What are you talking about?" Rick asked.

Sam figured Rick already knew about vampires—or monsters?—and decided to enter the room. Victoria was pacing, her attention on the smart phone in her hand as her thumbs were busy punching out a text or e-mail. Sam highly doubted she was playing a game; did she even know how? Ben stood in the corner, giving her the floor. He smiled when he spotted Sam.

Janie sat in a chair by the bed. Tears on her face. "You were trapped in your apartment after the blast. Anyone else going up there might have died trying to save you, or not acted fast enough and you could have bled out." She looked up and pointed at Sam. "He went in and was able to get you out. He not only saved you, but those firemen, too. Because the ceiling landed on him while he was getting to you. A ceiling! So don't tell me they're monsters. Monsters don't do that."

Sam fought back a grin. Janie was actually defending him. Maybe she was starting to like him after all. Too bad he couldn't say the same for Rick. His look of disgust said otherwise.

"They've brainwashed you, Janie. How can you not see that?"

"Are you serious? Have you not been listening? They can't brainwash us. We're different." She swiped the tears from her cheeks. "If you can't accept them, if you can't keep their secret, then I'll take my chances with the police and let them take you away until you can. It's the only way to keep you safe."

"What do the police have to do with this?"

"She thinks she's cursed," Sam said. Janie and Rick looked up at him. Even Victoria stopped her texting. "Everyone she's gotten close to has died and now your building was sabotaged. If you go missing, she's afraid the police will look into her past and discover the other incidents."

"Who died?" Rick asked.

"David and two others I was involved with," Janie said.

"But David was an accident. You said he fell asleep at the wheel from carbon monoxide poisoning."

"And it appeared the others died in accidents, too. But the police might think differently now. Because of your building. Because I'm cursed."

Sam approached the bed, keeping it between him and Janie. Any closer to her and he'd probably do something stupid like hug her. That probably wouldn't go over so well with her cousin. "You're wrong. You're not cursed. You're just being targeted."

"Targeted?" She shook her head. "What are you talking about?"

"I believe a woman is responsible for those deaths because she just injected me with a drug. One I'm assuming was supposed to kill me." And boy, was she going to be surprised when she saw him walking around.

Janie lurched to her feet. "You were injected? Are you okay?"

Rick snorted. "He's a vampire, what do you—ewww. If he was attacked, that means... You're sleeping with him?"

Exactly the reaction Sam thought he'd get if he'd hugged Janie. Guess it didn't matter after all.

"I'm not *sleeping* with anyone. Sheesh. I hardly know him."

To say his heart deflated a little was an understatement. But two steps forward, one step back was a lot better than the other way around.

"Ms. Robinson brings up a valid point," Victoria said. "How would this woman suspect you were together since you've only gotten reacquainted last night?"

"Did you tell anyone about our first encounter?" Sam asked.

"No. I couldn't. So…no." Janie sat. Her cheeks pinkened as if she had a reason to be embarrassed about that night.

"Then she must have seen us on TV. How else would she know I was here? Who hates you enough to come after you like that?"

She shook her head. "No one that I know of. I keep a pretty low profile."

"I'll say," Victoria muttered, her attention back to her phone.

Sam nearly laughed. While it had been difficult for Victoria to find Janie, it hadn't been for the…killer. Which meant this woman knew Janie. "How about when you were a candy-striper?"

"That was so long ago. And stuff didn't start happening until…David."

Sam couldn't mistake the look on her face and the pause. As if she were going to say "until you showed up in my life." And who was to say he wasn't the catalyst? Perry and he agreed another vampire wouldn't go to such extremes, but they could be wrong.

It would be so much easier if Sam could just read Janie's mind to see if the woman who stuck him was someone in her past. Or if he could transmit the image of the person he saw to Janie. But none of that was possible. "The woman was older. Fifties or sixties. Blue eyes. Wore glasses and had grey in her brown hair. She'd worn it up in a bun thing."

"A bun thing?" Janie snorted and quickly placed her hand over her mouth. "Sorry. She doesn't sound familiar, but I've been away almost ten years. People change."

"How do you know they aren't behind it all?" Rick asked, pointing to Victoria and Sam. "David died four years ago. He attacked you four years ago. Seems awfully coincidental if you ask me."

Sam nearly blurted that he hadn't attacked anyone, but that wasn't the truth. He *had* attacked Janie. Kissed her without permission. Not the kind of behavior he wanted to be remembered for. "I can tell you until I'm out of breath that I wasn't behind it all and you'd never believe me, now would you? But I'll tell you anyway. I had nothing to do with the deaths in Janie's life or the explosion at your apartment. I didn't know where Janie was living until yesterday, and I certainly had no idea she was your cousin."

"You're right. I don't believe you."

"Why?" Janie asked. "Why can you believe they're vampires but not good? Some people do bad things, evil things, does that mean all people are bad?"

"But they can control people. Maybe they're making them bad."

"Mr. Daugherty," Victoria said as she put her phone down. "The only way that could possibly be a true statement is if our numbers equaled mortals. They do not. It would take repeated suggestions from a vampire for a mortal to continuously do something against their nature. Only one vampire lives in Detroit. One vampire vs. the nearly seven hundred thousand souls that live here. Even if he tried, he would not be able to maintain that kind of control. We just want to live in peace, and that's a lot easier to do when the mortals follow the laws rather than break them."

Would Rick make the right decision? Not for Sam, himself, but for Janie.

* * * *

Janie snatched a tissue and blew her nose. She was through with crying for someone who clearly didn't care what happened to them. And she had vampires on her side. They could see that she wasn't charged with destruction of property, couldn't they?

"One?" Rick said. "There's only one here?"

She kind of found that hard to believe, too.

Victoria nodded. "There's only one of your kind here, too. That we know of, anyway. The odds were astronomical that you two should meet, but there it is. He did not want to hurt you. If he had, you would not be lying in this bed right now. Think about that, Mr. Daugherty."

Rick looked at Janie. "What should I do?"

Janie fought the urge to smack her cousin. Had he not been listening to a word she'd said?

Victoria answered for Janie's fist. "You have two choices. One, you can come with us to Atlanta. To learn and acclimate yourself with other vampires. You will be treated with the utmost respect and introduced to female vampires. Or two, you can stay with your cousin and Sam, since the two of them seem to be an item."

Janie blinked several times. Okay, now she was going to live with Rick *and* Sam? Where had that come from?

"Victoria?" Sam said. "Janie and I are just…dating."

Did it make her feel better that Sam was freaking out a little about them living together, too? Yeah. Yeah, it did.

"You can date while staying at the safe house. There are plenty of rooms to keep you separated if you so desire."

"Wait, wait." Janie's head was about to explode. "Aside from the Sam part and the safe house part, Rick can't stay with me. He has a job here and I live in Cleveland. In a hotel."

"Yeah, about that." Rick lowered his head. "I lost my job last month."

"What? Oh, Rick."

"If those are my only choices, I'm okay with staying with you and…*him*. I don't want to be locked up in Atlanta. And I don't want the police to suspect you."

"Those are your only choices for *now*," Victoria said. "Don't make me regret giving you one. If at any time you are out of line or tell one person what you know, Sam will start the process of sending your *Arsh* to Atlanta. Do I make myself clear?"

Rick blinked in confusion. "Arsh?"

Ben chuckled as he emerged from the corner. "She likes to cuss in German. That means 'ass.'"

"Oh. Right. Crystal clear," Rick said.

Victoria left the room with Ben following.

"Um, give me a minute, will you?" Sam turned and rushed out of the room, leaving Janie alone with Rick.

Now would have been the perfect opportunity to leave. No one was watching them. But it turned out Ben was right after all. She'd rather be with Sam than her stupid cousin.

"Are you really dating one of them?" Rick asked.

"Shut up. Just…shut up." Janie got up and headed for the hallway. Time to find out what the hell was going on.

* * * *

"Wait up, Victoria." Sam trotted down the hallway. Somehow he had to get Victoria to see reason. How could he date and live with Janie? And then watch Rick in the process? How were they ever going to connect with a witness? This day couldn't get any worse.

Victoria stopped and turned around. "Not here. In the waiting room."

Thank God it was late Saturday afternoon and the hospital wasn't that busy. The waiting room was still empty, aside from Perry watching the home improvement channel.

Victoria pointed to Perry. "Go guard Mr. Daugherty. He's not to leave."

"Bossy much?"

She leveled her ever popular glare at him.

"Okay, okay. Sheesh, Vic. I swear, you were more fun before you got married." Perry nearly collided with Janie on his way out. "Sorry, sweetheart. Guess I need to babysit your cousin. He doesn't bite, does he?"

As she stood there with her mouth ajar, Perry left, cackling in his wake.

"You two, sit down. Can I trust you to keep your hands off each other?"

From behind Victoria, Ben gripped her shoulders. "Honey, you're starting to sound like Barnet."

She closed her eyes for a bit and chuckled. "You're right. But I'm beginning to understand a little of what he went through with us."

"Except you had taken my blood. Blood I offered to you." He looked at Janie. "Have you offered your blood to Sam?"

"Offered? Noooo. But he fed from me."

Sam winced. Why couldn't she forget about that?

"Sam, do you have an insane desire to feed from her now?"

Desire? Yes. Insane? That was up for debate. "Not really. I mean, she smells great and all, but I have it under control."

"See?" Ben kissed Victoria on the cheek. "They're fine."

She grinned up at him. "My voice of reason." Turning her focus to Sam and Janie, she continued, "I know it seems like I'm putting you in a bind, but Ms. Robinson didn't want him taken away without his permission and I—we felt this was the best option for him."

"We?" Sam asked.

"Yes. I've been texting Barnet about the situation."

"Barnet is texting now?" Last time Sam saw the man, he still owned a flip phone.

"Sure seems like a miracle, doesn't it? Took the appearance of Perfect Mates, and maybe my prodding, for that man to get with the twenty-first century."

"Excuse me," Janie said. "You've mentioned this Barnet guy before. Who is he?"

"I'm sorry. I thought Sam filled you in. He's the Head of the Committee. And he will be arriving sometime next week so he can talk to Mr. Daugherty."

Sam exploded off his chair. "He's what?"

Victoria placed a hand on his chest. "Sam. Calm down."

He would calm down when she started talking some sense. "What did you do? What did you do?"

"You knew this was going to happen eventually."

Yeah, but not until after he had bonded with Janie. "I can't believe you did this to me."

"Sam?" Janie tugged on his jacket. "What's wrong?"

"Sit with her," Victoria said.

He'd rather take the chair and throw it against the wall. "Wasn't it bad enough I had to watch Dalton touch her? Now Barnet?"

"Dalton?" Victoria frowned. "What was he doing here?"

"He saw me on the news with Rick and came over to investigate. At least, that's what he told us." If only he had the sense to read Dalton's mind when he was getting Janie free to see if that was true. If the man was responsible for Janie's problem, Sam would finish him off, regardless of Committee rules.

"*Scheisse.* He was told to stay away from Mr. Daugherty. He should not have been here."

"That would have been a nice heads up." Sam paced the small room. "Anything else I need to know? How many other vampires do I have to worry about?"

"Sam, stop it. I understand what you are going through. More than anyone. Please. Sit."

Sam sat and lowered his head into his hands. What a nightmare. Not only did he have to babysit Janie's cousin, he would be forced to watch another vampire touch her. Didn't matter if Janie didn't react, Barnet could. And then what? Pull rank?

"Should I be afraid of Barnet?" Janie asked.

"No," Victoria said. "Sam's just…concerned with another male vampire being in your presence. But Sam, you seem okay with Perry being here. And I don't see Dalton hanging around. Shouldn't that tell you something?"

"That I've been lucky so far?" Luck that was quickly flowing away. "You know he's not only coming to talk to Rick."

"I understand your fear and feel bad I put it there. But he's changed. Does he want to know more about Perfect Mates? Sure, we all do. But his obsession has waned since he's gained more knowledge."

"While this subject is fascinating," Janie interrupted, "could we talk about something else? Like how Rick and Sam are supposed to live with me? I live in a hotel. Will that be…safe?"

She looked at him with concern in her eyes. Hotels weren't perfect, but he could survive in one. As long as he stayed away from the windows. And if they had connecting rooms, then maybe it wouldn't be so bad.

"We have a safe house in Cleveland," Victoria said. "You will use that."

Sam bolted off his seat again. "That isn't safe. Any vampire can use it. Even while we're there!"

"Are you saying I should be afraid of vampires?" Janie asked.

"No!" That was the last thing he needed: her afraid of him. He sat down beside her but didn't dare touch her, even though he wanted to with every fiber of his being. He'd said he had it under control and he did. If they didn't touch. "There's no need for *you* to be afraid. No one's going to hurt you. It's just…" *you might find someone more suitable than me.* He ran a hand over his face. If this was what life would be like before he took her blood, he certainly hoped if—no, when they started the bonding process they completed it quickly. He couldn't imagine sounding any more insane than he was already sounding.

"Just what?" Those sapphire blue eyes of hers implored him to continue.

He wanted to kiss her silly. Take her on the floor, regardless of who was in the room. But he couldn't lose control with her. He just couldn't. "Nothing. I'm sorry. I'm being an ass." He chuckled for good measure. "And a little protective."

"More like possessive," Victoria said. "But he means well."

Janie gave him a sympathetic smile and placed her hand on his arm. "So what happens now?"

Now? Oh, he only had to figure out how to win her over while fighting off every vampire who got a whiff of her whereabouts. Then there was the little issue of her so-called curse. Or rather, the woman responsible for killing Janie's loved ones. Somehow, dealing with an unknown deranged mortal seemed a whole lot easier to handle.

Chapter 12

One rendezvous coming up.

Janie had left Sam with Victoria and Ben and relieved Perry of his so-called babysitting duties. Seemed the vampires trusted her just as much as their own. She wasn't sure how she felt about that.

For the past hour she and Rick pretty much stared at the television. He might have cared who won the basketball game, but she couldn't give a flying fig. Hell, she wasn't even sure who was playing. All she kept seeing was Sam and how freaked out he'd become when he learned where they were staying. At the time she'd wanted to give him a big ol' hug, but for some reason she knew deep down that if she touched him, if they had skin contact, he might have lost what little control he had left. But would that have been so bad? Really? She was pretty sure she could find an empty room somewhere in this hospital.

"It's almost five," Rick said. "I guess we'll be leaving soon."

Five o'clock? She peeked out the curtain and nearly laughed. Had Sam or Perry put it into someone's mind to stick Rick in this room? It butted up against another building. Why there was even a window was beyond her. "How are you feeling? Are you up to travel?"

He shrugged. "It's not so bad. As long as I get pain pills. They'll let me have pain pills, won't they?"

"I don't see why not."

"Thank you for taking me in. I know you didn't have to do that. You could have let me go to Atlanta."

104

"And have you think some monsters were holding you hostage?" She tried to lace her words with sarcasm, but failed miserably. He probably still thought they were monsters. She should have let the vampires take him to Atlanta. Not only to keep him safe—especially if there was some kind of killer loose going after her loved ones—but to help Rick come to terms with vampires. Right now she couldn't tell if he'd actually changed his mind about them or if he was just biding his time to escape. The man was harder to read than an electronics diagram.

Rick clicked off the TV. "You know, since finding out they're real and actually meeting some of them, I'm feeling a little better. It's nice knowing I'm not going crazy. That Victoria chick was kind of scary, but Perry was nice."

"Yeah?" Her heart loved hearing those words from Rick's mouth, but her head didn't buy it. Was he for real or playing a game? "What about Sam?"

Distaste flashed across his features, so brief she would have missed it if she'd blinked. "From what little I've seen of him, he seems okay. I still can't believe you're dating him."

And there was the disgust she'd been waiting for. He did not approve of her and Sam. "Why? Because he's a vampire or because I hardly know him?"

"Because he could still be behind your...unfortunate incidents."

"Unfortunate incidents? Is that what they are now?" She shook her head. "He had no reason to kill those men because he could have just coerced them away." No, whoever killed them was human. But who? And why? What had she done to cause someone to hate her that much?

"I suppose that's true. So, do you think Perry is going to live with us, too?"

God, I hope not. And it wasn't because Perry was a vampire. It was just another guy she didn't know, living in a house she was practically forced to live in. The situation might keep Rick safe and familiarized with vampires, but would it just doom Sam? She still had her curse to contend with, and any sign of them being together only put a target on his head.

Perry entered the room with Sam on his heels. "Hey, Ricky, my man. Ready to take a trip?"

Sam smiled, but stayed at the doorway. Afraid to be near her or looking out for other vampires? With him it was a toss-up.

"I might not feel a hundred percent, but I'm tired of being here." Rick pulled the covers away and stood with a wince. The nurse had removed his IV and unhooked him from all the monitors earlier in the day. He grabbed the clothes his parents had brought over and shuffled into the bathroom.

Janie got up and went to Sam. "Do you really think it's a good idea? Living together? The last time someone asked me..."

Sam closed his eyes and leaned his head back. "You're not cursed."

"I don't know. Someone is after everyone I care about. Sounds cursed to me."

"Don't worry about Sammy," Perry said. "He's practically indestructible."

"Define practically," Rick said from the bathroom.

It was questions like that that made Janie wonder about her cousin. Sure, she'd like to understand, but probably for a completely different reason: she didn't want anything to happen to Sam. Why would Rick want to know?

Perry sat on the chair and put his feet up on the bed. "I'm thinking you don't need to know the specifics until you've been bonded to a vampire."

Did Perry feel the same vibes coming from Rick? Not that she blamed him for being cautious.

Rick emerged from the bathroom shirtless, but at least he wore his jeans. A big bandage covered the area where he'd been wounded. "What makes you think we're going to get bonded?"

"Because you're Perfect Mates. That's what you do."

Rick put his hands on his hips. "And we don't have a choice?"

"So, what's the plan?" Janie interrupted, giving Rick the stink eye. If he wanted to make a good impression on the vampires in the room, he was doing a lousy job. He did realize they'd report back to Victoria, didn't he?

Perry answered, "I am to drive you three to the Cleveland safe house, where I will drop you off and then head back to Dayton and return Johnny's car."

"He's not staying with us." Sam picked at the molding around the door and a piece broke off. "Shit."

He looked so miserable and couldn't seem to keep still. She just wanted to ease his worries if she could. "Can I speak to you privately?"

"Ah, Ricky-boy. I think she wants a little kissy face before we hit the road. What do you think?" Perry made loud, wet, kissing noises while Rick just looked disgusted.

Sam closed his eyes and shook his head. "Ignore him."

She had a feeling that was easier said than done. Perry seemed to live for the attention. She exited the room and led Sam down the hall, away from the nurse's desk, near the emergency stairs. Hopefully out of earshot of one nosy vampire.

"Alone at last?" Sam said with a sad chuckle.

"Are you okay? You seem so lost."

"I feel like all this information has been dumped on your head like a bucket of cold water. I don't want it to scare you off."

Misery covered his face and she wanted to wipe it clean. She palmed his cheek and reveled in the erotic wave. He closed his eyes on a sigh. Their acclimation earlier had done nothing to lessen the euphoria. At least not for her. God, to feel this all the time? She'd be a fool to give that up. "Do I look like I'm scared?"

"No." He grabbed her hand and kissed the palm. "You've been very level headed."

She leaned in close. Relished the scent that was all Sam. "I don't feel very level headed around you. Not so sure I want to. Are you ever going to kiss me again?"

"Oh God, I thought you'd never ask." He palmed her face with both hands and planted his lips against her own.

Erotic waves zapped all her erogenous zones. Her nipples hardened. Her core clenched. She wrapped her arms around his neck. He eased her back against the wall. The hardness of him rubbing against her had her groaning. If only they had snuck inside an empty room.

He plunged his tongue inside her mouth. Her knees gave out. Somehow he kept her upright as he devoured her mouth. When her tongue tangoed with his, something sharp pricked hers and drew blood.

His fangs.

He froze for the briefest of moments and the next thing she knew, he was across the hall. "Sorry about that. Caught me a little off guard."

The only thing she was sorry about? That she was no longer in his embrace and the euphoria had faded. But then she didn't really understand what he was going through. Or what urges he fought so hard to control. She slowly approached him and whispered, "Are you hungry? Is that why?"

Because if it was as simple as that, she'd gladly offer him a vein. How weird was that?

He grimaced. "In a way, but not for food."

If not for food, then what... "Oh." Which seemed like an understatement. The man had fangs and they came out when he became aroused. "Does this happen all the time you want to...you know?"

"No. Just with you." Still grimacing, he stood there and stared. Like he expected her to bolt.

Just her? Now she felt special. More special than the stupid Perfect Mate label.

"I like you, Janie."

"I kind of got that. I like you, too."

His grimace turned into a grin and he relaxed. "I don't want you to worry about my fangs, though. I won't bite you without your permission first. And I don't expect that for quite some time. I never would have asked to move in with you without knowing you first."

"I don't think we were given much of a choice. I just hate the way it looks. Because of me, your life and Rick's are in danger."

He placed his fingers against her lips, silencing her. And sending another zap of pleasure her way. "Nothing is going to happen. I'm the best bodyguard you could get, don't you know?"

"Unless the sun is out?"

He lowered his hand. "Yeah. Unless that. But she's not after you. And I'm not going anywhere in the daylight. We'll just have to make sure Rick doesn't either."

* * * *

Tricia sat in her car and her butt was growing numb. It would have been nicer to wait in the hotel foyer but she didn't want any witnesses, and who wouldn't remember a woman sitting in the foyer all stinkin' day. So she'd been sitting in the car instead, keeping it running every now and then so she didn't freeze to death. Eventually the slut would have to return to the hotel, and when she did, Tricia would make her move. Didn't matter if her cover was blown. Janie was finally going to get hers.

Tricia stepped out of her vehicle and stretched her legs. Thankfully the parking lot was sparse so there was no one to send strange looks her way. The empty lot was also a hindrance. If Janie spotted her too soon… Well, Tricia would have to make do if that happened.

That yellow SUV pulled into the lot and into the check in/check out area.

About damn time. Tricia quickly snatched her purse from inside the car and then froze. Wait a minute. What was her boyfriend doing with her? She banged the roof of her car. What the hell? He should be dead!

How did she miss him? She was sure she'd stuck him good. None of the drug remained in her needle. Damn it, damn it, damn it!

She couldn't expose herself now and ducked back inside her vehicle.

At least she had a backup plan. Just not the one she'd hoped to use. Someone was going to die tonight. The question was…who?

* * * *

Sam followed Janie to her hotel room. Luck was on his side for once. Rick's medication was still going to take some time so Sam suggested he bring Janie to pack up and check out while they waited. Of course, Perry was sure they'd do more than that. And while the temptation was there, it really didn't seem like the right time. Or did it? They were finally alone and this might be the only time they would have privacy for weeks.

Might as well be months. Or years. It would still feel the same. Hell, he'd been ready to take her in the hospital hallway. If she had suggested they find an empty room…

"Seems like such a waste." She laughed as she opened the door. "I don't think I slept here one night."

"I never sleep in them," he joked.

She looked over her shoulder at him, those blue eyes of her so mesmerizing. "No, I guess you don't."

"And that's why I'm the best bodyguard you could have."

"Except for the sun bit."

"Yeah, except for that." But as long as she was with him, there wouldn't be a problem. He'd just control whoever tried to hurt her. Or him.

She headed toward the suitcase on the floor, then stopped. "What the?"

He rushed inside, but no one was there. "What's the matter? What's wrong?"

"Sorry. Not a bodyguard thing." Abandoning the suitcase, she walked to the dresser where a vase of flowers and a box of chocolates sat on top. She picked up the note. "The flowers are for Rick and the chocolates are for you. Don't eat them all in one sitting. Love you bunches, Megan."

He examined each. Box was completely sealed. Flowers smelled pretty and a little earthy but nothing unusual. "Who's Megan?"

"My friend. She lives in Arizona. Wanted to come out here, but I told her not to. Insisted on having my room information instead. I guess this is why."

Arizona? "Were you friends when we met?"

"Oh yeah. She's the only real friend I've had since I left Detroit."

"And yet you didn't tell her about our encounter. Why?"

"Because I thought you were an alien." She laughed. "Teach me to watch *Roswell*, huh?"

"Ahh, but they were good aliens, weren't they?"

"You watched…?" She shook her head. "I guess I shouldn't be surprised. We do seem to have a lot in common, at least entertainment-wise. Part of the Perfect Mate thing?"

"Can't say." He sat on the edge of the bed. Should he sit here or in the chair? Did it even matter? God, he was going to go crazy. Her scent wasn't helping matters any, either. And to think he would be living with her. Living. With her. Without contact.

Janie picked up the suitcase and placed it beside him. "I'm really sorry about Rick. I want what's best for him. I just wish I knew what that was. I thought for sure he'd be okay with vampires once he met you. I mean, I was. Why wouldn't he?"

He couldn't stop the grin from forming if he'd tried. "You don't have a problem with vampires?"

"Well, I wasn't too fond of Dalton's reaction, but I'm thinking he was an anomaly. Barnet won't be like that, will he?"

"No. He won't be a problem for you. That's all on me. But I'll be fine." As long as her reaction rated in the Perry and Dalton range.

She pulled some clothes from the dresser and placed them in the suitcase. "I'm kind of disappointed we won't be able to go out on dates. Sounds bad, but I really don't trust leaving Rick alone."

"Yeah, I kind of figured that. But dating doesn't have to include going out. It just means getting to know one another." And having sex. Usually. But privacy would be at a premium once they were at the safe house. He stared at the bed. If only…

She grabbed his chin and warmth spread across his face. He hadn't even heard her move and now she was standing in front of him. Kissing him. Pushing him back against the mattress. Oh God, he was so hard for her. But was this real?

She pulled away and worked at unbuttoning his jeans. "I'm on the pill, but do I need to worry about disease?"

It *was* real. Hot damn. "No. Can't give or get." He gripped her upper arms. "Are you sure?"

"Yeah. Aren't you? I just assumed—"

"Shut up." He kissed her. Tasted her.

She unzipped his jeans and pulled him out. "God, you go commando." Palmed his testicles. The heat was glorious. Her hands even more so.

Once he came down from the stratosphere, he tugged her T-shirt. "Naked. We gotta get naked."

Sure, he'd like to take his time and undress her. Have her undress him. But he wasn't sure how long he'd last and their time was short already. Her smile and nod told him she felt the same way. Clothes flew every which way as they stripped.

His fantasy stood before him and he was almost afraid to touch her. What if she wasn't real? What if this was just another fantasy? "God, you're beautiful."

"You're not so bad yourself, Hot Cowboy."

"Hot cowboy?"

"That's what I called you that night. In my head. In my dreams. You've been in a lot of those. I want real now. Give me real."

Oh yes. Real. It was like she read his mind.

* * * *

Janie had never connected with a man as quickly as she had with Sam. And when he had longingly looked at the bed, probably wondering the same as her—if they'd ever have some alone time—well, she'd realized they were alone now. And after that kiss at the hospital, she wanted more. She wanted what she'd been fantasizing about, dreaming about. She wanted Sam.

He caressed her cheek, sending delightful zaps with his touch. Combed his fingers through her hair and fisted, pulling her head back. The power he held over her made her wet with desire. She licked her lips, inviting him. The next moment his mouth was covering hers. His tongue was exploring. And her knees gave way.

He lifted her and settled her on the bed. Covered her with his body and nuzzled her neck. She arched into him, secretly wishing he'd bite her. Taking the decision about bonding away from her. But he wouldn't do that to her. To them. She knew that much.

"You smell so good." He fingered her clit before inserting his finger inside her. "And you're so wet. I bet you taste good, too."

His finger—or fingers, as he slipped another inside her—did wonderful, evil things to her. She wanted more. So yeah, she was wet. For him. And if he really wanted a taste of her blood, she wasn't stopping him.

He moved down her body, spending a few moments with her breasts—pinching, then sucking the hardened nipples. Oh yes. Would he bite those? But no. He kept going lower and lower until he reached her sex. He inhaled deeply as if she were a fine wine. Keeping eye contact, he licked her.

She nearly shot off the bed. Okay, so maybe it wasn't her blood he wanted to taste. Holy shit. The erotic zaps were too much for her. The orgasm was building, building, building…

He sucked on her clit and inserted another finger.

Kaboom! She was a goner. Rode that wave until her brain settled back in her head. And once it did, he was on top of her. Entering her. And she was gone again.

He came almost as quickly as she had. Maybe next time they'd be able to slow it down a little. But man, what a ride. She'd never orgasmed that quickly. Or hard. She might have pulled a muscle.

"That was awesome. You're awesome." He kissed her as he hovered over her. Vampires could do that? And while her brain was working that out, her eyes told her the truth. His arms were holding him up. Oh thank God. She wasn't sure she could deal with a different vampire trait.

"Awesome or short? I feel like we kind of rushed things."

He laughed. "Next time I'll be sure to slow down."

Those fangs of his were extended once again and damn, she wanted him to bite her. The last time had been…orgasmic. With sex, she could only imagine. "What did Ben mean when he asked me if I'd offered my blood to you? Is that how we bond?"

"Not really. But it would start the process. To complete the bond, you'd have to take my blood."

"What?" Okay, that did not sound very…romantic.

He rolled onto his side. "You won't have to take a lot. Probably only a pin prick amount. We're not even certain if it matters who takes whose blood first, but of all the bondings I know, the Perfect Mate finished the process."

Which meant she had the control. She could live with that. "So you can feed from me and not bond us."

He placed his palm on her stomach and smiled. "That's sort of true, but if I start the process I could become…possessive, or more possessive, if not more paranoid about every unbonded male vampire that looks at you twice. You would also keep bugging me to complete the process. So if you're not ready to complete it now, why put ourselves through that kind of torture?"

She couldn't do that to him. And she really wanted to keep her wits about their relationship without some inane urge to bond. "This is all so strange."

"You think it's strange now. Wait until I take your blood. I hear the sex is insanely intense."

"But you took my blood already."

"Ah, but not with your permission. You have to be a willing participant, like you are now, by asking me to bite you."

"And then the sex gets *more* intense?" Holy shit. It had already been intense in the wham-bam-thank-you-ma'am version.

"So I've been told. It's not a decision we should take lightly, or delay once we start. So as much as I'd love to bite you right now, or as much as you'd like me to, I won't. You're not ready to start the process."

"But you are?" She placed her hand over his. This touching thing was contagious.

"Janie, I've been ready since the day I discovered you existed. But it's not about me. It's about us."

That had to be the sweetest thing anyone had ever said to her. She shoved him on his back and straddled his body. "How much time do you need to recover, Mr. Vampire?"

Her answer nudged her butt. Sweet.

"You ready for some slow this time?" he asked.

Was she ever.

Chapter 13

There's bugged and then there's bugged.

Sam rolled off Janie, but held onto her hand. The heat was glorious, but the sex had been mind blowing. Each and every time. And to think they'd done it three times.

She curled into his side. "You are way better than my dreams."

"Ditto." He liked that she'd dreamed of him. It had to prove she was his Perfect Mate. But that would be something she'd have to realize on her own. For them to work it had to be on her terms, and he had to keep reminding himself of that.

"Why did you say you were ready now? With the bonding?"

But hey, if she wanted to talk about it, he wouldn't stop her. "Because I can't imagine my life anymore without you in it."

"But we hardly know each other."

"I've been around a long time. I have never felt a connection with someone like I do with you. Never. I like being near you."

"I could say the same thing."

"But you've been married. Engaged. You must have loved them."

"I did. They were great guys." She chuckled. "Usually. But I never felt any passion with them. David had been a means of escape and I came to love him. Justin was someone I thought I wanted, but realized after he'd died I'd been using him as a replacement for David. Aaron, though, he was fun to be around. He made me laugh. But I had no plans on marrying him. Although he might have convinced me otherwise."

She rose on her elbows, using him for leverage. "You're different, Sam. I think I knew that that first night, even though everything you did should have made me angry."

He winced. "I really wish you'd forget about that night."

"Why? If not for that night, I wouldn't be here now. Not so sure I'd want to forget the best non-sex sex I'd ever had."

"But I attacked you."

"You thought you controlled me. Right? Having a little fun with your food, maybe?"

"See? That's why I want you to forget. I don't do that anymore."

"Would you have stopped if not for me?"

Okay. She got him there. Would he have stopped? Probably not. Shit.

"Hey, if I gave you a conscience, it's all good. I mean, you weren't going to do more than kiss, right?"

He shook his head. "I never did more than that. Kissing went with feeding. Sex was always consensual."

She kissed him lightly on the mouth. "And that's why I like you. Man, I could spend all night in this room with you, but then Rick and Perry might wonder what happened to us."

"I'm pretty sure Perry already suspected this was going to happen."

"Which means he probably told Rick. Ugh." She lowered her forehead to his chest. "That will make for a fun trip."

"It'll be fine." To get her moving, he lightly smacked her butt. But the softness of her skin, the warmth on his palm, he let his hand linger. Had he ever seen a nicer butt? He hadn't. But they had to get moving. "Come on, let's get you packed. What can I do to help?"

Slowly, she crawled to the edge of the bed. "You can make sure there's not too much water in the vase. I don't want it to spill in the car."

He found his jeans and took his time slipping them on while she got dressed. Damn, it was almost as erotic as watching her undress. Apparently three times was not enough. He was growing hard again. Before it became impossible, he zipped up. His shoes and shirt could wait. He picked up the ceramic container. "I don't think there's any water in here."

"What?" She peered inside as if she could see. "How stupid is that florist? Put a little in, then. I'll use my cosmetic bag to keep it upright."

As she finished emptying the dresser, Sam carried the vase to the sink. It was too tall to fit under the faucet. He unwrapped one of the plastic cups and filled it with water. As he poured it into the vase, a spider landed on his hand. Then bit him.

"Ouch." He squished the bugger.

"What's the matter? Get a thorn?" She came around the corner and screamed.

Spiders were pouring out of the vase and covering Sam's hand, each one biting him. "The shower!"

She quickly turned on the faucet and ran from the room. Holding onto the vase, he stepped in the tub and squished every arachnid he encountered.

Janie returned with a shoe. She pounded the sink. "Those look like brown recluses. What the hell are they doing in there? Should we get you to the hospital? They're poisonous."

"Don't worry about me. Make sure they don't bite you. I'm immune, remember?"

"Oh, thank God. Cause if you weren't…" She looked up at him with shiny eyes. "No!" She dropped the shoe and ran from the room, crying.

He made sure every last spider was smashed and washed down the drain. Who the hell wanted her dead?

Holy shit. She could have died. His Perfect Mate could have *died*.

* * * *

Spiders. There were spiders in the vase. How close had she been to touching them. To getting bitten? To dying?

Sam emerged from the bathroom, his jeans soaked in places. Pinkish welts appeared on his hand and arm. All because of her. Oh sure, he'd say it was someone else, but it was someone else because of her.

She ran into his arms, tears spilling from her eyes. "I'm so sorry. I'm so sorry. I'm so sorry."

He held her tight and she let his strength do what she couldn't seem to muster herself: bring calm to her life.

"This wasn't your fault," he said.

How could he say that? Of course it was her fault. None of this would be happening if it wasn't due to something she'd done to someone else a long time ago.

Holding her by the waist, he lifted her gently and placed her on the bed. Knelt in front of her. "Hey, it's going to be okay. We'll find out who's behind this. Who could you have pissed off, even a little? Megan?"

"No. Megan's been there for me. She'd have no reason. And how the hell would she get spiders from Arizona? I can't imagine a florist even going along with it. It has to be someone local. And they were in my room!" What else did she have to look forward to? Scorpions in her dresser? A snake in her suitcase?

Oh God. Not a snake.

"Were you a bully in school?"

"No."

"Bullied?"

"No. Having David for a friend kind of kept them away. He was a football player and quite muscular. I never had any problems at school."

"Then it has to be from your candy-striping days. That doctor who abused you. Dr. Crawford."

"Murdered. Remember?"

"Yeah, I know, but how about his family. Wife? Kids? Or maybe a mistress, another nurse?"

"I don't know. I never met or heard about them. But..." Shit. The one person who could probably help her was one of the last she wanted to see.

"But, what?"

"Liz. David's mother. She might know more about Dr. Crawford's family." She covered her face. "God, she's gonna hate me."

"I hardly doubt that. If anything, she's going to want to help find the person who killed her son."

"Do you really think David was killed?"

"If it weren't for the other deaths, no. But someone has been targeting your loved ones and today it appeared they were after you. I'm just glad I was here to prevent that from happening."

Having a vampire in her life was turning out to be a really good thing. She hugged him around the neck. "Me, too. Thank you, Sam."

"Come on. Let's get you out of here and talk to Liz. See what she knows." He stood and looked down at his wet jeans. "I've got another pair in the car. I'll get them and come right back." As he walked past the dresser, he picked up the box of candy. "Are you going to want this?"

"Hell, no. I'm almost afraid to go through the dresser now." She hadn't seen any bugs, but that didn't mean there weren't any.

"Then don't. Just stay on that bed and wait for me. I'll throw these out and be right back."

She scrambled onto the middle of the bed. Here she could stay. The covers were white and she'd be able to spot one of those spiders right away if one had survived. God, she hoped one hadn't.

* * * *

Sam inspected Janie's cosmetic bag. All clear. Her suitcase. All clear. As he went through each piece of clothing, he handed it over to Janie, who then folded and packed it away in her suitcase. When he reached her bra and panties, he picked them up and hesitated.

He'd been so close to telling her that he'd changed his mind. That he wanted to bond right away. Make her immortal and protect her from illness and injuries. Because what if one of those spiders had bitten her? And since one hadn't, some crazy person was out there hoping to strike again.

He couldn't lose Janie. Not after it had taken him so long to find her.

"Are you going to hold those or give them to me?" Janie asked.

"I don't want you to die."

"That makes two of us. But what does my underwear have to do with that?"

"Sorry." He handed over the garments. "I know I said I wanted to wait, but that was before…" Shit. What was he saying? "Never mind."

"Before my life was in danger?"

He nodded and picked up the next piece of clothing. Shook it.

"Actually, it's been in danger for eight years, hasn't it? And I'm still here. And now technically, your life is in danger. Sure, you're more hardy than I am, but you're not infallible. Will bonding change you?"

"Not like that, no." Too bad it didn't. She might be willing to do it if it meant saving someone else's life. But did he really want her that way?

118

She continued to pack the garments he handed her. "I like you, Sam, I really do, but if I were to become more hardy, like you, I want to make sure I'm doing it for the right person. We still might not be compatible. I like to snuggle in bed. You don't even sleep."

"Just because I don't sleep doesn't mean I can't snuggle. I'd love nothing better than having you sleep in my arms."

She smiled, probably picturing it. "Still, you said it yourself, this is a serious decision. And I still don't really know you. Like, you said you've been around a long time. How long?"

He shook the remaining garments and placed them on the bed. Nothing he could say was going to change her mind. Only time was going to do that. He prayed they'd have enough and would share whatever history she wanted to know. "I was turned during the war. Revolutionary."

She sat on the bed, her mouth open in a cute way. "Damn. And all that time you've been alone?"

"I'm not celibate. There have been women."

"But you haven't picked anyone to spend your life with. Why?"

Well, he had. But he'd screwed up. Okay, maybe there was some history he wasn't quite ready to share. He shrugged. "This picking is a two-way street, you know."

"I can't imagine no one wanting you."

"Yeah? You think I'm a catch?" Except she'd already caught him. Hadn't he told her so already?

She zipped up her suitcase. "So far I do. Yes."

"Okay, then." His heart lightened at that. He hadn't blown it with her yet. And if he was careful, he wouldn't at all. He was going to be vigilant.

"Revolutionary War? Really?"

"Yes, I'm *that* old."

"You're going to have to tell me that story some day."

"It's a date."

She placed her suitcase on the ground and attached her cosmetic bag on top. "Can you do me a favor? Just check around the dresser and make sure one of those spiders didn't sneak out earlier. I'd hate for the maid—" She shuddered.

"No problem." He couldn't blame her for the shivers. Those were some nasty arachnids. He still had the welts to prove it. A small cramp flittered across his abdomen. Drugged, sexed—oh yeah, sexed—and venomous spider bites had used up more energy than usual. He'd get some blood at the hospital. Plenty of workers to choose from.

But the day she agreed to bonding was the day he'd stop finding blood elsewhere. Her blood would become more potent; it would only take a couple of pulls a week to sustain him. Oh, he could still feed from other people, but from what he'd been told, Janie wouldn't like him doing it.

Using his phone, he turned on the flashlight and pointed it toward the back of the dresser. Nothing moved or crawled away, but there was a bump of some sort. He ran his hand over it, expecting to squish a bug. Instead, a metal object came free. He pulled his hand away and inspected it.

Oh shit. He got a bug all right. Just not the crawly kind.

"What is that?" she asked.

"Grab your things. We have to leave now. Someone's been listening." He smashed the item between his fingers and tossed the remains in the trash.

"Listening?" She stood frozen for just a moment when realization flashed across her face. "Liz!"

They'd just unleashed a murderer on another target, and who now quite possibly knew that vampires existed. Seemed the day *could* get worse.

* * * *

Tricia entered the foyer of the hospital, wearing the same disguise she had earlier. Hardly a soul in sight—meaning the cameras would definitely pick her out—but then hospitals weren't bustling so much on a Saturday night. Most people had the weekends off.

Or they were doing the nasty in a hotel room. God, how many times did those two go at it? But she couldn't leave until she knew her backup plan had worked. And as it turned out, she'd failed. Again.

The fact those two had figured out someone was behind all the deaths was unfortunate. Unfortunate for one Liz Delaney. But Tricia was ready to remedy that situation.

It was all that other garbage she'd heard that made her pause. Perfect Mates and vampires? What the hell was that all about? That boyfriend of hers was one crazy guy.

Except… He'd managed to escape a vase full of brown recluses as if they'd been ordinary spiders. Claiming he was immune. And that drug. She knew she hadn't missed. Was he immune to that, too?

But a vampire? She must have heard that wrong.

Tricia took the elevator to the third floor, keeping her head down low. The doors opened and she shuffled down the hall to the nurses' station. No one was manning the area. The board on the wall indicated which rooms belonged to Liz. A white lab coat hung on the rack. That would come in handy. Keeping her head down, she slipped it on and headed for the patient who still had an IV.

Long gone were the days of shared hospital rooms. Infection the big cause of that. So it was nice she didn't have to worry about a roommate. Not that that would have stopped her.

The man was asleep, but she couldn't risk him wakening. She pulled out the hypo meant for Janie and inserted the sleeping drug into the IV.

After a minute, she shook the man. No response. Tricia peaked out the door. Liz had returned to the nurses' station and was alone. Perfect. Tricia slipped into the bathroom, shut the door, and turned on the light. On the wall, beside the toilet, hung a cord. She pulled it.

No one was going to interfere with her plan. No one.

* * * *

Janie wished the car would go faster. Or that Sam would drive it faster. Or that teleportation was a reality instead of science fiction. But nothing of the sort would get them to the hospital any quicker.

After quickly checking out of the hotel, Sam had driven them to Liz's house, but she wasn't at home. To save time, Sam had called Perry while Janie had called the hospital, but Liz hadn't answered her page and the nurse on the line asked Janie if she wanted to leave a message.

Yeah, right. She could almost picture the message taker's face if she said, "Tell her to watch out. A killer is on the loose and she may be the next target." Instead, Janie asked that Liz call her right away. But she had a sick feeling that the message was much too late, that they were much too late, because if Liz wasn't answering her page… "I should have known she'd be at the hospital. We saw her late there the last time."

"Perry said he'd check the floor she works on. We'll find her."

No sooner had he said that, his phone rang, number unknown. Sam put it on speaker. "Perry?"

"She's on her dinner break," Perry said.

"What? Are you sure? Someone saw her leave?" If only she had Liz's cell phone number. But Liz hadn't owned one eight years ago, if she even owned one now.

"No, but it's on the schedule. And one of the nurses said she tends to go off campus to eat. Off campus. What a weird way of saying hospital."

"Did you check the rooms?"

"I didn't, personally, but I suggested, if you know what I mean, to one of the nurses to check the patients and call out if she saw Liz. All was quiet. Are you sure the bug was for you? I mean, couldn't it have been there awhile?"

"It's possible," Sam said, "but I'd bet my life savings it was planted for Janie. To hear if her little spider trick worked."

"Spiders. Blehhh. That's just creepy."

Sam glanced at Janie. "No kidding. We should be back soon. How's our patient?"

"Yeah, about him. Is your cousin always so twitchy?"

Janie prayed he wasn't asking what she thought he was asking. "Twitchy? Like in a tic?"

"No, no. Like one moment he's all happy to be alive and okay with vampires and shit, but then he goes and asks me what I can't do. I don't think I want him to know."

Shit. Exactly what she didn't need right now. "He has been known to waffle back and forth on issues. I was hoping he'd outgrown it."

"Okay, good to know. Anyways, I better get back before he notices I'm gone. He's got his pills and we're ready to go when you are. Good luck in finding Liz."

Sam disconnected the call. "You okay?"

"No. And I won't be until we find her."

Sam parked the car. "Do you just want to wait for her up on her floor, down here at the entrance, or start checking all the restaurants in the area?"

"If Liz didn't go to dinner, then she had to have been lured away. Right?"

"What are you thinking?"

"Perry said he had the nurse check the patients. I wonder if she checked the patients' bathrooms."

"Why there?"

"They have cords a patient can pull if they need assistance. If one went off and Liz went to investigate…would the nurse even bother looking in there if she were checking on the patients?"

"Okay, then. We'll go up. But you have to let me do all the work."

"You mean you'll do your vampire magic on them?"

He smiled. "Yeah, my magic. We don't want to draw suspicions if they're unwarranted. Because it's probable she has just gone to dinner."

Janie's gut told her that wasn't likely. It was just too coincidental. "Well, if anything, I am a friend from out of town and I can just sit around and wait for her to return."

Sam took her hand as they headed for the hospital. Kept holding it as they rode the elevator to the third floor. But even maintaining contact wasn't giving Janie any peace. She wouldn't get that until she saw Liz was okay. The doors opened and Sam pulled her along. As they maneuvered around the janitor's cart, screams came from the room on the right.

A woman of the cleaning-crew variety hurried out. "Oh my God, oh my God! Security! Someone call security!"

Janie rushed inside and stopped. A man was sleeping in the bed, but the bathroom light was on and the door stood open. A woman—a nurse?—was lying on the floor; her feet were the only things exposed from Janie's angle. The floor was covered in red. Red streaks lined the shower curtain. She took two more steps when Sam grabbed her around the waist and carried her into the hall.

"It's a crime scene. Don't touch."

"The red?" She knew. She *knew*. But she didn't want to know.

Sam whispered in her ear. "Blood. Too much. No heartbeat. She's gone."

Gone? Someone had died. But was it Liz? *Please don't let it be Liz.*

A nurse sped past. An announcement over the speakers requested security. A cry of Liz's name echoed from the room.

"Noooo…" Janie's legs gave out.

Sam maneuvered her to the stairwell door. His fangs were extended. "I'm so sorry, Janie, but we can't stay here."

"But Liz… And the police will want to know."

"Think about what we discussed in your room. I can't afford to have the police capture our listener before I've had a chance to wipe her mind."

"Her? You think a woman is responsible for all this?"

"A woman did inject me with something."

"But it could be a vampire behind it all, right? They could have controlled—" She stopped at the shaking of his head.

"A vampire wouldn't have bothered to inject me with something that couldn't work. And they wouldn't have needed to bug the room. They could have listened from out in the hall or from the room next door."

She conceded that round to him because it made sense. In the way vampires made sense. Which they didn't. Not to the general public. "Okay, but even if she was caught, no one will believe her."

"Doesn't matter. It's vampire business now. And since you're a Perfect Mate, you fall under our protection." He grabbed his stomach. "We have to go. Now."

"I can't. The police have to know what's going on. She can't get away with this."

"And she won't. We just have to catch her first."

"Don't make me leave her like this." The tears fell as guilt came crashing down. Guilt for not keeping in touch. For not saying hello when she'd had the chance. For not being able to get to her in time.

Sam wrapped her in a hug. "She's gone, Janie, and it's not your fault. We did our best."

Except their best hadn't been good enough. If only she could distance herself from everyone else. Would the woman leave her alone then, or would she become the next target? One thing was a fact: if this woman wasn't caught soon, Sam could very well be killed, hardy or not.

A security guard approached them. "Excuse me. Did you see what happened here?"

"No." She so desperately wanted to say more, but why bother? Sam would only erase the man's mind.

"She'd just lost a dear friend when all that happened," Sam said.

"I'm sorry for your loss, ma'am, but I'm going to have to ask you to leave the area."

"We understand. Come on, sweetie."

When they entered the stairwell, she asked, "Did you make him say that?"

A look of hurt painted his face. "Why would I do that?"

"So I would leave. So I wouldn't talk to the police. I don't see why I can't talk to them. Despite what you think, what's been happening to those around me is not vampire business. A sick-o human is behind it all." She sat on the step and covered her face. "Why won't you let me tell them to check into Dr. Crawford's family?"

"Because you have no proof. If anything, it'll just shine the spotlight on you. Let us find her first."

"And what? Wipe her memory? So she gets away scot-free?"

"She will be held responsible. You have to trust me."

Janie wanted to trust him, but everyone around her died. And Sam could very well be next. All it would take was this sick-o to believe he was a vampire and figure out a way to destroy him. Janie couldn't let that happen. And it appeared there was only one way to protect him.

Chapter 14

A shot to the heart.

Cleveland, at last.

Sam punched in the code and unlocked the door to the safe house. The one-story bungalow had three small bedrooms, one tiny bathroom, and a kitchen void of any appliances, but that had never bothered any vampire who stayed here.

Janie had been relatively quiet the whole trip. He figured she needed time to grieve, since she'd gotten confirmation that Liz had indeed been murdered. And while the trip should have given Janie some peace, her cousin had seen fit to complain. About being babysat to get food. To stretch his legs. To pee. If he was looking for some alone time, he was sadly disappointed. Sam was under strict orders not to leave the man alone. And apparently for good reason.

"You expect us to live here?" Rick pulled back a set of curtains to find more drywall. "Where are the windows? You don't have any fucking windows?"

Perry grinned as he shut the door. "Why am I not surprised he noticed that first?"

"It's a safe house for vampires, you idiot," Janie said as she dropped her purse on the coffee table and plunked down on the love seat. "Of course it doesn't have any windows."

Sam winced at the anger that rippled through in her words. He'd done what was best for the vampires. For her. He'd thought for sure the ride would have calmed her some. That she would have seen reason.

Rick stood in the kitchen. "They also don't have a refrigerator or oven. How are we supposed to eat?"

"Take out?" Perry said.

"Like you're going to let me out to do that."

"We'll figure something out," Sam said. "Why don't you go pick a room?"

As Rick took his meager belongings down the hall, Janie stood. "If I'm expected to live here now, I need my stuff from the hotel suite. And I guess I need to check out of that place, too."

"You live in a hotel?" Perry asked.

"A suite. It has a bedroom and a kitchen and I pay by the week. A lot easier than trying to rent an apartment for six months."

Sam dropped his bag on the floor. "You can do that later. Don't you want to rest?"

"Later? Like when it's sunny? Are you going to let me go alone?"

"You're not a prisoner."

"No, that would be me," Rick said as he returned. "And there are no sheets and blankets on the bed."

"Shut up," she said to him. "You've done nothing but whine the whole trip. Don't make me wish they'd taken you to Atlanta."

"You've been acting funny ever since you returned from your hotel room. Did he do something to you?"

No one had bothered to tell Rick about Liz's death. Janie wasn't sure how he'd treat that information and Sam had agreed.

"I'm just tired. So can I go to my hotel suite and get my stuff? I need my car, too."

"Your car?" Perry asked. "Didn't that get squished?"

"That was a rental. My car is still at the hotel."

"I'll take you." Sam turned to Perry. "Do you mind waiting? You'll still have time to make it to Dayton before sunrise."

"No," she said. "I want Perry to take me."

The pain in his chest couldn't hurt any worse if she'd shot him. He wanted to ask her why, but all that came out was, "Oh?"

"I realized I never really gave him a fair shake. You know, this Perfect Mate business. Figure I should get some alone time with him before I make any decision that would affect the rest of my life."

Or she'd already made a decision and just hadn't voiced it yet. Damn it. What'd he do wrong?

Perry leaned toward Sam. "I did not put her up to this. I swear."

"Right. Fine. I'll stay with Rick, then."

Janie picked up her bag. "Which room did you pick?"

Rick pointed down the hall. "The first one on the left."

She headed toward the bedrooms. A moment later she yelled, "You picked the only room with a bed?"

"I didn't know. I just picked the first room." Rick left to join Janie.

"What do you want me to do?" Perry asked. "I mean, I know how I'd feel if my Perfect Mate wanted to be with another vampire. I'd want to kill that vampire. You don't want to kill me, do you?"

"She's not my Perfect Mate." Not yet, anyway. And really, shouldn't she be one-hundred percent on board with him if they were to bond? Sounded good in his head. In his heart, not so much.

"Yeah, right. But really. What do you want me to do?"

"Whatever she wants."

"Shit. For real?"

"For real." And if it turned out Janie didn't want to be with him, he'd have someone rip out his heart. It would be irreparable anyway.

* * * *

Tricia pulled along the curb and parked the car. Using the borrowed iPad—sometimes friends came in handy—she'd been following the GPS signal of the trackers she'd placed on the yellow SUV.

Should have figured they'd come to Cleveland. That's where the slut lived. But what was this place?

The SUV was parked in the driveway of a one-story house. No lights shone from any of the windows. Had they just parked and slept? It was only midnight. Even she was still wide awake.

The four of them had come here. Why? Why didn't they stay in Detroit? Tricia understood why the slut would come here, and maybe the boyfriend, but Rick and that other fella? Something was going on. Did it have to do with that vampire business she'd heard? Is that why they were only seen outside at night? Could she do away with the boyfriend during the day? Like, blast a hole in that house? Wow, wouldn't that be something? She'd always wanted to destroy something big like that.

But what if she failed? What if she was caught? She'd come too close to being caught with Liz. If only the bitch would have cooperated. Instead she'd wanted to fight. Thank goodness Tricia had worn gloves. And a wig. She'd left no evidence behind. And she could leave no evidence this time, either.

The door opened, shining light on the small lawn. So they were still up. Must have light-blocking shades or curtains. Because...vampire, right? The slut and that other fella exited and climbed into the SUV. Leaving the boyfriend and cousin behind.

"Hmmm…" What could she do to a vampire at night?

* * * *

The hurt look on Sam's face had only made Janie's headache worse, but she really had no choice. The only way to keep him safe was to keep her distance. To keep her distance meant driving him away. And to drive him away meant implying she wasn't his Perfect Mate.

That she'd used Perry was unfortunate. But he'd already admitted to not having any urges around her. So it wasn't like she led him on or anything.

Perry started the engine. "So… Did you want to kiss me and see—"

"I do *not* want to kiss you." Shit. She *had* led him on. Janie rubbed her head, the ache was only getting stronger. "Sorry. I didn't mean to lead you on."

"Then what was that inside? Were you looking to hurt Sammy? Because you sure did a bang-up job."

She didn't want to hurt anyone. "Don't you get it? People die around me."

"Right. Sure. Where are we going?"

"Give me your phone and I'll put in the address."

"Well, I would if my phone was charged. And I'm not familiar with this fine city. So I'll have to follow you back. Will you know how to get back here?"

She pulled out her phone and programmed their trip, after notating the address of the safe house. "There. You're all set."

"Thank you." He drove off, following the directions from the WAZE app.

For the next several minutes the only soul talking was the app. Janie couldn't take the silence any longer. "What do you do for a living?"

Perry burst out laughing.

"What's so funny? Don't vampires work?"

"Oh, yeah, sure. Plenty of them do. I just don't happen to be one of them."

"Independently wealthy, are you?"

He laughed some more. "Not even. But seriously, I usually help the Committee. They even pay me, too. I suppose I should get my act together if I hope to snag one of you, huh? I just don't know what I'd like to do. It's been centuries since I worked."

"Centuries? Were you turned during the Revolutionary War, too?"

"No. I wasn't part of that…mess. I was turned before that. Think Jamestown."

"But you said you were born in the states."

"Minor technicality. I was born on land that became the United States."

"Wow. You're all so…"

"Old? Yeah. Because we're not just people. Sammy's not just people."

And now he'd maneuvered the conversation back to where she didn't want it and her heart hurt. "He's not indestructible, either. And now the killer knows he's a vampire."

"And you think she'll know how to kill him? That stuff isn't on the Internet."

"Oh? You can't die in the sun?"

"Well, yeah we can, but it's not like she can drag him outside."

"Or from decapitation?"

"Not necessarily. If the head is found intact and quick enough, you can reassemble it as long as you can get blood down the mouth to—"

"Shut up." Jane held her stomach. Her headache had been making it churn. Perry just added acid. "That sounds awful."

"It's not pleasant to experience, either."

"You were decapitated?"

"Almost. Almost decapitated. But see?" He stretched his neck. "Not a mark on me now."

Did she want to know how that came about? No, she did not. Her stomach wasn't doing so great with the headache as it was.

"You do know that Sammy is the best way to catch this killer, though. Don't you?"

"I know no such thing. I think the police can catch her, but Sam won't let me talk with them. And I have a feeling if I even try to contact them, you'll only get someone to erase their memory and destroy any documentation. Meanwhile, there's a killer on the loose, waiting to kill her next target. And I don't want to give her one."

"So you're trying to push him away, is that it? It's not going to work."

"Why? Because I'm a *Perfect Mate*?" She even used air quotes to emphasize her point.

"Because you're *his* Perfect Mate."

"We don't really know that." Although everything she'd felt when she was around Sam was pretty damn perfect.

"I think we do and I can prove it. Here, hold my hand."

She just stared at what he offered. "You just want to feel my warmth."

"Is that so bad? Then what are you afraid of? Finding out that you *are* Sammy's Perfect Mate or that you're not?"

She grabbed his hand. A nice electrical wave wove up her arm. Nothing erotic, just pleasant. Like a vibrator on her neck, not on any intimate parts.

He turned his head her way and fluttered his eyes. "Now do you want to kiss me?"

She snatched her hand back. "What is it with vampires and kissing?"

"See? You're not my Perfect Mate. If you were, you'd make me pull over and then ravish my body."

"Is that what you want to do to me?" Oh God. Maybe having Perry take her to the hotel was a mistake after all.

"Actually, no. That's the point. You're warm and smell great, and I like it a lot, but it's just… nice."

"So what are you saying? That I can't get rid of Sam if I tried?"

"Quite the opposite. I think you don't want to get rid of Sammy."

"I never said I wanted to. Just that I have to."

"You don't have to do any such thing. Why are you letting someone else dictate what you do in life?"

"Because she's killing the people I love!"

"Yeah, but you didn't know that before. Now you do. Just set a trap."

"Using Sam? I can't do that to him."

"Why not? You know he'd do it."

That's what she was afraid of.

* * * *

Sam found sheets and blankets on the closet shelf, packed in a plastic bag. Vampires never needed such things, but now with Perfect Mates in the mix, the Committee had seen fit to start stocking the safe houses to accommodate them, too. Apparently they were starting small.

He'd called Victoria about the lack of refrigerator and stove. And a second bed. She'd said the appliances had already been ordered and should be delivered on Monday. And that she'd look into getting the extra bed as soon as she hung up. When she asked if there was anything else, he almost didn't tell her.

But having more vampires on hand to find this killer was imperative now. So he told her what he suspected had been overheard and by whom. How much or how well the killer had listened in was not known. Victoria said she would start searching for Dr. Crawford's family and the latest kill and would get back to him as soon as she learned anything.

Sam handed the plastic bag to Rick. "I think you were looking for these."

Rick took the bag. "I'm sorry about earlier. I don't mean to be ungrateful."

"It's a lot to take in. I get it. But you aren't helping Janie any by being…disagreeable."

"I know. And I'll apologize to her too. In fact, she can have the bed."

"I don't think she'll take it. She's not the one recovering from surgery. Come on, I'll help you make it."

Sam tossed one corner of the fitted sheet to Rick and slipped his corner on. The last time Sam made up a bed was before the war, and even then it wasn't anything like it was now. Fitted sheets didn't exist back then.

"You've been a vampire a long time. Right?"

"I have."

"Does it hurt? To be turned?"

"Yeah, it hurts like hell. I truly thought I was going to die. Why do you want to know?"

Rick shrugged. "Just wondering what I had to look forward to, I guess."

Sam flicked the top sheet over the bed. "Look forward to? You can't become a vampire. You're immune."

"But I thought being a Perfect Mate—"

"Is just that. A mate who is perfect for a vampire. The only thing that will change for you is that you'll become immortal and not age. You'll still go out in the sun. Still eat regular food."

Rick's eyes widened as he finished tucking in the end of the sheet. "Really? That doesn't sound so bad."

"Didn't Victoria explain this to you?"

"She might have. If I'd given her a chance. Janie's right. I am an idiot."

Sam picked up the blanket when a thump sounded against the house. Followed by another thump.

"What was that?" Rick said.

Good thing the fake windows were made of Plexiglas. There might have been some serious breakage going on. Sam tossed the blanket on the bed and headed for the front door. "Stay here. I'll go check it out."

True, the house was not in the most favorable part of the city, but he couldn't imagine a street gang even giving this place a second look. Sam opened the door and stepped onto the small porch.

Two rocks lay on the front lawn. Now why would someone—

Before he could finish his thought, or even glance down the street, an arrow struck his chest. Pain flared and Sam quickly pulled the arrow free. "What the hell?"

He stared at the bloody tip. An inch closer to his heart and he would have—

Another arrow struck his chest. Sam's legs gave out. He fell to the ground, paralyzed. "Son of a bitch!"

* * * *

Tricia stood behind the bushes, frozen.

When she had rummaged through the back of Rachel's car, seeing what she might have to disable a vampire, she'd come across the archery set Rachel and she had used after their shopping trip.

It wasn't exactly a stake, but it was wood. She'd just assumed it would work the same.

The first arrow didn't seem to do any good, but the second... Wow, he'd gone down in a hurry. But where was the dust? The goo? Didn't vampires disappear when staked? It was the only reason she even bothered shooting the guy—he should have left no evidence.

So maybe he wasn't a vampire after all. Or they died differently in real life. Not that the killing was any less sweet. She just didn't want to get caught. Not until the slut got what was hers.

When Rick came to the door, Tricia crouched behind the bushes and headed back to the car, her heart beating a mile a minute.

* * * *

Sam concentrated on the sounds. Someone had shot him in the heart. They had to still be close by.

Bushes rustled across the street. Footsteps sounded inside the house. Rick's face came into view.

"You might want to step inside until it's safe."

Rick quickly retreated. "What happened?"

"Turn off the light inside. Do you see anyone across the street?"

The yard became shrouded. "No. It's too dark. Someone shot you?"

Sam was too stunned to come back with a smart ass remark. "Seems that way."

He should have known better. Been more alert. But no, he'd just stood there staring at the arrow like some dumbass instead of ducking back inside the house.

"How come you didn't turn to goo? Or dust?"

"Because I'm not a TV monster."

"Are you gonna die?"

"Not if you get this arrow out of my chest."

"Why can't you do it?"

"Because I'm paralyzed, you asshat." Ah damn. What had he done? It wasn't like he could hide his problem, though. "Please don't run away. It would only break Janie's heart."

"I wasn't considering it. Just wondering how I can get to you without getting hit."

Wow. Maybe Rick was coming around after all.

A car door opened and closed softly.

"Someone is in a car down the street on the right," Sam said. "Can you see them?"

"Damn, that's some hearing you got there." Rick peered around Sam just as an engine went off. "A car just took off down the street. No lights on, though."

Which meant no license number to check on. If it was even legal. "Damn it."

Holding his injured side, Rick stood over Sam. "I don't think I can carry you inside."

"Don't have to. Just remove the arrow."

When Rick tugged the arrow free, Sam nearly howled in pain. But at least he could move his fingers.

"So I guess you're the next target, huh?" Rick picked up the arrow Sam had dropped and looked at both. "Wonder how she found you?"

Sam had wondered the same thing. Only one thing came to mind. "Tracker. She put a tracker on the car."

The woman could be going after Janie next.

"Get my phone!"

* * * *

"There's my car." Janie pointed to the old SUV—nineteen years old and approaching 300,000 miles. The fenders were rusted around the edges and the white paint was faded in spots, but it was her baby. Thank God she hadn't driven it to Detroit, where it would have been destroyed. Eventually it would stop working, but she was prolonging that day from happening as best as she could.

"I can see why you got the rental." Perry parked beside it. "Don't they pay you enough?"

She laughed. "They pay me fine. David bought that for me when I was in college. As an engagement present."

"Did it look like that then?"

"What, you don't think it's pretty?"

"To each their own. Are you going inside to get some stuff or do that later?"

Just the thought of going inside after what had happened with the spiders caused her to shiver. "Would you consider coming in with me? Make sure it's safe?"

"Um…as much as I'd love to be in a room with you alone, I'm not so sure I want to see what kind of booby trap was left for you."

"Sam wouldn't hesitate to go in with me."

"Because you're his Perfect Mate. Do you get that now?"

In a way, she had. Sam would probably do anything for her. "You're leaving tonight. Right?"

"Already wanting to get rid of me, huh? Although you'll still have Ricky-boy hanging around. Don't know what kind of fun you and Sammy—"

"Are you ever serious?"

"Where's the fun in that?"

She shook her head. "You should dress more like yourself, then. You know, if you ever hope to catch that Perfect Mate's eye."

"What's wrong with the way I dress?"

"You look like you're ready for a round of golf. After being around you a bit, you seem more like a Hawaiian shirt and cargo pants kind of guy."

He stared down at his shirt, not saying a word. Wow. She'd managed to actually get the guy to shut up.

"If you won't go with me, I'll wait and bring Sam and Rick back later to get my things." And if there wasn't any booby trap, maybe convince them to stay here instead. Because…maid service. And a kitchen. And if she wasn't mistaken, the couch pulled out into a bed. "You gonna follow me back?"

Perry was still staring at his polo shirt, but nodded.

She opened the car door, but didn't bother to exit. In the movies and television, this was when the lonely suspecting person would climb into their car, start the engine, and then *kaboom!* Would that happen to her?

"Something the matter?"

She turned toward Perry and shut the car door. "Do you know how to check for bombs?"

"You think your car is booby trapped?"

"I don't know what to think." Her phone went off. She really didn't want to talk to Sam right now, but something could have happened to Rick. "What is it, Sam?"

"Hey, Janie. It's me, Rick."

136

She put it on speaker so Perry could hear. Although with his superb hearing, she probably didn't need to bother. "What's the matter? Why do you have Sam's phone?"

"He's a little bit paralyzed—"

"What?"

"He was staked?" Perry said.

"Yeah. With one of those archery arrows. Anyway, he wanted me to call and make sure you were all right. And to warn you that she's in town."

She placed a hand over her racing heart. "Is he okay?"

"He says he is. Just a little slow in moving right now."

"How the hell did she find us?"

"Oh, yeah. Sam thinks she put a tracker on the Xterra. Says you might want to destroy it. The tracker. Not the Xterra."

"Of all the ding dong days." Perry jumped out of the car and disappeared underneath.

She yelled after him, "Check my car, too."

"Hold on. Sam wants to talk to you."

A moment later, Sam spoke over the line. "Hey, Janie."

His voice sounded raspy, as if he struggled to breathe. Tears threatened to fall and she blinked them back. How could she do this to him? "Are you really okay?"

"I'm fine. Or will be as soon as I heal. I just want you to be careful."

Perry climbed back into the vehicle. "Hey, Sammy. You need to stop being target practice."

"Very funny."

"Yeah, yeah. Anyway, I found the tracker on Johnny's car, and Janie's is clear. No tracker. No bomb."

Sam screamed, "Bomb? What bomb?"

"I just said there's no bomb. It's fine. Her car is fine. We should return within the hour. Bye bye." Perry disconnected before Sam could say anymore.

She gave him the evil eye. "You just had to tell him about my fear, didn't you?"

"Hey, my job isn't done until I can frustrate the guy." He cackled as he dropped the bug into the cup holder.

"Aren't you going to destroy that?"

"Nope. Why let her think we caught on to her? You ready?"

She was more than ready to leave the hotel. Facing Sam was another issue. But no matter what Perry said, Sam's life was in danger and the only way to protect him would be to avoid being alone with him. Somehow, someway, she would do it.

* * * *

Tricia stumbled onto her bed. Home at last. Adrenaline had worn off hours ago and she'd been existing on fumes. The last fifty miles had been a bugger.

She'd been tempted to follow the GPS signal to the hotel and do away with Miss Slut and that other guy. Two men at one time? Did the woman have no morals? But it was late and Tricia didn't have a plan in place, and without a plan she could get sloppy. Besides, what fun would that be anyway? Janie needed to face another death. Grieve once again. Fear for her life.

And she should. Tricia would take care of that miscreant next and wouldn't even need Megan this time around. Trackers were a wonderful invention. Right now the slut and her cohorts were all back at that house in Cleveland. Even Janie's excuse for a vehicle.

Ah, but another one bit the dust. Well, not dust in the way Tricia had expected, but he was down and out and she'd gotten away completely. As usual. Now she could rest.

Because hell, it was Sunday. That's what people did on Sunday.

Chapter 15

Driven to destruction.

Janie rearranged the blankets on the floor of the bedroom next to Rick's. Sitting for hours reading had done a number on her butt and she could use more padding. Heck, she could use a chair. But the only chairs were in the living room and she wasn't about to go out there.

Because Sam was out there.

When she and Perry had returned from the hotel, Sam agreed to let the tracking device go for now. The woman already knew they were here and apparently they were staying. The hotel held too many innocent people and Janie had grumpily agreed not to relocate there. So no maid service. No room service. No pull-out couch. Instead she'd taken every blanket Rick wasn't using and had slept in one of the empty bedrooms.

Correction: tried to sleep.

Hard to do when her mind was only on Sam. And how he felt inside her. Didn't seem fair she had to give that up, but life wasn't fair—as her father always told her—and Sam's life was more important than a relationship. Eventually, she'd get him to see reason.

At least the television had cable or streaming abilities and there were football games on. That had kept Rick quiet. And she'd been able to go out earlier to buy breakfast and lunch for her and Rick, thanks to the fact that both vampires trusted her, or at least trusted she'd return to Rick. Sam, on the other hand, lost that sparkle in his eyes and his skin seemed more pale than usual.

She'd asked if he'd gotten enough to eat, but he claimed he'd gone out and took care of that problem as soon as he was mobile. So if lack of food wasn't to blame, it had to be her. Avoiding the man was making him depressed.

Wasn't doing much for her mood, either. Between grieving for Liz and sitting in a room with someone she could no longer have, she'd taken her book and crawled into a corner of her chosen bedroom. So far the book hadn't lifted her spirits, but at least it passed the time.

"He thinks you hate him now."

She dropped her book and nearly jumped out of her skin. Perry stood in the doorway and she hadn't even heard him approach. "Was there a reason you didn't leave last night?"

Although, his presence had made being with Sam a little less awkward.

"Sammy was in no shape to watch your cousin. But if you keep this up, he'll never be in shape."

"I only want what's best for him."

"Yeah? You think there's only one way to kill him?"

"What are you talking about?" She marked her page and slammed the book shut. "I'm trying to prevent that."

"Except what you're doing is worse than what that bitch is doing. Think about that."

"Perry, stop." Sam stood just outside the room.

Damn it. Now she would have to face him. Why couldn't Perry just leave her alone?

"You two are nuts." Perry turned and left.

Sam came inside and shut the door. "He's wrong. I don't think you hate me."

She froze. His scent overpowered her. Made her weak. If he came any closer, she wasn't sure she could keep her distance.

Instead, he slid down against the door and sat. Brought his knees up to his chest. "But you're wrong, also."

"How am I wrong?"

"You think I'm safe if you break it off with me, right?"

"Actually, I'm hoping she already believes she killed you." It was one of the reasons why Janie hadn't bothered going back to check out of her hotel. Oh sure, there was still a threat of the room being booby-trapped, but if she remained registered, Sam was safe. Right?

"Okay, say she does. What do you think will happen next?"

"Nothing. Because I never plan on dating again." It would be a hard and lonely life, but better than buying plots at the cemetery.

"Wrong. She comes after you."

"She hasn't come after me since I did whatever I did to her. Why would she start now?"

"But don't you see? She already has. Who do you think those spiders were for?"

Ah, damn it. Why'd he have to remind her of those? And why'd he have to keep making sense? "Then let her come after me, if that means she leaves everyone else alone."

"I'm not going to let that happen. I'll make sure she knows she didn't kill me."

"No." She grabbed her head. "You're free. Why would you do that?" If his plan was to frustrate her, it was working.

"Don't you get it? If she kills you, she might as well kill me, too. I don't want to live without you in the world."

"But you hardly know me." Why did he have to say words like that? Why? She tried to blink back the tears, but they fell anyway. Traitors.

He crawled toward her. Stopped within inches of her feet. "My body knows you. My heart knows you. My brain is looking forward to knowing more of you."

Ah, damn him and his words. "And how do you think I'd feel if something were to happen to you?"

"All the more reason we do this together. Fight her together. Live or die...together."

She couldn't handle another death. Especially his. "Do you think that's even possible? We don't even know who she is. And you won't let me call the police."

"We don't need the police. And if we have to go back to Detroit to find her, then that's what we do. But we do it together. And with a little help from my vampire friends."

"But this is my problem, not yours. I feel like I'm using you if I agree."

"It's *our* problem. I'm not going anywhere, Janie. I refuse to let that woman win. It would just be a whole lot easier if you were with me on this, though."

"Easier?"

"On my heart. I let you go before. I can't let you go again. Not like this. If it were because of another vampire, that would be different. Maybe. But you'd still be alive. And I would still have hope."

He moved closer. His scent enveloped her. His lips were inches from hers. "If it weren't for that woman, would you be fighting me on this?"

She laughed, hoping to camouflage the wild beating of her heart. "If it weren't for that woman, I'd probably still be married. Would you pursue me then?"

"I always told myself that if you were married, I'd leave you alone. Would I have gone through with it? I'll never know. Because you're not married. And I have no intention of leaving you alone."

He kissed her then.

Not a gentle kiss, either. He claimed her with his lips, and fireworks erupted inside her body. Didn't he realize how hard it had been to keep her distance? That she already wanted him?

He pulled away and brushed the tear off her cheek. "Janie. Please—"

"Stop talking." She grabbed his head and kissed him back.

* * * *

Tricia leaned back in her chair and smiled. People could be so…stupid. Or at least easily manipulated. And it hadn't cost her a dime, either.

She hadn't been totally convinced that she'd killed that vampire. When she thought more about it, the slut's cousin had been talking to him. So she'd gone back to the proverbial drawing board. If he was a vampire, would the sun kill him? And if so, how could she expose him and not get caught? Better yet, how could she get someone else to do it? So after having a nice breakfast with Rachel, Tricia researched the area.

Low and behold, a neighborhood site existed on the Internet where people chatted or complained about one thing or another. Two minutes later she'd created a new e-mail account and requested to join the group, using the address of the vampire house. Bing! She'd been accepted.

She'd scrolled through the postings. One man was livid. Was sure his girlfriend was cheating on him. Had given info about her and asked if anyone saw her to e-mail him.

She'd opened her new e-mail account. Typed in his address. Then composed her message:

I think your Amy has been cheating on you with my man. I'm heartbroken. I thought they were just friends, but after reading your post I now believe otherwise. She's been hanging around the house all the time and now that I'm out of town, they're probably boinking as I write this. Are you willing to confront the cheaters for both of us?

After hitting send, she'd left to refresh her coffee and returned to find an answer.

I knew it! If you give me the address I'll go over there right now and put an end to it.

Yep, easily manipulated. Or stupid. Social media was a Godsend. And so…anonymous. With glee in her fingertips, she responded with some suggestions on how to get even. The guy had to be on coke or something. He loved her ideas.

Then again, they were excellent ideas.

Whether the slut's boyfriend was a vampire or not, he could still die. The slut could die. And while that wasn't exactly how Tricia wanted it to end, at least she'd be in the clear.

Too bad she couldn't witness it. Or could she?

She e-mailed the guy again, hoping she wasn't too late.

* * * *

As Sam's lips were locked with Janie's, as warmth spread across his face and down his neck, he silently cursed. All day she'd been avoiding him and he'd let her, causing them both one miserable day. If he had talked to her earlier they could have been together in this room all day.

Okay, so maybe not all day. Rick or Perry would have put a stop to that. Perry, because it would be fun. Rick, because he liked to complain. A lot.

Janie ran her hand against Sam's erection and he nearly blew it in his pants, but he hadn't come back here for sex. Kissing was about all he'd planned. Hell, it was all he'd allow himself to hope for.

And when he'd noticed her tears, he was pretty sure he'd killed the kissing part. But she was kissing him now. And touching him. And he wasn't sure how far he should go.

Her scent came to life and his fangs extended. What was that bit he'd told her about not wanting to start the bonding process? Apparently his body had other ideas. At least his fangs did.

But there would be no taking of her blood tonight. Only because he'd promised not to. And not just to her. Damn it.

She held his face and paused kissing him. Her blue eyes were filled with desire. Her smile brought him joy.

She ran her thumb alongside one of his fangs. "I have a feeling you're as obsessed with my blood as much as I'm obsessed with these."

"You're obsessed with my fangs?" God. Why'd she have to say that? It was taking every bit of willpower to keep from biting her as it was.

"Why? Why do I want you to bite me so bad? And why does biting have to start the bonding process?"

Because their bodies were telling them something her head didn't want to acknowledge? "Because we're not tortured enough?"

She laughed. "Yeah. Tortured is a good word. I wish I knew what I wanted. My body is all like, 'do it, do it, do it,' but my head is like, 'are you crazy?' I like you, Sam. And you feel so good. But—"

"Stop. No buts. I can make it easier on you today. I'm not to sample your blood until after Barnet's visit. I kind of promised I'd keep myself...pure." But actually, it was keeping her available. Feeding from her now would diminish the effects Barnet and any other vampire would feel.

"So let me get this straight." She freed his shirt from his jeans and ran her hands up his abs, leaving a nice trail of warmth in their paths. "You're saying no to biting, not no to sex, right?"

"I'd never say no to sex with you. Never."

"Then get in me already."

She didn't have to tell him twice. The shirt was history in a fraction of a second. As he removed his jeans, his cell phone fell out of his pocket and proceeded to ring. Victoria was calling.

Janie looked at the display and laughed. "What timing. Go on. She might have news."

He answered it via the speaker. "Hey, Victoria. I got you on speaker and Janie's with me. What's up?"

"I found information on Dr. Ian Crawford's family. His wife is Patricia Crawford. Age 42. Daughter named Rachel. She's sixteen. They used to live in Troy, Michigan, but moved after Dr. Crawford's death. No forwarding address."

He slipped his jeans back on. Talking to Victoria while the boys hung out just felt awkward. "Forty-two? The woman who injected me was much older than that. Does he have any sisters? Maybe his mother is still alive."

"No sisters and his mother died ten years ago. So if his family is involved, the wife seems the likely candidate. The woman in the video from the hospital looked older, too. Could be a disguise, though."

"You hacked into the hospital?" Janie said.

"Of course." Victoria sounded insulted. Not that Janie knew about Victoria's excellent hacking abilities. "I'm sending you a copy of the video. See if it's the same woman who injected you. Although, she knew to keep her face away from the cameras, so I don't know if it'll do any good. But she left the hospital room they found the dead nurse in. So the police are on it."

"Is that going to be a problem?" Sam asked.

"Probably not. They have less to go on than we do."

"Were you able to determine the vehicle she was driving?"

"A Jeep, but I couldn't get a make on the plates, which means neither will the police."

A Jeep? "Was it green? Neon green?"

"Can't tell. Video's in black and white. Why do you ask?"

"I saw a neon green Jeep at Rick's apartment the night it blew. It was at the hospital, too."

A heavy sigh sounded over the small speaker. "Do you know how many people own Jeeps?"

Sam nearly laughed at the frustration in Victoria's voice. "About as many as Janie Robinsons exist?"

"Exactly."

"Would a license plate help?" He gave her the number.

"You could have led with that. Hold on." Clicking noises came from her end. "That license is assigned to a green jeep belonging to one Manuel Rodriguez. I'll check his address and see if there's a connection. But it's possible she stole it and it hasn't been reported yet."

"Do you have a picture of Mrs. Crawford," Janie asked. "Maybe I met her and didn't know."

"No. Not yet, anyway. I don't even have her current address. I might have to hack into the DMV. Won't that be fun?"

Janie laughed. "What? You can hack into a hospital and not the DMV?"

"I can hack into both. The hospital won't notice. The government is tricky. I don't want to get caught."

"Doesn't it seem strange that you can't find her picture?" Sam asked.

"Not really. She wasn't anyone before the scandal and she probably went into hiding after. And with a kid to consider, I understand. I gotta go. Let me know how it goes with Barnet."

Sam ended the call and rolled onto his back, groaning. He was so not ready for Barnet.

Janie's beautiful face came into view. "You keep telling me he's not a threat, so why do you keep groaning when his name is mentioned?"

Not a threat to her, but to him? It would cause him to groan every time. "I do not want to be paranoid. I want to be confident. But…"

She straddled his body. "But it's hard when you don't know where I stand, isn't it?"

Oh, it was hard all right. And he was growing harder by the second. Sweet Jesus, he had no control around her. "I don't want you to make a decision just to make a decision. It's my problem. I can deal with it."

"I'm not making a decision just to make a decision, but you should know." She ground her ass into his crotch and he nearly came. "You're the only vampire I want." She moved down his body, rubbing against his erection. Grabbed the waist of his jeans. "Now, where were we?"

He lifted up as she freed him from the confines of the jeans. He grew harder as she eyed his erection. God, he wanted in her. He sat up to undress her, but she palmed his chest and pushed him back to the floor. Ran her hands along his pecs. Tweaked his nipples.

"You do realize I'm already turned on, don't you?"

"I did notice that." She kissed him. Her soft tongue explored his mouth. It was a miracle his fangs stayed hidden.

She rained him with kisses. His face. His chest. Down to his belly button, where she stopped to run a finger down to his shaft.

"If you want me in you, you're going to have to stop." He was losing control, and fast.

"And wait, what? Ten minutes? I think I'll survive." She gripped him and took him in her mouth.

The moisture. The heat. And that tongue of hers. He arched, having her take more of him. And then she sucked. Hard. His orgasm practically exploded just as the front wall crashed in on them.

* * * *

Janie sat up. Sunlight reflected off the dust floating in the room. What the hell happened? One second she was tasting Sam. The next, she was flung across the room, blinking at the sun. And there was a truck in the bedroom.

What was a truck doing in the bedroom?

Someone cried out. No wait. Not just someone. "Sam?"

He was lying in the sunlight. Convulsing between attempts to crawl to safety. Except there was no safety. Not at this time of day with the wall gone. His skin was red and blistering. She grabbed the blankets and covered him, hoping that would be enough to stop him from bursting into flames. The bedroom door flew open. Perry stood outside the sun rays.

"I can't reach his mind. Gotta open the door. Ricky-boy, get over here!"

Can't reach whose mind? She turned toward the truck. The driver. Some guy her age was shaking his head in a daze.

She stepped on debris, which used to be the front wall of the house, and was able to yank the door open. The blacks of his eyes were huge. "What the hell are you on?"

He looked at her and blinked. "You're not Amy. Where's Amy? Amy!"

Moments later the guy shut up and tilted over to the side, as if he was asleep. Right now she didn't care if the guy died. Sam was hurt.

"Holy shit!" Rick said.

Perry pushed Rick into the room. "Help her get Sammy out of there."

She grabbed Sam by one arm pit and her cousin grabbed him by the other. Sam grunted and groaned each inch they moved him. When they reached Perry and shade, he was able to easily move him into the hallway.

"Is he gonna live?" Rick grabbed his waist and winced.

Oh God. Was that all it took? Just a little bit of sun to start the burning process? She lifted one edge of the blanket off Sam. One side was covered in horrible looking blisters. And in the process of moving him, they'd left a trail of blood from where he'd been. Her heart ached.

Perry patted Sam on the face. "Hey, Sammy. You still in there?"

"I'm here," Sam said. "Janie okay?"

His voice was strained, as if in pain—and why wouldn't he be in pain? His skin was burning!—but he seemed coherent. She leaned down so he could see her face. "I'm fine. But what about you?"

"He'll be okay once he gets some blood. Too bad neither of you Perfect Mates are bonded. He could heal in seconds instead of hours. But he'll live, regardless."

Sirens sounded in the distance.

"Sorry, Sammy." Perry lifted Sam, who howled in pain, and placed him in the back bedroom, where he'd be safe. "You two stay with him. I'll take care of that bozo. And the cops." He headed toward the hall and glanced at her over his shoulder. "Never a dull moment with you, huh?"

Perry shut the door. Rick turned on the light. "Did his clothes burn off?"

"No." She took the blanket and covered up Sam's nakedness. Winced when he jerked. "Sorry."

"Then why is he naked? And you're not?"

"I'm not having this conversation with you."

"Ohhh. Did he make you or did you—"

"Shut. Up." Janie sat on the floor and caressed Sam's hair. It seemed the safest place to touch him. His face was covered in angry red blotches. She suppressed a sob.

"I'm sorry. I didn't realize you two had gotten that close. I mean, Perry's been joking about it, but I thought he was just...joking. Are we safe with him if he needs to eat?"

"He's not going to eat us. He feeds off blood." And she had plenty to give to him. But would he take it? She brushed the hair from Sam's face. "Are you still there?"

He opened his eyes. "Not going anywhere."

"I want you to take my blood."

"No. Can't."

"I think healing overrules paranoia, don't you? And I promise not to give you any reason to be paranoid. Come on, Sam."

"No. Promised Barnet."

"Son of a—" She bit her lip. Was this some kind of vampire honor? "I think he'll understand."

"Barnet will understand what?" Rick said.

"Sam promised him that he wouldn't feed from me until after his visit. But I can't sit here and watch him be in agony until the sun sets. That's like three hours away." She eyed her cousin. A cousin who pretty much owed Sam his life. "Would you do it?"

Perry popped his head in. "Fair warning. It'll probably hurt. Sammy can't control the pain."

Oh God. Could Perry hear everything inside the house? He waggled his eyebrows as if he'd read her mind. She would worry about being mortified later. "It didn't hurt me when he did it that one time."

"Because you're his Perfect Mate. Of course it won't hurt. But Ricky-boy isn't his Perfect Mate and he's not bonded to a vampire."

"That makes a difference?"

"I don't know. That's why I said probably. Your call, Ricky-boy. Sammy will understand if you don't want to go through with it. Too bad I can't use bozo out there. Ooops. There's the police. Gotta go." Perry shut the door.

Janie looked at her cousin. "Well?"

Rick ran his hand through his hair. "I don't know. It hurt a lot the last time."

"But you didn't know what was going on. And you were bitten in the neck. Sam would take it from your wrist."

Sam mumbled, "He doesn't have to. I can wait."

She wasn't so sure she could. He sounded worse, not better.

"How much do you take?" Rick asked.

She answered for Sam. "He didn't take a lot when I saw him feed. Lasted for barely a minute."

"Okay. What do I need to do?"

Janie maneuvered Rick so that his wrist was up against Sam's mouth.

"Are you sure?" Sam asked.

"Yeah. Do it before I change my mind, though."

Sam grabbed Rick's arm and bit down.

Rick winced a little and then relaxed. About a minute later, Sam licked Rick's wrist.

"Thank you." Sam closed his eyes. His face was still blistery red, but Perry had said it would take hours. That amount of damage probably required more blood, too. At least Sam seemed more at peace.

Rick examined his wrist. The puncture wounds were fading. "That's it? That wasn't so bad."

Janie didn't know what she was more thankful for: that Sam would soon be out of pain or that it seemed her cousin was finally coming around.

Chapter 16

Promises to break.

Janie sat in the damaged bedroom and huddled inside her coat. The news crews departed awhile ago and the sun was near setting. Once it dropped out of sight, they were all to leave and buy wood or whatever to fix the hole the truck had left behind. Sam still wasn't looking very strong, but he'd said not to worry. That he'd be fine.

Fine, because he'd find someone else to feed from.

And that right there bugged the shit out of her. Why? *Why?* She'd known the guy two days. Two. Days. She had no claim on him. But every time she got near him, it was like her brain went on vacation and left her body in charge.

What was wrong with her? She'd never felt such an attraction to anyone before. Not Justin, not Aaron. Not even David. So why was Sam different? Why was it so hard to stick to her principles where he was concerned? This Perfect Mate business was giving her a headache.

"What are you doing back here?" Rick sat beside her. "Hiding again?"

"No." *Yes, you big liar.* "Just making sure no one comes in." Even the little voice in her head laughed at that.

"And if they do, then what? You plan on throwing some drywall at them?"

"If it comes to that."

Her cousin stared at the destruction. "Was that guy strung out or what? Perry said he truly believed his girlfriend was here, cheating on him, because someone e-mailed him and told him so."

"You mean Mrs. Crawford. Mrs. Crawford e-mailed him." And Janie was all but certain that the killer was the doctor's wife. It was starting to make sense.

"You don't know that for sure. Even so, who thinks like that? That's top-of-the-line crazy. How does she live without anyone noticing that shit? I mean, I went a little crazy and was called out right away."

"Maybe there isn't anyone in her life to notice. Or she acts different around them. Could it be she just blames me for her husband's death, even though my name was cleared?"

"It's possible, I suppose. Or maybe you looked at her funny or cut her off in traffic. Does it matter what the reason is? The woman is crazy. That's not on you."

Rick made a valid point. The woman had to be crazy to think Janie had done anything to warrant a death penalty for her loved ones. "I just hope we catch her before she kills anyone else."

"You mean Sam, don't you?"

"You forgetting you were a target, too?"

"Nah. How do you know it wasn't for you? Who knew you were there?"

"Megan. My work. Anyone could have called in pretending to be Mom or something to find out where I was. But I guess I could check tomorrow to see if anyone did call."

Rick nudged his shoulder against hers. "So… Are you going to do it? Bond with Sam?"

"Not any time soon."

"But do you want to? Do you love him?"

Love him? Her brain snickered. Nice to know it was back in control. "I hardly know him. But I do like him. So far."

"I guess you should if you're having sex." He bumped shoulders again and smiled. "Don't be mad, but I asked Perry if I could go back to Atlanta with him, so I could meet a female one. Or a few."

Janie didn't know whether to laugh or smack him. If he kept it up, he'd give her whiplash. "Now you want to be some vampire's Perfect Mate? What changed your mind?"

"Watching Sam around you. He'd do anything for you. Hell, you'd do anything for him, too, wouldn't you? I want that. I thought I had it with Julie, but I didn't. Probably because she wasn't meant for me."

"And being immortal doesn't factor into your decision?"

"Not really. Being immortal sounds interesting. Okay, it sounds awesome. But being immortally alone? Not so much."

"Exactly." Rick got it. Sam got it. Her brain got it. But her body? A body that didn't care about the consequences? Why couldn't it get it?

* * * *

Perry hammered in a piece of plywood. "I thought my carpentry days were over."

"Is that why you're so good at this?" Every time Sam suggested where the next piece should go, Perry had vetoed it and moved it someplace else. And he'd been right.

"You think I'm good?" Perry stood and examined the house. "Good enough for someone to hire?"

"Hire? Since when are you looking for work?"

"I'm not looking. Yet. But if I find my Perfect Mate, I need to be able to support her. Can't live on my charms alone."

Sam laughed. "You. Support her? Oh this I gotta see."

"Go ahead. Yuk it up. What about you?"

"What about me?"

"Can you support your Perfect Mate on a bartender's pay? Or are you planning on her being the bread-winner."

"First, I only work to keep busy. I've got plenty of money saved up, which I'm surprised you don't. And second, maybe Janie wants to work. I'm certainly not going to stop her."

"No one wants to work." Perry placed another sheet of plywood on the house. "Except, apparently you."

Sam nailed where Perry indicated. "Doesn't matter who's working. It's not like we've had time to discuss any of it."

"Yeah, but you certainly had time for some hanky-panky." Perry wagged his brows. "Did the sun hit your family jewels?"

"If you were so curious, why didn't you just look?" Sam shook his head. He certainly wouldn't have given a damn then. But luckily the sun had missed that part of his anatomy. Not that it wouldn't have healed like the rest of him, but the pain wasn't anything he wanted to experience.

"I'll take that as a yes. Sucks to be you." Perry grabbed another sheet and covered the last of the hole. "You sure you're up to being a target again? I mean, the smart thing would be to move someplace else. Put Janie someplace else."

"She has to go to work in the morning."

"And you're going to let her?"

"Perry, I don't own the woman. She's not a prisoner."

"But a mortal is after her. Not a vampire."

Sam nailed in the board. "And when I confront the bitch, I'll be able to control her and end this whole thing."

"I hope when you do finish her off, you take Janie on a vacation. Go someplace exotic and get bonded."

Sam loved that idea. Loved it a lot. Only one problem. "We still have Rick—"

"No, you don't. Ricky-boy asked me if he could go with me to Atlanta."

Holy shit. Was it possible he and Janie could actually go away together sooner rather than later?

A car approached and pulled into the driveway. Barnet climbed out.

No, no, no. Sam was not ready. Not by a long shot. If he could, he'd take Janie away now. But did he really want to be a coward about the whole thing? Regardless of what she said about not wanting to be with another vampire, she could still change her mind. And she could change it tonight.

* * * *

"What's with all that banging?" Megan asked.

Janie hadn't talked to her friend in what felt like ages, and now seemed like the best time to call since the guys were outside working, but she hadn't considered how noisy the place would be. Even from the back bedroom. "They're fixing the hole the car made."

Before Megan could get all bent out of shape, Janie told her what happened. Since it had nothing to do with vampires, why not?

"Oh, Janie. Did you lose another one?"

"Another one?"

"Boyfriend."

"What makes you think I'm dating anyone?"

"Because this kind of stuff only happens when you are. Don't get me wrong, I'm thrilled if you found someone else. I was pretty sure you'd given them up, though."

She'd been pretty sure, too. And while her brain and body fought it out, maybe talking about it would help. She just had to be careful of what to share. "Well, no, I didn't lose another one. And yes, there may be this guy."

"All right, Janie! How long has this been going on? And why haven't you told your best friend?"

"It hasn't been going on long at all. And it's too soon to talk about."

"But you like him."

Janie smiled. "Yeah, I do."

"So when do I get to meet him?"

"I told you. It's too soon."

"Fine, fine. Can you at least tell me how you met?"

The first time or the second time? Maybe stick with the second. "He rescued Rick from the apartment building blast."

"Oooh. A fireman? Wait. He lives in Detroit?"

"He's not a fireman. And he doesn't live in Detroit." She had no idea where he was from, either. Just another detail she was missing, although she got the feeling he moved around as much as she did. "He's here."

"In Cleveland? But you met him in Detroit? Janie, are you being stalked?"

Janie rolled her eyes as if her friend could see her. "It's not like that. We met four and a half years ago. He…wanted my number back then, but I was with David. It was just a coincidence we ran into each other."

Shit. This fudging the truth bit wasn't as easy as she'd thought. She'd nearly blurted about the bite.

"And a coincidence he lives in Cleveland?"

"He doesn't live here." *Shit, shut up already. You're only making it worse.* "But my rental was damaged and he gave me a ride home." Did that sound better? Believable?

"Janie…" Megan said it as if she were scolding a child. "This isn't like you. You've always been level headed when it came to men before."

Yeah. Tell it to her body. "I know, but he's different. I feel differently with him."

"Does he know about your luck with men?"

Janie laughed. She couldn't help it. "I told him about my curse. He doesn't believe in them. In fact…we think we know who's been behind it all."

"What are you talking about? They weren't accidents?"

"We don't think so." Just because Sam said not to tell the police, didn't mean she couldn't tell anyone else. "Remember Dr. Crawford?"

"You think a dead doctor is responsible? What? As a ghost?"

"Very funny. He's not responsible. But I'm pretty sure his widow is behind all the accidents. Sam, that's my guy, found a bug at my hotel when we were talking about who might know more about Dr. Crawford's family. I mentioned Liz Delaney." Just remembering David's mom brought new pain to her heart and tears threatened to fall. "Megan, she's been murdered. Just because I mentioned her!" Her eyes could no longer hold back the onslaught. Using her sleeve, she wiped her face.

"Oh, Janie, honey. I'm so sorry. What are you going to do? Have you called the cops?"

"I can't. I don't have any proof. But as soon as we locate Mrs. Crawford's residence, I think maybe I should go pay her a visit."

"Are you crazy? If she is behind it all, what do you think would happen to you if you confronted her? And how do you know Sam isn't behind it all? You said yourself you met him when you were with David."

"It's not him."

"How can you be so sure?"

"Because he's been attacked three times."

"Attacked? Or made to look like an attack?"

"Why would he do that?"

"Why does any man do anything? Maybe he's been stalking you ever since and has been doing away with your boyfriends. You need to call the cops."

Damn it. Everything Megan said was making sense. No one saw Sam get injected. Could he have manipulated someone to come into Janie's hotel room and put the flowers there? Had he even given her a chance to go near them? Same with Liz. Sam could have easily manipulated someone to kill her. They were in the same hospital. And the arrows. He could have also manipulated someone to shoot him knowing someone—Rick—was there to help. And just because Perry said the driver of the car hadn't been manipulated didn't make it so. Not if he was in on it. Shit. What had she gotten herself into? "I can't call the cops. I don't have any proof of anyone doing anything. I just want to talk to her."

Because if Mrs. Crawford was sane, or disabled, or anything to show she couldn't be behind it all, then it had to be Sam. Right?

"But you don't know where she lives?"

"Not yet. But I will."

"Well you can't go alone. That's suicide. Take Rick with you."

The hammering stopped. Were Sam and Perry finished already? Anything she said now was liable to be overheard. "I can't ask him to do that."

"Then I'm coming. I'm sure I can find a flight out—"

"No. No. It's not necessary. I was just thinking out loud. And you're right. Confronting her would be stupid."

"So when you find out where she lives, you won't go? You promise?"

"I promise." But that would be a promise she'd break. Problem was, getting away from Sam. Because she had to do this alone. It was the only way she could get answers. If Sam came along, he could very well manipulate Mrs. Crawford to say what Janie wanted to hear.

"What are you going to do with Sam?"

"I don't know." And that was the God's honest truth.

Chapter 17

Perfect illusions.

Sam opened the door to the back bedroom and found Janie sitting in the corner, his phone in her lap. "There you are. Barnet's here."

She looked up and smiled, but there wasn't any joy behind it. He'd done everything he could to reassure her that he had recovered, and before he and Perry had started working on the damage to the house, she'd seemed in better spirits. Only one thing could be getting her down.

He shut the door and went to her. "I'm sorry I got you spooked. It's really going to be okay. He's not a bad guy."

Might help if he really felt that way. Oh, not that Barnet wasn't a nice guy. He was. But that it was going to be okay. Maybe she was better tuned in to Sam than he'd realized. And that was a good thing. Wasn't it?

"I'm sure he's very nice." She handed him his phone. "I found this in the damaged bedroom. Victoria called. Hope you don't mind that I answered. I let her know about the latest attack."

"Thanks." He took the phone and slipped it into his back pocket. "Any word on Mrs. Crawford?"

She stood and straightened her shirt, but didn't look his way. "No. She hasn't been able to hack into the DMV yet. Just wanted you to know she's still working on it. Apparently you get antsy with news?"

He shrugged. "I might be a little impatient when it's something important. To me. Okay, so I'm a pain in her ass." Even that didn't get much of a smile out of her. Either he was losing his touch or she was really nervous. Would she relax if he told her his idea? "Hey, Perry mentioned that Rick asked to go to Atlanta."

"Yeah, he'd said something to me about that. It'll probably be good for him."

"It would. Especially if he's on board." He shoved his hands in his pockets. "So anyways, after Barnet leaves and we find Mrs. Crawford, do you think you can get some vacation time and the two of us can just take off and get to know one another better?"

No jumping for joy. No smile, even. Just a face deep in thought. "What if it's not her?"

He hadn't thought that far. Shit. What if it wasn't Mrs. Crawford? What if it was some mistress they didn't know about? "Then we'll go someplace private while Victoria investigates further. No phones. No Internet. For a whole week. What do you say? Do you have any vacation time?"

She stood there for the longest time, just staring at her feet, when she started to nod. "I do. I can ask when I go in tomorrow. Sure, that sounds good."

It would have eased his own nerves if she'd sounded more convincing, but that had to be because she was nervous about meeting Barnet. Right? Hell, this meeting couldn't end soon enough for Sam. But she'd agreed and he would let that carry him through the meeting.

Some of her warmth would probably get him through this, too, so he offered his arm, "Shall we?"

Janie shook her head and whispered, "Maybe it's best I don't go in there looking all horny."

Made sense to his head, not so much to his heart. He led her into the living room, where everyone had gathered like it was some damned inquisition. He indicated the one man she didn't know. "Janie, this is Barnet."

Barnet had been turned at the age of 42 and was more of a father figure than the Head of the Committee. He'd never talked about his turning, though, so whoever turned him was a mystery to Sam, if not all vampires. Wearing dark grey slacks and a light blue button-down shirt, Barnet approached and bowed slightly, as if she

159

were royalty. "It's an honor to meet you, Ms. Robinson. May I?" He held out his hand, but looked at Sam.

Oh great. The testing would begin. Sam took deep breaths. Had a vampire ever had a panic attack before? Probably not. He was such a wimp. *She agreed to get away. Get on with it.* Right. Right. Straightening, he forced himself to be the picture of confidence. Thank God Barnet couldn't read his mind. Not without touching anyway.

"Might as well call me Janie. And I know I should get used to this, but it still feels strange."

Barnet lowered his hand. "As it should. It's not every day our kind meet. And I am sorry if I've rushed you into anything, but once you and Sam bond, you won't affect anyone but him."

He spoke as if it were a done deal. Sam nearly laughed. That one touch could ruin all his plans. That one touch could bury him.

"No. I get it. Sam told me that you've been documenting everything to do with Perfect Mates. So have at it." She extended her hand.

Barnet took her one hand into both of his. Had she gasped in surprise or desire? Her scent intensified, answering his question. Desire, definitely desire. Shit.

"Oh my." Barnet inhaled deeply. "Wild meadows. Just like home. You are a dear, aren't you?"

Perry stepped up beside the Head of the Committee. "How warm is she to you? Is it lasting?"

"She's very warm. It's unbelievable how warm. I can see why—oh!" He abruptly released Janie and turned around.

"You okay, boss?" Perry stepped in front of Barnet and his eyes widened. He mouthed the word "boner" to Sam.

Oh great. Just what Sam wanted to know…not.

"How are you doing, Janie?" Perry asked. "You're scent is coming out in waves. Wanting to rip some clothes off now?"

Janie looked at Perry with disgust. "You're sick."

"Doesn't answer my question. How did Barnet's touch affect you? It's all for science, and he apparently can't speak right now."

"Shut up, Perry." Sam wanted to belt the guy but good.

"I'm fine," Barnet said as he turned around. "Sorry about that. Caught me off guard is all. I would like to know how my touch affected you."

She looked at all the men in the room. "Do I have to?"

"Oh shit, Sammy." Perry clapped Sam on the shoulder. "Guess you were right and I was wrong. I'm so sorry."

"Wait," Sam said. "She didn't say anything. Did you?" Of course she hadn't. It was her scent. Her lovely, lovely scent. Even he was getting a boner.

"Can I talk to you in private?" she asked him.

"You do realize we can hear everything you say if we want to." Perry grinned.

She gritted her teeth.

"Not helping," Sam said.

Janie glanced at Rick. Maybe it wasn't the vampires she worried about.

Barnet seemed to have gotten the clue, too. "Perry, would you and Mr. Daugherty please go outside so I can talk to Sam and Janie alone."

"Outside?" Rick piped in. "But it's cold."

"Why don't you get us some dessert then," Janie said. "Pie, maybe?"

Rick perked up at that. "Pie sounds good. You got some money?"

"I got it. Let's go Ricky-boy." Perry leaned toward Sam and whispered, "I expect a play-by-play when I return."

When Perry returned, he might find a dead vampire. Sam just wasn't sure who.

Barnet extended his arm toward the chairs. "Why don't we take a seat."

Janie sat on the love seat and Sam sat beside her. Barnet had already gotten his reaction from her and her from him, so would it be okay if Sam took her hand? Probably better to let her decide. He placed his palm up on the space between them, anticipating her warmth. But she either didn't see or didn't care.

Barnet sat in the chair, grinning. "This is the most amazing thing. I can see why someone would want to hide one."

Sam put his hand in his lap. "She's not a thing. And I didn't really hide her. I didn't even know where she was."

"You're right. I'm sorry. I wasn't talking expressly about you, though. I was talking in general. So, Janie, how did my touch affect you?"

Janie looked at Sam. "I pretty much got the same reaction that I get when I touch Sam."

Oh God. He hadn't thrown up in centuries, not since he'd eaten that meat pie. His stomach was now reliving that event.

Barnet's eyebrows rose. "You did? What exactly?"

"An erotic-like zap. Traveled up my arm. Made me…" She swallowed. "Tense."

Sam lowered his head. He knew he'd been too lucky with Dalton and Perry. That there were others out there who would affect her the same way he did. Others she might like better.

"Are you saying that you're attracted to me?" Barnet asked.

"No offense, but, no. Just that it felt good. Better than when I touched Perry or Dalton. The same as when I touch Sam."

The words were slowly killing him. Sam stood and paced the room. "So what does that mean? That you can become attracted to him?"

"I suppose if something were to happen to you or if you aren't the person I hope you are, that…maybe…I could become attracted to Barnet. Provided I like him as a person."

She only hoped? Hadn't he shown her who he was already?

"What if you had met me first, like Perry claims needs to happen? Do you think that would have made a difference?"

She shrugged. "I don't know. You're not exactly my type. No offense, but you do look like you could be my father. But I suppose if you were nice and persistent, I would take notice."

"So Perry's right?" Had Sam just gotten lucky in meeting her first? Or did he still have to win her over?

"I don't think that's what she's saying," Barnet said. "There's more to a relationship than good sex. Right?"

"Exactly. I'm thinking there's more to this Perfect Mate business than getting a pleasurable zap from one of you. You still have to like and respect one another."

She eyed Sam as if he wasn't worthy of being liked or respected. What had he done?

"Very well put. And something I shall keep in mind if for some reason you and Sam here don't work out."

If Barnet hadn't winked at Sam, he might have taken the guy out.

* * * *

Janie sat quietly while Sam roamed the room like a caged animal. She couldn't really blame him for that. Nothing she'd said could have possibly encouraged the guy that she was his Perfect Mate.

It might have helped if she felt like his Perfect Mate. Or rather, knew whether he was her perfect vampire.

Lying to him had been hard and she couldn't believe she'd gotten away with it. When Victoria had called with Mrs. Crawford's address, Janie was sure she'd hit the jackpot. No one had overheard her conversation. Keeping that information from Sam was necessary. If only to prove to herself that Sam wasn't involved. The only thing that could possibly ruin her getaway in the morning was if Victoria called to check in.

Barnet smiled at her. She hadn't lied about anything she told him. That zap she'd gotten? Wow. This whole vampire/Perfect Mate thing was mind blowing. If she had met him first, it was possible she would have been attracted. He was a nice man. A gentleman. He hadn't tried to abduct her or fight Sam. It was just his age that gave her pause.

Heck, technically they were all centuries old. Shouldn't matter what they looked like.

"Has Victoria told you and Rick about your lineage?" Barnet asked.

"Ben mentioned that we seem to all be related."

"We've gone so far back as to find a connection with Susannah Martin. She was hung as a witch during the Salem Witch Trials. But even that may not be the starting point."

"But you're just now noticing them? How can that be?"

"That's the question we've been trying to find an answer to. Victoria is under the assumption that you all fall under the same generational line from the starting point. That you all share the same great-great-whatever grandparents. Could be the tenth line. Could be the fifteenth. And that there aren't any Perfect Mates until that line. You, Rick, Sarah, and Ben are all on the same line from Susannah Martin. We're still trying to find Justin's line."

"Justin?" What did her late fiancé have to do with this?

"Not your Justin," Sam said. "He's Katarina's mate."

They'd only discovered five Perfect Mates so far? No wonder they didn't know anything. "So everyone on this line is a Perfect Mate? Even siblings?" Was Rick's brother going to be involved in all this? He was married. Had three kids.

"No. Not siblings," Barnet said. "So far. Ben's sister is not. Neither is Rick's brother. Do you have siblings?"

"Why should I tell you?"

"I have no intention of disrupting their life. It's our purpose to protect all Perfect Mates, just as we protect all vampires, but in order to do that, we need to know where they are."

"So you have no way of tracking them?"

"No. We must rely on our people to inform us of such a discovery."

Okay, so Sam didn't have some kind of beacon to find her. "Could they hide this information?"

"In the past, yes. A vampire can hide anything unless they're asked a direct question. But since the discovery of Perfect Mates, we now ask them at their yearly meeting if they've discovered someone they couldn't control."

"Every vampire shows up in Atlanta at one time?"

"Goodness, no. Wouldn't that be something? I mean yearly from their last meeting. We hold the meetings quarterly. Not every vampire has attended since we added this question, otherwise I would have known about you before now. Right, Sam?"

Sam lowered his head. "I guess so."

"You mean no one on the committee knew Sam had found me four and a half years ago? Not even Victoria?"

"I told Victoria back in June. After I learned Perfect Mates existed."

"And the rest of us would have known this March," Barnet said. "When he is due for his meeting."

March? If Sam had been stalking her, could that be why he revealed himself now? Why he wanted to take a vacation with her now? Stake a claim and get them bonded before his next meeting? She really needed to figure out who was behind all the deaths before she'd let that happen.

* * * *

Sam joined Perry and Barnet in the backyard. Janie had wanted to turn in early since she was getting up for work in the morning. Sam had offered to snuggle, to help her relax—or rather help himself relax—but she declined. Said if he did that she probably wouldn't sleep. Her words implied they'd have sex, but her inflection told him otherwise. That he just wasn't wanted.

"I'm sorry if my visit has been upsetting to you," Barnet said.

Sam kicked a pebble. "Just something I have to get used to, huh?"

"Not if you bond with her," Perry said.

Good plan, if he thought Janie was on board with that. But every minute she grew more distant. "So what now? Are Janie and I on our own?"

"I'm not happy with these attacks," Barnet said. "Do you think you can handle this on your own? I'd be more than willing to stay."

He would ask that. But this wasn't 1904 and Sam knew better now. "No offense, Barnet, but I really don't want you around."

"Which is the real problem with a vampire finding a Perfect Mate, isn't it? Is it because you took her blood?"

"I took it four and a half years ago, and she certainly didn't offer it to me."

"But you took it."

"And I had forgotten about her until the announcement was made." Or at least he'd made an effort. But really, could he ever forget what she'd done to him? Never.

"Had you? Really?"

Damn it. Why'd Barnet have to read him like a stupid fortune cookie? "Well, I wasn't out looking for her until then. What difference does that make?"

"Because I think her blood is still inside you. Affecting you."

"No. That's all happened since finding her. Sure, I thought about her before the announcement, but only because I thought she could be a liability." And he might have been tempted to look for her on his own—because yeah, he thought of her a lot—but only a stupid vampire would willingly seek a person who could out the entire vampire race.

"If that were the case, how come you didn't kill her when you discovered you couldn't wipe her mind?"

Damn it. Would the Committee ever let him forget that horrible incident? Janie wasn't anything like Alicia. She hadn't known anything. "It wasn't her fault I was too stupid to check first. Dalton didn't kill Rick."

"True, but he quieted the man and called for help. You didn't even do that. Which is a good thing, I suppose. I don't expect you know the answer. Just makes me wonder why."

Sam knew the answer all right. He never physically killed anyone and couldn't start with Janie. Not after the way she'd made him feel.

"I know why," Perry said. "Because she's *his* Perfect Mate. I took Sarah's blood before she bonded with Johnny. I had no problem with Johnny after that. According to your theory, her blood would have affected me."

Barnet turned toward Perry. "But didn't it? You're the only vampire I know who has this insane desire to get his own Perfect Mate. No one else seems to care."

"That's only because I've witnessed several bondings."

"You mean the same three that I also witnessed?"

Perry glanced down at Barnet's crotch. "Maybe it's not the blood. It's the touching. She's still affecting you, isn't she?"

Sam did not want to see if Barnet was sporting a boner. Did not. Did not. Did. Not.

Ahh, shit. He was.

Sam grabbed his head. "This is just great. And we let Dalton touch her."

"Sammy. She didn't react to Dalton's touch. She reacted to Barnet's."

"Not helping, Perry."

Barnet waved them off. "Stop. I'm sorry if my reaction has caused you to be upset. I have no intention of going after her. Which is why I think her blood has marked you somehow. But right now I'm worried about leaving you alone to face this attacker."

"I can stay," Perry said. "Sammy doesn't seem bothered with me and I don't think Ricky-boy is really ready to face more vampires right now."

"Victoria and Ben are still in Detroit. They've been helping, too," Sam said. "She's still trying to find a current residence for Patricia Crawford. As soon as we locate her and determine she's the culprit, I'll wipe her memory of all vampires. I hope she's responsible, because if she's not, I don't know where else to look."

And he wasn't so sure Janie would take that vacation without her problem solved first. If even then. Something had caused her to question his motives and he needed to figure that out pronto.

Chapter 18

Lying is the bane of all relationships.

The problem with being a regular, non-bonded vampire? Not being able to go out into the sun. It had never bothered Sam so much before, but then he'd never been involved with a mortal like Janie before. Made a big difference. Especially when said mortal's life was in danger.

But to tell Janie not to go into work? That would have been a major mistake. If he wanted her affection, and eventually her love, he couldn't behave like a caveman around her. So instead of telling her to stay, he'd sent her off with a kiss.

A kiss that barely warmed his lips, and if she'd felt anything he'd be surprised. Maybe he should have devoured her mouth. Put that zap in her body. Would she have stayed then? Probably not. Hell, he might have been slapped for the move. He'd done something to cause her to be distant. It was like she couldn't get out of the house fast enough.

Sam's phone rang. Ahh, Victoria. Maybe he could vent with her. He got up and moved to the back bedroom, not that that would have stopped Perry from eavesdropping. "What's up, Victoria?"

"I'm kind of hurt. I thought you would have called me with an update."

"Update? About what? Barnet? I'm not ready to talk about him." Although, maybe it would help if he did.

"Uh oh. He reacted to her?"

"They reacted to each other, okay? You'd be better off talking to Barnet about this. I really don't want to discuss this now."

"I'm sorry, Sam. So I guess you'll go out tonight to see Patricia Crawford?"

"You're losing it, Victoria. You never gave me her address."

"I gave it to Janie. She said she'd tell you. But that was before Barnet's visit. Maybe it slipped her mind."

His chest hurt. Janie had lied to him. No wonder she'd kept her distance. "Probably. This whole Perfect Mate thing has been confusing. Do you have a picture yet?"

"No. Just got lucky with the address. Found it under her daughter's social media site. Kids just don't realize you shouldn't share that kind of information. Is Janie at work?"

"Yeah." But for some strange reason, he didn't think that was the case. Probably why she'd been so distant. She didn't want to be caught in a lie.

"So, are you going out there tonight? Or would you rather I paid Mrs. Crawford a visit?"

If Janie was where he thought she'd gone, he'd rather Victoria was there to stop her. But he couldn't just say what he suspected. She'd just blame it on his paranoia anyway. "Would you do it, please? I just want this over with."

"No problem. Ben and I will head out there later."

"You can't go now?"

"Nope. For one, it's raining like crazy out there. I don't know what it is about daylight and rain, but it's like getting hit with liquid sunshine. Even with my enhancements. Don't wish to experience that again. And two, Ben and I are currently at the Ford assembly plant. He wants to see how the trucks are made and promised me it was all indoors and I wouldn't have to step out in that rain. Kind of nice that I can do this for him. Travel during the day, that is. One day you'll see what it's like."

"Yeah, sure. One day." If it ever happened.

"Is everything okay with you and Janie? Barnet didn't do anything, did he?"

"He was a perfect gentleman." A perfect gentleman who couldn't get rid of his boner. Sam shivered. "I really wish he hadn't been affected, but nothing I can do about that."

"Did you feel threatened by him?"

"What, are you now documenting everything, too?"

"Just curious." She laughed. "And maybe I'm documenting."

"Once I believed Barnet wasn't making a move on Janie, the urge to strangle him went away. How's that?"

"Sounds about right. We'll get this mess straightened out soon so you and Janie can start your life together."

Yeah, if they had a life together. "Call me after your visit, okay?"

"Will do."

After he disconnected the call, Sam brought up Janie's name and pressed to call. It rang twice before her voicemail picked up.

Busy at work or on her way to Detroit? He'd put his money on Detroit.

* * * *

With the windshield wipers flapping away, Janie pulled into the apartment complex parking lot and picked the spot closest to the entrance. She killed the engine, stopping the wipers and turning off the radio. The only sound remaining was from the rain pounding on the roof. Coating the windshield. No sign the rain would stop any time soon, either.

That she had managed to get out of the safe house without incident and was able to rent another car was a miracle in itself. Sam hadn't suspected a thing. He thought her mood had to do with Barnet's visit. If only that were the case.

She stared at the building through the watery windshield. According to Victoria, this was where Patricia Crawford and her daughter lived.

As Janie reached for her umbrella, her phone rang. Sam. Had he discovered her deceit? She sent him to voicemail. Why make the one lie any worse?

She so wanted to believe that Sam had nothing to do with David's or Justin's or Aaron's deaths. That he hadn't been stalking her all this time and finally decided to reveal himself because his annual meeting was approaching.

But thinking some poor widow was behind it all seemed…outlandish. Still, Janie needed to eliminate the innocent before she could discover the guilty.

She grabbed her umbrella and exited the car. If the temperature dropped any lower, the rain would surely change to snow. Then she might get stuck. Not that it mattered. Sam could find out about this meeting and do whatever after Janie faced Mrs. Crawford and got a real reaction.

Even one little look of hate or fear would probably be enough. Because if Mrs. Crawford recognized Janie now, then she knew who Janie was. And if she knew who Janie was, then the possibility remained that she might have revenge for her husband's murder in mind.

Which was very little to go on, but what else could Janie do? She'd almost told Victoria, thought maybe she could read Mrs. Crawford's mind, but what if Victoria didn't share what she learned? How would Janie know? A vampire would probably protect another vampire before protecting a mere mortal. How else would they have stayed hidden?

Janie entered the foyer and shook her umbrella before closing it. Mrs. Crawford's apartment was on the first floor. Janie walked down the hall and stopped at the door; her nerves were sending impulses to run. Which was silly. Wasn't it?

She lifted her hand to knock when the door opened. Janie stood frozen as her brain headed that way. "Megan?"

Megan eyes widened and she stepped out into the hall. "I thought you didn't have this address. Did you lie to me?"

"I got it after our conversation. What are you doing here?"

Megan dragged Janie to the front of the foyer. "Not here. You have to leave. Tricia can't see you here."

Not Mrs. Crawford. Not Patricia. But Tricia. "You're friends with her?"

Megan sighed. "She's my sister. Now go. I'll meet you at that restaurant on the corner."

"Sister?" All this time Janie had been friends with someone who was related to the person most likely responsible for all the deaths in her life? "I'm not going anywhere until you explain."

"Fine. Let's go outside, then."

"It's raining." Janie held up her wet umbrella as evidence.

Megan glanced at the staircase. "Upstairs. Third floor. Should be private up there."

Janie followed her so-called friend up the stairs. Not once had she mentioned a sister. And to have that sister be Mrs. Crawford? How could she have kept that information from Janie all these years?

When they reached the top, Megan spun around. "Why did you come here, Janie?"

"No, no. Why are you here? Were you warning her? Is that why you didn't tell me she was your sister?"

"It's not like that. She doesn't even know we're friends. I'm on a business trip to New York and after our phone conversation last night, I thought it would be best to make a pit stop here. See for myself if she was capable of what you said."

"What, you think she's going to admit it all to you?"

"No, of course not. But you have to understand. She was devastated when Ian was killed. Used to blame you for his death. So I befriended you. Just to see if her accusations had merit. I knew right away you had nothing to do with it. Ian was a jerk. I've always thought he'd treated Tricia like dirt, that he'd been fooling around on her, but I never had any proof. I was kind of glad it all came to light. Just not happy what it did to Tricia.

"But after a while, she stopped mentioning you. Stopped mentioning how bad her life was. Started concentrating more on Rachel. I was relieved. I really thought your life might have been in danger back then, but she never went through with anything. She's always been more bark than bite."

Janie fought back the tears that threatened to fall. "This whole time our friendship has been a lie?"

"No. Never. I might have become acquainted with you for the wrong reasons, but you've been a friend for me, something I hadn't realized was missing in my life. I saw no reason to stop the friendship."

"Or to tell me the truth?"

"I wasn't so sure you'd still want to be friends if you knew Tricia was my sister. But I swear, I was only protecting you at first. In case Tricia decided to go through with her threats. It was later when I realized you didn't need my protection."

"And none of those deaths seemed suspicious to you?"

"No. You said they were accidents, so that's what I thought. Plus, David's death happened, what, four years later? She was better by then. She's not involved. I truly believe she's forgotten you. But if those deaths were not accidents, you might want to look more into your new friend, Sam. Something doesn't sound right there."

Kind of hard to look into that which did not exist to the mortal public. Damn it. She didn't want Sam to be responsible. "Why can't I see Tricia? What's the harm?"

"It's been eight years, Janie. Eight years she's been able to forget. Seeing you might bring memories she doesn't need to relive. But if you really need to see her, I'll take you to her. She'll probably hate the fact that I've been friends with you all this time, but if it'll bring you peace, that's all that matters. I don't want to lose you as a friend."

She didn't want to cause Megan any problems. Wasn't sure where their friendship stood, though. "What's her state of mind?"

"She's happy. Involved with Rachel's life. One day I hope to get Tricia to date again, but I still don't think she's ready for that. But I have hope it'll be soon. She always sounds upbeat on the phone. And she was pleasantly surprised to see me out of the blue."

"You don't happen to know what kind and color of car she drives, do you?"

"One of those small SUVs. Silver. Don't ask me the make, they all look the same to me. Why? You saw the car? Did you get the license?"

It had been too dark for Rick to get the license and Sam claimed he hadn't seen the car, only heard it. But Rick said it was a car, not an SUV. Could Mrs. Crawford have been lying to her sister to hide the truth? Or was Sam behind it all? Janie's head hurt from all the speculation. Why couldn't anything come easy?

* * * *

Tricia shut her apartment door. Good thing the slut didn't take Megan up on her request. Then Tricia's fun would be over, and in a way she really didn't want it to end. But that slut was getting smart. Too smart. Only meant Tricia had to work smarter. Thankfully, that wasn't a problem.

It had hurt to hear those words from Megan's lips. Ian was not a jerk. And he hadn't cheated on her. Those other women, those sluts, had come on to him. But she would deal with Megan later, when she was no longer useful.

Tricia booted up her laptop. Thank goodness she'd seen fit to drive Rachel's car that night. And that she'd gotten away before anyone could spot the license. A mistake she would not make again.

They couldn't tie the crazy driver to her, either. Too bad that hadn't worked. Probably because the house was too big, too many rooms to hide away from the sun. None of the reports she'd read mentioned any coffins, though, so apparently they didn't "die" during the day. So if she were to try the sunlight thing again, it would have to be somewhere smaller. A place he couldn't find a hiding spot. That, or find another way to destroy the monster.

But first, she needed to get away. Because if the slut could find her, so could that vampire.

"Megan, you don't know how handy you've become."

* * * *

Janie turned down the safe house's street while the scents of pizza made her stomach clench. She had stopped at the pizza place on the way home like she'd promised this morning, but wasn't sure she could eat. Her moment of truth arrived and she found she couldn't lie to Sam again. Shouldn't have lied to him in the first place. And she wouldn't have if not for Megan.

Megan, who had been a friend for eight years. Megan, who had failed to mention a sister for eight years. A sister who lived in Detroit, even.

No wonder Megan had put the spotlight on Sam. She didn't want it shone on her sister. And Janie had fallen for it too easily. Because she'd trusted Megan. Because Megan had been her friend.

Which was another thing. Megan always visited her. Janie had never been to her place. Didn't even have her address, just a post office box number. It had never seemed strange before because Megan had said her trips were an excuse to see different parts of the country, since Janie's job never stayed long in one city. Could Megan have been living with her sister all this time? Was that it?

But now it was time to come clean with Sam. Maybe together they could drive back to Detroit and he could do whatever he needed with Tricia. If he could forgive her for lying.

Janie drove up to the safe house when the garage door rolled open.

Vampire hearing: a blessing and a curse.

The sun hadn't quite set yet and the angle was just right so the garage filled with sunlight. The rain either missed or hadn't reached Cleveland yet, but the western skyline was a glorious orange. So instead of Sam greeting her in the garage, Rick did. She grabbed the pizza box and climbed out of the car while Rick lowered the door.

"Sam said you were home. Didn't believe him. Teach me, huh?" He reached for the box. "What kind did you get? I'm starving."

"Your favorite." She followed Rick into the house. A house that now sported a refrigerator and stove. "Wow! When did these get here? You should have called me. I could have gone to the store."

"We did. Don't you check your voicemail?"

She might have if her brain was screwed on right or if she'd put the ringer back on. "Guess I got busy."

Sam emerged from the living room and leaned against the wall. "I'm surprised you remembered the pizza. How was Detroit?"

Rick had opened the box and pulled out a slice. "Detroit? I thought you went to work. Why'd you go back there?"

She ignored Rick's question but wasn't really surprised Sam knew. The man wasn't an idiot and Victoria had probably called him for news. The lie weighed heavily in Janie's heart. "Fruitless. I'm sorry. I should have told you."

"How was it fruitless?" Sam folded his arms across his chest.

She pulled out a chair and sat beside Rick. Glanced at the pizza that had set her mouth to watering when she'd picked it up. Now? Yeah, she wasn't eating. "Let's just say I ran into someone I know and they pretty much kept me from seeing her."

"Who'd you go to see?" Rick asked between chews.

"Mrs. Crawford."

"Holy shit!" Pieces of pizza flew from his mouth and he grabbed a napkin. "Are you nuts? Isn't she the one you suspect—"

"She is," Sam said. "I thought we were going to do this together."

"Yeah, well, I thought so too until I spoke with Megan. Now I don't know who to believe."

He frowned as he straightened from the wall. "You don't trust me."

"I don't know you." She stood and shoved her chair out of the way. There was no room to pace, so she turned her back on him. How could he expect trust in four days? Her brain just didn't work that way. But yet…her body trusted him. And if it came to her life, she knew she could count on him. Was that trust? Oh shit. What had she just done? She turned around.

Pain flashed in his eyes. "You stood up for me with Rick, back in the hospital. What changed?"

Before she could open her heart and apologize, his phone rang. He fiddled with the screen and placed the phone on the table. "What's up, Victoria?"

Was he trying to show her he had nothing to hide? Janie returned to her seat and nearly curled into a ball.

"I hit pay dirt. Got her picture. I'm sending it to you now."

The phone dinged. Janie got up to get a better look while Sam brought up his messages. His scent invaded her senses and she nearly buried her head into his shoulder. Yep. Her body certainly had no issues with Sam.

But her head cleared when the picture appeared on his screen. She pointed at it. "That's not Patricia Crawford, that's Megan."

"No," Victoria said. "That's Patricia Crawford. Straight from the Department of Motor Vehicles."

"But, but she looks just like her sister. Could they be twins?"

"Who is this sister and where does she live?" Victoria asked.

"Megan Reynolds. Tucson, Arizona. I think. Could be Detroit."

Sam turned toward Janie. "Is that who you saw in Detroit? The one who kept you from seeing Mrs. Crawford?"

"You went to Detroit?" Victoria asked. "And saw this woman?"

"I saw her sister, Megan. We've been friends for years. And yes, she looks pretty much like that picture. They have to be twins. Right?"

"It's going to take me awhile to do a search. In the meantime, Hubby has finished dinner and we've got a job to do. I know Mrs. Crawford lives with her daughter. Is Megan there, too?"

"She was this afternoon for a short while. Why?"

"Because Victoria and Ben are doing what we were going to do," Sam said. "I thought it was in Mrs. Crawford's best interest if I didn't get involved."

"Because of my visit?"

"Because if she is involved, I might kill her. You might not trust me yet, but I'd do anything to keep you safe." Sam stormed out the back door.

Perry popped his head in. "Hey, Vic. Need any backup?"

Victoria laughed. "You? Backup?"

"Hey, I can be useful."

"You want to be useful? Charge your damn cell phone." Victoria disconnected the call.

Perry frowned. "That seemed rude."

"Yeah, but was it the truth?" Rick asked.

"Aww, go back to eating."

As Perry returned to the living room, Janie picked up Sam's phone. Could she fix what she'd broken?

Chapter 19

To forgive, divine.

Being friendly with the apartment manager had its perks. When Tricia claimed to need gas, he'd lent her his car. When she wanted to borrow his iPad, he'd gladly handed it over. And when something in her apartment broke, she didn't have to wait a week to get it fixed. All she had to do was visit him at least once a week, bring one of his favorite treats, and chat for a few minutes. Not only did that raise her status as a tenant, she learned a lot about the building and other tenants. Information that had never been of much interest to her. Until now.

So after the slut left, Tricia paid a visit to her friend, Manny. Brought him one of her famous—to him—iced coffees. Listened to him go on about the problems with a former tenant and the mess they'd left behind. Then she promptly snatched the extra key to an empty apartment because dear old dumb Manny had them all displayed on a wall. Really, the guy didn't have any sense.

If Tricia guessed right, and lately she seemed to be doing that a lot, someone would be paying her a visit today. Someone of the vampire variety.

If only the websites she'd visited were about real vampires. There wasn't anything consistent about what vampires could or couldn't do. Because apparently no one believed they really existed. Sure, Tricia could tell them otherwise, but why bring attention to herself and possibly get tossed in the loony bin at the same time?

Since Tricia had never seen them out during the day, she could only assume that sunlight burned them. But could they read minds or control people? That Sam guy hadn't controlled her back at the hospital, but then he didn't really have a reason, now did he? Didn't mean he couldn't. All the more reason to avoid them.

She placed bugs around her apartment, just in case. Packed a bag with some toiletries and clothes and placed it in the empty apartment. Even grabbed a snack, spare pillow, and blanket. She wouldn't need to be in the apartment during the day, only at night. Or so she hoped.

Getting Rachel out of the house had been easier than expected. She was spending the next couple of days with her friend, so Tricia had one less thing to worry about. She locked up and headed to the unoccupied apartment down the hall.

Too bad she didn't have cameras, but that was an extravagant expense. If it turned out later that she would need them, then it would be bumped up to a necessary one.

The place was cold and she turned up the heat. At least the utilities were still on. The kitchen was her sole light source, though, but it was enough to read by. She turned the speaker on high so she could hear if anyone knocked on her door and opened up her book.

She hadn't read ten pages when the sound of a door squeaked open.

Tricia sat up straight. Already? That was quick. Okay, maybe not so quick. The sun had set over thirty minutes ago.

She didn't know whether to feel pleased or threatened.

"When's your mom coming back?" Mary asked.

"Shit!" Tricia tossed her book on the floor. What was Rachel doing back already?

"In a couple of days. Wait here, I'll go get my book."

A knock sounded on the door.

"Should I get that?" Mary asked.

"No-no-no-no-no!" Tricia ran to the door and peeked through the eye hole, but it was useless. Her apartment was too far away.

"Don't," Rachel said. "Let me." The sound of the chain being slid in place preceded the opening of the door. "Hi! You new here?"

"Let us inside," a female unknown to Tricia said.

178

The door snickered shut and the chain slid. The door squeaked opened.

Who was us and why was Rachel opening the door? Hadn't she taught that girl any sense?

"What are your names?" the unknown female asked.

The door squeaked shut.

"I'm Rachel."

"I'm Mary."

"Mary, sit down and take a nap."

Tricia clutched the doorknob. Damn it. It was vampires and they *could* control people. How many were there? They better not harm her daughter. God! She had nothing to fight them with, either. What was she going to do?

"Is your mother here, Rachel?"

"No. She's visiting a friend for a couple of days."

"I'm going to take a look around," a male said.

Oh shit. Was it that Sam guy? Tricia leaned her head against the door. There was nothing she could do. They would only take control of her, too, and then what? They better not hurt her baby.

"Relax, Rachel," the unknown female said. "I'm only going to ask a few more questions and then you'll forget I was even here."

Silence filled the apartment. What was going on? What questions were being asked? Several minutes passed. Several agonizing minutes.

"Ben, I'm finished," the unknown female said.

Okay, not the Sam guy. Had the slut wanted to protect him so she sent these two goons instead?

"I think we found our perp," he said.

"You do? Why? What'd you find?"

Silence. Were they talking in vampire or what? Tricia nearly pounded the door with her fist. She should have ended it this afternoon when she had the chance.

"*Scheisse.* And we just missed her. We can't stay here with these two. That look about right?"

"Yeah. You're amazing."

"You're the amazing one. Can't wait to tell Sam. Let's go."

Door squeaked opened and shut. Several moments passed. Tricia had turned the doorknob when her daughter spoke.

"There's no one there," Rachel said. "Didn't someone knock?"

179

"I heard someone," Mary said. "Maybe kids were playing games."

"Yeah, maybe. Let me get my book."

Tricia turned and slid to the floor. Rachel was okay. Her baby was okay. But those vampires would pay. No one messed with her family. No one.

* * * *

Sam sat at the picnic table on the patio. He'd never been more relieved at seeing someone walk inside the house as he was when Janie returned from her trip. But what did he do when she finally returned? Stormed out like some broody teenager.

He should rejoice. Should have picked her up and kissed her hello. Because she came back when she could have easily left. And he didn't think that had anything to do with Rick. Not anymore.

But damn it, it still hurt that she'd lied to him. Even though she might have had good reason. It wasn't like he'd given her months to get used to him. Or weeks. She'd known him for four days. Known about vampires for four days. And here he was, expecting loyalty?

Maybe the pain wasn't so much from the lie but from his expectations. Unrealistic expectations.

Janie stepped outside and huddled inside her coat, which she'd never bothered to take off. Her breath came out in wispy puffs. She sat across from him and placed his phone on the table. "I'm an idiot. Always said it should be imprinted on my forehead, because it's the truth."

Okay, he was wrong. Now he was the most relieved ever. Because she'd come out here looking for him.

He fought the grin that threatened to take over his face and pocketed his phone. "You're not an idiot. If anyone's an idiot, it's me. You have every right to wonder about me. About vampires in general. You've only known about us for a few days. I keep forgetting that part. Because I feel like I've known you forever."

A forever that started with the day he'd met her.

"Four and a half years is hardly forever in vampire years, is it?"

"It is when you finally meet the right person."

Her eyes glistened. "Still, you've showed me things you didn't have to and I should have taken that into consideration in my flawed thinking." Janie pointed to her head. "See, this brain of mine doesn't work quickly. And it overreacts. It's best you know this now. But it's not like I could give Megan all the details, you know? Not that it would have mattered. I truly believe she purposely misguided me. So that's what changed since I defended you with my cousin. My stupidity. I'm sorry. Can we just start over?"

"You sure you wouldn't want to know Barnet better?" Okay, kick him now. Maybe idiot should be tattooed on *his* forehead.

She folded her arms on the table and leaned forward, keeping her hands covered. "I'm not attracted to Barnet. If I recall, you caught my eye four and a half years ago. Before we touched. Before you fed from me."

"I did?" He'd been too busy acting nonchalant that night, he hadn't even considered she'd been eyeing him without the allure.

"Yeah. When you walked into the store. You were my hot cowboy."

Oh yeah. The name she'd given him. "But you were engaged to David."

"I was engaged. Not dead." Humor flashed in her eyes, but quickly faded. "But I wasn't out looking and I wouldn't have pursued you then. You didn't know that though, did you?"

He shook his head. "I didn't know anything about you."

"How come you didn't try to control me in the store?"

Now he leaned forward. He would have sat beside her, but wasn't quite sure she wouldn't bolt. "If I had, you certainly wouldn't be sitting here now, huh? But that wasn't the way I worked back then. You weren't just a meal. You were a game. Someone to have fun with. And if you hadn't asked where the ladies' room was, maybe I'd have tried. But you did, so I didn't have to."

"Fun?" She chuckled. "Was that the kissing part?"

He laughed with her. Glad she wasn't angry. "Yeah. I liked using my allure to get the girls to kiss me. Problem was, it didn't work on you. More like the opposite. Your allure worked on me."

And had basically been working every day since that night. Had it been her blood, her scent, or her touch that had kept him from forgetting her? Or could it have been the combination of all three?

"I don't know. I think your allure works amazingly well. Maybe in a different way than you're used to?"

Holy shit. He brought his hands up and rested his head in them. Gazed into those magnificent blue eyes of hers. "You're feeling something now?"

She leaned even closer. "All the time."

Could a guy come from just those three little words? She was testing his resolve and then some. He brought his hands down and folded them on the table again. His fingers itched to hold her hands.

"Is that why you didn't kill me or turn me in to the Committee? Because of my allure?"

"It'd be nice if it had, but it wouldn't be the truth. I didn't turn you in because I wasn't sure what the Committee would do. I mean, they could have left you alone, but they could have also killed you or kept you prisoner. I just didn't want to take that chance if I didn't have to. Plus, I thought I had covered my tracks pretty damn good. The only reason I got your credit card information was in case you mentioned what happened to someone and it became news. I needed a way to track you down. Not that it helped when I needed it."

"And I purposely made it hard for anyone to follow me. It makes sense that Patricia Crawford could and you couldn't, seeing as how Megan is her sister. I still can't believe she never told me."

"Did she say why?"

Janie shoved her hands in her coat. "Said she was afraid I wouldn't want to be friends anymore. And that kind of hurt. I thought I was a better person than that."

"So, you're saying even after knowing what she's done, you still want to be friends with her? Or was her fear founded?"

"She's been there for me. That's hard to throw away because of one little omission." She paused and looked down.

"What is it? What are you thinking?"

"That she never once asked for my help. Until today."

"Which is why you didn't press to see her sister?"

Janie nodded. "For Megan's sake, I hope her sister isn't involved. But if she isn't..."

"If she isn't, the person will strike again and then we'll catch her." Together. She got that, right?

She lifted her head. Her eyes shimmered with unshed tears. "So you forgive me? For lying?"

He'd forgive her for anything. "I do."

Her bottom lip quivered. "Thank you. And you don't have to worry about me doing it again. I never felt so lousy in my whole life. I don't know how people can live with lying. It's horrible!"

Her peaches-and-cream scent called to him and he took it as a sign. He stood and leaned across the table. "Does this mean I can kiss you now?"

She wiped her eyes. "A make up kiss? Most definitely."

She probably thought he'd just do it with the table between them, but instead he leaped across and landed beside her. As she laughed, he took her face into his hands, reveled in the heat, and gave her the kiss he should have given her in the morning.

She gasped and wrapped her arms around his neck. Pulled him to her. He devoured her mouth. Tasted the sweetness that was all Janie. But as her touch warmed him, the air around him became cooler. Not cold, but a definite difference. White flakes landed on his arm and turned to water. Snow. It was snowing.

"Did I lose you?" She pulled back and noticed the snowflakes as they drifted down. "Haven't you ever seen it snow before?"

"I've never melted snow before. Not since my turning."

"Oh. Why now?"

He shrugged. "You make me warm?" Seemed a whole lot simpler than stating that maybe she was his Perfect Mate. No need to add any more pressure to her life. "Victoria mentioned it was raining in Detroit. Did you run into snow on your way home?"

"No, but this isn't surprising. It's freezing out here." She hugged her coat on a shiver. "Does this mean you can tell that now?"

"Not like you can, but it's different. It's no longer not there." He stopped touching her. The warmth rapidly faded and the snow no longer melted on his skin. John and Victoria never mentioned this reaction. Did they even experience it?

"As fascinating as all this is, do you mind if we go inside? Soon I won't be able to melt snow, either."

He laughed. "Is that so? Then maybe we should warm you up. Don't want you to turn into a Popsicle." Although licking her would be fun. Crap. He really needed to stop thinking that way. He stood, hoping she wouldn't notice his growing erection, and helped her stand. "Since we aren't going to Detroit, how about we go on one of those dates I promised?"

"And leave Rick alone with Perry?"

"I think Perry would flip that around, but...yeah."

She gazed up at him with those beautiful blue eyes. "What did you have in mind?"

Kissing her some more. Making love to her. But those would follow a date, not be the date. So what could they do? Go to a movie? Before he could answer, his phone rang. He ushered her inside while he answered Victoria's call. "That was quick."

"Because she wasn't there."

* * * *

Janie went to the dining room table. Rick hadn't bothered putting the rest of the pizza in the refrigerator. Now that she'd basically made up with Sam, her hunger had returned. Amazing what a little apology could accomplish. Her body was certainly glad her brain fixed things this time. She sat down and grabbed a slice of pizza.

Sam put his phone on the table and put it on speaker. "What do you mean she wasn't there? Maybe she just went out to dinner."

"I wish," Victoria said. "Her daughter was there. Patricia told her she was going to visit a friend for a few days. But we do have good news. Seems she's your eavesdropper. Which means—"

"We found her?" Sam practically did a Snoopy dance. "Did you hear that, Janie? We found her!"

"I heard." Janie put the slice back in the box, uneaten. She'd never seen Sam so...happy. And she wanted to be happy, too. Happy they found the person responsible. But again, her brain was being cautious. "Are you sure, Victoria? How do you know?"

"Hey, Ben here. While Victoria was doing her mind-thing with Rachel, I searched Patricia's laptop. She's been in sites looking at how to kill a vampire."

"She what?" Janie's stomach clenched up again. That would be proof all right. Especially the part where Patricia was searching how to kill Sam. But the Internet? "There are vampire sites? How is that possible when you all don't exist?"

"Oh, these sites are for fictitious vampires," Ben said. "But really, they aren't all that inaccurate. And while some of the suggestions might not actually kill a vampire, they could do some serious harm."

Perry poked his head around the corner. "Well that explains the arrows. This woman's freaking me out. And I'm not even her target."

"Afraid you might get decapitated again?" Ben asked.

"Almost decapitated. I was almost decapitated. And yeah, I don't want to experience that again."

"Victoria, do you know where she is?" Sam asked. "Can you track her phone?"

"If Patricia has a smart phone, Rachel isn't aware of it. So no, I can't track her."

"Damn it!" Sam's joy had died a quick death. He paced the small room. "So in the meantime, we what? Sit around and wait for her to come here?"

"I don't know if that's what she's doing. If she overheard Janie and Megan talk, or if Megan confided in her, it's possible she's in hiding. We *will* find her eventually. She won't leave her daughter alone forever."

Would Megan have confided in her sister? Had she been confiding in her all along? She'd told Janie she'd only be in town for a few hours, while Rachel was at school. But if Megan was living there? Janie gripped her hands together. "Did Rachel see Megan?"

Please be no. Please...

"No. Doesn't remember much of her aunt so I couldn't get a visual, but knew her name is Megan. She hasn't seen any family members since her father's death. And she was only eight when he died so all those memories are fuzzy. It's just been her and her mom."

Janie loosened the grip on her hands. At least Megan hadn't lied about that. But how much was Megan involved? Or had Patricia been using her sister to get to Janie?

"This bitch sounds crazy. And sneaky." Perry rubbed his neck and shivered. "Sammy, you sure you want to stick around here? Maybe we should all go to Atlanta. She can't infiltrate Headquarters."

"I'm with Perry on that," Victoria said. "We know who she is and where she lives. In fact, there's an available rental on her floor and I nabbed it. That way we can monitor the building better. The Committee can take care of this. Or rather, Ben and I can. Crawford doesn't know us."

Janie snapped to her feet. "No. She's out there because of me. She's been killing because of me. I won't let anyone else get hurt because of me." She turned to Sam. He had to be on her side. "You said you wanted to do this together."

Sam gripped her shoulders. "I do and we will. I'm assuming since you went to Detroit you were able to get time off work."

If he thought she was going to take a break now, he was sorely mistaken. "I am not taking a vacation—"

"Not a vacation. Not Atlanta. And we're not waiting here like schmucks. We're going back to Detroit. And we'll stay in that apartment."

"What? Why?"

"To catch Patricia Crawford. Like Victoria said, she won't leave her daughter alone forever. And when she returns, we'll be there. And we'll catch her."

He was so full of confidence and it was rubbing off on her. It was about time they got the upper hand. Her curse would finally end and Patricia Crawford would get what she deserved: prison.

Chapter 20

What goes bump in the night?

"You're a brave man, Sammy. Or maybe stupid. I haven't decided." Perry tossed his backpack in the back of the Xterra.

Sam closed the door to the garage behind him, his bag in hand. He didn't need Perry upsetting Janie with his fears. Not when Sam had finally gotten her on board. "She's just a mortal."

"Yeah. A sneaky mortal."

"Only because we didn't know who she was before. Now we do. This will be over soon." And then he and Janie would be able to take that vacation. Maybe a cabin in the woods? That would be romantic, wouldn't it?

"Glad you're so sure. Just thinking about her coming here is giving me the willies. So I'm kind of glad we *are* going to Detroit. Don't need to be another one of her victims. Can you imagine if she'd thought about burning the house down?" Perry shivered.

Another reason they weren't staying. It really wasn't safe here anymore. He tossed his bag in the back of the SUV. "I feel bad about Rick. Bad enough he's caught in the middle of all this, but I don't think he's been healing all that well. Doesn't he seem pale to you?"

"We could always leave him with Vic and Teach. He'd be safe with them. So, we taking just Johnny's or are we taking hers, too?"

Sam turned toward the beat-up old SUV. When she'd brought it over from the hotel, he'd been surprised she still owned it. It really hadn't changed that much in four years, either. Thankfully she hadn't driven it to Detroit earlier and had rented a car instead. "I'm not sure it would make the trip. Why does she even keep this?"

"Because David gave it to her. Didn't you know?"

No, because Sam had never had a chance to really be alone with her and talk. "If he hadn't died, you think she'd still be married to him?"

"Does it matter? He's dead. You're not. But you don't keep stuff from people you hate. So don't suggest she get rid of it."

He hadn't planned to. If she wanted a memento of her late husband, why should he stop her? The man was no threat. "Then we'll leave her car here. Should be safe in the garage."

Something thumped above his head. "What the heck was that?"

"Probably raccoons or bats. I figured they got in when the attic was exposed from that stupid truck. But I told Ricky-boy it was the wind."

Sure it'd been windy, but could that cause something to thump around in the attic? "He's heard noises up there, too? When?"

"When you were in Janie's bedroom mooning over her scent."

"I wasn't—" Okay, maybe he'd mooned a little. But her scent had been the only thing that kept him from jumping out of his skin during her absence.

"I wouldn't be surprised if the attic held a lot of critters. But if I told him that, he might freak out. So I told him it's the wind."

"We should check it out."

"You can check it out if you want. I'd rather not find out what's living up there. Ignorance is bliss if you ask me."

"Afraid of a few raccoons?"

"It's not the raccoons I'm worried about. I've been attacked by bats before. That wasn't fun. But I can tell you who it's not. Patricia Crawford."

"I know she's not up there." Yeah, maybe the thought had crossed his mind, but no way could Patricia Crawford get inside the house now without being seen or heard, if she even in Cleveland. "Still, it wouldn't hurt to take a peek."

The door to the house opened and Rick popped his head out. "Hey, guys. Have you checked the weather lately?"

The snow had been light when Sam came inside with Janie, but since then the wind had picked up. He pushed the button to raise the garage door. As it rumbled upwards, snow blew inside. The driveway was still partially exposed—thanks to the wind—but the grassy areas were covered with the fluffy stuff.

"Holy shit!" Perry said. "Looks like a blizzard out there."

"Not quite that bad, but the TV reporters say snowmageddon is on its way," Rick said.

Sam lowered the garage door. Great. Another delay. Just what he wanted. Not.

* * * *

Janie sat on the blankets in her bedroom, her bag all packed. Not that she had much here. Thank goodness the safe house contained a washer and dryer. With detergent, too. Guess even vampires liked clean clothes. Soon life would go back to being normal—well, as normal as it could be with a vampire for a boyfriend—and she'd be able to return to her hotel room and the rest of her stuff. But not alone. Definitely not alone.

Perry was right. Patricia Crawford was a sneaky bitch and Janie wouldn't be surprised if her room had been booby-trapped. Sam wasn't worried, though. Said he'd take care of whatever she planted, if anything. And that after their vacation he would look for a job in Cleveland. Maybe find an apartment. He was planning for their future. A positive one. But something inside Janie—most likely her brain—was still itching to run.

In the past, she ran away when life got messed up, and look where that had gotten her: a person bent all out of shape, determined to enact her revenge. Or some such shit.

And while the vampires were a hardy bunch, Janie couldn't let them clean up her mess. Because it was her mess and people were dying. If she wanted a clean slate with Sam—and she really did—then she needed to face Patricia Crawford and put an end to all the madness.

But Janie also needed to face reality. She couldn't do it alone. And since she didn't have any proof to get the cops involved—yet—she'd have to rely on her vampire.

Yeah. Sam was her vampire.

Because there wasn't any other vampire she wanted. Heck, there really wasn't any other man she wanted. Sam was the only person to set her heart fluttering. Who set her blood on fire. Who would do anything for her. She just hoped "anything" wouldn't get him killed.

But since they were on the attack, the odds of him getting hurt were pretty darn slim. Or rather, nil, as Sam had said. She closed her eyes. *He better be right.*

Rick opened the bedroom door. "We might have a slight problem. Snowmageddon is headed our way."

The names forecasters came up with for storms almost made Janie laugh. Snow had been forecasted, but nothing major. Of course, that had been back on Thursday. A lot could have changed over the weekend. She followed Rick into the living room where Sam and Perry were watching the weather report on the television. "How bad is it?"

"It's not coming down super heavy yet, but the wind is blowing it all around. Perry and I can probably get to the store. I'm sorry. I should have paid attention to the weather earlier."

"Why just you and Perry? Why not all of us?"

"You want to go out in that?" Sam nodded toward the front door.

The wind howled outside, but without windows she couldn't make an accurate assumption. She cracked open the door and the wind nearly ripped it from her hands. Snow and freezing air blew inside, seeping through her measly sweatshirt. In a flash, Sam was beside her and shut the door. Vampire speed to the rescue.

She leaned against the wall and rubbed her arms. "If it's not safe for us, how is it safe for you?"

"If the car gets stuck, Perry and I can get back here on foot without much effort."

He made a valid point. "Do you really think the stores will be open? Or even have food?"

"You just make a list. We'll find something for you."

Lacking paper to write on, Janie asked for Sam's phone. He unlocked it with his thumb and handed it over. She opened the notepad. Wrote down some staple items—bread, peanut butter, that sort of stuff.

He came up behind her. "Twinkies?"

"Hey, if I'm gonna be stuck inside for awhile, I want something fun. I'm really wishing I had checked my messages now." Seemed her stupid days weren't over. If they ever would be.

"Had a lot on your mind. We both did. I'm sorry we have to postpone our trip, but I can't imagine Crawford traveling in this shit right now, so we'll be okay here."

She listed some perishable items then thought better. "What if we lose power? Is there a generator in the house?" Although why would a vampire need one? It wasn't like they could freeze or starve. Could they?

"If we lose power, I'll make a fire in the fireplace."

He couldn't be serious. She looked over her shoulder at him. "There's no fireplace here."

"Sure there is. There's a chimney, so there's a fireplace. It's just covered in drywall like the windows are. You'll be fine." He nuzzled her neck, sending erotic waves through her body. "Will you warm me up when I return?"

If he kept that up, she might not even let him leave. "But you don't get cold."

"I don't feel the cold, but that doesn't mean I'm not cold. My skin can freeze as well as burn. I just can't die from frostbite."

She turned and wrapped her arms around his waist. "I learn something new about you every day, huh?"

"Not hard to do. It's only been a few days."

And what she did know was that it wouldn't take two vampires to go food shopping. "You and Perry are planning on feeding while you're out, aren't you? That's why you both need to go."

He stroked her temple. Ran his fingers through her hair. "Busted. Does that bother you? My feeding?"

It bothered her more than she liked. "Not so much the act. More like who you feed from. And I know it's silly. It's not like I have any rights where you're concerned."

"You have all sorts of rights. You just don't want to take them." He brushed his lips against her forehead, lingering for a bit. Like he couldn't touch her enough. "But don't worry. Unless it's an emergency, I stick with the men."

"Because you don't trust yourself with women?"

"Because the women aren't you."

"Oh." Sometimes he just said the sweetest things.

"I suppose we should get going. I just hate leaving you." He kissed her temple. "Not because you make me warm." Rubbed his cheek against hers, each brush of his whiskers making her nipples harden. "And not because of your lovely scent." He tenderly kissed her cheek as if she'd been hurt. When was he going to kiss her lips already? "You're a thief. Did you know that?"

A thief? Where did that come from? "What did I steal?"

"My heart." He kissed her mouth and her world exploded.

If she was a thief, then he was one, too, slowly taking bits of her heart. And if she wasn't careful, if her brain didn't put a stop to it, he'd have the whole damn thing before she knew it. But kissing her like this, as if he worshipped every part of her mouth, made it very hard for her brain to fight the attraction. And her body couldn't be more pleased.

"Break it up, love birds," Perry said. "It ain't getting any better out there."

Sam ran his thumb across her lower lip. "I want some more of that later."

Yeah, later. Suddenly being snowbound didn't sound all that horrible. She followed the guys to the garage and raised the door. Damn wind had blown the snow against the house and was now blowing it into the garage. Sam gunned the SUV to plow through the mini snow wall. As soon as he was in the clear, she lowered the door.

Holy crap, but it was cold out there. She closed the door and rubbed her arms as she headed for the living room.

"So, do you want to watch weather, or weather, or maybe some weather?" Rick asked as he flipped through the television stations.

She plopped down on the loveseat. "I don't care."

"You've got it bad for him, don't you?"

"He is growing on me."

"It used to be like that with Julie and me. Now that I know I'm not going crazy, if I clean up my act, you think she'd take me back?"

"I thought you were interested in meeting some female vampires. Of being someone's Perfect Mate."

"I don't know what I want. But I miss Julie."

"Well, then, clean up your act and see what—"

A thump sounded from the garage.

She stood. "What was that?"

"According to Perry, it's the wind. I think raccoons or something is living in the attic, but he didn't seem interested in finding out. I think he's a little afraid of them."

"If that noise was from a raccoon, he might have a reason. It sounded big."

The power went out. Darkness engulfed them.

"Holy shit," Rick said. "I can't see a God-damned thing."

Neither could she. Having a house without any kind of windows was like living in a box. Janie pulled the phone from her back pocket and turned on the flashlight app. Shone the light to the front door. Bracing for the wind, she cracked it open. Lights were on across the street. She quickly shut the door. "We must have blown a breaker or a fuse." A breaker she could reset. A fuse would be a problem. Hell, were there even spare ones in the house?

"Think the wind can do that? Or a raccoon? Maybe that Crawford woman is here."

"Not even she is crazy enough to drive out in this weather."

"That you know of."

"Fine, say she did. How'd she get in the garage? That's where the panel is. That must have been the noise I heard. Let's go check it out."

Rick grabbed onto her shoulder from behind. "Just in case you lose the light. Or there's a raccoon."

She laughed. It had been ages since she'd heard Rick cut a joke. "Just don't throw me at it, okay?"

"Then what good are you?"

She lit a path to the door leading to the garage. She opened it and swung the light inside. Her car was unharmed, so nothing had fallen on it. But if she remembered correctly, the panel was located on the back wall.

Something sizzled as pain exploded in her side. She dropped the phone and fell to the ground, unable to utter a word.

"Janie!"

Another sizzle echoed inside the garage and Rick fell down beside her.

Footsteps. More than one person. A click and the lights came on. Janie blinked at the sudden brightness. Dalton and another man stood over her.

Or rather, another vampire. The dark haired stranger had blue eyes that sparkled the same as Sam's and Perry's did.

"I told you the stun gun would work," the stranger said. "Now tie her up."

Dalton pulled some zip ties from his pocket and secured her wrists behind her back. She couldn't even resist; her muscles no longer obeyed her commands.

The stranger held ties in one hand and cupped Rick's face with the other. "Hot damn. You were right, Dalton. The warmth is incredible. And he smells…" He inhaled deeply. "Heavenly. Sorry I have to do this to you, but since I can't control you, I have no choice." He secured Rick's wrists behind his back.

Dalton crouched down and caressed her face. No pleasurable zap. No zap at all. Like she'd taken all he'd had to offer. But he closed his eyes briefly and smiled. "You will be okay as soon as we get you out of here."

Her only consolation was knowing these two had no plans to harm them. At least not right away. But what would the stranger do when he realized Rick wasn't gay? And would Sam or Victoria be able to find them before that happened?

* * * *

Sam took the corner maaaaybe a little too fast. The Xterra slid in the snow, the four-wheel drive useless at this point. He braked and turned the wheel, narrowly avoiding a collision with a white lump of snow. Or in this case, the car under said lump.

Perry released his grip on the dashboard. "That's the third time you've done that. I know you're in a hurry to see your Perfect Mate, but can we do it without the near accidents?"

Sam almost blurted that Janie wasn't his Perfect Mate. He'd gotten so used to saying it that it'd become rote. But why deny the truth? She was. And once they got some alone time she'd come around. See, he was perfect for her, too. Then he almost blurted he wasn't in any hurry, but that would have been a lie, too. And either statement would have only fueled the fire under Perry. Sam had to keep that flame low if he and Janie were to have any privacy during this storm.

"If you two were bonded already, we wouldn't have had to suffer through all that. Why are mortals so crazy goo-goo over a little snow?"

Sam couldn't argue with the man there. He'd never seen such a zoo at the grocery store before. "This is hardly a little snow. And even if we were bonded, she still has to eat."

"Yeah, but I'd be in Atlanta with Rick and you two would be off making out like bunnies."

"Not with Crawford still in the picture."

"But don't you see? You get bonded, Janie is protected. I would have thought you'd have convinced her of that by now."

"And that's a good reason to get bonded? I shouldn't have to convince her. It has to be her decision."

"Yeah. In the meantime, she could die while you wait."

It was the chance he had to take. At least Janie couldn't go anywhere during this storm. Not that she seemed to want that. Not after their goodbye kiss. So he might not be able to convince her to bond for protection, but he could make himself irresistible. And it would start with some hello kisses. Hell, he could kiss her all day long.

Sam finally made it to their street—without a slide this time—but as he approached the safe house, the garage door was open and Janie's SUV was gone.

"Whoa, Sammy. I thought you two made up."

"We did. Something's wrong." Sam put the SUV in park and jumped out into the snow. He practically slid into the garage. Janie's cell phone was on the floor. He picked it up. The flashlight app was on.

Perry entered the house and returned a moment later. "They aren't here, but I don't think they left voluntarily. Someone dumped her purse on the floor."

"To get the keys? How did Crawford grab them both, though?" Had they totally underestimated this woman?

Perry looked up. "Maybe it wasn't Crawford?"

The attic access was open. "You mean, maybe it wasn't a raccoon or bat making that noise. Damn it. Give me a boost."

Perry linked his hands together for Sam's foot. He lifted Sam through the opening. Sam then lowered his arm to raise Perry.

Not much insulation was installed over the garage. But what was here was squished. Perry picked up a piece. "Someone's been up here awhile."

Sam sniffed the air. "Dalton?"

"Yeah, I can smell him. Someone else, too, but I don't know who. Shit. Think Dalton told a female about Rick?"

"And they took Janie, too? Why?"

"To keep her quiet, or…"

"Or maybe Dalton didn't believe us." Sam gripped one of the beams and cracked it. "I'm gonna kill him."

"You'll have to find him, first. You call Vic and I'll get the car out of the street." Perry dropped down through the access hole.

How was he ever going to find Janie? Her phone was here. And her SUV certainly didn't have any kind of GPS. It was just too damned old. Sam pulled out his cell and called Victoria.

"You must be psychic. I was just getting ready to call you. Ben and I have to go back to Headquarters. Are you going to be able to handle Patricia Crawford on your own?"

If he was psychic, none of this would be happening. "Janie and Rick are missing."

"What? How?"

He quickly explained what had happened. Tried to keep his cool, but everything in him was dying.

"Okay, okay. I'd tell you to calm down, that we'll be able to find her, but I know words are useless to you right now. Hold on while I ping Dalton's phone."

Dalton's phone. Yes! He'd forgotten she could track everyone. One of the reasons every vampire had a phone. Sam had been so sure that Dalton wasn't a threat. Instead, all the guy had done was stall. Stall enough to find a female willing to help him. The few moments Victoria needed passed like an eternity.

"His phone is showing up at his residence."

"But he was here. I can smell him."

"I'm sure he was. He just doesn't have his phone."

Damn it. Now what? Wait! "Someone else was with him. Does Dalton have any female friends?"

Laughter burst out over the phone. "Sorry. It's just that, he's a recluse. He doesn't have any friends. Part of that was Anton's fault. In fact, he shouldn't have turned Dalton at all. His IQ just isn't all that high. But we didn't have any say in that at the time."

The Committee didn't have a say in too much until Barnet took over. He gave the vampires structure. Goals to be better people.

"How about Anton?"

"Anton didn't have any female friends, if you know what I mean."

"He was gay?"

"Oh yeah. Big time."

"But Dalton is straight."

"Dalton was his slave, not his lover. Hold on, let me check out something."

"Why did we even allow slavery? Shouldn't that have been abolished when the Civil War ended?"

"Does it matter? Every slave that was turned is no longer a slave. Well, aside from Dalton, and he became free after Anton's death. Like I said, he shouldn't have been turned, but Anton promised he'd treat him well and Dalton never complained."

Sam could only shake his head. At least there weren't any vampire slaves now. That shit just wasn't right.

"I got a hit in your area. Tucker Anderson. He was one of Anton's lovers and his phone is on the road just outside Cleveland."

If Victoria was here, Sam would kiss her. Tucker and Dalton were dead men. They just didn't know it yet.

Chapter 21

In case of an emergency...bite.

Janie leaned against the side window in the back of her SUV. Her wrists chafed from the zip ties that Dalton had secured too tightly and her teeth were chattering. Her sweatshirt and jeans were not enough insulation to keep her warm. Especially when it didn't seem the heat was turned on at all.

"Do you think you can turn on the heat?" While Rick was also tied up and coatless and probably as cold as she was, at least he wasn't stuck in the back. The stranger had placed Rick in the back seat and then had promptly sat beside him.

"Oh, where are my manners? Dalton. Heat."

Dalton glanced at the dash. "Where's it at, Tucker?"

Tucker smacked Dalton on the side of the head "Can't you read?"

The car swerved, pitching Janie forward, but Dalton recovered quickly. "No. Master Anton never taught me."

"God damned idiot."

Janie wasn't sure if Tucker was cussing out Dalton or Anton.

"There." Tucker pointed to the knob. "Turn it toward the red and turn that one until the fan comes on." He sat back and smiled at Rick. "Slaves, what are you gonna do with them? I could never figure out why Anton bothered turning him."

"Dalton is your slave?" Rick asked.

"Not mine. No. He's on his own. I only check in on him occasionally since he belonged to Anton. Good thing I did, too.

Else, I might not know about you." Tucker ran his nose along Rick's neck. "God, you smell good. Hold still while I take a taste."

Rick backed up as far as the door let him. "Why?"

"To see if you taste as good as you smell, why else? If I don't like it, no use in us bonding."

"We're bonding?" Rick glanced at Janie. She shook her head.

"You're a Perfect Mate. And I'm a vampire who wouldn't mind having someone at their beck and call. Especially a looker like you. Man, I'm already getting hard." He grabbed his crotch and Rick looked away.

Janie's stomach churned. The guy was not only a kidnapper, he was an idiot to boot. She couldn't keep quiet any longer. "It doesn't work like that."

Tucker narrowed his eyes at her. "Who asked you?"

Rick shook his head at her. "Leave her alone. Go ahead and take your taste."

It wasn't the blood taking that bothered Janie as much as what Tucker expected in return. Nothing had happened when Rick had fed Sam. Neither one had gotten any urges. But Tucker was gay, or at least bisexual. How much would that matter?

Rick gritted his teeth as Tucker latched onto his neck. The vampire groaned for a moment, then pulled back. Blood trickled down Rick's neck and Tucker lapped it up, as if he wanted every drop.

"That has got to be the sweetest, most erotic thing I've ever tasted. Yeah, I'm keeping you. Now it's your turn." Tucker bit into his wrist and placed it at Rick's mouth.

Rick turned his head, smearing Tucker's blood across his cheek. "I'm not taking your blood."

"You will or your friend will die."

"She's mine," Dalton said. "You promised."

Tucker wiped his bloody wrist on Rick's shirt. "Dalton. Pull over."

"But—"

"Now!"

The few cars that were behind them passed by as Dalton pulled over to the side. If only she could send a signal for help, but anyone who stopped would only be sent on their way by one of these two vampires. And frankly, she wasn't sure Tucker would leave a Good Samaritan unharmed.

Tucker pulled a stick from the inside of his jacket. In a blur of speed he stabbed Dalton in the chest.

Dalton didn't struggle. He just slumped in his seat behind the wheel. "Why? You promised."

"I promised only if you behaved. I can see now you won't." Tucker leaned over the front seat and opened the passenger door. Grabbed Dalton by his shirt and flung him outside. "You better hope someone finds you before the sun finishes you off."

"Shit," Rick muttered.

No kidding. She'd just lost her main ticket to staying alive. Janie closed her eyes and took deep breaths. Now was not the time to panic.

Tucker shut the door and moved back beside Rick. "Now, where was I?"

"Don't hurt her. Please."

"What is she to you?"

"My cousin."

"Ahh, so family." Tucker bit into his wrist again. He brought it up to Rick's lips. "Is she going to be my family, too, or will I need to toss her in the snow with Dalton?"

Rick wrapped his lips around Tucker's wrist and gagged.

Tucker leaned his head back and groaned. "That's right, baby. Take my blood."

On his third gag, Rick pulled away and lowered his head. "I think I'm gonna be sick."

Tucker either didn't hear Rick or didn't care. He just breathed deeply. "God, you smell even better now. You want the bottom or top first? I don't care which."

"I'm not having sex with you…here." Rick recovered nicely, but Tucker was having none of that.

"Yes, you are. I don't care if she watches. You're my Perfect Mate. You'll do what I say."

"And if I don't?"

"Then I guess you didn't take enough of my blood." Tucker bit into his wrist again.

Janie couldn't take it anymore. "Stop it! He's not your slave."

Tucker snarled at her. Oh crap. What had she done? She scooted toward the back of the SUV, as if it would make a difference. He pulled the tazer from his pocket.

"I'll take your blood," Rick pleaded. "I'll take it. Just don't hurt her."

Tucker stuck the gun in Janie's chest and pushed the button. Pain ripped through her body and her vision greyed in and out. She slumped over.

"No! Janie!"

Another sizzling zap echoed inside the vehicle, but the tazer wasn't directed at her.

"Sorry, baby," Tucker said. "I'll make it up to you later."

A door opened and closed, sending snow and cold air into the SUV. The hatch opened and she nearly fell out of the vehicle. She shivered, but not so much at the freezing air.

Tucker grabbed her face. "I've had enough of you, family or not. Once my blood takes hold, he'll forget all about you. I already have." He waited a beat—probably for a car to pass—grabbed her by the sweatshirt and flung her toward Dalton.

She landed on her back, her arms taking the brunt of the fall. Snow puffed up around her. She couldn't move. Couldn't blow the snow off her face.

Tucker slammed the hatch shut.

And she couldn't even scream Rick's name as her SUV drove out of sight.

* * * *

"He pulled off about five miles ahead of you," Victoria said. "Turned right."

Sam had kept the line of communication open since Victoria could track Tucker's phone. And while he was thankful he had a lead on Janie, at their current speed, it would take nearly ten minutes to get to her. The roads were practically impassable, and the snow was making it harder to see. Sam's feet itched to run, but going on foot wouldn't get him there any faster. "Do you know what's around that area?"

"Possibly old motels. Hard to tell."

"They could be looking for a place to hunker down," Perry said. "This weather is crazy."

Sam could only hope that was what Dalton and Tucker were doing. He pushed the SUV as fast as he dared and reached the exit in eight minutes.

"They stopped," Victoria said. "Less than a mile from you. Right side of the road."

In this weather they could be feet away and Sam wasn't sure he could see Janie's SUV. Most of the cars were completely covered in snow.

"There's a motel." Perry pointed to an old motor hotel sign lit on the right.

Praying he was in time, that this was the correct place, Sam turned and trundled through the snowy lot. There, parked in front of a room, was Janie's SUV. "Thank God."

He lined up behind it, blocking it from exiting.

"Sam," Victoria said, "I know how you're feeling right now, but remember—"

Sam disconnected the call. He didn't need a lecture of what not to do. Because frankly, he didn't care. Getting Janie back was the only thing that mattered.

"You just cut Vic off." Perry grinned. "Awesome. So, what's the plan?"

Sam grabbed one of the stakes Perry had whittled from a broom handle during the drive. "I'm busting down the front door. I stake Dalton, you do whatever to Tucker."

"Subtle. I like it." Perry took the other stake. "But make sure you know what room she's in first. Don't need to be kicking all the doors down, get my drift?"

Sam nodded. They started with the room in front of Janie's SUV and listened. As soon as he heard Rick's voice, Sam lifted his leg and connected with the door jamb. Splinters flew.

A naked Tucker jumped off the bed where a semi-naked Rick lay. "What the fuck?"

No sign of Janie. Shit. Had they gotten separate rooms?

Rick rolled away from Tucker, panting and holding onto his bandage. "Thank God you're here. That guy is crazy. You have to find Janie."

Sam helped Rick stand. "Is she in another room?"

"No. That bastard threw her out into the snow."

In the snow? Where she could die? Sam rushed the vampire and ran into Perry. "Let me at him."

"Be reasonable. You kill him you might never find her."

Yes. Find Janie. That had to come first. *Then* the vampire would die.

* * * *

Snow continued to coat Janie as she tried unsuccessfully to move any part of her body. If the effects of the tazer had worn off, she couldn't tell. Everything was numb. Her fingers. Her toes. Especially her lips.

"Miss Janie."

Dalton had been calling her for the past several minutes, but she'd been unable to answer. That stun gun had scrambled every nerve in her body. Now that she was starting to think clearer, she gave talking another try. "I'm here."

It wasn't much, and certainly not loud enough to be heard by a mortal over the wind and snow, but apparently loud enough for the vampire.

"If you can get this stake out of me, I can get us to safety."

Janie started laughing and ended up crying. How the hell was she supposed to get a stake out of a vampire when her hands were tied behind her back? That didn't take into account of actually crawling through the snow to get to him. But she could try. Better than lying in the snow and waiting for death to come.

Slowly, she sat up. Everything hurt and the wind was wicked. If she wasn't frostbitten yet, she would be soon. Her sweatshirt and jeans weren't enough to keep that from happening. She rolled to her knees, but as she went to stand, a gust of wind knocked her over. Not willing to give in to defeat, she used the wind as leverage and stood.

"Keep talking, Dalton, so I can find you."

He sang some song she didn't recognize. The man had been nothing but trouble in her life, but his baritone voice was lovely to hear. Fifteen steps later she fell on top of his body.

"Thank you for finding me, Miss Janie. I know I don't deserve it."

"Don't thank me yet. I have no idea how I'm going to get that stake out of you. I can barely feel my fingers as it is."

"But you are willing to try and for that I will be forever grateful."

If she failed, forever for him would be sunrise. She didn't like the guy but that wasn't a reason for a death warrant. She rolled onto her side, keeping her hands free. Then inched her way back toward Dalton's head, figuring she'd hit the stake one way or another.

"You're almost there," he said.

Her arms bumped against something hard. She wiggled to get her hands on the stake, ignoring his grunts of pain.

"You got it. Just pull it upward."

Easy peasy…not. But maybe if she rolled. She fisted the stick as well as her frozen hands would allow and took a deep breath. This would either work or it wouldn't. She didn't want to think about the consequences if it wouldn't.

She rolled forward, away from his head.

Dalton screamed.

Shit. Had she killed him? The stake was loose in her hand, though. No longer attached to Dalton. She dropped it and sat up. The snow around Dalton's chest was turning pink. "Did it work? Are you okay?"

"Yes, it worked. I can move my fingers now. But in order for me to help you, I'll need some blood to heal."

Blood. Right. And she was the only mortal around. She didn't want to start any bonding process with Dalton, but if she didn't give him her blood, she could very well die in the storm. She'd already lost sight of the highway.

"Fine. You can use me. Can you break these ties first?" Sure would make it easier to offer her arm.

"Not strong enough." He sat up and rolled on top of her. Bit into her neck.

Oh, God. What had she just done? Those were her last thoughts as the cold took her away.

* * * *

Sam left Perry with the car, Rick, and a staked Tucker and headed out on foot. According to Tucker's memories, courtesy of a little mind meld from Perry, Tucker had staked Dalton and thrown both him and Janie off the side of the road. Less than a mile from the exit.

Sam knew exactly where that was. Victoria had mentioned Tucker's phone blip had stopped for a bit, figuring they'd gotten stuck in the snow before moving on again. Sam had even seen what remained of the tracks off to the side. And to think she was out there—freezing—and he'd driven right on by.

He'd left on foot, traveling the shortest distance between the two points. A path the SUV wouldn't be able to make.

As he approached the area, he called out. Janie might not be able to hear him, but Dalton could. Sam couldn't imagine Dalton not answering.

"Mister Sam," Dalton yelled. "Over here!"

Sam expected to see two human-shaped snow mounds, not Dalton hovering over Janie. "What happened?"

Blood stained his face. "I don't know. I only took a little. And now she won't wake up."

God, he'd taken her blood? With or without her permission? Sam couldn't think about that now.

He yanked the vampire off her and shook her gently. "Janie?" Her lips were bluish, but her heart was still beating and she was breathing. But for how long?

"Stay away from her," Dalton screamed. "She's mine."

"Like hell she is." Sam lifted her. Her hands were secured behind her back, but he'd have to take care of that later.

"She is. She said I could have her blood. I can feel her."

Damn it. Not the news he wanted to hear. "If you want her to live, then get the hell out of my way."

"You're not taking her away from me. When she wakes up, you'll see. She belongs to me."

Sam headed back toward the motel as fast as the snow would let him. If it weren't for the fact he was slowed by carrying Janie, he might have lost Dalton in the storm, but the vampire kept up with them all the way.

As soon as Sam reached their vehicles he called for Perry.

Rick opened the door. "The tub is full of warm water. Is she still alive?"

"Yes." Sam placed her on the bed. Bit through the zip ties. Two red welts appeared on her tender skin. If Tucker wasn't already staked, Sam would have beaten him senseless. Hell, he might do it anyway. He rubbed her wrists. Heat spread up his arms and her scent came alive. At least Dalton's feeding hadn't taken that away. That had to be a good sign.

As Rick went to close the door, Dalton zipped inside.

"I thought you weren't going to unstake him," Perry said.

"She'd already done it. See if you can find some juice somewhere." Sam removed her shoes. Kicked off his own.

Perry eyed Dalton. "You fed from her?"

"To save her. She's my mate."

"Holy shit."

Sam didn't want to hear any more. He lifted Janie and carried her to the bathroom. Shut the door. Cradling her against his body, he stepped in the tub and sat with her, clothes on and all. If the water was warm, he couldn't tell. Either she wasn't affecting him or she was just too cold. They weren't bonded yet—if they ever would be—but their skin-to-skin contact might generate some heat.

He made sure the water covered her body, pulled her arms out of the sweatshirt, and lifted it over her head. Removed his T-shirt and wrapped his arms around her. "Please wake up, Janie."

Her neck displayed two small holes. Dalton hadn't even bothered healing her. Sam bent over to lick the wounds, but stopped. Wasn't sure if he should or could. So instead he spit on his fingers and applied his saliva that way. The holes shrunk and eventually disappeared. He washed the dried blood from her neck.

A while later a light rap sounded at the bathroom door. "Sam? It's Rick."

Sam covered her breasts with the wet sweatshirt. "Come in."

Rick stepped inside holding a can. "Machine had apple juice."

"Thanks. Just put it on the counter." Sam had no idea how he would get her to drink it if she didn't wake up. "You look like you could use some juice, too. How are you feeling?"

"I'm okay. Perry got me a can. But I'll feel better once Janie wakes up. Call me when she does, okay?"

"Stay. Please. I need someone to make sure the water stays warm enough. I can't tell when it gets cold."

"Okay." Rick sat on the toilet seat. "Those two vampires are kind of nuts, aren't they?"

"Can't argue with you there."

"What's going to happen to them? Are you going to kill them?"

Sam very much wanted to kill them both, but would that make him, and possibly all vampires, monsters in Rick's eyes? In Janie's? "It won't be up to me. I'll let the Committee decide."

He'd have to thank Perry later for stopping him when he had.

"Is she bonded to him? Dalton?"

"Not unless she took his blood, and I don't think she did." But Sam's fear? Dalton might have started the bonding process, and she could possibly want him to finish it.

"Does that mean I'm bonded to Tucker?"

Sam rubbed Janie's arms under the water. "You'd have to accept his blood for that to work. Not have it forced upon you."

"But I did. He was going to hurt her, so I told him I'd take it. But I don't feel any different. Well, a little grossed out, but no desire to be with the guy."

"Then it's because you're heterosexual and he's not. He didn't hurt you sexually, did he?"

"You saved me from that. And I'll be eternally grateful." Rick stuck his hand in the tub. "Water's getting cold."

Rick turned on the spigot and opened the drain. Janie stirred in Sam's arms.

"Get the juice."

Rick opened the can and handed it over.

Sam pressed the can to Janie's lips. "Come on, sweetheart. Take a drink."

She pushed his hand away. "I don't want any blood."

"It's not blood. It's apple juice. Please, Janie. Drink it for me."

She blinked her eyes open. "Where am I? Why am I all wet?"

"You're safe," Rick said. "Sam found you and is warming you up. You need to drink. Dalton might have taken too much blood."

She covered her face and cried. Whether they were tears of relief or sorrow, Sam couldn't tell. But his heart ached with each sob.

"You're okay now." And he would make sure she stayed that way.

Chapter 22

The stomach never lies.

Tricia logged into her account. Last time she'd checked, both SUVs were at the house. Now the map showed them just outside Cleveland, stopped near the highway. Had they started to come to Detroit and the weather stopped them? Detroit lucked out and had only gotten rain. Cleveland, on the other hand, was getting hammered with snow. Tricia could only take that as a blessing.

Meant she had time to get her plan in gear. Those vampires must think they're so smart, being able to control people with just a look. Well, she wouldn't let them look at her. Hopefully she had something that would prevent that.

She grabbed the step stool and carried it to her closet. The top shelf was too high to reach without help and she stepped up. Boxes of letters and Rachel's crafts took up most of the space, but over by the wall, in the corner, was a square box.

One of the first things she'd sold after Ian's death was his motorcycle. When he'd bought that blasted thing, she had insisted he wear a helmet, too. He'd argued with her—why doctors thought they were above getting hurt was beyond her—but had finally caved in. Whether he had actually ever worn the thing, she'd never know, and she had chided herself for forgetting about it at the time of the sale.

She opened the box. The bright blue helmet even had a shaded visor. Heck, she could wear her sunglasses under it for added protection.

No one was going to control what she did.

All she needed was to surprise them so she could take out the vampire. Or at least immobilize him. The arrow worked last time, why not this time? After he was down, the slut would be a piece of cake.

In a way she was sad that it would end soon. It had been her life for so long. But those vampires never should have touched her baby girl, and for that they would pay. They would all pay.

* * * *

Sam carried Janie's satchel and a small bag and entered the bathroom where Janie—wearing nothing but a towel—sat on the toilet seat. Her lack of attire caused his body all sorts of commotion, but he did his best to ignore it. "I hope you packed everything. Perry just grabbed your bag. Maybe once you get dressed you can climb into bed where it's more comfortable?"

And where she might be covered from head to toe and unable to tease him. Oh, who was he kidding? She could wear a snow suit and he'd still be turned on by her body. Because he was turned on by her.

"Unless you can get a private room for me, no. And I don't mean kicking someone else out to do it."

"I know what you meant." Bad enough Tucker had done that to the occupants of this room, but in a way it was a blessing. If not for that action, Sam would still be out looking for her, or stuck on the road somewhere. He handed over her satchel and his gaze might have lingered on her cleavage. Yep, still turned on. "Unfortunately, all the rooms are taken."

And was that really so bad? The more people around, the less likely he'd do something stupid, like talk her into bonding with him. He was sure vampires and bonding were the furthest thing from her mind.

She opened the bag. "Some reason why you're still wearing wet clothes? I thought you put your bag in the car."

He looked down at his legs. "Shit. I didn't even think about it."

"I get that you don't feel the cold, but don't they bother you being wet?"

"Normally, yeah. But I've had other things on my mind." Like her, being naked under that towel. And man, if that weren't the wrong thing to think. His cock thickened with need.

She looked down at his crotch and it twitched from her perusal. "I guess you don't suffer from...shrinkage?"

Shrinkage? It took him a moment to catch on. His growing boner wasn't helping his thought process any. "Nope. Lucky, huh?"

"Lucky someone," she muttered.

"You mean you. Lucky you. There isn't anyone else I want to be with."

"Why is that? Because I'm a Perfect Mate?"

"No. It may have been the catalyst, but since I've gotten to know you more, I like you. A lot. I just hope after tonight that you can feel the same toward me."

"You think because Dalton took my blood that I won't? Can't?"

He couldn't lie to her. "I don't know."

Although, after tonight he'd certainly know the answer to that. He just wasn't in any hurry.

She shook her head. "You vampires are a clueless bunch, aren't you? I wasn't attracted to Dalton before and I'm not attracted to Dalton now. If anything, I'm madder than hell at him. He's done nothing but ruin Rick's and my life."

Her statement pleased him to no end. "What he did to you was uncalled for."

"Except stupid me gave him permission."

"Not to hurt you." Hoping to put a smile on her face, he opened the small bag. "I brought the groceries in. Do you want a Twinkie?" A tear slipped from her eye and brought him to his knees. "Please don't cry. It'll get better."

She swiped the tear away. "How? A crazy lady is after everyone I care about and I'm stuck in a small hotel room with four vampires. One of which wants to mate or bond or whatever. I wish I could just run away and never be found again."

He knew she didn't mean him. Deep down, he knew that. Didn't cause his heart any less pain. He so badly wanted to caress her cheek. Hold her in his arms. But what if she rejected him? Instead, he placed the bag on the floor beside the tub.

"How long do you think we'll be stuck here?" she asked.

"Weather reports indicate we're in this storm for another couple of hours. But then we have to wait for the plow trucks to come through—"

"So, tomorrow. Which means you vampires are stuck here until tomorrow night."

"Yeah, that sounds about right." He didn't like the way she said that, though. "You're not thinking of leaving earlier, are you? You and Rick are safe with Perry and me."

"It's not you and Perry I'm worried about. Can you just leave me alone for a little while? So I can get dressed?"

He stood. "Sure. Need anything else?"

With a shake of her head, he managed to tear himself out of the bathroom and emerge into the main room where he faced Dalton.

"I need to see her," he said.

"I don't think so."

"She's mine."

"She's not anyone's. Get that through your head." Okay, so maybe Sam wanted her to be his, didn't mean she was or should be. But damn if he'd let anyone bother her while he was there. He planted his body in front of the door when he noticed a lack of a person. "Where's Tucker?"

The guy had been staked and shoved in a corner earlier. Now? Nowhere to be seen.

Perry grinned. "Put him in the Xterra. Even found some tape and taped his mouth shut. I'm tempted to do the same thing to Dalton."

"Yeah," Rick said. "He's getting on our nerves."

"She let me feed from her," Dalton said. "That makes her mine."

Sam fisted his hands, but kept them by his side. "She let you feed from her to save her life, dumb shit."

"There is one way to shut him up," Perry said. "Let him see her."

"Are you crazy? He nearly drained her the last time."

"I did not take that much from her. I am still weak."

"You are?" Perry said. "Then she's not yours, is she?"

"She is. I feel her pull."

"The same pull you felt before you took her blood, I'm sure. If she were yours, her blood would have given you more strength than from a normal feeding."

"Are you sure?" Sam asked. "When I fed from her four years ago, I didn't get anything like that. And you fed from Sarah before she bonded with John. Did her blood do that to you?"

Perry rolled his eyes. "Sammy, Sammy, Sammy. You gotta learn to keep your mouth shut. I was trying to help you here."

Sam shook his head. He was still living in the past, when Perry had only thought of himself, so it was hard thinking the guy had changed. But the man was beginning to become a good friend and confidant and Sam would try to remember that.

"Which means Miss Janie is mine."

"Will you shut up about that?" Sam kept his hands fisted, so tempted to throw that punch. "You want to end up in the car with Tucker?"

"Listen." Perry stood and slapped his hand on Sam's shoulder. "He's not going to stop whining until he sees her. What's the harm? She didn't have any reaction before. What makes you think she will now? I mean, she didn't take his blood."

"She has to take my blood?" Dalton asked. "So Tucker was right? Or are you lying again?"

"I'm not lying. Swear to God." Perry lifted his hand, palm outward. "And Tucker was partially right. To complete a bond, the Perfect Mate has to want to take the blood. Not forced down their throat like Tucker did to poor Ricky-boy, here. Do you feel any different?"

"Just more disgusted." Rick stared at Dalton. "As if that were possible."

"I did not mean to hurt you," Dalton said.

"You don't mean to hurt a lot of people, but you manage to do a good job of it."

Rick's words were directed at Dalton, but Sam couldn't help but wonder if they didn't apply to him, too. How much of Janie's life had he messed up unintentionally?

* * * *

As the guys argued out in the main room, Janie got dressed. There weren't enough clothes in her bag to kill the chill that had permeated her bones. Would she ever be warm again? She turned on the tap and ran her hands under the warm water.

Her vision greyed out and she grabbed the counter. The apple juice hadn't really helped, but could she eat? She should probably eat. She dried her hands, sat on the toilet seat, and opened the bag Sam had brought her. Chips and Twinkies. She chuckled. Well, they had been on her list. She opened the box and pulled out a

Twinkie. Her stomach churned. Yeah, that wasn't going to happen. She put the Twinkie back.

It had been thoughtful of Sam to bring her clothes and food. But why'd he have to go and think that because she'd offered her blood to Dalton that she would feel anything toward that vampire? If anything, he'd given her an upset stomach.

This whole Perfect Mate business was starting to give her a headache. She'd love nothing better than to get in her car and drive off. Get away from vampires. Get away from Patricia Crawford. A hermit lifestyle was starting to sound pretty good. No one would get hurt, then.

Janie swiped at her wet eyes. No one but her. Because she had to face it. She liked Sam. She liked him a lot, and the thought of never seeing him again hurt. But would it hurt less if the reason was from a choice she made rather than from his death? She bet it would.

Angry voices filtered into the small bathroom. Walls were super thin—and the vampires were definitely not whispering—so it wasn't too hard to make out what the discussion was about: her. She'd had enough. Time to put this puppy to bed. Slowly she stood, waited to make sure the room didn't move, then yanked open the door.

Sam spun around but Dalton was the one who spoke. "Hello, Miss Janie. You look much better now."

No thanks to him. She looked up at Sam. "I'm surprised you didn't just stake him. Or better yet, taze him, so he can see what that feels like."

Sam pulled out the stun gun from his jacket pocket and twirled it in his hand a couple of times before handing it over. "You can have the honor."

She believed he actually meant it, too. She took the gun. It was lighter than she expected. "Does it work on vampires?"

"Oh, it works."

"Why would you want to hurt me?" Dalton asked.

"Why shouldn't I hurt you? You hurt me. You hurt my cousin."

"I didn't want to hurt you, and your cousin was an accident. But since you gave me your blood, don't you feel the pull? The need to be with me?"

The room spun slightly and she blinked the dizziness away. Standing this long was a mistake, but if she sat he just might take it as a weakness or her giving in to his theories. And they were just theories. "No. I'm getting more vibes from Sam than you."

The end of Sam's mouth curled up. Yeah, she was getting all sorts of vibes from him. And his scent. It had come alive as soon as she'd entered the room. If Dalton emitted anything, Sam's scent overpowered it. Or her nose just didn't care.

"Then we should touch." Dalton held out his hand.

The last time she touched him, he'd nearly dragged her away. "And if I say no? Are you going to force me like Tucker forced Rick?"

"He'd have to get past me first." Sam stood beside her.

Perry moved to the door. "Me, too."

"Me, three."

She'd forgotten all about Rick. He stood by the bed, holding two stakes. Or were they parts of a broom handle? He tossed one to Sam.

Dalton took a step closer, but when Sam growled, he stepped back. "What Mister Tucker did was wrong. I know this now."

She put her hands on her hips. "You don't think you did anything wrong?"

"Mister Tucker lied to me. If I had known he was lying, I wouldn't have done what I did. Just touch me and you'll see. The bonding process has started."

"And what are you going to do when you discover that we are not in the process of bonding?"

"But we are."

"That's not an answer," Sam said.

Dalton lowered his head. "If Miss Janie is not drawn to me after we touch, I will leave and wait out the storm elsewhere." He looked up. "But will you be honest in your reaction?"

"I haven't lied to anyone yet about this Perfect Mate business. I don't plan on starting now." She held out her hand while her stomach churned. "Let's get this over with."

* * * *

Perry's cackling loosened a snort from Sam. Dalton's expression hadn't hurt any, either. The man had wanted proof and got it. He couldn't leave the room quick enough.

Janie grabbed her stomach and sat on the bed. "I'm glad you find this so funny."

"But you upchucked all over him," Perry said between laughs. "Priceless."

"I'm just glad you didn't get any on the floor, or I'd be sick right now," Rick said. "Man, you hit him good."

Sam had only seen projectile vomiting in movies and television. Didn't really think it could happen. Boy, did Janie prove him wrong.

She continued to hold her stomach and leaned over. "I didn't mean to."

Damn. Was she actually ill? He knelt in front of her and tucked a strand of hair behind her ear. "Are you okay? Maybe being outside all that time got you sick or something." He looked to Rick. "Does she feel hot to you?"

"I'm not hot," she said.

Rick placed the back of his hand against her forehead. "She's right."

"If anyone's hot, you are," she said to Rick. "Why aren't you lying in bed resting?"

Now that the drama was over, Sam took a good look at Rick. "You are looking kind of pale."

Rick held his hands out. "Don't go deflecting. I'm not the one who threw up."

"No, you're the one who recently had surgery," she said.

"Well..." Perry interjected. "Sammy or I could help heal his wound quicker. Probably only take a couple of licks."

"What?" Rick asked. "You can do that?"

Sam kept forgetting how little these two knew about vampires. "We can't heal inside you, not without opening up the wound first. But yeah, we can easily seal the wound so it won't rupture."

"And reopening the wound is not a guarantee we'll get everything," Perry said. "But it certainly can't hurt. Well, I mean, it probably will hurt, but... Ah, you know what I mean. It's your decision."

Rick ran his hand over the bandage. "Does doing that bring on some kind of blood lust for you guys?"

"Ricky-boy, be serious. If it did, don't you think Sammy would have attacked you back when you fed him?"

"Oh. Yeah. But...how much will it hurt?"

Perry sat in the chair and propped his feet on the bed. "Depends. We'd have to re-cut you to heal deep. Sealing the

215

wound probably won't hurt at all. But just sealing it won't make the pain inside go away. So a lot of pain now or irritating pain for several days or weeks or however long it takes for you to heal."

"Why didn't you offer this to him earlier?" Janie asked.

Still kneeling at her feet, Sam took her hand and tried not to get a reaction, but of course his body had other ideas. Especially when his touch garnered a gasp out of her and she didn't yank her hand away. "We wanted to, but if he had escaped, and we were pretty sure he was going to try, we couldn't afford to have people notice his miraculous healing."

"Plus, the wound would have slowed him down," Perry added.

"Hey, I wasn't going to escape. Where the hell would I have gone that you couldn't find me? And I wasn't about to leave Janie with you two."

Janie turned around. "So I was an afterthought, huh?"

"You know what I mean." Rick's smile turned into a chuckle.

She squeezed Sam's hand. "How long will it take?"

"Not long. Why?" He couldn't help but hope she wanted some privacy with him. Even if it was in the bathroom. Not that it was all that private, but sometimes looks could deceive the mind if a person was distracted enough. And he'd like to distract her a lot.

"So you heal him and then we can go to Detroit?"

Sam sat beside her on the bed. "Did you forget about the storm?"

"I didn't forget. And Detroit isn't that far away."

"Okay. But if we got stuck in the snow—"

"But would we really get stuck? I mean, if we did, couldn't you and Perry push us out? Who's going to notice your strength? And I'm sure the roads are being plowed as we speak. I can't believe it'll take that long to get there."

"She's got a point," Perry said. "I heard a plow go by a few minutes ago."

"Plus it's not snowing in Detroit. Patricia Crawford will not expect us to leave Cleveland during this storm," she added.

Perry chuckled. "If we leave the GPS tracker here, she'll think we just moved to someplace she couldn't find us."

"What? You still have it?" she asked.

"Yeah. Didn't want her to think we caught on to her."

"What about Dalton and Tucker?" Rick asked. "We leaving them behind? Please say we're leaving them behind."

"Dalton's long gone now," Perry said. "Not that he's much of a threat. We'll have to take Tucker. Unless the Committee says otherwise."

How did this happen? First they were talking about healing Rick, next about facing Crawford? And how could she even be up to a trip to Detroit? She'd nearly froze earlier. Sam grabbed his head. "This is crazy. We don't even know if Victoria has the apartment yet."

"What?" Perry said. "Your phone suddenly not working?"

She took his hand in hers. "You sound like you don't want to do this. If you've changed your mind—"

"I haven't changed anything. But you nearly died out there. I don't want to rush you."

"I'm fine, Sam. Really. And it's not like I'm going to do any work sitting in the car. I'll sleep. I promise."

He couldn't argue with her and make sense. But he had almost lost her. Again. Suddenly facing Crawford seemed more of a risk than a victory. A risk of losing Janie one way or another. Because without Crawford in her life, would she have a use for him? It helped that he still affected her, but would that be enough to keep her?

Perry jumped up and rubbed his hands together. "So, Ricky-boy. Which one of us gets the honors?"

* * * *

Tricia placed the box by the front door. She had everything for a miserable night in that empty apartment. Hell, she should have been over there already, but she kept remembering something else to take and the next thing she knew, she had filled the box.

But before she left, she would take one last look at the GPS signal. It'd be nice if she could take the computer with her, but the thing was too big—something Rachel always complained about. Maybe it was time to get a laptop, or an iPad like Manny's. Certainly would be easier to lug around. But those items didn't come cheap. God, she hated being poor! If only there were some way to get the slut's money, but that would require some serious hacking skills and her skills were limited. It was amazing she could use the software for the GPS.

Tricia brought up the program. Good, they were still at the motel. But wait. Only two green dots were there. Where was the third?

She'd stuck two trackers on the yellow SUV, thinking that if they found one, they wouldn't bother looking for another. And it seemed she'd thought right. She would have done the same on the slut's beater, but she'd only had one tracker left. Good thing she stuck that in a completely different place. Because if they found one on the yellow SUV, they'd probably look in the same spot on the beater. God, she loved it when things worked out her way.

Except where was the third tracker? They wouldn't dare destroy it and give themselves away. They'd want her to think they hadn't moved. She zoomed out. Shit. There it was. Moving toward Detroit. So who was braving the weather to get here?

Whoever it was, it most likely involved a vampire. Probably two. She had no time to lose. Tricia logged off and picked up the keys to the empty apartment. She could just wait until they arrived in Detroit, but those other two vampires could return earlier. The thought of spending the rest of the night in that empty apartment gave her the shivers, but what choice did she have? She couldn't very well let them find her at home.

She opened the door just as Manny walked past.

"Oh, hey, Mrs. C. Good news. Someone's rented the apartment down the hall. Now I just have to find the stupid keys. Can't believe I misplaced them again."

Tricia swallowed. Damn it. Her hideaway was taken. "Do you mean these keys?" She held them out. "I found them in the hallway and was just headed your way."

"Hey, yeah, that's them. Must've dropped them. I swear, I'd drop my head if it weren't attached. Thanks, Mrs. C."

So much for her hideaway. Or was it? She hadn't locked the door. "When are the new renters moving in?"

"I was told to have it ready tonight. I'm just glad I found the keys. I was afraid I'd have to call a locksmith. You're a life-saver."

Manny headed back toward his apartment. Tonight? Who moved into an apartment on a Monday night? Vampires, that was who.

Well, she should be safe in her own apartment. They couldn't get in without Rachel's help the last time, which meant they didn't have any special skills in breaking and entering. But no way was she sleeping in her bedroom. Nope, the couch would do.

Chapter 23

A piece of cake's not always easy going down.

Another city, another hotel. Janie woke up on the king-sized bed. Rick was sleeping on another next to her. Driving through the snow had been a bit stressful making sleep near impossible, but at least they hadn't gotten stuck. Eventually they'd driven out of the storm, as the roads were clear the last hour of their trip.

They'd left her SUV back at the hotel in Cleveland. She'd hated leaving it behind, but it couldn't be helped. It really wouldn't have made it through the snow. But they'd stopped at this hotel because the only safe house in Detroit belonged to Dalton and going to the apartment now wasn't wise. Sam didn't want to risk having Crawford spot the SUV. She may not have been home when Victoria and Ben visited her apartment, but that didn't mean she wasn't home now. Later, Janie and Rick would pick up a rental.

The only light source in the room came from the television. Perry was nowhere in sight, but Sam sat on the floor, leaning against the foot of her bed—his head the only part of him she could see—and watching some nature show. Or maybe it was an ad. The sound was turned down so low, it might have been muted. Was this what she had to look forward to if they were to bond? He'd be up all night while she slept soundly? Or would he lie in bed beside her? She couldn't imagine that would be much fun if he couldn't sleep.

Of course, she wasn't sure how much sleep she'd get if he lay in bed with her. One touch and she'd be all over that body. Probably a good thing they weren't alone.

"Good morning," she whispered, so as not to disturb Rick. She did her best to ignore the trunk in the corner of the room. A trunk that held one staked vampire.

Leaving the TV on, he turned and smiled. "Actually, it's close to afternoon. Sleep well?"

She would never tire of seeing his face light up like that. Like she was his whole world. Hell, he was pretty darn close to being her whole world. And the funny thing? Her brain wasn't arguing with her body anymore.

She glanced at the clock. Eleven fifty-three. "I guess I did. Where's Perry?"

"He's downstairs playing on a computer, I'm sure. I reserved a rental. You and Rick can pick it up at four."

She crawled to the foot of the bed to make talking a little bit easier. It had nothing to do with wanting to be closer to him. Oh, not at all. Okay, now her brain was coming up with excuses. When did that happen? "You have any idea what we're going to do once we get to the apartment? I can't imagine it's furnished."

"Well imagine it." He placed his elbow on the bed, but didn't touch her. "Victoria arranged to have a rental company furnish it with the bare necessities. Frankly, I'm hoping we don't need to stay there. I figure I knock on Crawford's door, control her, read her mind, and wipe her memory. Easy peasy."

Janie chuckled. "Easy peasy? Really? If she's even home, why would she open the door to you? She already knows what you are. You also have to assume she knows Perry, too. You might have to break in."

And why wasn't he touching her? Rick was asleep, and so what if he caught them kissing? Maybe if she ran her hand through Sam's hair, he'd get the message. She lifted her hand just as the door swung open. Figured. Opportunity lost.

Perry entered and turned on the light. "Wakey, wakey. I ordered food for you mere mortals, so don't say I didn't do anything. And we won't need to break in because the superintendant has a key."

Rick stretched. "Where are we breaking in?"

"Get with the program, Ricky-boy. No one's breaking in." Perry kicked the door closed and dropped a bag onto the desk.

"You heard in the hallway?" So much for privacy. Janie could have sworn they hadn't been speaking that loudly. Rick had slept through it. But then Rick wasn't a vampire with super-hearing, which meant Tucker probably heard it all, too.

Sam frowned. "He only heard us because he was listening. Which is rude, you know."

"Hey, I brought breakfast." He slipped off his coat, revealing his new Hawaiian shirt and cargo pants, and tossed it on the chair.

Once they'd managed to leave the snow storm behind, they had stopped at a 24-hour Walmart to get some clothes for her and Rick and the trunk to put Tucker in. When Perry had spotted the shirts, he grabbed one for himself and then searched for the cargo pants. Janie smiled at the new Perry. "I like it. It suits you."

Sam raised his eyebrows. "So you're the reason he went back to that outfit?"

"What do you mean? He used to wear them?" No wonder the guy looked shocked when she'd suggested he wear a Hawaiian shirt.

"Yeah, but he only owned the one shirt and one pants. Wore them even when they got holes. Let his allure cover the fact he looked like a *bum*." Sam turned to Perry as he emphasized the last word. "I hope you keep better care of them this time."

"I have no intention of looking like a bum. But I gotta be me. Just took your girl there to make me realize that." Perry bowed to her. "So, thank you."

Wearing grey sweatpants and a white T-shirt, Rick climbed out of bed and rubbed his stomach. "I can't believe I don't hurt anymore. Not even a scar. Thanks again, Perry."

"It was my pleasure. No, really. You tasted pretty good there. Can't wait until I get my own Perfect—"

"Shut up!" Janie, Rick, and Sam said simultaneously.

"Gee. Gang up on a guy, why don't you?" Perry jumped. "Holy shit. What was that?"

"Your phone?" Sam pointed to Perry's side pocket. "It just vibrated."

Perry reached into his pocket. "So it is." He chuckled. "Man, if I'd have known it did that, I'd have kept it charged more often." He placed the phone up to his ear. "Hello, Vic. To what do I owe the pleasure of your call?" He frowned. "Okay." He turned toward

Sam. "You heard her, so I'll just..." He nodded toward the doorway and then left the hotel room.

"What was that about?" Janie asked.

Sam sat beside her on the bed. "Committee business, I think. She didn't want me, or Tucker, to overhear."

"Perry's on the Committee?"

Sam snorted. "Hardly. But he does do work for them. You might want to see what he brought to eat. If it's not edible, you can order room service."

"Oh, it's edible," Rick said, peering inside the bag. "Just not healthy."

Janie climbed out of bed. Staying in a room full of men—one of which she was more than interested in—she'd opted to sleep in a T-shirt and yoga pants. "And you care about healthy, why?"

"I don't. Figured you might."

"You figured wrong." At this point, she just wanted food. Didn't care what it was. "Ooh, donuts." She pulled out one with sprinkles on it and grabbed a napkin.

Perry returned, still frowning. "Something's come up. I have to go back to Atlanta. Vic will meet me at Johnny's and we'll take Bozo back in the company van."

"What? How come?" Sam asked.

"I can't say. Yet. Orders. But it has nothing to do with Crawford or Perfect Mates. Or even Bozo, over there."

"When do you have to leave?"

"Sunset. Which means I won't be able to help you guys. I've also been told to bring Ricky-boy with me."

Sam had told her earlier that Victoria wouldn't be able to help them with Patricia Crawford, that she'd been called back to Headquarters. Janie hadn't worried so much about losing the additional help because Perry and Rick were still here. But to lose them, too? Could Sam handle it all on his own?

Rick pulled a chocolate donut from the bag. "Me? Why?"

"I think you know why. Are you going to be a problem for me?"

"No." Rick grabbed a napkin and sat on the bed. "But man, I'm gonna miss all the fun."

"Fun?" Janie gave her cousin the crazy eye. "You think confronting a killer is fun?"

"Not that part. Watching them control her. I mean, she won't be dangerous, will she?"

Sam stood and shoved his hands in his pockets. "If we get control, no she won't. But it'll probably be more boring than fun. What do you think will happen when we read her mind?"

Rick shrugged and took a bite of his donut.

Janie placed her uneaten donut and napkin on the desk. "So you can wipe her memories and get her to confess to everything without any help from Perry?"

"Oooh, she has a point," Perry said.

Sam put his hands on his hips. "I'm not a newbie. I know how to erase memories and place a command."

"I'm not saying you are, but when was the last time you actually dug into someone's mind?"

"Dug?" Sam's eyes widened and he plopped down on the bed.

"I take it digging into someone's mind isn't easy?" She kept picturing a vampire taking a tiny shovel and digging, and she couldn't shake the vision.

"For some, it's very easy. For others, not so much," Perry explained. "And then there are some mortals who are easier to manipulate than others. If Crawford has an easy mind, even the most inexperienced vampire would be able to dig without a problem. But if she's like most mortals, it'll take some finesse. I doubt Sammy here wants to turn her into a vegetable. I mean, unless you do, then it won't matter."

"A vegetable?" Rick asked in the middle of chewing and spewed crumbs all over his shirt.

"Bad analogy. More like a baby. You gonna clean that up?"

"What are you, the maid?" Rick held up the bottom of his shirt to catch the crumbs and headed for the bathroom.

Sam stood and paced. "Why do I need to dig into her mind? She doesn't really know what we are. No one told her. She's only suspected. And she's only suspected for a short amount of time. I don't think digging is warranted."

"But what about Janie?" Perry asked.

"What about me?"

Sam stopped pacing. "Yeah, what about her?"

"Crawford has years of memories concerning Janie. Years of wanting and getting revenge. Having her confess to that won't take a simple command. You need to instill guilt, a little more after each memory, and to do that you'll need to dig to get to those memories."

"That doesn't sound so bad." Sounded more confusing than dangerous, but then she wasn't a vampire and they were.

"It isn't, with practice. How often have you done it, Sammy?"

"Once."

"And?"

Sam closed his eyes shook his head.

"Bummer." Perry slapped Sam on the shoulder. "But all is not lost. We've got a few hours before Ricky-boy and I have to hit the road. I can tell you what to do. If it doesn't work, you'll just have to…" He glanced Janie's way.

"What?" she asked. "Turn her into a baby?"

Perry ran his finger across his throat.

Shit. "You can't just leave her that way?"

"Nope. A total mess of the mind would cause someone to investigate. And a curious doctor is a dangerous thing. The last time some stupid vampire left someone like that behind, the Committee had to step in and clean up the mess. Caused them to add this particular rule. Now I'm not so sure an investigation would lead to us, but the vampire nation won't risk it. So we can't leave her like that."

Janie couldn't ask Sam to kill. This wasn't his fight. But could she do it?

* * * *

"Damn it!" Tricia hit the tower unit as if that would do any good.

Every hour she'd checked on the GPS signal. Every hour she'd get the same results. One car was still in Cleveland and the other…nothing. Either the tracker was damaged or they had parked in a garage. But where? How close were they?

The last time she'd gotten a read on the SUV, it was still an hour out of Detroit. And as hard as she tried to stay awake during their trip, sleep had eventually claimed her. When she awoke, the signal had disappeared.

She should have spent more and gotten the system that tracked the routes. But then she wouldn't have been able to buy three and she hadn't thought the vehicles would be so hard to find. Those stupid people!

Garage. Yeah, they had to be in a garage. But where? There was a garage not too far down the street. Could they have parked there while she slept?

The front door opened with a clank. Oh hell. Were they here now?

"Mom? Can you undo the chain, please?"

Tricia placed a hand on her racing heart. Not vampires. Just Rachel.

"Hold on." Tricia closed the door and slid the chain free. "What are you doing here? I told you to stay with Mary."

Rachel tossed her backpack on the couch. "Mary pissed me off. Besides, I can take care of myself. What are you doing here? I thought you were going away." Her eyes widened. "Oh shit. Do you have a guy here?"

"Watch your language. And no, I don't have a man here. Why would you think that?"

"Motorcycle helmet?"

Tricia turned to where Rachel was pointing. "That was your father's. I was doing some cleaning and came across it."

"Oh. Then why did you want me away? You know, it's okay if you're dating."

Tricia nearly laughed. Her? Dating? Yeah, right. But if it got Rachel to go back to Mary's... "You're okay with me dating?"

"Yeah. You deserve to be happy, Mom. I worry about you."

"I don't want you to worry about me. I just want you to go back to Mary's."

Rachel flapped her arms to her sides. "Mom... I can't."

"Why not?"

"She accused me of stealing her boyfriend."

Mary had always seemed a little melodramatic, but she wasn't delusional. "Did you?"

"No! That's what I kept telling her, too. I can't help it if he asked me out and not her."

"Then I'm sure once she calms down she'll come around. Unless... You didn't accept, did you?"

"I..." Rachel lowered her head.

Oh no. Her worst nightmare was coming to life. "Rachel Crawford. I thought I taught you better than that. Mary's your best friend, isn't she?"

"Yes."

"You need to break off that date and apologize to her. Friends are gifts. You can't just throw them away like dirt. And certainly not over some boy."

"But, Mom. I like him."

Her daughter would not be a slut. Would *not!* "Doesn't matter. You need to do what's right. Don't disappoint me."

Rachel hugged Tricia. "I'm sorry, Momma. I'll break off the date and apologize to Mary."

Tricia's heart ached. Rachel hadn't called her "Momma" in ages. "That's my girl. That's the girl I raised. Your daddy would be so proud." It always helped to throw that in every now and again. Not that Ian had ever noticed his darling daughter.

Rachel pulled away and wiped her eyes. "How long do you need me to stay away?"

"Just until Saturday." That should be long enough. "We'll do something special together then, okay?"

"I love you, Momma."

Tricia caressed her daughter's cheek. "I love you, too, baby."

Tonight. This would end tonight. If those vampires didn't come to her, she just might have to go to them. If she could find them. *That helmet better work.*

* * * *

Sam leaned against the headboard of Janie's chosen bed and basked in her scent. She and Rick had left awhile ago to pick up the rental car. And while he'd put the time she'd been gone to good use, he wanted, no, needed her to return. If only to lift this funky mood he found himself in.

Because all this talk about digging had only brought back memories of how he screwed up before and caused the Committee unnecessary action.

Sweet, sweet Alicia. She'd been a lovely woman. Fought for women's rights. And she kissed with a passion... Well, better than anyone had up to that time. He'd been smitten.

Sam always wondered if anyone other than the Committee knew of his involvement in that horrible incident. If Perry knew, he didn't let on. Not when he told Janie about the rule. And not even during their little training session—if Sam could even call it that— when it had been just the two of them in the hotel room. In fact, Perry didn't even ask Sam who the unfortunate diggee had been. Ever since Victoria's phone call, Perry's mood had been subdued.

Probably just as well. Sam didn't need Perry's harassment about his one and only disastrous dig.

"Did I lose you, Sammy?" Perry perched his butt on the desk and crossed his arms.

"I was so sure this would be a piece of cake."

"Actually, it is a piece of cake. I can't keep that shit down. Now if you'd have said it was like drinking blood, that I would have gotten."

Sam chuckled. Okay, maybe Perry wasn't so subdued after all. "How the hell am I going to do this?"

"Does it matter? Really? I doubt Janie is going to give a flying fig whether you succeed or not."

"She wants the woman to pay for her crimes." And Sam so wanted to give her that.

"And she will. One way or another."

Those words were not very reassuring.

A few minutes later, Janie and Rick returned. Their mission accomplished. Some kids laughed in the hallway. One of these days Sam would like to laugh again. To be carefree like those kids. And that day *could* come after he dealt with Crawford. Or it could never come again.

She tossed the keys to him. "Sorry it's not yellow. You'll have to do with an incognito silver. Have you heard anything about Megan?"

Perry pointed to Janie. "See? Even she thinks yellow is the wrong color for a surveillance job."

Sam ignored Perry. "I got a text from Victoria that she's still working on it." A text. Like he didn't warrant an actual phone call. But then he'd have asked why Perry had to leave and Victoria probably didn't want to have that conversation. So the text made sense. He didn't like it, but he understood it.

Perry wheeled the trunk to the door. "You ready to go, Ricky-boy?"

"Yeah, I guess I am. Not like I have a lot of stuff." Rick hugged Janie. "Glad I could have a last meal with you."

"You're not going away forever, doofus. I'll see you as soon as this is over."

"Yeah, don't," Perry said. "At least not for a few weeks. Take some time to decompress. Get to know one another. Go be bonded or whatever. Don't worry about Ricky-boy. I'll take good care of him."

Sam could have sworn that Perry was warning them against coming to Headquarters. How bad could it be down there? Well, it couldn't be that bad. He was taking Rick.

Perry slung the bag strap over his shoulder. "Now, you two don't do anything I wouldn't do."

"Oh?" Janie placed her hands on her hips. "What wouldn't you do?"

He thought a moment, then cackled. "Not a damn thing."

When the door shut, silence ensued. Sam closed his eyes. His confidence was shot. What happened to that cocky vampire who thought Crawford would be easy peasy? Where was he now? Sam wanted him back.

Janie turned and spread her arms. "Alone at last?"

"I guess we are."

Frowning, she sat on the bed. "Sam? What's the matter?"

Pick her up. Kiss her silly. Make love to her. If only those would work.

"If I screw up the digging, I'm going to have to kill her. I'll be a killer." He was pretty sure he could live with that, he'd do anything to protect Janie, but could she bond with a killer?

She took his hand, which was probably not wise on her part. Heat spread up his arm and wrapped around his heart.

Better yet, pick her up. Grab your things. And get out of Dodge. Ha! Like she'd go for that.

After a brief gasp and a smile, she became serious. "She's the killer. Not you. But if it comes to ending her life, I'll do it. I won't put that on you."

Had the woman lost her mind? He jumped to his feet. "You will do no such thing!"

Not that he'd thought she could even go through with it, especially if Crawford looked like Megan. But still.

"She's my responsibility. My mess. Not yours."

Not that again. He sat beside her. "You're wrong. That woman is not only a threat to you, she's a threat to all vampires."

"Yeah, but you don't need to dig to erase that part, now do you? It's not like it's gonna matter anyway. Right?" She palmed his cheek. "You *will* succeed digging into her mind. And she *will* go to prison."

She had so much faith in him. Why couldn't he, too?

"You're thinking of your last dig, aren't you? How bad was it?"

"Bad." Did he want to tell her? Turned out he did. Maybe then she would understand.

Chapter 24

Luck, be a lady tonight.

The sun had set. Tricia kept vigil at the peep hole. It would have cost her a hundred bucks if she'd used her own credit card—*thank you, Megan*—but even if she had, it would have been money well spent if she succeeded in ending this. And she would end it. Her string of luck told her so.

At four o'clock, the luck had started when the SUV appeared on her app. A hotel. It came from a hotel. And since it was still daylight, that meant the bitch was alone, probably running an errand. She wouldn't dare come to the apartment without her vampire friends. Tricia had quickly gathered up her stuff and set off for the hotel.

Lucky break number two: she'd arrived at the hotel before the bitch returned. Parked her car where it couldn't be spotted and entered the hotel.

Lucky break number three: two middle-grade boys had come from the pool area. Tricia promised them each ten bucks if they could follow the slut to her room. The boys had been happy to help, and not a minute too soon.

Janie had returned in a rental car and that cousin of hers followed in the SUV. Tricia laughed. Were they hoping to sneak into the apartments, was that it? Oh, if they only knew.

Lucky break number four: the room directly across from the slut's had been free to book. And Tricia booked it. But now she had to wait, and the wait was nerve wracking.

The only thing that could ruin all her plans was if they all left at the same time. But with two cars now, would that really happen? And what do you know? Lucky break number five.

The blond vampire and the slut's cousin left. But for how long? They were both carrying overnight bags and the vampire was pulling a trunk. Were they leaving the lovebirds alone? Or just putting the bags in the car and would return for more? She'd give them twenty minutes. Twenty more agonizing minutes.

* * * *

Janie took Sam's hand. The erotic zap was there, but she willed her body to stand down. This was not the time for sex. This was the time for listening. And offering comfort. Because if Sam ever needed comfort it was now. She knew all about bad memories. "Tell me about it."

"Her name was Alicia. I met her—or rather, fed from her—in Chicago, spring of 1904."

"Kissing bandit strikes again?" At first, knowing he'd done that, it had bothered her. Now that she knew he no longer did it, she could make fun of it. Let him know it didn't bother her anymore.

He squeezed her hand. "You know me so well. She affected me. Not like you do, but more than anyone had at the time. I wanted to see more of her. So I called upon her without the allure. Surprised me that she accepted my invitation."

"Why would that surprise you? You're a great guy. Pretty hot looking, too."

"I don't know if she would have used those words to describe me, but she seemed to like what she saw. And she didn't have any problems with just seeing me at night, either. By summer, I was sure she was the one, so I told her what I was. And the fact she didn't run off screaming only confirmed my belief. I finally asked her to turn. Be my wife. She agreed, but asked for time to get her affairs in order. It was a valid request, so I didn't suspect anything at the time. Then she started to grow distant. Cautious. I should have known something was wrong when I touched her and always found her singing a tune in her head."

"She knew you could read her mind?"

"Yeah. I told her that. I told her everything."

Sounded like a woman hiding a secret. "She didn't want you to turn her."

"I don't know. It turned out she'd told her brother, who had this fascination with Dracula. He wanted to meet me. To capture me. Unfortunately for her, she had underestimated my power. Or she thought I wouldn't control her if given the opportunity."

"Because you have to protect your kind."

He nodded. "Didn't make what I had to do any easier. Her brother's memories were easy to erase. I basically had him forget seeing me and having any conversations with his sister. But I couldn't do a simple mind sweep on her. I'd known her too long. Told her too much. I'd heard about digging and was so sure I could do it. So sure I could do anything back then. So I dug into her mind. I was such a fool."

She caressed the back of his lowered head. "I already know that didn't work. What happened to her?"

"I broke her. Her mind... It was gone. I dug too deep. Disconnected something important. What? I have no idea. I just know I couldn't fix it. I couldn't fix her."

"So you had to kill her?"

"I couldn't. Not Alicia. I loved her. So I left her with her brother."

She gasped. "That was you Perry talked about?"

"The one and only. Doctors got involved. Articles got written up. And then her brother started remembering... I panicked. The Committee was headquartered in Chicago then, when Barnet was just a member, and I confessed all. They were furious with me, but not so furious to turn me into an example of what not to do. So instead they made me help clean up the mess and added that new rule. Said next time they wouldn't be so lenient."

Her poor Sam. No wonder he'd been so restless, so worried. "I get why you couldn't kill Alicia. But you aren't involved with Patricia Crawford. And she's nothing to me. Frankly, I don't care what happens to her. Does that make me a bad person?"

"No. Just makes you human. But you also have compassion. Even for those who have done you wrong."

"And you think, what? That if she became helpless that I wouldn't want to see her dead? I have no problem with following orders that make sense."

"Even if she looks like Megan?"

"Is that what you're worried about? I know she's not Megan. And besides, you might not mess up this time. Ever think of that?

You're older, wiser now. Right?" She'd meant it as a joke, but he didn't smile.

"Older and wiser? Yeah. Experienced? Nope. It's not like I've had practice. I just want to do this right. I want you to get your justice."

Or maybe he was afraid she wouldn't want to be with him if he had to kill. But it wasn't like he was setting out to commit murder. He wanted to prevent it. She released his hand and stood. Took a deep breath. "You've already said we can't tell the police. And I know, without proof, they wouldn't listen to me. So please, don't let my wishes stop you from doing what needs to be done. If you can get her to confess, great. If not, so be it. I can live with that. It won't be a deal breaker, you understand? I just want it over."

He swung his legs to the side of the bed and took her hands in his. "I know you do. I do, too." He chuckled softly. "Perry told me that if we were bonded already, none of this would be happening. We'd just disappear and she couldn't bother you anymore."

And Perry spoke a lot of crap. "That's not true."

"Oh, I know. But it was a nice thought." He kissed her palms as if they were precious, and her chest clenched. "I know you need your time, that you're not ready to bond, but I love you, Janie. In case you had your doubts, know that."

Love? How could he love her so soon? She pulled her hands away. "Why? Because you get a reaction when we touch?"

"No. It might have been the start, yeah, but not the reason. And it's a lot of little reasons, actually. How you can still love your cousin even though he tends to piss you off. Or how you can love your friend, Megan, even though she's been lying to you. How you can even forgive me after assaulting you."

She placed her fingers against his lips. "Stop. I'm not that person."

He gingerly wrapped his hand around her wrist. "Yes, you are."

"No. I'm the person who runs away."

"From what? Commitment? You have three relationships that say otherwise. I just want to be the last."

"But I run when it gets bad."

"Yeah? It's pretty bad now. Why are you still here? It's not like I've kept you a prisoner."

All Janie's life, at the first sign of trouble, she would run first, think later. Except for now. Why was that? Was it because she was tired of running? Or because of the man sitting in front of her, looking at her as if she were the only person in the world?

He loved her. Hell, he was willing to *kill* for her, and even that kept her rooted.

God, could she be in love with him, too?

"I'm here because of you." She would die if anything happened to him.

"Okay."

He was probably afraid to say any more. Not that she could blame him. She sat on the bed beside him. "But I'm scared. I'm scare of bonding. I'm scared of Patricia. I'm scared of losing you."

Her track record with men was pretty sad. Sure, Patricia Crawford was to blame for that. And now they knew she was out there. But that didn't mean Patricia wouldn't succeed a fourth time. Janie closed her eyes. That curse thing was starting to sound believable once again.

He touched his temple against hers. "Would it make you feel better to know that I'm scared of the same things?"

She pulled away and stared into those beautiful brown eyes. "You are?"

"Patricia is one scary bitch. She could easily do something crazy and take us all out. And bonding is no guarantee you'll love me back. Which is why I'm not asking you to bond right now. No matter how much I want it." He laid his arm across her shoulders and nuzzled her neck. "But you can do something to ease my fear where Crawford is concerned."

She closed her eyes as waves of pleasure coursed through her body. "I want to help. What can I do?"

"Stay here. Where it's safe. Let me do this alone. And then we can take all the time you need."

Alone? She played with the coverlet on the bed to focus on something other than his lips. He made sense, but to let him do it alone…that just didn't seem right. "If you have to kill her, won't you need help in disposing the body? Or cleaning up the mess?"

He laughed. "Sweetheart. I'm not going to shoot her. If I fail, it won't take much to have her commit suicide. I'll just make sure she writes out a confession before I go digging."

"You can do that? Get her to write a confession?"

"That'll be the easy part, because she won't be around to contest it. Can you live with that?"

He was willing to do so much for her. Maybe too much. "You said we'd do this together. Why are you changing your mind?"

"Because I don't want you to get hurt. I don't trust her. If I were the police, would you be asking to go with me?"

"No, of course not. I'd just get in...the...way." And she'd probably get in Sam's way. Especially if she became a distraction. Damn it. She didn't want to be a distraction.

"So you'll stay here?"

She nodded. He trusted her with his secret, the least she could do is trust him to finish this.

He cupped her face and desire raced through her again. "Thank you." He kissed her. Just lips against lips, but he lingered a bit before pulling away. "God, what you do to me. I love you, Janie."

He stood and she grabbed his arm. She couldn't let him leave without knowing. "Sam? Please don't die. Okay? Because... Because I love you, too."

"Janie." He lifted her and kissed her thoroughly. Devoured her mouth. She wrapped her arms around his neck and couldn't pull him any closer.

"I'll end this for you. I promise." He kissed her one last time and then sprinted out the door.

She plopped back onto the bed and stared at the place he'd been sitting. Already, she missed him.

A knock sounded at the door. The key cards sat on the night stand.

Janie picked one up. "Did you forget your key?" When she opened the door, her mind fritzed out on her. "Megan? What are you—"

Her words were cut off as her friend shot her with electricity. Damn. Another tazer. Was there a sale on them or something? Pain burned in her belly and her legs gave way. Oh shit.

* * * *

Tricia laughed as she shut the door. "Megan will never be here for you again."

Yes, it was her lucky day. The vampire had left the slut alone, making her job so easy. But wherever that vampire went, he would return. She had no doubt about that.

"Time to get to work." She picked up the dropped key card off the carpet and pocketed it. Walked over to the window and opened the curtains. When the sun had set, it had shone through her windows, which meant that orb would rise and shine through these. "Perfect. This will do nicely."

Tricia grabbed the moaning slut by her T-shirt and dragged her to the bed. No use making the woman comfortable. She wouldn't live much longer anyway. But what could she be secured to? Tricia knelt and looked under the bed. Legs were not bolted to the floor, so they wouldn't work. Ahh, but the frame was welded to the legs.

Tricia pulled the hand cuffs and some duct tape from her bag. Slapped a piece of duct tape over Janie's mouth and secured one part of the cuff to her wrist. Looped it around the frame and then slapped the other half to her free wrist. Not only was she secure, she'd have a good view of the window.

Tricia couldn't have planned it better. She headed back to her room and retrieved the rest of her gear. When she returned, Janie was picking at the tape across her mouth.

"Ah, ah, ah!" Tricia zapped the slut again. Boy, did that feel good. The woman flopped like a dead fish. "Guess I gotta do a better job with that flap trap of yours." Tricia wrapped the duct tape across Janie's mouth and then around her head. Taped her fingers, too, just in case.

The only thing that could go wrong was if the vampire didn't return before sunrise. Then Tricia would have to kill the slut without the fun. But that was highly unlikely since he'd left his bitch behind. If he was like most men, he'd be back. Oh yeah, he'd be back.

* * * *

Sam entered the apartment Victoria had rented. Crawford wasn't in hers and while he'd thought about just waiting there for her, wasn't sure if the daughter would show up first. The fewer people involved, the better. Besides, he'd be able to hear whenever Crawford returned. Hopefully, it wouldn't be long.

And then he could go back to Janie. She loved him. Had actually said those words. And that she was willing to let him do this alone meant more than she'd ever know.

His phone went off. Wow, Victoria was actually calling? "Hey, what's up?"

"Is Janie with you?"

"No. She agreed to stay at the hotel while I wait in the apartment across the hall. Crawford hasn't returned yet."

"Wow. That's good. She'll be safe there. The reason I called, I finally found a picture of Megan. I'm sending you a copy."

Sam put the phone on speaker and opened his messages.

Victoria continued, "It's hard to tell since this picture wasn't taken in the same year as Patricia's, but I think—"

"They're identical twins. She really exists."

"And she lives in Arizona, just like Janie said. Sure wish I knew what her involvement in all this was."

"Well, it won't matter. I won't leave until I end this." One way or another, as Perry had said.

"Hopefully it won't take long. I know how badly you want to get back to Janie. Call me when it's over."

"Sure. I'm surprised you actually called and didn't just send a text."

She laughed. "I thought about it."

"Is Perry okay?" Seemed a whole lot easier to ask that.

"Perry's fine. You know how he can be when he can't tell everyone what he's doing. But it's Committee business and it has nothing to do with him or you or Janie. That's all I can say at this time. Please understand." Victoria disconnected the call before Sam had a chance to ask more questions.

Secrets. How many more secrets did the Committee have? Probably just as well he wasn't on the Committee. He wasn't sure he'd be able to keep them all to himself. Hell, keeping Janie a secret all this time had practically killed him. The day he was able to unload on John was the day a huge weight had been lifted.

Which meant no keeping Megan's identity from Janie. He brought up Janie's number and smiled at her photo. When he took his phone to snap the picture, she'd been holding a slice of pizza and had stuck her tongue out.

She'd wanted him to delete it. He made it her contact picture. She'd rolled her eyes when he showed her. He was never going to delete it because in that moment he'd captured the real Janie Robinson. One he hoped would surface more often after this fiasco was finished.

Because she loved him. She'd said so.

He hit the call button. It rang several times before ending in her voicemail. She was probably in the bathroom or something. "Give me a call." And just for the heck of it, he ended it with, "Love you!"

Twenty minutes later, still no call and no Patricia. He called Janie back. Ended up in her voicemail again. Something was wrong, his bones told him so.

Shit. They'd been so sure to remove the tracker from the Xterra. What if there was another one? A backup? Or what if Crawford had bugged something else?

The what ifs were going to kill him. Sam rushed out of the apartment to the rental car. Breaking all kinds of laws, he high-tailed it back to the hotel. If he was wrong, he was wrong. But at least his worry would go away.

After he parked the car, he ran inside, trying not to bring too much attention to himself, and made it to the stairwell. Out of sight of any cameras, he took the steps several at a time.

He opened the door to their floor and stopped. Took a calming breath. Stealth was called for here. Taking long, quiet strides, he approached their room and listened.

The television was turned on loud. He concentrated. Two heartbeats. Definitely two.

Damn it. Janie wasn't alone. What should he do?

No, not damn it. He was a vampire. He was the powerful one here. But he wouldn't rush in there like some newbie vampire. All he had to do was open the door a crack and take control. Whoever was in there with Janie would be under his command. And if that someone was a friend, he'd apologize later.

He slipped the key card into the slot. Unfortunately, he couldn't quiet the motor that unlocked the door. Had the television drowned it out? Too late to worry about that now. He opened the door wide enough to get a view of the dresser and sent the command to fall asleep.

No one fell. Maybe they were sitting. Or lying on the bed. He opened the door wider.

He could only blame his confused brain for hesitating. Someone was sitting on the chair, by the window. Wearing a motorcycle helmet, and pointing a—

An arrow struck his heart and his legs gave out on him. Another, then another, then another followed suit. He crumpled onto the floor, landing on his left side.

"Who are you?" Which was a stupid question. Who else would it be but Patricia Crawford?

She kicked his legs out from the doorway and shut the door. "Hello. Sam, right? Isn't this the prettiest little bow you've ever seen? It's really fast, too." She put the weapon down and taped his mouth shut. "Let's get you in position."

Sam sent mental commands to the woman to no avail. Either the helmet was blocking him or she was insane. Maybe a combination of both? Whatever, he was unable to stop her.

She grabbed his right arm and pulled, but he barely moved. "Man, you're heavier than you look."

He was facing the wall and he couldn't see her, but she seemed to be searching for something as she moved about the room. Her "Ah-ha" confirmed she'd found it.

She shoved something against him. Managed to roll him up on top, but not without grunting. "If you put my back out, I may just kick you in the family jewels. Heck, I might do it for the fun of it." She laughed. "You won't be needing them anyway."

His head had flopped to the right and he now had a view of the bathroom. Empty. Janie wasn't making any noise, but her scent was strong and so was her heartbeat. She was somewhere in the room.

Each time Crawford touched him, he'd tried to take control. But between his clothes and her gloves, there hadn't been any actual skin contact for him to connect. Damn it. How did this woman know so much?

Something clicked above his head. A handle? Oh, she put him on Janie's suitcase. Crawford lifted the case enough to get the wheels working and wheeled him to the window. He passed Janie, who was cuffed to the underside of the bed closest to the window. Her mouth was taped up, but she was blinking as if she'd been unconscious. When she finally saw him, her eyes practically bulged out of her head.

He tried to reassure her that he was okay. But was he? Really?

* * * *

What was it with people and their stun guns? Every time Janie came to, Patricia would zap her again. Apparently the woman didn't want her making any noise to warn Sam.

Janie came back to the living for the fourth time just as Patricia, wearing a motorcycle helmet, dragged...Sam? Oh shit. How'd she get the drop on him? And why wasn't he controlling her? Was it because of the helmet or because she staked him before he got a chance? Could he even control her in that condition?

Four short arrows protruded from his upper left chest. Blood had oozed from the site, but he didn't seem to be bleeding anymore. At least he wasn't leaving a trail behind. He tried to reassure her with his eyes, but how was he going to help if he couldn't move? And couldn't control Patricia?

She dumped him over by the window and positioned his head to face Janie. "Wouldn't want you to miss the agonizing look she has when you finally burn."

Would he really burn if he was dressed the way he was? Or would just his hands and face burn? He could survive that, couldn't he? But Patricia dashed those hopes goodbye when she pulled scissors out of her bag. She ran the scissors up each sleeve of his jacket until she could remove it from his body. Cut open the legs of his jeans to just above his knees and exposed his legs. Snipped the sleeves to his T-shirt. Cut his shirt from the bottom to expose his torso. When she reached his upper chest, Sam moaned.

"Aww, does that hurt?" She wiggled the stakes and Sam wailed behind his taped mouth. "So nice to know you can feel pain. I had wondered. But these things are much too loose." She took her shoe and hammered the stakes in deep. He wailed with each whack.

Tears formed in Janie's eyes. They were going to die because of her. Just like David and Justin and Aaron and Liz. Because she'd run instead of facing the consequences of her actions all those years ago.

Patricia didn't remove the rest of his jeans, which were more like shorts now. Or even unzip him. Good thing. She probably wouldn't take kindly to him going commando. Hell, she had kept calling Janie "slut" with each taze.

Patricia put her hands on her hips and looked out the window. "I sure hope it's a nice sunny day tomorrow. But will it matter if it isn't?" She looked down at Sam. "Will you even burn if the sun is behind clouds? Like you'd tell me the truth if you could speak. Guess we'll just have to wait and see, huh? Now excuse me while I go back to my room and take a little breather. This helmet's kind of hot."

That helmet had to go. But would it matter? Once the door across the hall shut, Janie worked the tape from her bottom lip. Her fingers were taped, but her thumbs were free. With the TV blaring, she didn't even bother to whisper, not that she could talk all that well to begin with. Good thing Sam had vampire hearing. "Is the helmet keeping you from controlling her? Blink once for yes, two for no."

He blinked once.

Hmmm… Janie had been keeping her legs curled up and Patricia hadn't bothered walking far enough away to avoid being tripped. And if Janie did it right, maybe Patricia would fall into the dresser and crack the visor open, or at least free it a bit for Sam. It had to work. It just had to.

"I'm going to trip her, okay? When she falls, the helmet should move some, if not crack. Will that be enough?"

He blinked his eyes several times.

"You don't know?"

He blinked once.

Maybe he just didn't want to get her hopes up. But what else did she have if not hope? "Be ready to take control anyway. Okay?"

He blinked once.

She stood the best she could with her hands stuck under the bed. Pinpricks spread through her legs. Four zaps to the system and her inactivity had caused her legs to fall asleep. She practiced several times shooting her legs out and squatted every few minutes to keep the circulation going. To have enough strength to actually take the woman down. Patricia had been gone nearly thirty minutes.

"Do you think she left?"

Sam blinked twice.

"Yeah, that's what I thought. She probably took a nap."

Maybe Patricia wasn't planning on returning until just before sunrise. There might not be enough time to save Sam then. Before Janie could come up with another plan, the door across the hall shut. Finally. Janie sat up straight and pulled her knees up to her chest.

Patricia entered the room and tossed the crossbow onto the first bed. "I'm bored. This isn't as entertaining as I thought it would be."

She walked over to Janie and crouched down. "Too bad we're not someplace secluded. Then I could remove this…tape. What'd you do?"

Oh shit. Janie forgot to replace the tape. But then, maybe she could use that to her advantage.

While Patricia was inspecting the tape, Janie took her legs and shoved them into Patricia's chest. The woman flew across the room and the helmet hit the dresser with a clunk.

Had it worked? Had Sam taken control?

Patricia stood. "You bitch!"

Damn it! The helmet was just as secure as ever.

Patricia pulled a knife from her bag. "If I didn't want you alive to see him burn, I'd kill you right now. So instead, he'll receive your punishment." She plunged the knife into Sam's thigh.

He wailed behind his tape and tears sprung from Janie's eyes. "Stop! Don't hurt him!"

Patricia yanked the knife free and pointed the bloody tip at Janie. "You've been nothing but a thorn in my side since the day you came onto my husband."

"He harassed me. I didn't—"

"Liar! You and Megan, both. If you two had actually met, I bet you'd be friends."

If we'd met? If? "What?"

"You mean you haven't figured that out yet?" Patricia leaned her head back as far as the helmet allowed and laughed. "When you came by my apartment I thought for sure I'd blown my cover. Boy, you really *are* gullible."

"You're...Megan?" Janie lowered her head. Her friend for eight years had actually been her...enemy?

"Ding, ding, ding! Give the girl a prize!" She paced. "It's your fault, you and your slutful ways. It's your fault Ian's dead."

"I did not kill your husband."

"You might as well have. He was ready to commit suicide because of what you did. I couldn't have him do that. Then what would I have? Certainly not his insurance. His social security. My only mistake was not making sure you didn't have an alibi."

"You killed your husband?"

"No! You did, you twit. Can't you hear?" She threw the knife in her bag. Pulled out the tazer and tape. "I'm tired of you two. Sunrise can't get here soon enough so I can see the pain on your face when you watch him die. And I'll certainly enjoy the pain on your face when I kill you. But apparently I can't leave you alone like this. And I certainly can't trust you not to kick me again." She zapped Janie. More than once.

The pain was so great, Janie's world went dark.

Chapter 25

Nothing worth having comes easy.

Sam could do nothing but wait. Wait for Janie to wake up. Wait for the sun to rise. Wait to die.

Because if the sun rose before Janie could get free, he would surely die. But first, she had to wake up.

After tazing Janie, Crawford had kicked Janie's knees and only stopped when she noticed Janie wasn't reacting. Guess it wasn't "fun" then. And to make matters worse, she taped Janie's ankles together before leaving for the other room. Probably to get a breather from that helmet.

Could Janie even move? All he needed was for her to stretch her legs out.

The clock on the nightstand read 11:57. Maybe someone would complain about the television still being on. But the hotel hadn't been all that busy on a Monday night; he could only imagine how empty it was on a Tuesday.

Janie stirred.

He had spent his time waiting by pushing the tape away from his lips. It was not an easy thing to do. Sure, his mouth wasn't paralyzed, but it wasn't at 100% either. His tongue could move to speak—none too smoothly—but for other measures, it didn't have much strength, or saliva. At least the tape wasn't strapped around his head like it was with Janie. It might actually come free. But unless Crawford left for good, he couldn't risk his work being seen. Not yet, anyway.

He could speak, though. Probably not intelligible words, but noise all the same. "Janie?"

She shook her head as if getting the cobwebs free. How many times total had Crawford tazed her? She'd zapped Janie twice before the kicking show. At least once to get Janie in the room, for sure. Once when Crawford surprised her? Damn, no wonder it was taking Janie so long to wake up.

Too bad he hadn't been tazed. It would have incapacitated him just as much as a staking, but he could recover from that without any help. And he could have faked it after it wore off. But no. Crawford had to go and stake him. Again.

Janie moved her legs and gave a muffled cry. Or maybe she cursed. He couldn't blame her for either. And now he would purposely cause her more pain.

Because while she was unconscious, he had spotted the key on the carpet. Janie must have freed it when she kicked Crawford. If Janie could get to that key and unlock her cuffs…

No use in finishing that thought. She needed to be able to *reach* the key first.

"Janie." When he got her attention, he rolled his eyes in the direction of the key. "Key."

She looked at the door.

"No. Floor. Key." He stared at the key.

Her eyes widened. She grabbed the bed frame and sat up. Took her thumbs and worked the tape on her bottom lip. Crawford had secured it better, but not enough for his Janie.

"How long has she been gone?" she whispered.

"Hour. Still across hall."

She nodded and then stared at her feet. Her shoes would make it difficult, if her knees didn't already have that job.

"How bad knees?"

"They've been better." She took a deep breath and pulled on the bed frame. But her angle wasn't quite right and she had no leverage. She pushed herself onto her feet. Tears streamed down her face, but she got the leverage she needed. The bed moved an inch.

She collapsed onto the floor and buried her head into her arm.

He couldn't tell her to stop. Both their lives depended on her getting that key. But he hated seeing her in such pain. If only they had bonded, she'd be partially healed by now.

He'd remind her of that after they got free and had been bonded for a decade. At least.

She repeated the process two more times. Moved the bed two more inches. She then stretched her feet out. They covered the key.

The door across the hall closed. Janie's eyes widened. "Maybe she'll think I was trying to get to you."

She then moved the cuffs as far as she could get them toward him and whipped her legs on a curse against his own.

Her legs landed on his, creating skin contact. The heat was glorious. The pain in his chest subsided. Her touch was magic.

The door opened and Patricia emerged. "What the? Can't leave you two alone for a minute can I?" She aimed her tazer at Janie and stepped closer. Looked down. "What's this?" She picked up the key. "Awww, were you trying to get the key? Guess the bed's not going to stop you after all."

She placed the key on the dresser. "You know, I was thinking that I'm going to have to miss all the fun if I want an alibi. Would the whole room go into flames when you do? That would be sweet, but someone could come and save Janie if she wasn't caught on fire right away. And since you two lovebirds seem to want to be close together, then that's what I'll do. I think the radiator will hold you much better anyway."

She zapped Janie and the electricity passed through him where they touched. It was only brief, but damn, it'd hurt. *Oh, Janie.*

"At sunrise the vampire will go up in flames and you'll go up with him." She turned to Sam and held up his phone. "Your friend has been trying to reach you, but I can't seem to send him a text without your fingerprint. So be a dear."

Be a dear? As if he had a choice in the matter.

Still wearing gloves, she placed his thumb on the phone, which opened it up. "Let's see… Yes, I got it. I'll tell him you're fine, just busy with your…what did you call her? Oh yeah. Your Perfect Mate. You vampires are so strange."

* * * *

Perry drove down the alley behind Johnny's bar and parked behind the Committee's van. Driving was a pain. One accident and they'd been stuck in traffic for hours. Traveling with mortals only made it worse. Or maybe it was just this one particular mortal. If Ricky-boy wasn't whining for a drink, he was whining to take a piss. The only break Perry ever needed was to fill up the damn car so he could be on his way. Which wasn't even necessary for this trip. The Xterra could make it to Dayton from Detroit on one tank of gas.

When he got a Perfect Mate, she wouldn't have to stop so often. Well, except to have sex. Naturally.

As Ricky-boy climbed out of the car, Vic appeared at the back door to the bar and waved him inside. The only reason she was still here was so Perry and Ricky-boy could hitch a ride to Atlanta after dropping off Johnny's SUV.

Perry pulled out his phone and tried Sam's number again. Again he ended up in voicemail. He stuck his head out the window. "Hey, Vic. Give me Janie's number."

She sauntered over to the driver's door. "I'm not giving you Janie's number if she doesn't want you to have it."

"How do you know she doesn't want me to have it?"

"Because you don't have it."

Perry growled. "Then do me a favor and call her, okay? Sammy's not picking up."

"He could be busy. He was over at the apartment waiting on Crawford. Janie stayed behind at the hotel. She's fine."

"He's waiting on Crawford? She wasn't there?"

She rolled her eyes. "Didn't I just say that?"

"Then you definitely need to call Janie. What if Crawford found her and she thought it was Megan and—"

"*Gott.* Shut up. I'll call her." Vic took her phone, pushed a button and laid it out flat on her palm. The call went into Janie's voicemail.

"I don't like that," Perry said.

"Maybe they're together now."

"And you don't think Sammy would have called you if he'd confronted Crawford? I'm going back."

"You can't go back."

"What? You think Barnet wouldn't approve? He'd approve this shit."

"I don't know what Barnet would approve or not approve since he's gone missing."

"And how many times do I have to say it? He's not missing. He's just embarrassed after his reaction to Janie." And it had been quite a reaction. Even Perry hadn't gotten a boner after touching her. Which should have been his first clue that she wasn't his. Still…

"And I hope that's all it is. But whatever has happened, he's not answering his phone and we can't locate him. Protocol states we bring you in for the fifth vote."

And if that wasn't the stripper popping out of a birthday cake. Him? A voting member of the Committee? Had hell frozen over? Barnet must have gotten delusional, since he'd been the one who'd picked Perry.

She opened the back of the Xterra and pulled out the trunk containing Tucker. He would stay staked until they reached Headquarters. "Call the hotel. See if someone can go into the room and check in on her."

Perry nodded. Yeah, he could do that. He brought up the hotel information when his phone vibrated and chimed. "What was that?"

Vic shook her head. "You got a text. Don't you ever use that thing?"

"Never had a need until now." He brought up his messages. "It's from Sammy. Says he's fine being with his Perfect Mate."

"Okay, then."

"Why didn't he call?" He climbed out of the SUV and opened the back of the van for Vic to load the trunk.

"Because he's busy and doesn't want to talk? Trust me, when you find your own Perfect Mate, you'll understand." She shut the back of the van and returned to the bar.

Were they doing it like bunnies now? Hot damn. He texted Sammy back. Perry smiled as he headed inside the bar. One of these days he'd get his own Perfect Mate. But how much longer would he have to wait?

* * * *

Her head split. Her knees throbbed. And her mouth was one big cotton ball.

Janie blinked back to consciousness, but something was different. The room was quiet and dark and she was on her stomach lying across… "Sam?"

Of course, the words wouldn't come out, just a muffle. Patricia had re-secured the tape, damn it.

"Hey." The tape was still across his mouth, but his head had been moved to face her. Apparently, Patricia hadn't noticed his tape had gotten looser.

Janie went to grab the radiator, but couldn't spread her hands. "Damn it. She taped my thumbs." She spoke as if the tape made it possible for anyone to understand her. Which they couldn't. Because her voice came out all muffled. Damn it. She rested her head on her outstretched arms. Now how was she going to free her mouth? There must be something she could use. Using the hand cuffs for leverage, she pulled to sit up, but not only did her wrists scream in pain, her legs were stuck.

"Sorry. Should have warned you. She also taped you to me, so you couldn't avoid being burned. She left an hour ago, by the way. And yes, I've tried calling out for help, but as you can see that didn't work. My voice isn't all that loud anyway."

Because he was weak. Would her blood help him? Sure, it would start the bonding process, but did that really matter? She couldn't let them lie here and die.

Using her tongue, she freed her lips the best she could. Hopefully his superior hearing would understand her. "Would my blood help?"

Which was probably the stupidest question she could ask him. Of course her blood would help. But how the hell was he going to take it with his mouth taped shut?

"While your blood *is* special, even it won't remove these arrows."

"But you could yell louder and get someone to remove the arrows." Nice to know her noggin still worked after all those tazes. God, she never wanted to be tazed again.

"Yeah, about that. I don't think it's going to matter. Perry…" Sam closed his eyes.

"Perry, what?"

"While you were out, Crawford used my thumb so she could send a message to Perry on my phone. Told him I was fine with my Perfect Mate."

"Yeah, so?"

"Perry responded back saying it was a good thing he suggested on the way out that no one be issued a room up here. Crawford thought that was funny. Probably made it easier for her to leave us alone, too."

"So…no one's coming." It was up to her to get them out.

"Seems so. And no one's come up here since I arrived."

She laughed. She actually laughed. Or maybe she was just becoming hysterical. "So taking my blood won't do any good, will it?"

"I didn't say that. You just have to remove the stakes first."

And she just needed to wish for her fairy godmother. "How do you suppose I do that? Hello." She shook her wrists. "Cuffed to the radiator."

"With your mouth? If you can remove my tape, I'll be able to remove yours."

Okay, that made sense. Her face burned in embarrassment. Maybe her noggin wasn't working too swiftly yet. But as she bent her head toward his, the most she could do was kiss his cheek. If her lips were exposed, that was. Could she move him closer to the radiator? Would that help? "She didn't tape you to anything immovable, did she?"

"No. Just you."

The last time she tried to move Sam, she'd needed help. Now? She just needed more leverage. "If I roll back on you, I might be able to use my feet to move you." Provided her knees worked at all. "But I'm afraid I'll break the arrows." And breaking the arrows would be bad. Very, very bad. She had no way to dig them out.

"Actually, I don't think that's possible. She pounded them in pretty good."

"Right. Here goes nothing." Slowly, she rolled onto her back as far as her legs allowed. He moaned, but that could have come from the arrows or having her butt rubbing up against his crotch. Maybe later she'd ask him which. Using the hand cuffs as leverage, she pulled her feet in. The pain in her knees brought tears to her eyes. No! She wouldn't give in. Another tug and his legs moved. Yes! It wasn't much, but it sure motivated her to keep going.

Each tug only gained her a fraction of an inch, and maybe crippled her for life—she didn't need knees, did she?—but eventually she got the lower part of him close enough to the radiator to give her arms some slack. She rolled back onto her stomach and took a breather.

"You're doing great."

"Yeah. Just call me Superwoman." Her next trick probably wouldn't warrant such praise. After her lungs stopped burning and her heart calmed, she hooked her elbow around his neck, pushed off with her toes and yanked. It only took two more yanks to get her face next to his.

"Hey, handsome." She'd never worked out so hard, and with the tape blocking her major airway, her lungs suffered. What she wouldn't give for a decent breath.

"Hey, beautiful. You doing okay?"

"Never better," she said between pants. "Let's see if I can get that tape off now." Using the top edge of the tape on her face, Janie rubbed against the side edge of the tape on Sam's cheek. A couple of cheek-to-cheeks later, she still hadn't gotten hold of the tape, but whenever their skin touched, desire shot through her. Of all the times to get horny. Even Sam was being affected, if the hardness in his crotch was any indication.

She managed to finally catch the sticky part and let her rip. His mouth was now free and his tape hung from her face.

He dropped his fangs. "Now you. Slip your tape under my fang. It should be sharp enough to cut the tape."

She could see it not only cutting the tape, but her face, too. Well, she wanted him to have her blood. Did it matter how? She brought one side of her mouth to his and hooked the top of her tape on his fang. Little by little, the fang sliced it free. Didn't even nick her skin. Score! She used her upper arm to remove it from her mouth. Ahhh, air. She took in a deep breath.

"What's next, Hot Cowboy? Blood?"

"Not yet. Now here's what you might consider the gross part. Removing the stakes."

Gross? More like impossible. She hadn't really gotten a good look at them until now. Four stakes, surrounded with the remnant of his shirt. Some form of arrow, actually, but thicker. And imbedded deeply after Patricia had pounded them into him. "Man, she sure did a number on you. Couldn't she just shoot you with one?"

"That would have made life easier, wouldn't it?"

"Nothing worth having comes easy. Right?" And he was certainly worth having. At least she didn't have to worry about living without him. If he went up in flames, she'd go right along with him. Okay, why'd she think that? That was so not going to happen.

Thank goodness the ends were flared. Gave her something to sink her teeth into. But as she pulled, the leverage was all wrong. And it seemed his skin had healed over the mini stakes.

His moaning as she touched the arrow didn't help matters any, either. Oh, he tried to be quiet, but when something hurt, moans escaped. A couple of tugs loosened the arrow. And it only took a bazillion more tugs to get it free. Very little blood oozed from the hole, so it turned out not to be as gross as either of them thought. Yay?

"How much time do we have?" She was situated where she couldn't see the clock, but the sky was an inky black.

"It's a little after four. You have plenty of time. Don't worry. You're doing great."

A little after four. Sun rose at eight. Three more arrows. Was it possible they would get out of this alive after all?

It took another two hours to remove the next two arrows. Apparently there wasn't any kind of learning curve involved. Bummer.

She reached for the last arrow. It was cracked along the side where the previous arrow resided. "What happens if I leave in a splinter?"

"If a splinter is imbedded in my heart, then it's like I'm still staked. Why?"

"This last arrow is cracked."

"How bad?"

"Can't tell." Wasn't much where it met the skin, but what if there was more damage inside?

"Guess we'll find out when you remove it." He didn't have to tell her to be careful, because he knew she would be.

"Right." She went to work, but this one was imbedded deeper. Stuck on bone. Damn, one little misstep and it could be all over for him. For her. She'd gotten it half-way free when she took a breather. The sky wasn't so inky anymore. She went back to work. That little crack turned into one big split. She spit out some wood chips.

But she didn't come this far just to quit. The split was beyond her control. Removing the arrow was not. She could do this.

When the last arrow finally came free, she rested her head on his shoulder. Hallelujah. "How long before you know?"

"Give me a moment."

She could give him more than a moment. Counted to sixty. He still wasn't moving. "Oh no. I left a piece in there?"

"No. I can move my fingers. See?" The fingers on his left hand moved.

"Oh thank God. Time to feed, right? So feed already."

"You're going to have to come to me. I can't bend my head."

She moved toward him, but her neck wouldn't reach his mouth. All this work and she'd failed? "What the hell? Shit."

"Shush. Just kiss me."

Kiss? They were going to die and he wanted to kiss? Then he flashed his fangs. Oh, right. Her lips had blood, too. D'oh! Could she be any more dense? She placed her lips against his. He nicked her bottom lip and sucked. Oh, sweet Heaven. If only the charge that went through her would burst the cuffs free from her wrists. Or the tape from her legs.

"I love you, Janie." He held her head, leaned forward, and fed from her neck.

Oh God. It was better than she remembered. Better than her dreams. The orgasm wasn't a complete surprise, but the intensity was. She shorted a fuse.

Chapter 26

Beating the clock.

Sam finished feeding when he blew his load in what was left of his jeans. Holy shit, that was intense. And her blood was so much better than he remembered. Was it because she had offered it to him instead? He licked the site of his bite, but Janie was limp in his arms. Oh crap. What had he done?

He shook her. "Janie? Wake up."

She came to on a gasp. "What the hell was that?"

"Did I hurt you?" He didn't think he'd taken that much, but she was injured. He should have taken less.

She gazed up at him. "Are you kidding me? That was the best orgasm I've ever had. Did I pass out?"

"Yeah. Kind of scared me." Had either bonded vampire mentioned that particular trait? Of course not.

She laughed. "Sorry. But you have to promise that we'll do that again. When we're not trying to save our lives, that is."

"You got it." He moved his arms. Flexed his fingers. He was slow, but it was progress.

"What about me?"

"I'll get you free as soon as I can."

"Not that. Your blood. Don't I get your blood?"

Not even in his fantasies had he thought she'd want to complete the bond now. "You sure you want to finish the process? I mean, I'm okay with waiting."

"I'm not. I was stupid. We still have a way to get out of here. I'm not even sure we'll beat the sun. I don't want to spend another second not being your bonded mate."

If his vampire eyes could tear up, they would have. "I think that's the loveliest thing you've ever said to me." He pricked his finger and offered the bloody tip to her. She took it in her mouth and sucked. God, he loved her mouth.

He caressed her cheek. "Do you feel different?"

"Not really. Should I?"

"I don't know. But your knees should heal faster now, if they're not already healing."

"Now that you mention it, the throbbing has subsided. My headache is gone, too. Holy crap. Am I immortal now?"

"Yes, my love. You're stuck with me forever." Sam closed his eyes. They were bonded. Actually bonded. Now if he could only get them free before the sun rose. The sky wasn't so dark anymore, but he wasn't moving as freely as he'd hoped. It would be awhile before he could even think about cutting her free from him. Thanks to not only the staking, but the stabbing, too. That woman liked her knife and had stabbed him four more times before she left for good. Wasn't skimpy on the tape, either, when she'd attached his leg to Janie's. He probably could start unraveling the tape, but that required sitting up.

"How come you're not getting up?" Janie would narrow in on his predicament.

"I will. Just give me a minute." Although it would most likely be several minutes, if not an hour. But an hour would take him past sunrise. He didn't have that long. Then he remembered a conversation. "Although, Perry said…"

"What did Perry say this time?" The inflection of her voice said she didn't have much faith in anything Perry had to say.

"That he'd healed in record time when he took blood from a bonded Perfect Mate." In fact, he'd taken Ben's blood after getting caught out in the sun.

"A bonded Perfect Mate?" She lifted her head, eyes wide. "Hey! That's me!"

"Yeah." He laughed. He couldn't afford to take from her neck again, though. Hopefully he wouldn't need much. "Give me a kiss."

She rolled her eyes. "You and your kissing."

What could he say? He loved to kiss. No, strike that. He loved to kiss Janie. He would never kiss another woman again.

She obliged and he nicked her tongue. Gave it a good sucking. A jolt of power surged through his body. Holy shit. Perry hadn't been kidding.

She pulled away. "If I could, I'd rip the rest of your clothes off. I've never wanted you more."

"Save that for when we get free." He sat up. Damn, he'd never healed so fast in his vampire life. He tore the tape binding them together and scooted out from under Janie just as the sun broke the horizon and lit up the room. He yanked the curtain closed, shutting off the damaging rays. That was close. Granted, he could probably tolerate the sun now, but why test it so soon? He had forever to do that.

Yeah. Forever. With Janie.

The key was still on the dresser. A miracle! He removed her cuffs.

She rolled onto her back and stretched her arms. "Ah, freedom. What's next? Sit around and wait for sundown so we can get Patricia? That'd be fine with me. I could use a nap."

He removed the tape from her right hand. Once uncovered, she worked on the other while he removed the tape around her ankles. "I'm thinking a confrontation during daylight hours will be better. She definitely won't expect to see me then, and according to Victoria, I should be able to tolerate the sun better. As for your tiredness, that's your healing process at work. You might be out for a few hours."

"A few hours?" She sat up and rubbed her knees. "They're still sore, but I should be able to walk."

"You won't have to." He picked her up placed her on the bed.

"Will I fall asleep right away or do we have time to...?" She wiggled her eyebrows.

"I thought you were sore."

"I'm not that sore. Especially if I let you do all the work."

He laughed. Life with Janie was going to be sweet.

* * * *

Janie sat up on her elbows. Yeah, her knees hurt, but watching Sam remove what little was left of his clothes trumped any kind of pain. They were bonded. She was immortal. And she couldn't be happier.

Now if she could only get this stupid tape out of her hair. "You think shampoo will get this out? Or maybe conditioner?" Luckily, she had both.

He crawled on top of her. Inspected the tape. When he tugged, she yelped. "Can your knees stand for a shower? Or would you rather make love in the tub?"

Thing was, the bed was getting too comfortable and no way was she sleeping before she got her release. The orgasm she'd had earlier only seemed to get her more horny. Or maybe it was his blood. Or maybe it was just him. "The tub sounds wonderful."

Before she could even think about swinging her legs over to the side of the bed, he lifted her and carried her to the bathroom. She could get used to this kind of service, especially since she didn't seem to be a burden to carry.

He settled her on the toilet seat and started the tap. She went to remove her shirt, but he held her hands down. "Let me."

Crouching in front of her, with his glorious body on display, he ran his hands under her shirt and lifted the garment toward her head. She reached out to touch him, too, but as she raised her arms, he pulled the shirt up and over her head, trapping her arms behind her.

"That's not fair."

"You'll get your turn." He lowered one strap of her bra and exposed her breast. Cupped the orb and then sucked on the hardened nipple. She leaned her head back. Damn, she'd end up having another orgasm before they even had sex.

Was this what bonding was all about, or was it love? She certainly loved what he was doing to her.

He pulled his hand away as if she were on fire. And frankly, she felt pretty hot. His erection bobbed against his thighs. "I didn't believe them. Damn."

"Didn't believe who? About what?"

He grinned. Almost evil like. "You'll find out. Let's get that off your hair first."

After placing all the stuff they might need on the edge of the tub—and the razor worried her the most, would he cut her hair?—he set to work on her clothes. Removing them quickly, efficiently. Without the seduction. She wasn't sure whether or not to be offended. But then the tape would snag on something and pull her hair. She just wanted it off. He stepped into the tub and lifted her from the toilet. As he held her against his body, he lowered them into the warm water and became her back rest. Ahh, she could lie like this forever.

Turned out the conditioner worked best and no razor was needed. With the use of her comb Sam was able to remove the tape. Oh, he might have played with her breasts a few times, too. Not for any length of time, though. Almost like he was experimenting. What? She had no clue. But it sure made her want to scream at him.

With the tape history and her hair now clean, he slipped around her to get on top, sloshing water onto the floor. He kissed her forehead, each eye, nose, and finally her mouth. But it was just a light peck. "I love you."

"I love you, too." And she really did. She never loved anyone as much as she did him, and without learning every minute detail of his life. "But are you frustrating me on purpose? Get in me already."

That evil grin returned. He then entered her. Pulled out. Continued the in and out thing in the slowest way possible. "What do you feel?"

She felt loved, but suspected he hadn't meant that. And while she wouldn't have minded him speeding things up, the steady rhythm was pretty hot, too. Like nothing she'd ever felt before. Not only was she feeling him enter her...could she be feeling her around him? Holy shit. Dual rubbing. Dual intensity. She grabbed his shoulders. "Oh God, Sam. What is that?"

"Shared experiences. Like it?"

"Love it." She bared her neck. "Do it."

He bit her. Her mouth flooded with the most exotic taste. Was that what she tasted like to him? No wonder he loved it so much. He finally sped up and she exploded. Or was that him? Whatever. They were so doing that again.

Once she woke up.

Chapter 27

Biting the curse.

Sam sat outdoors. In the middle of the day. Okay, maybe not *out*doors, but in the backseat of the rental car. That was the same thing, wasn't it?

At least it was cloudy. He wasn't sure his eyes could take that much light without sunglasses. But he'd buy a pair first chance he got.

Being bonded was better than good. It was awesome. And while Janie had conked out again after their first bout of love making, he'd like to think it had to do with the sex more than the healing.

Maybe he'd been mean to her not mentioning the shared experience beforehand, but he hadn't really believed the stories until he experienced it himself. And what an experience. If he hadn't been warned, he might have freaked out a little. Okay, maybe a lot. Man, he'd almost passed out.

After her "nap," he'd ordered room service, fed her, and then made love to her all over again. He'd also been warned about the addictive quality of it. But what an addiction to have.

By one o'clock, they were ready to finish this whole ordeal. Janie had picked him up in the covered drop off area. But as she drove off, his hand had been exposed for a brief moment. Nothing happened. No searing pain. No blisters. Her blood was like a miracle cure for him. Because they were bonded.

When he'd checked in with Perry during Janie's nap, he'd asked about sun exposure. Was Perry still able to go out into the sun after that one feeding? He wasn't, but Victoria and John were. Whether that was because they were bonded or just fed from their Perfect Mate regularly, no one knew.

Sam wasn't sure to be happy or worried about that. Barnet and the Committee still needed to make rules regarding vampires and their Perfect Mates. Sam didn't want Janie or any other Perfect Mate to be beholden to give their blood to just any vampire. They weren't objects to be used.

The world looked so different during the day. Much more alive. He'd never seen so many people out and about at one time. And now he was part of them. In the daylight. After centuries in the dark. It was so cool.

As she pulled into the apartment complex, she passed a neon green Jeep—even brighter during the day—with a familiar plate number. "Holy shit, there it is again."

She stopped the car. "I told you there were lots of green Jeeps."

"No. It's the same one. Damn it. I should have realized."

"But the owner of the car doesn't live here."

"Maybe he doesn't get his mail here, but he lives here. I just didn't put the names together. Manny Rodriguez is the superintendant, here. Manuel Rodriguez. I wonder if she borrowed his Jeep."

She turned around in her seat, her face a shade paler. "Megan, or rather, Patricia called me. Right after Rick left the car, she called me. Oh God." Janie placed her hand over her mouth. "She was watching. All this time she was watching. And she wanted Rick to die."

He took her hand and squeezed it. "She won't have a chance to do it again. That's why we're here, right?"

She nodded and turned around. Drove up to the covered entrance and dropped him off.

He waited by the entrance while Janie parked the car. When she returned, the smile that had been on her face most of the morning had vanished. Had he done that to her? He palmed her cheek. "I shouldn't have said anything about that Jeep."

"No. I'm glad you did. She's evil. She's always been evil. And you're going to stop her." She placed her hand over his. "One way or another. You got that?"

Man, he was not going to tell Perry he was right. Sam smiled. "Yeah. I got that. Let's go."

He stopped at Crawford's door. One heartbeat sounded from inside. Rachel's school didn't let out until three, so very likely Crawford was inside. He pulled the key to their apartment from his pocket and handed it to Janie. Grabbed her hand and spoke telepathically, because they could do that now that they were bonded. *"You go on and I'll be back when I'm finished."*

She shook her head. *"No. I'm going with you. We do this together. Always. Together. If she has to die, I'm there with you. I won't let you do this alone."*

Never in a million years would he deserve her love, but he had it and would cherish it forever. *"She won't answer the door for us, though."*

Just then a woman emerged from another apartment. Sam took control and had the woman knock on Crawford's door while he and Janie stood off to the side.

The chain slid free and the door squeaked opened. Sam took control of Crawford and sent the stranger on her way. He and Janie entered the apartment.

"That was too easy," Janie said as she closed the squeaky door with her hip.

"Because she thinks we're dead." He ordered Crawford to sit on the couch. He sat beside her and wrapped his hands around her head.

First, the easy part. He erased all mention of vampires and Perfect Mates from her memories. Erased the fact she'd even bugged the room. Let her believe he was just another boyfriend. He then manipulated her memories of each attack on him, making her wonder if she had messed up or he was just lucky.

Next, to confirm what they suspected. He asked her a series of questions for her to answer truthfully. She admitted to fiddling with David's car, causing it to fill with carbon monoxide. She'd lured Justin to his job and pushed him off the ledge. She'd sent that drone into poor Aaron. And had set it up so that when Rick turned on his bedroom light, the furnace next door would blow. She just hadn't expected the building not to burn.

That last part startled Sam. Damn. How close had he and Perry triggered that? Thank God they hadn't needed the light.

"Oh my God." Janie wiped a tear from her cheek. "She doesn't even sound sorry."

Hopefully he could change that when he dug into her mind. "Get a paper and pen. But don't touch anything. Can't afford to have our fingerprints here."

"Right." She went down the hall and came back with the items, using a tissue to protect her prints. She placed the pen and paper on the dining room table.

Sam sent Crawford to the table to write out the confession. Had her sign and date it. Not too hard for him to accomplish since she was responsible for the crimes. If he were planting these events in her head, her words wouldn't ring true and her writing would appear forced.

Now came the hard part. Instilling guilt for all those crimes she'd committed. How easy would it be to just mess up on purpose? The woman really didn't deserve to live. But Sam had never purposely harmed another person. Wasn't sure he could start now. Wasn't sure he wanted to. He had a long life to live with Janie. Guilt wasn't invited. No, he would do everything he could to succeed.

* * * *

Janie paced while Sam worked on Patricia. She still couldn't believe that Patricia had pretended to be Megan all these years. She felt like she'd lost a dear friend and it hurt. Frankly, she kind of wished Sam would fail. She just wanted the woman gone.

Someone knocked on the door. Janie peeked through the hole. What the hell were they doing here? She turned toward Sam and mouthed, "Police."

Sam stood and grabbed her hand, leaving Patricia at the table in a daze. *"I can't control them through the door."*

"Are you done with her?"

He shook his head. *"Go to the bedroom. Wait for me."*

She slipped inside a room, out of view of the living room. Sam appeared within seconds. She grabbed his hand. *"What's the plan?"*

"Wait and see what they want. I can finish after they leave."

Police knocked again. "Mrs. Crawford. It's the police. Please open up."

The door squeaked open. "Hello, officers. How can I help you?"

"May we come in? We have some questions about Friday night."

The door squeaked closed. "Friday night? What about it?"

"I'm Detective Corso and this is my partner, Detective Armstrong. A Jeep belonging to one Manuel Rodriguez was spotted at the scene of a crime. The building that exploded Friday night. We're trying to find everyone who was in the vicinity, hoping someone saw something. He claims you borrowed his vehicle that night. Is that correct?"

She squeezed Sam's hand. *"Or they're hoping to find the person responsible, right? Too bad they can't read that confession."*

Sam's forehead crinkled.

Oh shit. He probably thought she didn't trust his abilities. *"I didn't mean it like that. I don't care if the police are involved."*

Then a smile spread across his face and he kissed her. *"I hadn't even thought of the confession. I love that mind of yours."* He then concentrated toward the living room.

"Hey, Corso. Come look at this."

"That's not yours. Leave it alone," Crawford said.

Sam covered his mouth, muffling a snicker. *"I made her think they're doing an illegal search."*

"Mrs. Crawford," Detective Corso said. "Were you getting ready to commit suicide?"

"Yes. No. What are you talking about?"

Janie buried her face into Sam's arm to keep her laughter from escaping. He was doing an excellent job of making Patricia sound crazy.

"Mrs. Crawford, I'm placing you under arrest for murder and attempted murder." He then read the Miranda rights. "Armstrong, bag that confession."

"Confession? I didn't write any confession. I didn't do anything. That bitch! She's framing me. This is a set-up."

They left the apartment against Patricia's wishes. She let them know it, too.

Janie looked up at Sam. The man she was bonded to. The man she would love forever. "What just happened?"

"As luck would have it, the police got involved. I just gave them a little nudge in the right direction. It's what you wanted. Right?"

It was only what she wanted if it made his life easier and apparently it did. "Will it stick?"

He shrugged. "Guess we'll find out when they call you. Your name is on that confession."

"It won't matter if they see me?"

"You don't look any different since the bonding. In ten years or more you'll have a problem, but not now."

Because she wouldn't age. "So it's over?"

"I'd say it is. Looks like you finally bit the curse."

"No. We bit it. Together." And she looked forward to a long and happy life with her Perfect Vampire.

Thank you for purchasing this book.

Sign up for Stacy McKitrick's newsletter to receive new release announcements, sneak peeks of future books, and bonus content. She sometimes even gives stuff away. You can find the signup form on her website: http://stacymckitrick.com

ABOUT THE AUTHOR

Stacy McKitrick always had stories in her head; she just never knew what to do with them. Then one day she decided to give writing a try and discovered the passion she'd been looking for all her life. She waved goodbye to accounting and now spends her time writing romance featuring vampires and ghosts. All with happy endings, of course. Born in California, she currently resides in Ohio with her husband. They have two grown children. You can learn more about Stacy at her website www.stacymckitrick.com.

www.ingramcontent.com/pod-product-compliance
Lightning Source LLC
Chambersburg PA
CBHW061604100726
47898CB00002B/513

* 9 7 8 1 7 3 3 1 7 6 2 0 0 *